Child of the State

Catherine Lea

Copyright © 2016 Catherine Lea
Published by Brakelight Press

ISBN: 978-0-473-34500-6

Child of the State is a work of fiction.

Names, characters, businesses, places, events, and incidents are either the products of the author's imagination or used in a fictitious manner. Any resemblance to actual persons, living or dead, or actual events is purely coincidental.

Cover Design, Elizabeth Mackey
Formatting, Polgarus Studio
Editing, Sara J. Henry
Proofreading, Linda Au

DEDICATION

For my girl. You'll always be with me.

PROLOGUE
CARRINGWAY WOMEN'S PRISON, OHIO—AMY

Amy knew she should have gone to Stacy the second she'd opened the box. All night she'd lain there in her cot, listening to every sound, frightened they'd come after her, and wondering who else knew. Because somebody did.

Why she'd even gotten stuck in that stupid job was anybody's guess. She'd applied for the prison sewing program. Would have helped if she knew how to sew, but others on the same work scheme didn't know how to sew when they started, either. They got lessons.

Amy still couldn't make a buttonhole worth a damn so she got stuck in dispatch, sending out boxes of garments in the truck that turned up twice a week. Her job was to pack the boxes, check the details on the packing slip, seal the boxes up. Most boring job on the planet—or it was until that particular box came back, returned from wherever and marked *Attention Dispatch Department*. The only person around with any authority to accept the box was Trish Tomes, the prison officer overseeing the project.

Amy had been going through the box, looking at every item. She was just holding a silk blouse up to the light, checking she wasn't imagining things, when Officer Tomes appeared behind her. Amy just about peed her pants. She yelped and pressed the blouse to her chest to try to slow her heart down. The woman had the stealth of a cat. Didn't matter how hard you listened, you'd turn around and there she was, standing right behind you.

Officer Tomes took the blouse from Amy, holding it up to the light while she looked it over. Then she dug through the box, frowning as she brought out other garments and checked them.

"I'll take care of this," she told Amy.

"But these are ours."

"I said I'll take care of it. Now go back, seal up the last of those boxes." Her tone implied she wasn't going to say it again. She gathered up the returned box and took it back to her office. When Amy looked up the next time, she could see her on the phone, talking to someone with that sour look on her face, every now and then glancing accusingly across at Amy.

But Amy wasn't stupid. She'd already tucked one of blouses down the front of her prison jumpsuit, then slept all night with it tucked under her mattress. Now here she was standing in line for breakfast with the blouse down the front of her jumpsuit while she waited for Stacy. What she'd discovered was something big—she just knew it was, and Stacy was the only one in this joint Amy could trust. She was also the one who'd know exactly what to do.

After several minutes, the doors opened and Stacy's crew entered, lining up for their breakfast trays, all chattering and checking out the tables to see whether anyone had been stupid enough to sit in their seat, then looking back down the line to see who they might be eating with. Amy fell into line with her heart jumping and her hands shaking. She waited until her oatmeal and juice box had been set on her tray, and when she turned, she caught Stacy's eye, indicating for her to sit with her.

As soon as Stacy came over, slid her tray onto the table and sat down, Amy looked left and right, and said, "Gotta talk."

Stacy dug her spoon into her oatmeal, screwed her face up in disgust as she stirred it around. "Sure. Go ahead."

Amy leaned forward and hissed, "I'm talking *real talk*. In private."

Stacy looked up from her tray, her expression grim. "Are you okay?"

Amy gave the adjacent tables another furtive once-over. Satisfied they weren't being overheard she leaned forward again. "I found something."

Stacy straightened in her seat, lifting her head and letting her gaze casually navigate the room before settling back on Amy. "Go on."

Amy took another quick glance back over her shoulder. "Can't. Have to show you. Bathroom."

Stacy got up and returned her tray to the counter along with her uneaten oatmeal, and pushed through the swing doors, heading in the direction of the bathroom. No point in leaving the meal until she got back. You leave your food unattended in this place, you never know what might have been added to it while you were gone. Amy followed, placing her food tray back with her breakfast untouched, giving the area another wary scan before following Stacy.

When she got to the bathroom, two stalls were closed. A toilet flushed and Nyla Guthrie stepped out and looked from Stacy to Amy and back. "What?" she said in an accusing tone.

"Nothin'," said Amy.

"It's nothing. Don't worry about it," Stacy told her.

Nyla gave Amy a sour once up and down, then pushed through the bathroom door going back to the dining room, leaving Stacy and Amy both watching the second stall.

Impatient, Stacy went across and banged on the door with the side of her fist. "Hey, hurry it up, will ya?"

The toilet flushed and Cissy Pettameyer stepped out, a picture of ingratiating sweetness. "Good morning, ladies," she said with a sly smile as she moved to the basin and washed her hands, checking her face in the mirror.

Neither of them spoke, just watched her.

"Be like that then," Cissy told their reflections, and ran a smoothing finger along one eyebrow. "I'm just trying to be polite."

Neither Amy nor Stacy was taken in. Cissy was a poisonous, two-faced gossip who spread stories at a rate that would make the black plague look slow.

Stacy stuck one hand on her hip and shifted her weight. "You done?"

Cissy turned and ran her eyes right down to Stacy's prison-issue shoes and back. "I guess."

She jerked her head towards the door. "Then get out."

After Cissy had gone, Stacy opened the door and peered out, then closed it, leaning against it so no one else could enter.

"So what's so important? Are you okay, Amy? Is someone giving you a hard time?"

"No, it's not like that. I'm fine. But when I was working today, a box came, addressed to the prison, like they do sometimes. It had a Faulty Goods sticker on the side, so I figured it was just stuff coming back that had stitching problems with them or something." She paused and dropped her voice to a whisper. "But this was in it." She reached down into the front of her jumpsuit, pulled the blouse out, and handed it to Stacy.

"What is it?"

"You look," Amy said, hugging herself and jerking her chin toward the blouse in Stacy's hands. "I didn't know who else to tell."

Stacy checked the seams, the sleeves, the buttonholes, and her eyes came back up to Amy, questioning.

"Keep lookin'," she said.

Stacy turned the garment, checking the collar, then the neckline. Her jaw dropped and she looked up, eyes wide.

"Well, holy shit," she said.

CHAPTER ONE

FOUR MONTHS LATER
DAY ONE: 1:56 PM—STACY

The car rounded the last bend into Becker Street and came to an abrupt halt. Right in front of them was a pack of reporters and TV crews surrounding the front gate and stretching halfway down the street. By the look of them, they must have had the place staked out since dawn. The instant the first person spotted the car, the crowd was in motion. In a matter of seconds the car was swamped, microphones and cameras pressed to the windows, reporters and news anchors pushing and elbowing each other and yelling questions while a couple of cops tried unsuccessfully to hold them back.

Stacy sat up in the back seat, peering out at the commotion. This was something she hadn't expected. This could be a problem.

She twisted around, looking out the side and rear windows, watching the chaos outside while Mrs. McClaine, who was sitting next to her, leaned forward, directing the driver to pull in as close to the front gate as possible. Meanwhile, Penny Rickman, Mrs. McClaine's secretary, got out of the car behind them and cut her way through the crowd, also pointing and yelling over the rabble, ordering security to push the media back and form a guard around the car while Stacy and Mrs. McClaine got out.

There was nothing like this when Stacy was sentenced three years ago.

As she'd left the courthouse that day, a handful of supporters had lined up along the front steps, shouting and waving placards that said things like: "No mother should be in prison for wanting her child," and "Where's the justice in this country?"

Didn't make one iota of difference because she'd already been tried and sentenced. Seventeen years old she was, and on her way to Carringway Women's Prison with a sentence of five years for assaulting the social services lady who'd taken her son away. And that was the last she'd seen of the outside world—would have been for the next two years, if it hadn't been for the governor's new early release program.

Now, here she was free again—or at least, she would be if all these reporters weren't surrounding the place.

The car door opened to a semicircle of space made by a wall of security guards. Stacy flashed Mrs. McClaine a glance, and when she got the okay Stacy got out, head down, hand shielding her face from the flash of cameras. The security guards closed in, forming one compact unit, and together they moved in through the front gate, up the front steps, and onto the porch.

While Mrs. McClaine turned to answer questions and pose for the cameras, Stacy took a second to ease the tension out of her shoulders, look the place over. Seemed kind of ironic that after all these years, here she was back at the very house she'd run away from in the first place. Gayleen Charms never would have made Mother of the Year. Child Services knew the house better than the mailman. Having a child at fifteen might have been the best thing that ever happened to Stacy, but being a teen mom hadn't been at the top of Gayleen's list of career choices. Gayleen had wanted to be a dancer. She wanted to live in the big city under the bright lights.

From the minute Stacy was born she knew she'd been the biggest mistake Gayleen ever made, that she'd ruined her mother's life. Fourteen years of being made to feel like trash finally made life on the streets a way more attractive prospect. Which was why Stacy had run away.

Standing here now, the place looked no different—same crappy house with the same dirty white paintwork, same clutter all over the front porch, same broken railing her mother still hadn't fixed in all the time she'd lived here. One of the conditions of Stacy's release was that she must live at this address for a minimum period of six months.

Like hell.

Stacy didn't intend to stay six minutes. The instant she got the chance, she'd be out the door and looking for Tyler.

Behind her, the reporters and TV crews were packed like sardines outside the gate, all out across the street, and two doors down. Walking out the front door wasn't an option. She'd have to come up with something else. And she had to do it quickly. Tyler's school was out at 2:30. She had no idea where his foster home was, so if she missed him, she'd never find him.

One of the security guards leaned in and knocked on the door. When there was no response, he looked to Mrs. McClaine, who nodded, so he pressed a finger into the doorbell and leaned on it. Inside they could hear the chimes ring through the house. Stacy folded her arms in tight and hung her head while they waited.

Still no reply. Mrs. McClaine leaned across and rapped on the glass panel in the door. Again they waited, with reporters shouting questions and holding up phones and taking pictures. Mrs. McClaine cut a look across at Penny Rickman, as if to say, "I thought you said she was home," to which Penny Rickman shrugged and made a face that said, "She was. She answered the phone, said she'd be here."

Outside the gate, a couple of police were cutting through the crowd, ordering the media back, away from the gate. When Stacy turned to follow the action she caught a glimpse of Penny's watch, and her heart flipped. It was later than she thought.

Her plan had been to use her mother's car to pick up Tyler, then take him straight to Wayne's. That's what she'd told him in the letters she'd had smuggled out. If traffic was light, getting to Tyler's school in time would have been a breeze. But Gayleen hadn't answered the phone when she was supposed to. She'd picked up twenty minutes after the appointed time. And now they were running almost a half hour late.

All those months' planning had come down to this. Heat flashed across Stacy's forehead and a bead of sweat trickled down her back.

Penny looked to Mrs. McClaine, eyebrows raised, and Mrs. McClaine replied with a quick nod. But just as Penny reached for the knob, the lace curtain flicked aside, the door swung open, and Gayleen Charms filled the entranceway.

She was just as Stacy remembered, a little fatter around the middle, long dyed blonde hair hanging past her shoulders, faded jeans and a low-cut top exposing a withered and deeply lined cleavage, bare feet.

"You're late," she said by way of greeting. No "Sorry, I didn't hear the bell," or "Hello, Stacy, it's good to see you."

That was hardly surprising. Gayleen had only agreed to have Stacy live back with her because she thought there was a buck in it. Then she'd found out otherwise and had been less than cooperative ever since.

Stony faced, she stepped back and opened the door wider, an unspoken invitation to enter. Elizabeth McClaine stepped in over the threshold, followed by Stacy, then Penny.

The inside of the house hadn't changed, either—same battered old sofa, same threadbare rug, same smell of musty furnishings overlaid with stale cigarette smoke and cooking grease.

Gayleen went back to an old velour armchair where she'd apparently been sitting—leaving Mrs. McClaine to close the door—while she plopped herself into the seat and picked up a lit cigarette from an overfull ashtray. After tapping the ash off, she took a puff and finally looked up—steely blue eyes, deep lines around her lips from years of smoking, no smile. From her expression, anyone would have thought they'd come to raid the place.

"I expected you a half hour back," she told them through a cloud of smoke.

Mrs. McClaine dipped her head by way of acknowledgment. "I'm sorry. We got caught in traffic. But it's so nice to meet you at last, Mrs. Charms. I'm Elizabeth McClaine, custodian of the Charles McClaine Foundation. And this is Penny Rickman, my secretary," she added, gesturing to the woman next to her.

All eyes went to Penny, who was looking around as if she'd found herself in a toxic wasteland. As soon as she realized Mrs. McClaine was looking at her expectantly, she snapped to, suddenly all business. She switched her briefcase from one hand to the other, addressing both Elizabeth and Gayleen at once.

Stacy dug her teeth into her upper lip to stifle a smile while Penny went straight into automatic mode.

"I'm afraid Governor Straussman hasn't been able to make it today. He has an urgent meeting downtown. He sends his apologies. Kay Heathers from Child Services is on her way over." Penny lifted her left wrist to check the time. "Matter of fact, she should be here any minute now."

Gayleen's barely concealed sneer went from Penny's face, down her sleek gray business suit to her shiny black pumps and back up again.

"Then you better take a seat, and get on with it," she said, nodding at the sofa behind them. "Sooner I can get all a' them reporters outta my front yard the better."

Penny Rickman glanced back at the threadbare seating, then at her boss. Mrs. McClaine lowered herself to sit on the edge while Penny hovered like a dog that can't make up its mind which way to lie, then perched alongside Mrs. McClaine, saying "Thank you," and positioning her briefcase close in beside her as if someone might steal it.

Stacy circled the room slowly, picking up ornaments from the dresser and replacing them. All her grandfather's things. Gayleen must have just carried on after he died like nothing had happened.

Behind her, her mother was already complaining about the crowds outside, droning on about her privacy being invaded and people trampling the lawn. Stacy had stopped listening. Instead, she moved across to the front window, angling her head so she could see the street. Even more reporters were arriving.

Shit!

Acting as if she was reveling in a trip down memory lane, she wandered casually through to the kitchen and peered out the window over the sink into the back yard.

Nothing but grass. No rear fence. Just like it was when she lived here. Wasn't the best situation, but it could work.

Out in the living room Mrs. McClaine was going through the conditions of Stacy's release, the curfews set around her work program, and explaining how Stacy's ankle bracelet would monitor all her movements via satellite and cellular networks. All the same old *blah blah* she'd heard from the guy who fitted it. She hadn't listened the first time because she hadn't planned to wear it long. But if she didn't leave now, she'd never make it.

"I'm just going to the bathroom," she called.

Mrs. McClaine called back, saying, "Okay. Then maybe you should get some rest. If we need you, we'll call," and went on listing off the conditions. Judging by Gayleen's reactions, Mrs. McClaine must have felt like one of those diplomats you see on TV, trying to talk nice to a bunch of people who just wanted to start another war.

But the longer they took, the better for Stacy.

She made her way quickly to the back of the house and stood outside the bathroom looking back. Penny had moved from the living room into the kitchen, and Stacy could hear her still talking on the phone.

Walking quickly past the bathroom, she ducked into her mother's room, quietly closing the door behind her.

What now?

Gayleen's purse lay where she always kept it, on the nightstand beside the bed. Stacy unzipped it and emptied it on the coverlet. A pile of old receipts fell out, along with a pack of cigarettes and a Bic lighter, sunglasses, a pack of gum, and her money purse. No keys. Stacy stuck her hand into the purse and felt around. Right at the bottom, she found a photograph, caught in a pocket in the lining, and pulled it out. It was a picture of Gayleen as a young woman: platinum blonde dyed hair, low-cut blouse, cigarette in her hand—the good-time girl.

Yeah, we all remember those good times, Stacy thought bitterly and shoved it back.

Next she turned to the dresser and started opening drawers. In the third drawer down was a stack of folded scarves. When she lifted the top one, she spotted a wisp of hair. She pulled the drawer out further and there was Gayleen's old wig. Straight out of the eighties. She put it on and tugged it into place, securing it with one of the scarves. Then she checked her reflection in the mirror. It wasn't perfect, but it would do.

With the scarf and the wig on, she crossed to the closet and rummaged through the pockets of two coats before finally locating the car keys.

Out in the living room she could hear her mother blabbering on and on to Mrs. McClaine and Penny Rickman—still sounding like she'd rather stick pins in her eyes than have her only daughter come live with her.

Stacy rolled her eyes to the ceiling. From the minute Stacy's living arrangements had been suggested, Gayleen had thrown herself into a blue funk, like her life was about to be ruined all over again by her useless daughter and her retarded kid—which was how she referred to Tyler.

But Gayleen need never have worried. Before the day was out, Stacy and Tyler would have both vanished into thin air, and Gayleen would never have to see them again.

CHAPTER TWO
DAY ONE: 2:16 PM—STACY

Sliding one hanger after the next, Stacy went right through the closet, looking for something she could use. She yanked one of Gayleen's old house dresses from the hanger and pulled it on over her clothes and patted her pocket—a quick check for Tyler's toy car: Lightning McQueen, a little red die-cast racer with "95" and a lightning bolt on the side. She'd carried it ever since he gave it to her the last time she saw him. Still there, thank God. That was the one thing she never wanted to lose.

A look in the mirror told her she looked like someone living on the streets. When she shoved on the sunglasses, no one would have known her. Just the look she'd been going for.

With her hand on her head to keep the wig and and scarf in place, she tiptoed to the back door, eased it open, and slipped out, gently closing it behind her. Down the back steps, along the rear of the house. Sure enough, the old green '67 Chevy that Gayleen had inherited along with the property was parked in front of the garage at the side of the house. Hidden from street view by a couple of overgrown shrubs, Stacy made a beeline for the car, head down while she unlocked it. As she pulled the door open, two reporters at the end of the driveway turned, heads swiveling her way. Next thing, they were moving quickly down toward her, calling, "Hey, you there!"

Stacy slipped into the car, stuck the key in the ignition, and twisted it. The car grumbled into life.

The gauge told her she had half a tank of gas. *Could be worse.*

In the rearview mirror she could see the two reporters moving up on her. She slammed the car in reverse, laid one arm along the back of the seat while she turned, and pressed her foot on the gas. The car roared and shot backwards, forcing the two reporters to leap aside. She stamped on the brake, then pushed the gear stick into drive.

Out on the street, people had begun turning this way, craning to see down the narrow driveway. A few reporters took photos while others yelled questions with their hands held up like kids on a class outing. She ignored them and turned her attention to the front again, lifting her head so she could see over the steering wheel while she pressed her foot to the pedal, harder this time.

The car lurched forward so fast her head snapped back and she almost hit the side of the garage. Her foot slipped off the gas and the car jerked to a stop. She twisted the wheel hard, pressed her foot down, and the car lunged forward again. Clinging to the wheel, and keeping her foot steady, she steered down the strip of grass between her mother's garage and the neighbor's, then turned across Gayleen's back yard.

In the rearview mirror she could see five reporters now, all following her down the driveway. She ignored them and kept going.

The car bounced over ruts with rocks scraping the underside, followed by the hiss of grass brushing along beneath her.

A woman standing on the neighbor's back porch yelled something.

Stacy didn't flinch. She just kept going; she had to concentrate. Three years since she'd driven a car; it was like flying a freaking spaceship. The thing rocked and bounced, the body swaying like a fairground ride over the ruts and ridges. When she hit a ditch that formed the boundary between her mother's place and the rear neighbor's, the wheels lost traction.

A jolt of panic scorched down her spine and she hit the gas again. The car roared and the wheels spun. Behind her, she could see the journalists closing in and taking photos. Another blast, and the tires found solid ground. The car bucked under her and leaped forward again, up over the edge. She clung to the wheel and headed down the side of the rear neighbor's house, across a flower garden, and around to the front. When she reached a bend in the driveway, she spun the wheel and headed for the street. In the rearview mirror she spotted the homeowner running down the front steps behind her, yelling, "Hey! What are you doing?" then turning with his hands laced over the top of his head in anguish while he surveyed the damage the car had done.

"I'm sorry, I'm sorry," she muttered, but she didn't stop. As soon as she hit the curb, she slammed her foot down and swerved out into the street with a squeal of tires, only to see a young woman crossing the street right in front of her. She jerked the wheel around, missing the woman by inches. The woman leaped aside and held up a cell phone, snapping photos—but Stacy had her foot to the floor, heading east.

Behind her she could see the homeowner running into the street to join the woman, the two of them watching her disappear around the corner into Lester Street. As she slowed to cross the intersection at the end of her mother's street, she could see the media trucks with people crowded around, pressing in on her mother's front gate. She took the first turn right, ripped off the wig and the scarf, and sped off.

This may have been the dumbest idea she'd ever had. But it worked. Now here she was—a half hour behind schedule, but if she hurried she could still make it.

A wave of relief rolled over her. She lowered the window and let the wind blow through her short brown hair.

The sweat on her face stung in the chill air, and her muscles twanged like piano wires. She sucked in a deep breath and tried to relax. But as she turned toward the freeway, a cop car coming the other way sent another blast of adrenaline down her spine and another wave of sweat flashed over her forehead. She slowed the car, took her elbow off the window frame, and kept her eyes fixed on the road ahead. On the other side of the street, the cop pulled over, watching her as she drove by.

"Shit!"

A look in the rearview mirror told her the cop had swung a U-turn and was now following her. She tapped the turn signal and swung a left. The cop followed.

Her heart rate kicked up into high gear and heat prickled across her scalp. She ran her tongue around her lips, and blew out a long, slow breath while she kept driving. The cop signaled right and turned. She watched in the rearview mirror, then cast her eyes back to the road in front just in time to see brake lights in front of her. She stamped her foot on the brake, snapping her head forward and stopping inches from the car in front.

When she checked behind her, the cop had gone. She was in the clear.

An uneasy smile broke across her face and her shoulders sank in relief. Now she had no time to lose. The instant the light changed and the car in front took off, she planted her foot, swung the car into the right-hand lane, and headed south.

She had four minutes to get to Tyler.

She knew exactly where his school was. She'd recognized it in the background of the photograph someone had left in her cell. It showed Tyler standing outside the school with a wisp of fine, dark hair blown back from his face, a troubled frown lifting his brows to a peak on his forehead. He was with a woman Stacy guessed was either his teacher or his foster mother—both of them looking down the street, perhaps waiting for a car, or waiting to cross.

Around the periphery of the shot, someone had circled Tyler with a red Sharpie, then drawn lines representing crosshairs that bisected over his heart. On the back was written *He's first, you're next*. Now only two questions blazed in her mind: Who else would have known where he was? And could she get to him before they did?

CHAPTER THREE
DAY ONE: 2:21 PM—ELIZABETH

Elizabeth snatched her phone from her purse, answered the call, and listened. Frowning, she excused herself and stepped towards the hallway, away from the din outside.

"I'm sorry, can you repeat that?" she said, pressing one finger into her other ear.

"Mrs. McClaine, it's the Cleveland Central Station. We've been monitoring the bracelet on Stacy May Charms."

Elizabeth looked toward the front windows in frustration. With the commotion out there, she could hardly think, let alone hear. "Yes, what is it?"

"The bracelet is showing that Miss Charms is outside the designated area. Can you confirm her presence for us, please?"

"Oh, for goodness' sake," she growled and massaged her forehead. Between the media circus and the pressure she'd been under from every politician who'd put their vote to the program, she could feel a headache coming on. The guy on the phone repeated the request.

"Yes, yes," she snapped. "I heard you the first time. Just wait a minute, will you?" Turning to Gayleen, she said, "Would you excuse me a moment, Mrs. Charms?"

Penny Rickman frowned and got to her feet. Elizabeth gestured for her to follow her to the kitchen. "If you'll hold the line, we're checking with Stacy now."

She rested one hand on her hip and lowered the phone while she waited for Penny, who entered the kitchen behind her, hands spread questioningly.

Elizabeth let out a frustrated sigh. "It's the bracelet. There's a problem. Go and ask Stacy to come in here. We'll have someone do something about it or it'll be setting off their alarms all hours of the night."

Penny disappeared to the rear of the house.

"Ah, Mrs. McClaine, can you confirm Miss Charms is with you?" the guy asked again.

"Yes, I can. If you could just hold a minute," Elizabeth replied.

Penny came back. "She's not here. I can't find her."

Elizabeth put her hand over the mouthpiece and whispered, "What do you mean she's not here? She has to be here somewhere. Have you tried the bathroom?"

"That was the first place I looked." They both looked to Gayleen, who was approaching from the living room.

"What's the problem?" Gayleen asked.

Elizabeth said, "May I?" and headed for the hallway without waiting for a reply.

"Hey, excuse me. What are you looking for?" Gayleen demanded as she followed along, peering into each room after Elizabeth. "What are you doing? This is a private house."

"Where is she?" Elizabeth asked no one in particular.

"We're looking for Stacy," Penny told Gayleen. "Have you seen her?"

"Course I have," Gayleen replied like they were both nuts. "She's right here." She followed Elizabeth as she made her way to the back of the house, opening doors to the bathroom, the bedroom, the storeroom, and leaving them all standing open.

"So where'd she go?" Penny asked Gayleen, like it was her fault. "I thought she was in the bathroom."

"I didn't say she was in the bathroom. You said she was in the bathroom."

Elizabeth let out an irritated huff and put the phone to her ear. "Can you hold the line a second? We're just trying to locate her."

"According to the reading, she's outside the area," the guy said again.

"Yes, I heard you the first time. Penny," she said, and pointed to the back door. "See if she's out back."

Penny leaned out, looking across the back yard. "Nope. But there are car tracks to the rear of the property and a bunch of reporters out there. Do you have a car?" she asked Gayleen.

The woman pushed past her to the back door, saying, "Course I got a car. What are those reporters doing in my back yard?"

"I don't believe this," Elizabeth groaned. "I'll call you back," she told the guy on the phone, then hung up as she stepped out to join Penny in the back yard. There a garbage can had been knocked over and tire marks led to straight across to the neighbor's place, and about half of the crowd was milling about.

Elizabeth pressed her fingers to her forehead while she did a 180-degree turn, scanning the entire yard, boundary to boundary with reporters closing in, calling questions and shoving phones in her face. "Please stay back," she called. Then she turned to Penny, voice lowered. "This is ridiculous. How could she just drive off without anyone seeing her? Where are the security officers?"

"Good question."

"Mrs. McClaine! May I ask you a few questions?" It was one of several reporters who pushed out from the crowd with his phone held up.

"I want them offa my property right this minute," Gayleen told Elizabeth, jabbing a thumb over her shoulder. "And I want my car found. Anything happens to that car, you'll be the one paying for it."

Elizabeth held up both hands, fending off the questions. "I'm sorry, not right now." Then turned to Penny, hissing, "Get them out of here."

While Elizabeth stood surveying the damage, Penny began herding the crowds back, both arms rolling like she was rounding up sheep. "Would you mind moving back? This is private property—"

But one of the reporters interrupted her, shouting over her shoulder, "Mrs. McClaine, can you confirm this is a photo of Stacy May Charms driving a green '67 Chevy down St. Clair Avenue five minutes ago?" He was holding his phone aloft.

Elizabeth spun around and pushed through the crowd with her hand out. "Excuse me, give me that."

"You're welcome to it," he said and passed it to her with a smug smile. "But it was uploaded on Instagram just a couple of minutes ago."

Penny leaned over her shoulder. "Holy shit," she blurted out, in a rare lapse of public composure.

Elizabeth handed the phone back to the guy. "Find out who put it up there, and get it off the internet before anyone sees it," she told Penny, who was already dialing her cell phone.

Almost at once, the cordless phone in Gayleen's hand rang. Gayleen hit the call button, put the phone to her ear, finger stuck in the other so she could hear. "What?" She nodded, then said, "Yes, it is." After a short pause, she said, "I have no idea, but Mrs. McClaine is right here. You can talk to her about it." She shoved the phone at Elizabeth, saying, "It's for you. It's Governor Straussman. He's asking if you have access to Twitter."

Penny pressed the key on her phone, abandoning the call, and looked to Elizabeth, who took the phone, swallowing hard and muttering, "Oh, dear God."

"Elizabeth," Penny said quietly, "given the current events, I don't think 'Oh, dear God' even scratches the surface."

CHAPTER FOUR
DAY ONE: 2:39 PM—STACY

Stacy pulled the Chevy around the last corner to find the school almost deserted except for a handful of kids still playing out front, waiting for their parents or nannies under the watchful gaze of two teachers.

Ever since the McClaines' daughter, Holly, had been kidnapped five years back, every school in the state had increased after-school security. No one wanted to be responsible for the abduction of another kid. The security didn't bother Stacy. She knew it would be like this. It's what she'd planned for. She wasn't dumb enough to try to snatch Tyler out of the teacher's grasp like the stupid girl that had snatched Holly McClaine. She didn't have to talk to anyone. All she had to do was to get a lock on the car that picked Tyler up, then follow them.

This was definitely the right place. But now, looking around, it was becoming obvious that she'd wasted too much time back at Gayleen's. A car rounded the corner and stopped. The last three remaining kids whooped and squealed and raced towards it. The rear door opened and they threw their backpacks in and jumped in after them, and the car pulled out and drove off. In a matter of minutes, the school yard was empty and the two supervising teachers were making their way back across the yard to the main door.

Stacy cursed and thumped the steering wheel with the side of her fist. How could this have happened? How could she have come this far to miss him by a matter of minutes? Originally, it wouldn't have mattered. When she'd first applied for the program, the release date was a Monday. Stacy could have come back the following morning and waited again. But delays in the paperwork and all the bureaucratic bullshit had meant the release date was delayed. Now it was Friday. Coming back Monday wasn't an option. She had an 8:30 a.m. appointment with her parole officer. From that point on she'd be with her employer, or her mother or somebody every second of the day. It'd be days, maybe weeks, before she got this chance again. By then it could be too late. Tyler could be dead.

Across the road two elementary school boys trailed a girl of around eighteen or so down the street. Maybe their older sister or their after-school babysitter, too busy texting on her phone to notice the kids shoving each other back and forth and fighting. Stacy got out of the car and followed on the opposite side of the street to the next corner where the girl had walked on, almost out of sight of the boys, who had stopped to grab sticks from alongside the sidewalk and started a play sword fight.

Stacy checked the road both ways and trotted after them.

"Excuse me!" she called after them. When the girl kept walking, she ran up behind her and called again, louder this time.

"Hey, excuse me."

The girl turned around and yanked earbuds from her ears and looked up. The two kids stopped fighting and also turned their attention on Stacy.

"You talking to me?" the girl asked as Stacy approached.

"Yeah," she replied, trying to sound casual. "Listen, do the boys here go to the elementary school back there?"

They both looked back in the direction of the school, then at the boys. The bigger of the two was punching the smaller kid, who said, "Leave me alone, Darin. I'm telling Mom."

"Shut up, you two," the girl told them, then turned back to Stacy. "Yeah, so?"

Stacy stuck her hands on her hips, and surveyed the empty street, not quite sure where to go from here. "Okay, so my friend's boy goes to that school, and she asked to make sure he got picked up today. But I got caught in traffic, so I'm late. I thought maybe your boys might know if somebody picked him up already."

The girl gave her a curious once-over, her gaze stopping briefly on the crude tattoos across the knuckles of Stacy's right hand, so Stacy folded her arms with her hand tucked down and hidden.

"Whyn't you go ask the teacher?" the girl asked.

Stacy glanced back at the school again. "All the teachers just went back in. And all I want to know is if one of your boys knows him—knows if he got picked up. That's all." And she shrugged like it wasn't a big deal.

"Who got picked up?" Darin asked, giving the little kid another thump on the arm as he approached.

"A little boy that goes to your school," Stacy told him. "His name is Tyler Charms. Do you know him?"

Darin's lip hooked up in a sneer. "Yeah. He's in the special needs class. He's a retard," he said, and elbowed his brother, who tried unsuccessfully to hit him back.

"He's not a retard," Stacy snapped before she could stop herself. Modifying her tone, she added, "He has learning difficulties, that's all."

"Quit hitting your brother, Darin," the girl told the older kid.

Stacy tamped down her frustration. "So hey, Darin. Do you know if Tyler's mom picked him up from school already?"

Darin gave her a grin that was altogether too sly for someone his age. "No."

Then his brother piped up, saying, "His mom's in prison. Tommy Redmond said she killed a lady."

Darin sneered at him. "Shut up. You don't know nothin'. But I heard his mom's real crazy. She goes around at night, *killing people*," he told Stacy.

Stacy gave him a cutting look and kept the response she'd like to have given him to herself. She slipped her hands into her back pockets and scanned the street again. "Listen, all I want to know is if Tyler's gone for the day. Can you tell me or not?" Her tone came out a little harsher than she'd meant.

Darin didn't seem to notice. He'd picked up his stick again and struck a pose, as if to strike out at some unseen foe. "Yeah, he went early. Cory West said a lady from Child Services came and got him. Cory said he's going to a retard school."

The girl looked up from where she'd been scrolling through her phone, cocked her head to one side, and frowned at Stacy. "Who'd you say you were again?"

Stacy looked down at the phone in the girl's hand. Up until now, her thumb had been constantly swiping at the screen, shifting from one image to the next. Now it was paused on one picture. When their eyes met and locked, Stacy knew she'd been found out. She plucked at the short, spiky hair over her forehead and backed away, saying, "Ah, doesn't matter. I'll call his teacher. Thanks."

Then she turned, quickly crossed the street, and walked straight past the car so the girl wouldn't connect her with it.

"Hey, wait a minute," the girl called.

"Sorry, gotta run," she called over her shoulder. She broke into a trot and took a left down the next street where she dropped down behind a parked car, leaning with her back to the rear wheel, forearms on her knees with her head back and her eyes closed.

Automatically, she felt her pocket, then pulled out the toy car and turned it in her fingers. For the first two years she was in Carringway, the Child Services lady had brought Tyler to visit. Every other weekend Stacy had sat cross-legged on the floor next to him, watching him run that same car back and forth. A few words here and there. It took a good part of the visit to even engage him. By the time he'd notice her, the hour was almost up and her heart would sink. Did he even notice her? Did he even care? She'd almost given up. Thought she'd lost him. Then it happened. The Child Services lady had told Tyler it was time to go. Just like she always did. Normally, she'd take his hand and he'd walk out the door without a word or a backward look. But this time was different. This time Tyler got up to leave, but when he got to the door, he stopped and came back to crouch beside her.

"For Mommy," he said and pressed the little red car into her hand.

The Child Services lady came back and crouched next to him. "But Tyler, that's your very favorite car. Are you sure you want to give it away?"

Again, Tyler pushed the car at Stacy, a little more firmly this time. "For Mommy."

Stacy's heart just about melted. She enclosed his hand with the car in both of hers and kissed it. "I'll keep it safe, baby. I promise," she'd told him. "When you come home to live with me again, it'll be waiting for you."

That was the last time she'd seen him. After that he'd changed foster homes, changed Child Services case workers, and for a whole bunch of reasons the visits had petered out to nothing.

The memory of his small hand in hers, that stern look in his eye as he gave her his most prized possession brought a lump to her throat. She swallowed against it, pulled herself back to the present, and peeped out from behind the rear bumper. The street was clear. She checked each way, just to be sure, then got to her feet.

The lady from Child Services, the kid on the street had said. If the lady really was from Child Services, Tyler was safe for the moment, but the chances of Stacy finding him had just grown infinitely smaller. So that took away one problem and added another.

But what if Wayne had arranged to have him picked up? She'd written to him, telling him that the second Stacy was out, Tyler's life was in danger. She'd given him a brief outline of her plan—to pick Tyler up after school, then hand him off to Wayne to take somewhere safe, somewhere no one would ever find him. Didn't matter what happened to Stacy after that. Long as her son was safe. It meant Wayne would also be laying his life on the line. But what father wouldn't do that to protect his son? So maybe, just maybe, he'd gotten someone to pose as a lady from Child Services to come pick Tyler up.

But why would he do that? Why wouldn't he pick him up himself? Maybe he had another plan. Maybe there was a reason he couldn't do it.

There was only one way to find out. She got in the car, did a U-turn, and headed for Walton Street.

CHAPTER FIVE
DAY ONE: 3:45 PM—ELIZABETH

Elizabeth walked straight into her office and placed her briefcase next to her desk.

"Where the hell do we start?" she said and fell into her chair, swiveling it to lean both elbows on the desk, forehead cradled in her hands while she went over her calendar.

Before Penny could reply, the phone in the outer office rang. She went back to the reception area and looked at the screen of her phone.

"Thirty-seven missed calls," she announced.

Elizabeth switched on her computer, let out an exasperated sigh, and sat back. "Pick up the messages. Just give me the important ones. Delete the rest."

The calls had begun on Elizabeth's cell phone almost the second her call with Walt Straussman had ended—newspaper reporters from all over the country, TV networks, women's magazines—all one after the other until she'd switched her phone off. How they'd gotten her private cell phone number was anybody's guess. Now she'd have to change it again. The curse of social media. And not the only curse, considering the excruciatingly short time the uploaded video had taken to go viral on Twitter.

Elizabeth was sitting at her desk massaging her temples while she waited for her email to download, when Penny knocked and came in, shuffling through a stack of *While You Were Out* notes.

"A Detective Delaney asked if you could give him a call. 'As soon as you can,' he said. And Mr. McClaine wants to speak to you—Mr. Charles, that is," she said, identifying him as her father-in-law, rather than Elizabeth's ex-husband, Richard. "Four calls from Walt Straussman," she added with an ominous flick of the eyebrows.

Elizabeth extended her hand and Penny passed the messages to her.

"Thanks, I'll call him right away." Elizabeth stacked the messages neatly, then set them to one side while she placed both hands on the desktop and breathed out slowly, taking a second to gather herself. From almost the moment Stacy went missing, the barrage of media attention had put a light to a fuse, and the political backlash had started. Until then, Elizabeth hadn't really considered just how many state departments, how many state services, individuals, and organizations Stacy's disappearance would affect. Not to mention her father-in-law's credibility. She didn't want to speak to him, much less see him. As for the governor, even thinking about how this would affect him brought the taste of bile to her throat. She blew out a slow breath.

"Are you okay?" Penny asked in genuine concern as she collected up a stack of faxed documents from Elizabeth's fax machine. "You look pale."

Elizabeth pressed her lips together momentarily before reaching for the phone and hitting "2," the governor's private speed-dial. Then she sat back, composing herself while she waited for the call to connect. "Just give me a second. I'll be fine."

First things first: she needed to speak to Walt Straussman again, start ironing things out with him. It was the last call she wanted to make right now, but it was imperative she put a plan of damage control into place. The line opened and the phone had rung twice when the little buzzer on her desk sounded, signaling her that someone had entered the outer office.

"Whoever it is, throw them out and lock it," she told Penny as the call clicked through and Walt's messaging kicked in.

Penny exited to the front office while Elizabeth waited for Walt Straussman's recorded voice message to finish, but Penny returned almost at once, saying, "I'm sorry, Mrs. McClaine, it's Detective Delaney. He'd like to speak to you immediately."

Elizabeth let out a weary sigh and her shoulders sank. She hung up and leaned back in her chair, head high, arms laid gently along the armrests of the chair, with her legs crossed, attempting to look unruffled, despite feeling ten years older than she did this morning. "Show him in."

Apart from an extra sprinkling of gray around the temples, Detective Lance Delaney looked no different than when Elizabeth first met him five years ago when he'd been the lead detective in the case to find her missing daughter. He was tall and thin, with a shading of stubble across his hollowed-out cheeks, and still looked as if an unseen burden weighed him down. There had been times in the past when Elizabeth had wondered what that burden was; others when she thought she was better off not knowing.

He nodded in greeting, saying, "Mrs. McClaine," and closed the door behind him.

Elizabeth reached across and closed her calendar. "Detective Delaney."

"You mind?" he said, indicating the chair on the other side of her desk.

She opened one hand in invitation. "Of course."

He took a seat, hands on his knees as though exhausted, and looked around her office before speaking. "I don't suppose you're wondering why I'm here."

Elizabeth dropped both forearms on the desk and gave him a deadpan look. "I wouldn't exactly need second sight to figure it out, would I?"

A brief head-dip in acknowledgment. He gave her a second, then looked up. "I don't envy your position right now."

"No kidding."

"The media's gearing up for a field day on this. They're knocking down our doors already, wanting statements. Do you think you're up to all this?"

She leaned back in her chair. "No. But if you're asking me if this'll drive me back to the bottle, save it until tomorrow. I have a horrible feeling there's worse to come."

"I don't suppose you have any idea where Stacy may have gone?"

"You're kidding, right?"

"I had to ask." He gave it a beat, then said, "Any ideas or theories about why she might have run? Any threats you were aware of? Maybe trouble she'd gotten in?"

"Not a thing."

"No indication she was planning anything?"

"Oh, please. You can rephrase the question a hundred different ways, the answer's still the same." Elizabeth swallowed back the bile she felt rising in her throat. She felt sick.

Perhaps picking up on it, Delaney said, "We'll find her, Elizabeth. Just be patient."

"*Patient*, he says. Lance, this isn't about my reputation. There's a little boy out there who's waiting for his mother to come home to him. I'll be the first to admit that Stacy didn't always make the best choices. Good grief, she had a child at fifteen. And yes, she was stupid enough to write a bad check. But it was for *groceries*. So they could eat. C'mon. She had a child with a lot of challenges to take care of."

"Elizabeth, Stacy May Charms didn't go to prison for writing a bad check. She assaulted a Child Welfare worker."

"Who came to take her son away from her."

Delaney said nothing, just held her gaze.

When she realized there was no point in attacking him, she shook her head and waved it away. "I know, I know. It's not your fault. You're just doing your job."

"Then we'd better get some details down, shall we?" He took a tablet from his pocket and consulted the screen, swiping it from side to side. "You good to go?"

She nodded.

"Then let me just confirm: You picked up Stacy May Charms from the prison at 11:45 this morning. Is that correct?"

Oddly wounded by how readily his demeanor switched from sympathetic acquaintance to public official, she gave it a moment before answering.

"It was *supposed* to be 11:45. That was the time we had scheduled, but her mother wasn't picking up the phone to confirm she was home. I have no idea what the woman was doing, but we had to wait another twenty minutes before we could get through. We didn't leave until after the release procedures had been completed and that took until 12:15."

He paused with his pen over the tablet screen. "At exactly 12:15?"

"You want the time to the second?"

He looked up.

"Yes, 12:15."

He nodded and tapped it into the screen. "And her parole officer is Nancy Pattrenko, correct?"

"That's correct," Elizabeth said, wondering why it mattered. Stacy would hardly have fled to go to her parole officer. "I'd like to make it clear that I intend to make my own inquiries into Stacy's disappearance. I have an awful lot riding on this program—not least of which is my position with the Charles McClaine Foundation." She looked away towards the windows and winced at the thought. What damage this could wreak on the foundation's name didn't even bear thinking about.

Delaney never looked up, just kept making notes in his tablet.

"Understood. And you're welcome to carry out your own inquiries. However," he said and paused to catch her eye, "any information or evidence you obtain in regard to this case must be passed along to my office. Are we clear?"

Elizabeth picked up a pen, rolled it in her fingers. She felt like a recalcitrant student at the principal's office. "Yes, we're clear."

He waited a beat, then nodded. "I believe Tyler Charms was picked up from his school by Child Services."

"That's correct. Kay Heathers was on her way to meet us when she got the news. According to the message we got from the department, she went straight to Tyler's school and collected him."

"And took him back to his foster home." A statement, not a question, so he obviously already knew.

"I believe so." Elizabeth leaned forward to catch his eye. "Lance, I interviewed twenty-four women in Carringway. Right from the first meeting, I was in awe of Stacy May. I mean, really in awe. Tyler has brain damage. He has learning difficulties, developmental delays, coordination problems. There's no saying where the problems will end. That's a tough outlook. I should know, I've been there. And yet, Stacy loved that child unconditionally from the word go. Every time I spoke to her, I sat there thinking, 'Why couldn't I have…?'" She dropped her gaze, felt her lip tremble while the memories of her own failures as a mother threatened to rise up. Determined not to let herself go down that track, she swallowed hard and gathered herself. "Anyway, I thought this program was the perfect opportunity for her to turn her life around. Which is why she was the successful applicant."

When he simply nodded and kept tapping, she lifted her head but couldn't see the screen.

Eventually, his eyes came up to meet hers. "This isn't about you and Holly, Elizabeth. This is about someone else's choices. And you can't change them."

Elizabeth felt her heart drop. If only he could have seen Stacy May the way she did—how strong she was. If only Elizabeth had always had that strength.

Ignoring her silence, he went on, saying, "Do you remember her mentioning anyone she might contact when she got out? Anyone she might trust enough to go to?"

Elizabeth kept her eyes fixed on the pen she'd found herself repositioning on her leather-bound blotter. "From memory, I don't think she had any friends at all. Certainly no one on the inside from what I could see. I heard some of the inmates turned on her when she applied for the program. Jealousy, I suppose."

Delaney gave her a wan smile. "You wave a free pass for release at a prison full of desperate people, you're bound to create resentments."

She lifted a look on him but said nothing. She knew the Department of Corrections and the police deemed the program "politicking where politicians and do-gooders had no right to tread."

Delaney checked through the details he had and nodded once. "I think that's everything for now." He leaned to one side, tucking the tablet into his jacket pocket, eyes on Elizabeth. She was waiting for him to abruptly get up and leave the way he always did, but instead he said, "How's Holly? She must be, what, eleven now?"

Elizabeth felt her mood lighten at the thought of her daughter, how Delaney had worked night and day to find her when she was kidnapped.

"She's fine. And yes, eleven years old already. I don't know where the time went. One day all she talks about is *Sesame Street*, next thing I know it's all about clothes and shoes and makeup. Just like any little girl, I guess." She smiled at the memory of finding her daughter clomping through the house in a pair of Elizabeth's spike heel shoes, bright red lipstick smeared across her round, flat face, her favorite toy tucked under her arm. "And then there's Arthur, her teddy bear. She takes him everywhere with her." Her smile faded as the reality hit home. "To think I almost lost her."

They sat in silence for a moment, eyes downcast. That dreadful time five years ago was Elizabeth's worst nightmare. Any mother's worst nightmare.

"I don't know…" she began and cut herself off while she groped for the words. "I don't know if I ever thanked you."

Another sad smile turned one corner of his mouth up. "It's my job."

"You did more than your job."

He nodded once. "And yes, you did thank me."

An awkward silence spooled out. Then Delaney got up, adjusting his jacket. "Well, I think that's all for now. There's bound to be a lot of media attention on this."

"As if there hasn't been already," she said and made a face.

"Oh, and I'll ask you to refrain from speaking to the press." He lifted his eyebrows and added, his tone firm: "And this time, I mean it."

She flicked a glance up, then shifted her attention to align the message pad on her desk with the blotter. "Understood."

"And if I need to get in contact with you?"

"Penny will give you my new cell phone number."

He turned for the door, but Elizabeth stopped him, saying, "Lance, if there's one thing I'm sure of, it's that Stacy is devoted to that child. She won't go anywhere without him. Wherever she is, she'll be searching for him."

"Then after three years in prison, and with so little contact with him over the last one, I'd say she's either a very devoted mother, or an exceptional actress. Thank you, I'll see myself out."

The moment Delaney left the office, Elizabeth leaned her elbows on the desk, fingers massaging her forehead as she consulted her calendar. Already the day felt as though it had lasted a month. She also knew it was just the beginning. She checked her watch, lifted the phone and punched in the number she now knew by heart. When the line picked up, she said, "I'd like to speak to Warden Glassy, please." The line clicked through and rang once. Warden Jennifer Glassy answered just as Penny entered the room with a note in her hand. Elizabeth waved her to a seat.

"Jennifer, it's Elizabeth McClaine."

"How are you, Mrs. McClaine?"

Mrs. McClaine, not *Elizabeth*. Plus her tone was on the frosty side of cool. Elizabeth dropped her head onto one hand.

"I'm guessing you've heard," she asked.

A chilly beat before answering. "About Stacy? Oh yes, I certainly have."

"I'm convinced there was something going on behind the scenes—something we didn't know about that made her run."

"Well, that's become very ... apparent. Although in light of what's happened, perhaps she'd been planning this all along. We'll be sure to ask her when the monitoring company tracks her down and brings her back and the whole program is scrapped."

Elizabeth squeezed her eyes shut. That barbed comment had hit the mark. But bickering over the whys and hows wasn't going to get them anywhere.

"Jennifer, I know you've been one of the greatest advocates for this program. I know you saw the benefits. You see how many young women whose lives could be turned around. You were one of the biggest supporters right from the start, long before anybody else. We would never have made it this far if it wasn't for you. And I know Stacy wasn't your choice of representative for this program."

"Stacy May Charms is headstrong, determined, and resents any kind of authority. I thought we had applicants who would have been more suitable for the program. That's all."

"Stacy was a good mother in a bad situation. All she ever wanted was to look after her child."

"Which she could have. If she'd let the Child Services worker take Tyler into care until the mess with the bad check was ironed out. Jail is no place for a little boy. But, *no*. Stacy wasn't going to have anyone tell her what to do. So she attacked the Child Services worker who was only trying to help her."

Elizabeth could feel her hackles rising. "I believe Stacy *pushed* her."

"Doesn't matter. The woman fell, hit her head and needed hospitalization. Since Stacy was nearly eighteen, she was charged as an adult. That's how the law goes, Mrs. McClaine. You break it, things don't always go the way you want."

"But all the characteristics you just listed—the strong-headedness, the determination—they're the exact qualities I was looking for in the applicants. Whoever the first successful candidate for this program was, she had to be passionate, and dedicated to the care of her child, no matter what."

"Your point being?"

"My point being that Stacy has those qualities in spades. Every time I spoke to her, I was even more convinced."

"Yes, it's incredible how convincing these women can be."

"Oh, come on, Jennifer. You don't believe it was an act any more than I do. I think someone, somewhere, has said or done something to frighten her. It's the only thing that would explain her taking off like that."

"If she was so terrified, why didn't she say something? Why didn't she come to me?"

"That's what I intend to find out. But I need your help."

A tense silence stretched. Then Jennifer Glassy sighed down the line and said, "That'll depend on what you need."

Elizabeth outlined her plan, then hung up. Penny, who'd been listening, let out a relieved breath.

"Sounds like that went better than I thought it would."

"It did, but we don't have much time. Have my car brought around. We're going back to the prison."

"What? Today? I thought you were going to the Business Awards dinner tonight."

Elizabeth swung around on her chair, snatched her coat from the stand, and shrugged into it. "So I'll be fashionably late. I hardly think anyone's going to miss me for the first hour or so. It'll be all long-winded speeches by Clay Farrant and Christine Wentworth smooching up to anyone that smells of cash so his company floats at the highest share price."

"You can hardly blame her. I heard her employment package includes a substantial share issue. She'll be worth millions overnight."

"Don't worry, he'll see that she's worked for it. What time do the awards start?"

"Are you sure this is a wise decision?"

Elizabeth looked up at her. "I'm on the Business Awards committee. What else do you think I'm going to do? Hide in my office with my tail between my legs?"

"It starts at eight." Penny checked the time. "I'll have Katy put out your dark blue business suit, the *take-no-prisoners* one. You show so much as a ruffle you may as well wear a matching noose."

Elizabeth lifted her briefcase from the desk and snapped it closed. "Under the circumstances, I might already be wearing it. But I refuse to back out now. This isn't about the Cleveland business community, or about Clay Farrant's egotistical puffery and self-promotion. This is damage control. Anyone who's anyone will be there. I'm going to see to it that each and every political backer who supported this program—supported me—knows that nothing has changed, that we're still on point."

Penny's eyebrows shot up. "Whoa! That's going to be some hard sell."

"I know. So the sooner we find Stacy May Charms, the better the chance I won't spend the rest of my life in social and political purgatory with just a leper bell to keep me company."

CHAPTER SIX
DAY ONE: 4:17 PM—STACY

The whole stretch of Walton Street was pretty much deserted when Stacy pulled up outside Wayne's house. That meant nothing. You could never be too careful. She stayed in the car, twisting around in her seat so she could peer up at the house, then up and down the street. When she felt safe enough, she got out, locked the car and walked quickly up the front path. Keeping her head down, she hurried up the three front steps to the door, knocked, and waited.

Stacy had met Wayne three days after she ran away from home. He was sixteen, good-looking, and streetwise. Stacy thought she'd found the love of her life. Eleven months later, when Tyler was born, all that changed. Tyler came out of the womb with the cord wrapped around his neck and his face the color of thunderclouds. The doctor said he had brain damage due to lack of oxygen, and that if Stacy had been in the hospital like she was supposed to be, instead of the back of Wayne's car at two o'clock that morning, things might have been different.

Wayne had tried to get the cord off the baby's neck but when he couldn't, he'd panicked and run, leaving Stacy holding the baby, so to speak. Wasn't until she managed to loosen the cord that he took his first breath.

From the second she looked down at her newborn son with those great big eyes that were still swollen shut, those rosebud lips, and his tiny fingers clasped around hers, she knew right away that he was the first thing she'd ever loved—really loved.

Sitting in that car, Stacy made Tyler a promise: that she'd never be the kind of mother Gayleen was; that he would always have a good home; that anything he got would be his alone, not second-hand crap that someone else had worn first. And that no one, *no one* would lift a hand to her child. They'd have to go through Stacy first. That was the kind of mom she was going to be.

Didn't exactly turn out that way. If only she'd made better decisions in her life.

Wayne's place looked like he'd put some work into it since she was last here. A two-story, single family house, it had a porch with a love seat angled to catch the sunset, new paintwork across the front, windowsills highlighted in a shade of royal blue, and a freshly dug-over garden along the front containing flowers that looked like daisies. Didn't look like anything Wayne would do. Last time she saw this place, it looked fit to be demolished. Then again, time changes a person. If anyone knew that, it was her.

When she got no reply from her first knock, she knocked again, a little harder this time, then moved to the side window and peeped in. No movement. Checking the street, she slipped the key out of her back pocket, inserted it in the lock. It turned. She gave the street another once-over, then twisted the handle and pushed the door open.

The living room smelled faintly of dog, bacon, and freshly tumble-dried laundry. She moved to the kitchen where a single cereal bowl sat in the sink, but the counter was clear and wiped down. A couple of wilted flowers sat in a jelly jar on the windowsill. Under a cat flap in the back door, someone had spread newspapers across the worn linoleum. A neatly laid-out toolbox full of screwdrivers and wrenches stood open on the floor next to the dining table, on which a lace cloth had been laid. Set in the corner of the table was an array of photographs in black frames. Most of them featured a blonde girl, probably in her late twenties, standing next to a big lumberjack-looking guy with brown curly hair, his arm around her. Then it hit her.

Oh, jeez, Wayne's moved.

Now what?

When her eyes dropped back to the toolbox, she spotted a pair of tin snips neatly slipped into a compartment down the side. Taking the opportunity while she had it, she snatched them up and set her foot on one of the dining chairs, sliding one edge of the snips down under the bracelet, and squeezed hard on the grips with both hands. The blades snapped through the strap, and the display on the bracelet tweeted and flashed. The strap sprang apart and the device clunked to the floor.

Stacy picked it up and inspected it. The display was still active. Soon as she left, she'd get rid of it. But she had to find Wayne first. She stuck the bracelet into her jeans pocket and scanned the room.

A phone sat on the sideboard, plugged into the wall jack next to it. Stacy opened the first cupboard, and sure enough, phone books were stacked there, the edge of the pages showing dark smudges where someone had thumbed through them. She pulled one out and opened it to the Ls. The only Lettes she could see in the area was J. D. Lettes—Wayne's witch of a mother. If she called Janice Lettes to find out Wayne's address, first thing the woman would do was call the police, have them waiting at whatever address she gave Stacy. She flicked to the Bs, ran her finger down the column until she found what she was looking for.

According to the listing, Curta Brixton lived in an apartment on Terrence Avenue. Curta had been out of prison on parole for almost a year now. Chances were good that her place was the first one the police would search. But it was a chance she had to take.

She was just lifting the phone, using one finger to mark the listing, when the sound of a vehicle pulling in down the side of the house made her swing around. She replaced the receiver and crossed to the side window overlooking the driveway, leaned alongside the frame, and peeped out. A blue tow truck rattled into the driveway and came to a halt with a squeak of brakes. The logo on the hood and door depicted a snarling grizzly with the words *Traynor Towing—You Better Call The Bear* circling it in yellow italics.

"Dammit!" With her heart rate ratcheting up the scale again, she pivoted back against the side of the window and searched the room for escape: her choices were either upstairs or out the back door.

When she peeked out again, the driver's door creaked open and a big guy in a plaid shirt and Indians cap got out—the guy in the photos, she realized. And here she was in his house, with no good reason to be.

She heard the truck door slam shut, so she ran for the back door. She flicked the back door latch and ripped it open to find an enormous boxer dog bounding up the back steps. She slammed the door and the dog jumped up against it, howling and barking. But when she turned to press her back to the wood frame, the tow-truck guy was standing in the front doorway, gaping at her with a startled look on his face.

He swiped his cap off and ran his hand through his hair. "Who are you and what are you doing in my house?"

Stacy kept her back to the door, and raised both hands—part surrender, partly telling him to keep his distance. "Listen, there's been a mistake." Behind her, the dog was having forty fits, hurling itself repeatedly against the door, causing the upper glass panel to rattle and the cat flap to clatter. Any minute the thing would break the glass.

As he approached, the guy tilted his head, looking past her, and yelled, "Get down, Luther."

The dog went quiet but for a few whimpers and the guy turned his attention back to Stacy. "You're damn right there's been a mistake. Who are you? What are you doing here?"

She straightened and tucked her hands into her pockets, nervously watching him. He tossed his cap on the sofa as he passed it, shooting her accusing glances as he strode into the kitchen. He pulled open the refrigerator, took out a can of Coke, and snapped the top open before turning back to her with his hip leaning against the kitchen counter.

Stacy folded her arms, hugging herself while she tried to think up a good lie. "I'm sorry, I thought my ah … friend was living here. He was, last I knew. I guess he must have moved out."

The guy took a swig of Coke, and frowned, the corners of his mouth pulled down. "So you broke in?"

"No, no. The front door was open," she lied, silently thankful she'd had the presence of mind to stick the key back in her pocket. "That's why I thought he was home. I just opened the door and walked in. Anybody could have." She thumbed over her shoulder towards the dog. "And besides, he wasn't here when I got here. I wouldn't have come in if he was."

"Luther always comes to work with me." He angled his head, regarding her with suspicion. "So who's this friend you're looking for?"

"Wayne Lettes. He lived here like, a couple years ago or something."

When the dog let out a bark right next to her, Stacy's heart just about jumped out of her chest and she leaped aside. She looked back to find the dog had stuck its head through the cat flap. She clapped both hands to her chest and bent briefly at the waist. "Oh, jeez, I wish he wouldn't do that."

"Get back, Luther," the guy growled. He crossed to the door, waiting for the dog to retreat. "Well, I wouldn't know where this Wayne Lettes is, but he ain't here now, only me and Luther. 'Scuse me." He reached past Stacy for the door handle. "Back, Luther, back," he ordered.

Stacy could hear the dog whimpering and moving about, his huge feet thumping on the wooden porch in excitement. The second the door opened the dog burst in like a hurricane, stumpy-tailed rear end wagging, big cinderblock head and slobbery jowls all over the guy like he hadn't seen him in months. The guy bent over and pounded his side with the flat of his hand, making a hollow thump that looked painful, but the dog responded with a look of ecstasy.

The guy grinned. "Don't worry about this guy. He's a big baby at heart."

The dog spun around and lunged at Stacy. She threw up both hands in defense, but the dog jumped up, front paws up on her chest while it subjected her to the same slobber treatment his owner had, leaving a trail of drool down the front of her shirt and jeans. "Whoa! Easy there, fella," she said, turning her face away and giving him a tentative pat on the head.

"Down, Luther. Away to your bed," the guy ordered and pointed to the living room.

Luther's excitement vanished in a snap and his head dropped. He turned and trotted to the living room, where he leaped up onto the sofa and collapsed with his head on his paws, watching them, one black eyebrow up, then the other.

Stacy let out a silent breath of relief and wiped her hands down her front. "So I'm guessing you're the Traynor on the truck, huh?"

"Philip Traynor. Folks call me Bear. And who are you?"

Stacy nodded. "Bear Traynor. Right. Okay well, I'm, ah … Shelly—Shelly Shay … just call me Shelly."

Bear said nothing, just turned and went to the living room where he opened a drawer in the dresser and took out a stack of envelopes, all bound together in with a rubber band.

"Well, then, Shelly, when you find your Wayne Lettes, you can give him his mail. And tell him to change his address. I swear, he gets more mail than I do."

He ambled back and handed the stack to Stacy. She gave the wad a cursory flick through, noting the familiar envelopes, and her heart sank. Most of them were addressed to Wayne in her own handwriting.

"Shit." She looked up. "I mean, *dammit*. He didn't get my letters. How long's he been gone?"

"I've been here just over two years."

She flipped a couple of them over, only noticing now that the envelopes had been torn open, and the flaps taped back down. A flash of panic went down her spine as she flicked through the rest of them. "Some of these have been opened," she said and looked to him.

Bear leaned against the kitchen counter, ankles crossed as he lifted his Coke can again. "Wasn't me," he said. "They all came like that."

He was about to take another swig when his gaze dropped to the pocket of her jeans and stayed there. Following his line of sight, she could see the bracelet peeking out.

Their eyes met.

"How long have you been here?" he asked flatly.

"'Bout two minutes before you got here."

"Then I'd really like you off my property, if you don't mind. To my reckoning, the cops should be here in around..." He checked his watch and frowned like he was doing some mental calculations. "...three minutes."

"What? Here?"

"Near enough. We're in a cellular black spot, but they'll have tracked you almost to the door."

Her eyes widened. "They can trace these things that accurately?"

"They didn't tell you?"

She shrugged. "I guess, but—"

"And was it you removed it?"

"Well, who else was gonna? I thought it would just switch off when I cut the strap."

"Seriously? The second you tamper with that thing, the bracelet sends out an alert. That's how they know you're trying to remove it."

She took the bracelet out of her pocket, only now realizing the severity of the situation. "Holy shit."

"Empty your pockets."

"What? Why?"

"I wanna know if you took anything before I kick you out."

Stacy lifted her chin, looked him defiantly in the eye. "I don't steal stuff," she told him sharply. "I'm only here because I thought Wayne lived here."

"Then I'd like you to go. Believe me," he said, "the instant you cut that thing off, whatever problems you had before, they just tripled."

CHAPTER SEVEN
DAY ONE: 4:49 PM—ELIZABETH

Despite the fact that Elizabeth had left her office immediately after speaking to Warden Glassy, rush hour traffic was already mounting and the hour drive back to Carringway Women's Prison took fifteen minutes longer. The prison came into view in the distance as she turned off the main road. It was an angular building of concrete and glass, gardens tended both inside and out. The structure might have been mistaken for the headquarters of some international manufacturing company, were it not for the twenty-foot fencing topped with razor wire that ran around the perimeter.

The complex had been state of the art in private prison construction when it was built eight years ago by her father-in-law's company, C.J. McClaine Construction. At the time, she was still married to Richard. She remembered the long nights he'd put into winning the contract. Now, on reflection, she realized that was probably about the time when the marriage had begun to founder.

Elizabeth checked the rearview mirror, then swung the car into the dedicated road built for traffic to and from the prison. The rain that had been threatening all the way here had cleared by the time she pulled to a halt at the barrier in front the prison entrance. The guard exited the gate house at the side of the roadway and rounded the car. He bent at the driver's side, one hand on the roof as she lowered her window.

"Yes, ma'am."

"Elizabeth McClaine. I'm here to see Jennifer Glassy," she told him.

"She's expecting you. Drive straight through and park in the private parking area around the south side of the administration building," he said, pointing.

She raised the window, and as soon as the barrier lifted, she drove through the gates she'd driven through not six hours previously, under entirely different circumstances.

Jennifer Glassy looked up as Elizabeth was escorted into her office. Despite looking tired and ill-tempered, she gestured Elizabeth to the visitor's chair opposite and gave her a brief smile. No doubt Elizabeth's close ties with the governor were the reason Glassy had agreed to Elizabeth questioning some of the women. Under the circumstances, that agreement could be withdrawn at any minute. Elizabeth had to make the most of the opportunity while she had it.

"Thank you for seeing me at such short notice," Elizabeth said and lowered herself into the chair, waiting until the prison officer who'd accompanied her had withdrawn and closed the door before adding, "and I appreciate your assistance."

Jennifer Glassy leaned back in her leather chair and folded her arms. "I don't know what you're hoping to find. Even if any of these women know anything, I very much doubt they'll tell you."

"To be honest, I didn't know where else to start. I'm hoping Stacy might have confided in someone about what she had in mind. I find it hard to believe she'd spend six months planning all this without telling another soul."

Glassy let out a cynical chuckle. "If we were talking about anyone else, I'd agree. There are very few secrets in prison. Everybody knows everybody else's business. Information is currency. You know something, you can trade on it. One thing I'll say for Stacy May Charms, she knew how to keep her mouth shut. Which is why she earned a reputation for being trusted."

"Yes, and I understand that. But what if one of her friends figured it out—guessed what she was up to? You said yourself, gossip is rife here. If I can convince one person to open up and cooperate, it might give me a place to start."

Jennifer Glassy tilted her head briefly, her expression skeptical as she reached for a file folder sitting off to one side of her desk. She drew it across in front of her and opened it, saying, "You can try. I don't like your chances. I made a list of inmates who have agreed to speak to you, but by the time she was released, she didn't have too many friends."

"Is that because of the program?"

Glassy plucked a sheet of paper from the file, passed it to Elizabeth and closed the file again. "As she progressed through the various stages and passed the academic and program requirements, resentments arose. We expected that. The successful applicant was never going to win the title of Miss Popularity. But that just seemed to make her all the more determined. Personally, I didn't think Stacy would last the distance." She shrugged in resignation. "To her credit, she did. I'll give her that much."

"Do you know if she had any particular disagreements or rivalries that might have aggravated tensions with the other inmates?"

The warden leaned forward to square up the file on her desk, avoiding eye contact. She let the question hang for a moment, maybe debating the best way to answer it. "About four months ago, we had a … an incident, during which we discovered drugs were being smuggled into the prison. We carried out a thorough investigation, and with some fast thinking by some of our officers, we found the culprit and dealt with the situation swiftly, and surely." The expression in her eyes hardened along with her tone. "The following day, a friend of Stacy May's—Amy Dixon—died as a result of a drug overdose. Amy had gotten clean, she was doing well. Then, all of a sudden, she OD'd. Stacy was…" Jennifer Glassy looked away to her left and drew a breath while she searched for a word. "…furious, devastated. She was only two months into the program at the time. Up until that point, she'd been doing okay, but something about Amy's death seemed to cross a line for her, made her even more determined to turn her life around. After that, she put everything she had into acing all the required programs. And as you know, the work paid off. I guess you could say that was the story of Stacy May's life."

"And what happened to the person who was smuggling the drugs in?"

Again, her eyes dropped to her desktop. When she hesitated, Elizabeth thought she wasn't going to answer. Then she said, "The supplier turned out to be one of our own contractors—a physical therapist working for a company called Cavalier Health and Wellness. Not one of their proudest moments. Or ours," she added in a low voice as she shifted the file back to its original spot.

"You have a physical therapist on site?" The surprise in Elizabeth's voice rang clear.

"Right now, we have three inmates in wheelchairs. By law, we're required to meet their needs."

Elizabeth nodded. "I see," she said, wondering where this slotted into the picture.

Jennifer Glassy lifted her head and folded her hands in her lap, clearly discomfited by the subject. "Naturally, her services were immediately suspended and Cavalier fired her. Once we knew where to look, the evidence against her was overwhelming. She's currently spending time at the taxpayers' expense in the Ohio Women's Reformatory Prison."

"Is there any chance she could have been in contact with Stacy? Maybe threatened her if she thought Stacy was the reason she got caught?"

The warden lifted her chin with a look of steely determination. "No way. Last I heard, she'd taken quite a beating from a couple of the inmates. Now she spends most of her time in protective custody. There's no way she could have had any communications with Stacy. Or anyone else," she added in a firm voice.

"I imagine the incident must have put a lot of pressure on you."

Another tight silence. Then she said, "You could say that."

It seemed the conversation was freezing up, so Elizabeth turned her questioning back to Stacy. "So what if Stacy was afraid for her life? Is there anyone she might have confided in?"

Jennifer Glassy let out another skeptical chuckle. "I'd be surprised. Like I said, she knew how to keep secrets—including her own. But if you check the list, you might like to speak to Cissy Pettameyer. She was in the same work detail as Stacy. Cissy keeps an ear to the ground and she just may have heard something."

Elizabeth found Cissy's name fourth on the list. "The name sounds familiar. I think I remember interviewing her." Elizabeth made a mark next to the name.

"You did. Cissy was one of three women who made it through to the final cut. Cissy and Stacy weren't close, but Cissy has an ear for gossip. She's cautious, but she might tell you what she's heard with the right amount of prompting. You never know."

"Thank you."

"I also added Nyla Guthrie to the list. You haven't met her. She didn't apply for the program, but she requested the opportunity to speak to you."

Elizabeth looked up. "That sounds promising."

"Don't get your hopes up. She and Stacy came to blows. They had to be separated. Stacy wound up in the hospital with a couple of broken ribs. Nyla could be just playing games. She's cunning and manipulative—likes to think she's in control. But she was adamant she wanted to talk to you."

"You think she could know something important?"

"Let's say Nyla has a lot of influence within a certain crowd. Stacy inadvertently stepped across the line when she first got here. Nyla put her in her place. Nothing serious. It's what happens. Things seemed to simmer down; in fact, they seemed quite close for a while—hanging together, in the same work detail, always with their heads together. But something happened between them four months ago after Amy died, and for Stacy's safety, we placed her into a different dormitory and a separate work group. I never found out what the disagreement was about. But that's not surprising."

"Stacy was already in the program by that time. Why wasn't this flagged to me?"

"No reason to. Stacy didn't fight back. Just stood there and took the beating, by all accounts. Yes, she wound up with a couple of broken ribs, but nothing you'd have noticed. And she begged me not to let it affect her application." She lifted one shoulder in concession. "I didn't think it should count against her."

"Would anybody else know what the disagreement was about?"

"No idea. You can try Nyla, but I wouldn't bank on her saying anything. It could have been because one of them used the other one's soap on the wrong day, or someone spoke to someone else they shouldn't have—who knows? There's always friction in this place. Two thousand women all locked up together, it comes with the territory."

"Do you think Nyla was involved in this drug ring?"

Glassy leaned forward on her elbows. "Mrs. McClaine, when I say we did a *very* thorough investigation, we carried out cell inspections, personal strip searches, drug dog inspections, we tore the place apart. If there had been anyone else involved, believe me, I'd have found the evidence."

Elizabeth nodded, acknowledging the unintended implication that Jennifer Glassy didn't know her job. "I'm sorry. I didn't mean—"

"No offense taken," she replied, although clearly there was. "But believe me, Nyla's influence stretches a long way. She's been here a long time, and she knows all the ins and outs of the place. If Stacy had crossed her badly enough, it wouldn't matter if they were in separate dormitories, separate work details—separate continents—Stacy wouldn't have lasted two minutes. Nyla would have found a way to get to her."

"She has that much control?"

"Not control, Mrs. McClaine—determination and time. You wouldn't believe the lengths these women go to, the detailed planning they put in to get what they want. If they'd used the same initiative to carry out the crime they were in for, they'd never have been caught in the first place."

Elizabeth consulted the list again. "Who's Eileen Caston? Sixth on the list?"

Glassy lifted a pen and leaned back, rolling it back and forth in her fingers. "Eileen didn't apply for the program, but she has requested the opportunity to speak with you."

"May I ask why she didn't apply?"

"She would have failed the application criteria."

That was obviously all the warden was prepared to say.

"I see Eileen was in Stacy's work detail."

"Only for the last four months. They worked two benches away from each other, but they seemed on good terms. I got the impression that since the bust-up with Nyla, Stacy deliberately cut herself off from her usual circle, but she seemed to get along with Eileen. But then, Eileen doesn't involve herself in the tittle-tattle that most of the women do."

"May I ask what the work program entailed?"

"Sewing. We have a contract for low-cost industrial garments and a little fashion wear. Each of the women is paid for their work, and they can use that money as they wish. Unless they have expenses or outstanding fines they haven't paid. Then it gets channeled to pay those.

"I can tell you this much, Mrs. McClaine: Stacy May Charms is a lot of things, but she's nobody's fool. She's a survivor. She knew who to get along with, who not to cross, how to work the system. A lot of women trusted her with personal information. I think you'll find that what you're searching for isn't what Stacy was told—it's what she wasn't."

The prison officer who escorted Elizabeth to the interview room was introduced as Trish Tomes. She was somewhere in her early forties, short dark hair brushed harshly back from a face devoid of all makeup apart from a smear of lip gloss. She wore the standard gray prison uniform—a cotton jacket with her name embroidered on the left lapel, plain gray pants, nightstick and cuffs on a leather belt, black leather shoes—and walked with her shoulders military square, hands clasped behind her back.

They entered Cell Block C and walked for some minutes in silence. When they paused in front of a solid steel door, waiting for the remote security mechanism to activate, Elizabeth grabbed the opportunity while she had it, saying, "How well did you know Stacy May?"

They stepped through the doorway between metal detectors, and Trish Tomes signaled the security camera above the door. The door slid closed with a faint click as the lock engaged, and they turned and walked on.

"Well as I know any of 'em. I oversaw the work detail she was assigned to." She gestured for Elizabeth to turn down the next corridor.

"The warden told me she was a seamstress in one of the work programs."

Trish nodded. "Yes, she was our best sewer—fast and very precise, which is what you need. Got through twice the work some did, but then, they're all pretty good now."

"She learned to sew in here?"

They stopped at another door. Trish made the same gesture at the camera, and the door clicked and slid open. As they stepped through, she said, "She had no idea of how to sew before she got here. She did some classes and took to it like a duck to water. A lot don't. No matter how hard they try, they just can't sew a straight line."

Elizabeth's heels echoed off the sterile gray walls as they walked on together. How women could be locked up years in here without going insane, she had no idea. The few hours she'd spent doing interviews here had been more than enough for her. Which brought her to another question.

"Warden Glassy said Stacy had a friend, Amy Dixon, who died. She said Stacy was very upset."

A burst of air escaped Trish's lips. "That's one way of putting it. Amy was a good kid. She'd worked hard to get clean. I don't think she'd have made it without Stacy. Then when those drugs were around, she must have gotten hold of some, and overdosed. Hell of a thing to happen. She was only two months from release."

"Warden Glassy also tells me Stacy was friendly with Eileen Caston and that they worked together."

Trish let out a bemused chuckle. "I wouldn't say they were exactly friends. Eileen doesn't make friends. She likes to think they're more like *admirers*. You'll see what I mean. But, yeah, Stacy got on okay with her."

They paused at a door and Trish looked up to nod at yet another camera. Again, a click of a lock.

"In here," Trish said as she reached for the handle. Before she opened it, she leaned her shoulder to the door and turned, dropping her voice. "First on your interview list is Nyla Guthrie. Take anything she tells you with a grain of salt. She's got a real way with words, but believe me, she's a troublemaker."

Then she pushed the door open and they stepped in.

CHAPTER EIGHT
DAY ONE: 5:14 PM—ELIZABETH

Elizabeth would have picked Nyla Guthrie to be in her early thirties. Heavyset through the shoulders and neck, she bore a pale scar that cut a crease in her left cheek, giving her an unintentional lopsided smirk.

Her shoulder-length brown hair had been pulled back in an untidy ponytail, and three teardrops had been tattooed beneath her left eye, a permanent testimony to her time in prison.

Nyla sat in a plastic chair, arms folded across her chest, ankles crossed under a Formica table, smug look on her face, while a second guard leaned against the back wall, watching her. Trish ran through a flat round of introductions, then gestured Elizabeth to a green plastic chair opposite Nyla.

"Officer Reynolds is on C-Block duty today," Trish said, indicating the uniformed woman on the other side of the room. "Thanks, Kathy. We're good from here."

Kathy Reynolds straightened, nodded at Elizabeth, then jerked her head toward the corner of the room, an unspoken request for Trish's ear. The two turned away, whispering in brief conversation. When they broke, they shared a knowing look. Trish nodded, then Officer Reynolds bid Elizabeth a brief goodbye and withdrew, closing the door behind her.

The door locked, and Trish Tomes turned her back to it, hands behind her back, eyes fixed straight ahead.

Elizabeth took the seat, sliding it up to the table and depositing her briefcase next to her. She could feel Nyla Guthrie's eyes on her. The intensity of the glare made her skin crawl. Heeding Trish's caution, she avoided any eye contact until she was ready. She wanted to make sure she got the upper hand, if possible. Finally, confident she was in control, she leaned both elbows on the table, hands clasped under her chin, and met the woman's gaze. "Thank you for seeing me, Nyla."

A snide smile hooked back one side of Nyla's mouth while she ran her eyes from Elizabeth's elbows to the top of her head and back before speaking. She tipped her head. "Breaks up the day."

Elizabeth folded one arm over the other on the table. "I believe you and Stacy May Charms were friends for a while."

One eyebrow went up and she snorted out a bitter laugh. "Is that what you heard?"

Irritation blazed down Elizabeth's spine. She steadied her tone and looked the woman directly in the eye. "I also heard you and Stacy May had a disagreement. Or did I get that wrong?"

Nyla tilted her head, her dark eyes studying Elizabeth. "Not everybody gets on in here. I don't believe *not getting on with people* is in breach of the penal code. Or maybe it is now. I been here so long I wouldn't know."

Elizabeth refused to react. "I assume you know Stacy has broken her parole and disappeared. We're very keen to find her."

Nyla scratched at the side of her mouth and folded her arms again. Elizabeth went on. "This program was a lifeline for Stacy. She was already released. She was supposed to be seeing her son on Monday. She had *everything* going for her. Do you have any idea why she'd risk all that by running?"

"Why would I? I'm not her personal keeper."

Glassy was right, Nyla was playing games with her. "I thought she was a friend of yours."

Nyla shifted in her seat, clearly amused. "Lady, you don't make friends in this shithole. You make allies, or you make enemies. That's it. Nothing in between."

Elizabeth reined in her mounting irritation. "Nyla, I'm pretty sure you know what'll happen when the police find her. If there's anything you can tell me that could help Stacy, this is the time. Now, do you have anything for me or not?"

Nyla rocked her head right back and studied the ceiling a moment. "Umm, maybe. Maybe not."

A bolt of anger flashed through Elizabeth. "Then, I'll take that as a *no*," she said, and stood up, picking up her briefcase. "If you have nothing to tell me, then I don't have time to waste playing games. Goodbye."

But just as she turned for the door, Nyla called after her. "Hey, maybe you're just not asking the right questions. Ever think of that?"

Elizabeth hesitated. Was this another game? She turned a glare back on Nyla—one that said, *I'm listening, but you'd better not be wasting my time.* Then she spoke aloud. "So what happened between you?"

"We're talking three years here. Can you be a bit more specific?"

Elizabeth raised her eyes to a point just above Nyla's head. "Quit screwing around, Nyla. I lobby politicians for a living. You think I can't play this game? I'd leave you for dead. Now, the fight you had with Stacy. You broke two of her ribs. Talk to me or I'm out of here."

A sly grin curled up one side of Nyla's mouth. She looked off towards the windows, and slipped her hands in her pockets. After a long breath, she brushed something off the leg of her prison uniform. "It was nothing. Just prison shit, that's all."

Elizabeth crossed to the table, and stabbed her finger onto the scratched surface, midway between them. "Nyla, I didn't ask to see you, you asked to see me. I'm trying to help Stacy. If you've got something to say, say it."

The other woman grinned, seemingly enjoying the moment. "Or what?"

"Or you can go back to your cell and I'll find someone that will help me. Last chance, because I don't have time for your bullshit."

"Fine," she said and leaned forward with her upper body across the table, arms folded, eyes fixed on Elizabeth. "When you find Stacy—and you will—tell her I said, *Amy's got what she had coming to her.* Tell her that, word for word. Then watch the look on her face. I wish I could see it myself."

Elizabeth brushed herself off, as though that would rid her of the past ten minutes. "What a complete waste of time," she told Trish as Nyla was escorted from the room.

"I told you. She's playing you. Kathy Reynolds has gone to get Cissy. Might take a while, her work detail ends in a half hour." Trish dropped her voice and angled herself a little closer. "Watch her as well. She's all sweetness and light. But she's a whole different animal to Nyla. You gotta watch for the subtext."

"Thank you. I'll take that into consideration," Elizabeth said.

When the radio on Trish's left shoulder crackled into life, she excused herself and stepped aside to answer it. She snapped a few comments, then ended the connection with the flick of a switch.

"Nancy Pattrenko, Stacy's parole officer just called in. Looks like they've got a location for Stacy May Charms' ankle bracelet."

Elizabeth rocked her head back, shoulders sinking in relief. "Oh, thank God. Where is she?"

"The bracelet has been traced to within fifty or so feet of the corner of Walton and Cane Streets up near Cleveland Heights. The police have been notified and they're on their way. I doubt they'll find Stacy there, though. The guy tracking her said the device is registering that someone's tampered with it, and the location is stationary."

"Meaning what?"

"Meaning she's removed it."

Elizabeth turned away from Officer Tomes, squeezed her eyes shut, and cursed under her breath.

CHAPTER NINE
DAY ONE: 5:45 PM—STACY

Gayleen's car was a heap of junk. The steering was heavier than Stacy remembered, and the driver's seat suspension had given way under a succession of drivers' rear ends over the years. Stacy had to sit up, back ramrod straight with her head lifted high just to see over the steering wheel. She drove slowly, sedately, down every back street she knew, until she located the rent-controlled apartment block where Curta Brixton lived and parked across the street.

Again, she waited, checking the street before getting out. Parking right outside Curta's probably wasn't the smartest move. If time was on her side, she'd have parked further away and walked back. But every minute she wasted, the closer they'd get to Tyler. So she entered the Terrence Street lobby and went straight for the stairs, taking them two at a time until she reached the sixth floor, where Curta was last registered in the phone book. She exited the stairwell and walked quickly along the first hallway, checking over her shoulder every now and then while counting off apartments until she got to 6F.

She paused, held her breath, and knocked.

No response, so she knocked again, harder this time.

"Hold your damn horses," she heard Curta's voice call from inside.

"I only got one pair of feet." At which point the lock clicked, the door opened, and Curta stood framed in the doorway with a waft of air smelling of freshly baked cookies rolling out around her. At almost sixty, she was still as wide in the girth as she'd been the previous year when Stacy last saw her, gray hair still a mass of coarse curls pinned back from her face with a clasp, dark eyes narrowed in suspicion. She wore a cotton flowered dress to just past her knees, house slippers, a dish towel clutched in one hand. She peered out, face set in a scowl until realization hit her. Her eyes widened in surprise and she clapped a hand to her mouth. "Stacy May? That you under that hair, girl?"

Stacy glanced around and whispered, "Yeah, it's me, Curta. Can I come in?"

"Oh, my Lord, it is you." Curta grabbed Stacy in a bear hug, squeezing the breath out of her. When she released her, she took Stacy by the shoulders, holding her at arm's length, looking her over. "What in heaven's name are you doin' here, girl? They let you out? Last I heard you was in some kind of program for early release. But what you doin' here?" Then remembering herself, she glanced around, shoving Stacy past her through the door, then followed behind, saying, "Get inside, outta the hallway there. There's all kinda lowlife in this here block. How nobody got killed yet, I don't know."

After another quick check along the hallway, she closed the door and turned to Stacy, fists on her hips. "Now, lemme get a good look at you. You lost more weight. You been pumping that iron? I tol' you, you ain't never gonna wind up looking like Arnie. You gonna wind up all scrawny, with them veins all stickin' out like you see in the magazines."

Stacy snatched the wig off and ran a hand through her hair. "Curta, I can't stay long. I need some help."

Curta's expression became serious. She took Stacy's hand. "Come over here inta the kitchen and tell me what's happened. I got some cookies in the oven and I don't want them to burn. Sit down over there," she said, pointing back to a tiny dining table with two chairs set on either side while she waddled across to the stove. Using the dish towel to open the oven door, she slid out a tray that she set on the stovetop. A wave of heat rolled out of the oven, filling the kitchen with the smell of cookies so delicious it made Stacy's mouth water. She hadn't eaten since breakfast, hadn't even thought about it until now.

Tossing the dish towel on the countertop, Curta pulled out a chair, and sat facing Stacy, her cheek resting on the knuckles of one hand, face set in concern.

"Now, what's happened? What do you need?"

Stacy hardly knew where to begin. She took a deep breath, eyes searching just above Curta's head, then said, "I got out on the program. You heard about that, right?"

"It's been in all the papers. My, oh my, you shoulda seen what some of them political reporters are saying about that Elizabeth McClaine. They're saying she don't have any right saying who gets released and who doesn't, and asking what does she know about anything, anyway. Then there's others thinks it's a great program, helping young mothers get back with their kids again. Been seesawing like that for months now."

Stacy waved it away. "Doesn't matter. The program's gonna get shut down anyway. No one else'll get out after this."

Curta sat back and folded her arms and frowned. "Why do you say that?"

"'Cause I ran. I broke parole, cut off my leg bracelet and ran."

The older woman's mouth dropped open. She glanced around as if an explanation might come from elsewhere before pinning Stacy with a challenging glare. "Are you crazy? Why would you go and do a stupid thing like that for?"

"It's a long story, and even if it was short, I can't tell you. You know Amy died."

"Yep. Heard about that, too. I'm sorry. I thought she was doing good."

Stacy leaned forward, met Curta's gaze, dropped her voice. "She was doing good. She was murdered."

"I heard she overdosed. That's what they said."

Stacy shook her head. "Amy was clean. She promised me she wouldn't go back to drugs. And she wouldn't have. She found something. And I think she was murdered because of it."

The skepticism was clear on Curta's face. "You know who?"

"Nope. But it'll be the same person who gave me this." Stacy reached down the front of her sweater, pulled out the photograph of Tyler and handed it to Curta.

Curta picked up a pair of green plastic-rimmed eyeglasses and slipped them on, adjusting the angle of them before lifting the photograph to study it through narrowed eyes. After some moments, Curta flipped the photograph to read the scrawled words on the back. When her eyes lifted, her disgust was clear. "Who would do such a thing?"

"I don't know."

Curta handed the photograph back, then removed her eyeglasses, folding them and placing them back on the table. "He is such a sweet boy. Looks like you all the way down to his toes and back. You know who took the picture?"

"Nope. It wasn't the one who left it for me. It's someone on the outside."

"So there's two of them?"

"Has to be. This means if I ever open my mouth or get out from where they can keep an eye on me, I'd never see Tyler alive again. They gave me this to prove they know where he is and that they can get to him."

The older woman leaned back hard, placing both hands to her face and dragging them down her cheeks before folding her arms across her broad chest, regarding Stacy with concern. "So why didn't you tell someone? Why didn't you go to the warden, tell her what you knew?"

Stacy gazed at the photograph, feeling a physical pain cut through right from her chest to her throat, pin pricks threatening to draw tears in the corners of her eyes. She tucked the photograph down into her bra again.

"I did. I went to Glassy straight after Amy died. I told her Amy wouldn't do drugs. I told her she'd spent so much time trying to get off them, it's the last thing she'd do. But she said she'd done an investigation and the evidence was all there. She said Amy must have gotten hold of some of the drugs and overdosed."

"Was there any drugs?"

"Oh, yes. They found a spent syringe in Amy's bed. But she wouldn't have done that. I know she wouldn't."

Curta leaned forward and gently placed a hand over Stacy's. "You sure? Wasn't the first time that girl got clean. She had the devil inside her. You put drugs in front of her, she'd have stomped her own mother to death to get to them. That's how it takes a hold. Addicts ain't the same people they was before they started using."

Stacy was shaking her head. "I don't believe that. She wouldn't have. She was murdered."

"Did they find any other drugs in the place?"

"Yep." She met Curta's gaze, and said, "There was a stash in the clinic, in Lois Hankerman's locker."

Curta's mouth dropped open in a gasp. "Lois Hankerman? Why in sweet Jesus's name would Lois do a thing like that?"

"She didn't. She was set up."

"So what are you gonna do now?"

Stacy lifted both shoulders and dropped them. "Find Tyler. Run. What else can I do? I don't know what I'm up against. I don't even know who's coming after us. Could be anyone."

"What about that Mrs. McClaine? Can't she help?"

Stacy made a dismissive face. "Like I said, I don't know who I can trust. Maybe she knows all about it. And if she doesn't and she finds out, she'll go asking around, and maybe she'll be the next one down in the morgue with a tag on her toe."

"So what you gonna do? Soon as you show your face, they're gonna throw you straight back in the can, no questions asked. Maybe if you tell me what happened, I can go and tell the police, explain it like you did right now."

"I can't ask you to get involved. And seriously, do you think they're gonna listen to you? No offense, Curta."

"Where you gonna go next then? I'm assuming you got a car." Curta angled her head, eyes narrowed on her. "You do have a car, don't you?"

A hesitation while Stacy looked away. "Not exactly. I borrowed my mom's."

Curta drew her head back, chin down and mouth puckered in silent reprimand. "And by *borrowed*, I'm thinkin' she don't exactly know."

Stacy winced. "I'm thinking she does by now."

"Then knowin' your mama, so will the police."

Curta twisted her mouth while she considered the situation. Then she heaved herself to her feet and crossed to the dresser where she fished through the contents of a glass bowl before returning and placing a key on the table. "Then you're gonna need this."

"What's this for?"

Curta pushed the key toward her and sat down again. "My car. It's old, but you can use it till you get yourself organized. It's a blue Toyota, the license plate number's printed out there on the tag."

The key lay on the table between them. Stacy pushed it back. "Don't be stupid. I can't take your car."

"Don't you start arguing with me, girl. You take it. I ain't taking no for an answer."

"What about you?"

"Me? I hate driving the thing. I take the bus everywhere. Do the car good to have a run." She leaned forward, expression serious. "Now you take it, y'hear?"

Stacy picked up the key and put it in her pocket. "Thank you."

Curta reached across, laid her hand over Stacy's. "I wish you'd let me help you. There must be something—"

"Please don't ask. I can't let you do anything else. I shouldn't have even come here, except I need you to do something for me."

"Name it."

Stacy took out the scrap of paper where she'd noted the phone number for Janice Lettes and handed it to Curta. "Call her. Ask her where Wayne's living now. Make something up, like he's won a prize or something."

"So who's this?"

"Wayne's mother. If I call, she'll slam the phone down or call the police or something. If you call, she won't recognize your voice. Just ask where you can find Mr. Wayne Lettes. Better still, tell her you've got a parcel for him, and you need to redirect it from his old address," she said and wrote the last address she had for Wayne on the note.

While Curta made the call, Stacy went to the window, tweaked back the lace curtain, and looked out. Down in the street, it looked all the same as usual, no cops, no sign of anything amiss. Just business as usual. Maybe they hadn't thought to look here. Maybe they were still searching the gully where she tossed the bracelet from the car and her luck was holding out.

Curta put the phone down, and Stacy turned to her. "What'd she say?"

"I told her I was from the mail department. I hid my number like they showed me when I got the phone, and she said he lives down in Rainbow Drive. Here's the number." She gave it to Stacy. "So what's Wayne going to do? Last you told me, he was a good-for-nothing waste of space."

"I need him to locate Tyler. It's the only way I'll find him. And thank you."

Stacy folded the notepaper and stuck it in her pocket.

"You're leaving already?"

She nodded. "I have to. If the cops turn up, you haven't seen me."

"Wait up a second. You're gonna need these." Curta went back to the kitchen and returned with a brown paper bag of cookies.

"Thank you. I mean it."

Curta's face began to crumple. She rubbed the heels of both palms into her eyes and said, "You need a bed, you need anything at all, you come back here, okay?"

"I can't ask you to do anything else. You've done too much already."

"Anything I do for you, girl, is cause I want to. I never got a chance to thank you for what you done for me in Carringway."

Stacy met her gaze with an annoyed frown.

Curta held up both hands in surrender. "Now, don't look at me like that. Blame Nyla Guthrie. She told me what you did, keeping Cissy off my back with all her poisonous stories. Then getting Nyla to stick up for me when I was down. I swear, there was days I could see the very bottom of that pit. I wouldn't'a survived another minute in that place if it wasn't for you."

A tense silence spooled out. "Nyla should have kept her big mouth shut."

Curta lifted her head, unrepentant. "She told me the day I got out, and I'm glad she did. She said I owed you big time. I already knew that."

Stacy eyed her now, a little annoyed that Nyla had spoken out of turn, but a little warmed by the knowledge that everything she'd done had been worth the effort. "Yeah, well—don't go telling anyone else. People are gonna start thinking I'm going soft."

She reached for the door with her heart rising into her throat. This could be the last time she'd ever see Curta. She bit down on her lip, glanced back at her old friend, nodded once, and left without saying goodbye.

CHAPTER TEN
DAY ONE: 6:12 PM—ELIZABETH

Elizabeth remembered Cissy Pettameyer as soon as she was escorted into the room. Sure enough, Cissy had made it to the final cut, but to Elizabeth, something about her demeanor didn't feel right. The woman was too sweet by half, as though every minute she was angling for something. There was nothing Elizabeth could put her finger on, but every interview with Cissy had left Elizabeth feeling as though she'd been duped in some way. That didn't matter now. What she needed was information.

Somewhere in her late twenties, Cissy had a picture-perfect complexion, dark, smoothly arched brows, and shoulder-length blonde hair that looked as if it had just been styled into a neat bob, with a little tortoiseshell barrette holding one side back off her face.

She sashayed in like a model on a runway, hips swaying, little smile on her face as she swung around to thank the prison officer who'd accompanied her. As the door closed and Officer Tomes turned to lean her back against it, again staring at the opposite wall as though she wasn't there, Cissy slipped into the seat opposite, a wide smile on her face, ankles crossed to one side under the chair, hands loosely clasped on the table in front of her.

"Oh my, it is so nice to see you again, Mrs. McClaine. I'm so sorry about the circumstances, though. I wish they were better."

"It's very nice to see you, too, Cissy. And thank you for agreeing to speak to me," she added while she rummaged through her briefcase and brought out her notepad, placing it on the table for something to do while she grounded herself.

"Oh, believe me, it is no problem, Mrs. McClaine. Anything at all that I can do to help is my pleasure."

"I won't take up too much of your time—"

Cissy interrupted, saying, "Well, as you know, time is something I have plenty of, Mrs. McClaine. So don't you worry about that." The smile had lost something of its wattage, leaving Elizabeth to suspect it was some kind of underhanded sarcasm.

She ignored it and came straight to the point. "Do you know of any reason Stacy might have broken her parole and run? I mean, do you remember anything, any incident that might have happened before she was released?"

Cissy leaned forward, dropping her voice. "Well, I do remember some months back, something did happen, and I just didn't think too much of it until now," she replied with a slight crinkling of her brow.

"And what was that?"

She took a deep breath and lifted her eyes to the ceiling while she thought. "Let me see, now. I was in the bathroom, just outside the dining hall in B Block. It must have been about six o'clock in the morning. Those of us who have earned our place on a work detail, we all get up at 5:30 every morning without fail," she explained. "Heaven help anyone that lays around in the mornings in this place when you have a work program to get to. Not that I would, anyway, but—"

Sensing Cissy would ramble on endlessly, Elizabeth interrupted her, saying, "Cissy. I'm sorry, but can we get to what happened?"

Cissy pressed her hand to the chest of her jumpsuit and dropped her head briefly. "Oh, I'm so sorry. I'm just running off at the mouth here. Anyways, I was in the bathroom stall, you know, just sitting there, when all at once I heard the bathroom door open and Stacy May and Amy came in—I knew it was them because I could hear them talking. There was only one other person there. I didn't know who, because she was in the next stall. Next thing, I heard the you-know-what flush, and Nyla's outside my stall saying something like, 'What are you looking at?' or something. And then Amy said, 'Nothing,' like she was scared—which she had every right to be. That Nyla is not to be trusted. So anyway, then Stacy told Nyla it was 'nothing to worry about,' or some such, like she might tell her later on, although I doubt it because Stacy never let out a word about anything to anyone. Everybody knew that."

Elizabeth frowned. "When was this?"

Cissy placed a forefinger to her lips, eyes narrowed while she thought. "I think that was the day before Amy overdosed. Or it could have been the day before that. But I have the impression it was the exact day before, because we had a big shipment due out, and I remembered them talking."

This flew in the face of what Elizabeth had been led to believe. "So you're saying that Nyla and Stacy were on reasonable terms?"

The snort Cissy let out was almost out of character. "Reasonable terms?" she said with another wide smile. "They were like that," she said and held up her crossed fingers. "Always together whenever they could be, heads almost touching, whispering away. Ask me, there was more to it than just being friends, if you get my meaning. But that would be nothing new in this place," she added, brushing something from the table in front of her onto the floor.

Struggling now to fit this new information with what she knew, Elizabeth shifted in her chair. "I thought Stacy and Nyla had a fight. Stacy wound up with broken ribs, and they were separated into different dormitories and work details."

A knowing smile tweaked back the side of Cissy's mouth. "Yeah, that's what everybody said—big fight, terrible bust-up. But I heard something different. I heard it was all a big act. They were friends before, friends after."

"Why would they stage a fight? I believe it was Nyla that requested they be separated."

"That's right. Worked on some. Not me," she said, and tilted her head to one side.

"So what did Stacy and Amy talk about in the bathroom?"

"I have no idea. Stacy told me to get out. I assumed that's because she and Amy wanted to talk. Well, I have every right to be in that bathroom as much as anyone, so I just took my sweet time. But to my way of thinking, it must have been something important because Stacy threatened me, that if I didn't get out, she'd do something terrible."

Elizabeth's eyebrows shot up. "She threatened you?"

"Yes, ma'am. I was so afraid, I left quick as I could."

"And you didn't hear any of what they were saying?"

"No, ma'am. You have a threat on your life in this place, you take it seriously. I left. Stacy peeked out after me to make sure I was gone. I thought about sneaking back and listening, but honestly, it was just not worth it."

To Elizabeth, she didn't look afraid. Then again, it had been four months ago.

"Thank you, Cissy. I think this has been of enormous help," Elizabeth said, although, in fact, she didn't know what to think.

"Ma'am, if you don't mind my saying, I think this program is a wonderful opportunity for young women with children to make amends for their crimes, and take all due care of the children they've left behind. I hope Stacy's foolishness doesn't jeopardize it. For your sake," she added with a wan smile.

"Thank you, I'm sure it won't."

Elizabeth made a point of lifting her briefcase and placing the notepad back into it, signifying their meeting had come to an end.

But Cissy went on. "I am such an admirer of the governor. You know, most politicians are too busy trying to lock more people up instead of trying to help them get their lives back again. Hardly a one of them ever wants to address the problems in the community that gets people locked up in the first place, let alone how to get them out."

Rising to her feet, Elizabeth locked her briefcase and lifted it to her side. "It was nice meeting you again, Cissy. Thank you for your help."

Just as Elizabeth turned, Cissy reached across the table to place a hand on Elizabeth's arm. They both looked down at the hand, and Cissy removed it.

"Mrs. McClaine, I'd like to reapply for this program, and I'd like you to know how much it would mean to me." Cissy was on her feet now, words tumbling out, desperate to get her point across. "I got to the final cut and I'd be an excellent candidate for it. And I wouldn't run. You could count on me—"

Elizabeth cut across her, saying, "I'm sorry, there's nothing I can do now. You'll have to reapply through the appropriate channels, Cissy. Goodbye."

As she went to move off, Cissy grabbed her again, this time wrenching her around to face her.

"That should have been *me* out there. I wouldn't have run off—"

Elizabeth stiffened. "Get your hands off me."

Trish Tomes was already moving towards Cissy, baton in hand, shouting, "Siddown, Cissy."

Trish took Cissy around the shoulders, pulling her back in a headlock. "I said get back, Cissy. Right now."

Cissy tried to slither out of the headlock, but Trish adjusted the hold. "You bitch!" Cissy shrieked at Elizabeth. "You use people up and then spit 'em out when you're done with them. You can go screw yourself, Elizabeth McClaine. I hope you never see Stacy May Charms again. And I hope you all rot in hell."

The door flew open and Officer Kathy Reynolds crossed quickly to assist Officer Tomes, who now had wrestled Cissy to the floor, one knee in her back as she writhed and kicked out, shouting obscenities.

"Mrs. McClaine, would you please exit the room?" Officer Reynolds said as they pinned Cissy to the floor, one on either side of her.

Elizabeth didn't need telling twice. She slipped out the door, hand on her heart, and leaned on the wall outside, waiting for her blood to stop pounding in her ears and her breath to return to normal.

She lifted her phone—no reception. Cursing under her breath, she started back in the direction she'd come from, only to realize when she got to the first door that she was just as much a prisoner in this place as the inmates. Behind her the two officers wrestled Cissy out through the door and dragged her backwards along the hallway with Cissy pedaling against the floor and spitting expletives and threats at anyone within range.

"Wait right here, Mrs. McClaine," Officer Tomes called over her shoulder. "You'll be safe here and I'll be back in a jiffy."

"No hurry," Elizabeth called weakly. Then she reentered the room she'd just been sitting in and lowered herself back down onto the plastic chair, staring at the bars on the windows while she calmed herself. Despite the well-lit corridors, the distant sounds of chatter and footsteps echoing down nearby hallways, regardless of the security systems, the prison officers or the steel doors surrounding her, even in her darkest days, Elizabeth had never felt so vulnerable.

CHAPTER ELEVEN
DAY ONE: 6:27 PM—STACY

Stacy had exited Curta's building to find one police car parked in front of Gayleen's car, a second right behind. One of the officers was on his radio, obviously calling it in while another was bent down, looking first through the passenger's window into the front and then the back seats of the car.

Stacy ducked back into the lobby and waited, wondering how she was going to get out, when a woman appeared from the stairway with a trash bag, rounding the bottom banister and disappearing down a short hallway. Stacy followed to an alley with trash cans lined up, waiting for collection.

She slipped past the woman who was depositing her trash into one of the cans, then followed the back alley into the next street.

Curta's car was parked in a slot three blocks down—an older model Corolla with a dented passenger's door and four parking tickets stuck under the windshield wiper. Stacy plucked the tickets off, unlocked the car, and after a quick scan up and down the streets, slipped in behind the wheel.

First attempt, the car's engine sounded like the battery was on its last legs. It groaned over a couple of times, like an old dog woken for work. Stacy held her breath and tried again, gently turning the key and pressing her foot to the accelerator, just like Wayne had showed her all those years ago.

The car spluttered once and died. She turned the key once more, easing her foot to the floor so she wouldn't flood the engine, and this time the engine cranked over twice and burst into life.

"Thank you, thank you, thank you," she whispered as she put it in gear, released the parking brake, and pulled out.

Rainbow Drive sounded as though it would be in an up-market neighborhood, but Stacy knew better. It ran east from Euclid and cut through an area that had once been voted the worst neighborhood in Cleveland. She checked the door locks and drove the back streets. Fifteen minutes later, she slowed and turned into Rainbow Drive, ducking her head to look over the two-family frame homes on either side of the street until she found the place. She did a U-turn, then pulled over, and looked the place over.

"Here we go again," she said as she checked the wig in the rearview mirror, slipped the key from the ignition, and got out of the car.

She waited for a couple of cars to pass, then trotted across the street, up to the front door, and knocked.

This was more like it. Same kind of structure as the one she'd just left, only here the paintwork was peeling and the gardens overgrown with weeds. In the corner of the porch was a kid's bike with a rusting pink frame, a buckled rear wheel, and handlebars with a Cinderella motif that was barely recognizable under the dirt. Why Wayne would have a kid's bike there was anyone's guess. Maybe one of his friends' kid's—which would fit. They'd all be the age where they were getting hitched and having families by now.

From somewhere inside she could hear a kid wailing. She checked up and down the street, dropped her head, and knocked again.

"I'm coming, for chrissakes," Wayne yelled from the other side of the door.

A smile caught the side of Stacy's mouth. *What on earth had he gotten himself into?*

The door opened and Wayne stepped into the doorway, his face unshaven and gaunt, hairline a little farther back from when she'd last seen him. He looked like he'd lost weight.

A scowl puckered one side of his face. "What are you doing here?" he said and looked over her shoulder, then up and down the street before coming back to her.

Behind him, the child let out another unearthly howl from somewhere inside the house. Wayne glanced back, yelling, "Shut up, will ya?"

The kid let out a few sobs and Wayne turned his attention back to Stacy, leaning one forearm on the doorframe like he was barring her from entering. He looked worn out.

Tough, she thought.

"What do you want?" he said.

Feeling like the whole street was watching, she drove her hands in her jacket pockets, hunched her shoulders briefly, and said, "Ah, can I come in?"

Wayne gave the neighborhood another quick scan, said, "No, you can't. What are you doing here?"

"I got out on a release program."

His face registered disgust. "I heard. So what are you doing here?"

"I need to find Tyler. Can you let me in?"

Behind him the kid started screaming again.

He glanced back and huffed in irritation. "No, I can't. I gotta go." He went to close the door but she slammed her hand against it, fingers splayed, and one foot in the doorway, stopping him. He opened it again, his face coloring in anger. "What!"

"Can't you even tell me where he is? I gotta find him."

"How would I know?"

"You're his father. When's the last time you saw him?"

Wayne did a dismissive palm up. "I dunno. Two years back, maybe."

"Two years?" she said, aghast. "What have you been doing you can't see your own son for two years?"

"Why would I want to see him? He's retarded. He doesn't know me from a stick of butter."

"He's your *son*," she began, but the sound of a car pulling into the driveway cut her off. They both looked over to see a beaten-up silver sedan pull up.

"Oh, shit." Wayne pressed his finger and thumb to his eyes. "Why don't you just go?"

The young woman driving got out: sharp features, dirty blonde hair pulled back in a ponytail showing a strip of darker hair where the dye was growing out. She slammed the car door and looked up, regarding Stacy and Wayne with a sour expression while she went to the rear passenger door, opened it and unfastened a baby from the car seat. Setting the child on one hip, she grabbed her purse and slammed the door shut before heading for the house.

She climbed to the top step, wiping a trail of snot from the baby's nose with a balled-up tissue, and stopped next to Wayne, looking Stacy over. The kid had scarlet cheeks and red, puffy eyes. Didn't take a genius to see he had a fever.

"Who's this?" the woman asked Wayne, tipping her head in Stacy's direction, like she'd just come home to find the trash spilled out all over the porch.

"It's nothin', Cher. Why'n't you take Justin inside? I'll deal with this," he told her.

"Like hell," she said. "I wanna know what's going on."

Wayne looked away briefly, obviously irritated, then gestured dismissively in Stacy's direction, saying, "This is Stacy May." He folded his arms and looked away down the street.

Cher gave her another once-over, scowling at Stacy while she hiked the kid on her hip, adjusting his position. "So what do you want? Better not be money."

Stacy gave Cher a sullen up and down in response. Noting the ring on her third left finger, her mouth dropped open and she swung around on Wayne. "You're married? When were you planning on telling me you got married?"

Cher leaned in. "I'm not married to him. *Yet*," she added and cut Wayne an accusing look.

"So whose are the kids?"

"Me and Wayne's, whose do you think they are?" Cher told her. "And don't think you're coming in. Just because of you and your stinkin' kid, we can't even afford a decent place to live. Now if you don't mind, I want you offa my porch, and offa my property." She pushed past Wayne, taking the child inside. They could hear her moving down the hallway, hushing the other child and telling him, "It's okay, it's okay, Mommy's home now."

"Great parenting skills," Stacy told Wayne.

"What the hell would you know? You been stuck away in prison, sitting on your ass all day twiddling your thumbs while someone else looks after your kid."

"So how are Tyler and me costing you?" She knew he didn't pay a penny toward his son's care.

He looked away. She knew that look. It was the one that said he'd been caught in a big, fat lie.

"Oh, I see." Stacy stuck her hands in her jacket pockets, nodding theatrically.

"She's got the wrong end of the stick is all," he said in a petulant tone, still avoiding her gaze.

What did Stacy care? Cher wanted to live with a lying ass who couldn't even visit his own son, that was her problem. "So how do I find Tyler?"

He spread his hands. "I don't know. How would I know?"

Stacy bit back her fury and turned to let her gaze drift. When she turned back to him, she said, "Okay, so here's the deal: you call up the Child Services lady, ask if you can see Tyler, then you call me, tell me where you're told to meet. Okay?"

He scowled and snorted. "And what do I get out of this deal?"

"Cher never finds out that we're not the ones getting your money. How does that sound?"

Wayne sniffed and dashed a knuckle under his nose, obviously giving it some thought while he regarded the area over her shoulder. From inside the house, Cher yelled, "Wayne! Are you coming in here, or am I locking you out there?"

"I'm coming," he yelled over his shoulder. To Stacy, he said, "You got a phone?"

"No. I'll call you. Give me your number."

He disappeared for a moment, came back yelling over his shoulder, "I said I'm coming." Then muttering, "Goddamn woman, drives me insane. Here's my cell. Call me later and I'll get a day set up."

"Not day—time. I need to see him tonight."

"Tonight? How'm I supposed to make an appointment for tonight?"

"It's tonight or we don't have a deal."

He considered it, and sighed. "I'll see what I can do."

"Don't just see. Do it," she said, and he slammed the door without another word.

Stacy skipped back down the steps and crossed the street to the car again.

So far, so good. But now she had other things to organize. A phone she wouldn't have to buy, for one thing. If she could find Caitlin O'Hare, that would be half the problem solved. Caitlin had been in prison with Stacy for six months after a drug raid found her in possession of twenty-five tabs of ecstasy, and a decent-sized bag of crystal meth. She'd also amassed seven cell phones so she could contact any of the seven dealers she used. Last Stacy heard, Caitlin was living in an abandoned warehouse on the edge of East Cleveland. If she could find her, Stacy might have half a hope of evading the police long enough for Wayne to set up the meeting. Or at least that's what the plan had to be. Because right now, she didn't have anything better.

She twisted the key in the ignition and pulled out, heading east.

CHAPTER TWELVE
DAY ONE: 6:51 PM—ELIZABETH

Despite the promised "jiffy," it was almost fifteen minutes by the time the heavy steel door slid aside and Officer Kathy Reynolds reappeared, escorting a plump woman wearing a prison jumpsuit. Elizabeth would have put Eileen Caston somewhere in her early to mid-forties. She wore no makeup and her hair styled into a square-cut bob reminiscent of all powerhouse women of the early 2000s, nails short with no polish but obviously cared for. Despite the attire and their surroundings, she carried herself with assurance, an almost imperceptible smile lending her an air of authority.

Elizabeth stood as they entered.

Officer Reynolds closed the door behind them, saying, "Mrs. Mc-Claine, this is Eileen Caston."

Eileen Caston gave Officer Reynolds a tight nod, as if dismissing staff. "Thank you, Officer Reynolds."

Kathy Reynolds replied, saying, "Please, take a seat, Mrs. McClaine. Eileen, you sit on the other side, hands to your side of the table."

"Very well," Eileen said, pulling out a chair opposite Elizabeth. She lowered herself into it, and sat with her hands loosely clasped in front of her, head slightly tilted.

Elizabeth positioned her notebook open in front of her, laying the pen on top. "Thank you for agreeing to see me. I don't know how much you know about me or the trust I'm custodian of."

Eileen returned a self-assured smile. "I'm acutely aware of who you and your family are, Mrs. McClaine. I'm a financial economist by trade turned journalist later in my career. Top honors student straight out of Harvard. Probably only a few years after you."

"I see," Elizabeth said, trying to hide her surprise.

Eileen lifted her chin, clearly relishing her moment in the spotlight, but continued in the same mild manner. "I worked for three of the biggest banks in America until the Fannie Mae and Freddie Mac debacle, at which time I began writing a financial column, analyzing the business and future funds markets, discussing trends in the commodities markets, you name it. My column appeared in five of the top financial magazines in the country over a period of twelve years under my pseudonym, Eileen Grant."

Elizabeth drew in a sharp breath at the recognition of the name. "I read your columns. I enjoyed them immensely. I know my father-in-law made several very astute investments based on your predictions."

Eileen dipped her head in self-congratulatory acknowledgment. "Thank you. I like to maintain a healthy interest in the business comings and goings outside these walls, although I hardly think the four financial magazines the authorities allow me each month would give me a detailed view," she said, aiming the comment directly at Kathy Reynolds, who reacted with a lopsided grin. Eileen continued, saying, "History, however, has a habit of repeating itself, so I guess formulating predictions is only a matter of extrapolation and guesswork. That said, I'm usually right. So yes, Mrs. McClaine, I'm very well aware of who you are, where you've been, and what you're doing now."

"I'm impressed. But how on earth…" Elizabeth began, then stopped herself. How Eileen Grant ended up here was not up for discussion.

Seemingly picking up on it, Eileen said, "I understand, Mrs. McClaine. No doubt you've been instructed by the warden not to make enquiries into the personal lives of inmates, or into the circumstances behind their incarceration."

"Those were the conditions of my speaking to you, yes. My apologies."

A tight smile crept onto Eileen's lips. "I can appreciate your curiosity. My last employer did an admirable job of hushing up the circumstances of my sudden departure. As a result, while all the information is in the public domain under my own name, it certainly never made the evening news." She cocked her head but didn't elaborate further.

Elizabeth lifted her pen, still feeling a little star-struck. "I assume you know why I'm here, then. I believe you worked alongside Stacy May in her work detail."

"That's correct."

"And you ... sew?"

"Ironic, isn't it?" Eileen replied, the smile widening. "You'd think they'd put me to work analyzing the financial reports of the prison's myriad moneymaking schemes and work ventures. But I don't suppose they're too eager to find another Shawshank Redemption playing out within its walls."

Elizabeth's own smile widened. She found herself warming to the woman and wondering if a little digging when she got home might unearth how someone like Eileen Grant had gotten herself into this situation. "I guess you're right. So what can you tell me about Stacy? Do you have any idea what might have been going on? Why she fled?"

"I can't tell you much, but I'm happy to help any way I can."

"Thank you."

Eileen lifted an expectant gaze to Kathy Reynolds who was standing in the same position Trish had been earlier, back to the door, eyes straight ahead, pretending to be invisible. "Kathy, I wonder if you could give us a moment."

Kathy smiled. "Against regulations, Eileen. You know that."

"Pity," she told Elizabeth, but said nothing more.

"Do you know what was going on?"

"You could say it's … extrapolation, on my part. Without more solid evidence, there's nothing I could swear to on a Bible."

Getting information out of Eileen Caston AKA Grant was like pulling teeth. She seemed more than happy to talk, provided she herself was the subject. Elizabeth made a point of closing the notebook in front of her and leaned on her elbows on the table. "I see. Then do you know anything about the drugs that were smuggled in? One of the inmates, Amy Dixon, died as a result of an overdose shortly after."

"I believe that was the story. And, of course, I assume you knew the warden's sister was found guilty and sentenced to ten years in the Women's Reformatory."

The news hit Elizabeth like a punch to the chest. "Lois Hankerman was Jennifer Glassy's sister?"

Obviously pleased she'd told Elizabeth something she hadn't known, Eileen tilted her head, a smug smile lifting the corners of her mouth. "Incredible how the finer details get lost when it's so close to home, isn't it, Mrs. McClaine?"

"But surely the warden wouldn't be allowed to employ her own sister."

"Lois wasn't employed by the prison, per se. Or perhaps the authorities either overlooked it, or made some concession. Who knows?"

"And do you believe she was guilty? If you, say…extrapolated?"

"From what I heard, Lois Hankerman had the contacts, but frankly, if you'll excuse the expression, she didn't have the balls. So even based on that assumption, I'd say no, she was framed."

"Do you know why?"

"People are usually framed to pass blame, or to get rid of them because they know more than they should. Perhaps, if you can convince the authorities, you should ask Ms. Hankerman herself. I'm certain that after the plea bargain she eventually accepted, she's had more than enough time to reconsider her hasty decision, so she may agree to speak to you."

"Thank you," Elizabeth said, but her mind was scrambling, trying to find where this part of the puzzle fit. She made a mental note and moved on. "Who would Stacy go to on the outside? Any friends, acquaintances who might help her?"

The smile dropped. Now that they were veering off the subject of Eileen Grant and her brilliant career, she was less interested in the conversation. She shifted in her chair, breaking eye contact for the first time.

"I'd say Curta Brixton would be a good bet. Or perhaps Caitlin O'Hare. Caitlin was a drug addict. I can't see her ever making anything of herself, but Stacy always got along with her. I think she'd feel safe enough calling in a favor from her."

Eileen inclined her head, watching as Elizabeth wrote down both names. "Mrs. McClaine, let me give you some advice. One of the things I learned in journalism is that you always start with the Who, What, How, and Where. But most importantly, you have to discover the Why. You'll find it's not always about the money. But it's almost always at the root."

"Again, thank you."

"I think we're ready," Eileen told Kathy Reynolds as though they were at a restaurant, and she was signaling for the bill.

Officer Reynolds stepped forward and took Eileen by the elbow as she rose, then escorted her to the door. After signaling for the door to be unlocked, there was a click and the door slid aside. But just as Eileen stepped behind officer Reynolds, she paused to turn an unflinching gaze on Elizabeth.

"Mrs. McClaine, just for your information, I'm serving two life sentences here with no opportunity of parole. I stabbed my two young children to death in their beds as they slept. I tell you this because you need to understand that, regardless of the circumstances, nothing, and no one, is ever what it seems on the outside. There is no magic wand, Mrs. McClaine. There never was."

And with that, they left Elizabeth sitting at the table, a wash of horror rolling through her like a heavy tide after a storm, and wondering where on earth to go from here.

CHAPTER THIRTEEN
DAY ONE: 7:02 PM—STACY

The place Caitlin O'Hare had chosen to live in wasn't exactly what Stacy would have called suburban Utopia. It was an old concrete building with broken windows and graffiti scrawled across every surface, even some that seemed out of reach. The ice cream manufacturer that once ran a business from here had closed up some years ago and the place had been used by drug addicts and runaways ever since.

Stacy drove past the place, found a parking spot a block down, then trotted back, entering the building through a narrow gap where the chained and boarded-up front doors had been wrenched apart.

Inside was a maze of steel open-frame walkways and stairways that probably led right up to the open-framed roofing two floors up. The place was filthy. Dirt had blown in over a number of years and piled up, collecting in the corners and against the housing where the manufacturing equipment had once stood, and at the foot of the dozen or so concrete columns holding the roof up.

Initially, the building looked deserted. If Stacy didn't know better, she'd have thought she'd got the wrong place. Treading softly, she made her way into the center of the open warehousing area and did a 360-degree turn, scanning the place for life. Lighting in here was poor. The upper windows had been boarded up, but to her left, she spotted a doorway leading to what must have originally been the offices.

Checking over her shoulder, she moved across to find a narrow hallway. Sure enough, leading off left and right was a series of offices. Moving slowly along, she peeked into each one, noting the wall-to-wall mattresses, coats, and assorted rugs used as blankets, shopping carts stacked with forty-two flavors of crap.

Up ahead, she heard movement.

"Hello? Anybody here?"

A gaunt-looking guy with the pinched expression of a habitual user appeared at a doorway. Dressed in a dirty pea jacket over jeans and high-topped sneakers with holes in both toes, he looked like he hadn't bathed in months.

"I'm looking for Caitlin O'Hare," she told him. "I was told this is where she hung."

He folded his arms across his chest, hands tucked under his arms, shifting from foot to foot while he scanned the hallway. "Who wants to know?"

"A friend."

Angling his head, he said, "What kind of friend?"

Stacy could see where this was going. She casually checked behind her, making sure there was a clear path to the exit. "Just a friend, that's all."

He dashed his sleeve across his nose and flicked a look to the doorway. "You got any meth on you?"

She let out a sigh and balled both fists, ready. "No, I don't have any meth on me. I'm not that kind of friend."

He sniffed and considered his response. "What about money? You got money?"

"Nope, no money either."

His eyes met hers. "Then what are you doing here?"

"Stacy May? Is that you?"

She whipped around to find Caitlin standing in one of the open doorways she'd passed.

Stacy let out a relieved breath. "Holy crap, Caitlin. You sure know how to dig up the best addresses."

"She's okay," Caitlin told the guy. "I was inside with her."

The guy gave Stacy an accusing look, then disappeared back to where he'd come from.

"Over here," Caitlin said, motioning Stacy over. "Ignore him. He's paranoid. Anyone comes in, he thinks they're trying to plant something in his brain or something. Freakin' weirdo."

Stacy followed her into the office she'd appeared from, and Caitlin closed the door. "What are you doing here? I thought you were in for another couple years or something."

"I got out."

"Well, *obviously*. So did you finally make parole?" Caitlin flopped down on a filthy mattress and scooted back against the wall, knees up with her arms around them, like a kid waiting for a story at bedtime.

Slipping her hands in her jacket pockets, Stacy went to the window and peeped. Beyond the dirty glass was an empty parking lot. "Nah, I got in a fight. I wouldn't have been up for parole for another year. I got out on a new program for inmates with kids."

"Shit. If I'd known about that, I woulda not let my mom talk me into having the abortion that time. Maybe if I'd'a had a kid out there, I'd have gotten out sooner."

"Maybe if your mom didn't talk you into that abortion you wouldn't have been on drugs, which is what got you put inside in the first place." The sharpness in her tone surprised even Stacy.

"She did what she thought was best."

"Yeah, sure."

What she thought was best for who? Stacy wanted to ask. Instead, she moved around the cluttered office with its filthy floor and graffiti-covered walls, then across to the few possessions Caitlin had, all jumbled up into three cardboard cartons. "So how'd you wind up here anyway?"

She shrugged. "You gotta live somewhere. And this was easy. I don't get any shit from anyone."

"What about your mom? Weren't you supposed to go back and live with her?"

The break in eye contact told Stacy everything.

"We decided I'm better on my own."

"Yeah, sure you are."

Obviously eager to change the subject, Caitlin said, "So tell me about this program. What'd you have to do?"

"It's a little like parole, with curfews and such so you can go to work and earn enough money to keep your kids. And you have to pass a whole bunch of tests and do your school work and wear a leg bracelet so they can track your movements." Caitlin's eyes dropped to Stacy's ankles. Stacy followed her line of sight, then said, "Oh, I cut mine off."

Caitlin's jaw dropped, aghast. "Are you nuts? Do you know what they do if you cut those things off?"

Her eyes widened briefly at the irony. "Well, I do now."

"One of the guys that was living here got another two years in the slammer for hacking his bracelet off. Did it with a machete, the big dumbass. Sliced a chunk out of his leg doing it. Blood everywhere. You shoulda seen his face. It was hilarious," she added with a wry chuckle. "Cops followed the trail of blood and picked him up at the hospital."

Stacy couldn't help but smile. "Listen, I'd love to stay and chat and all, but I need some help."

Caitlin patted the dirty mattress next to her. "Come, sit down. Tell me what you need."

Stacy lowered herself to a crouch in front of her, forearms rested on her knees. "A phone. You got one?"

"I got three."

Stacy straightened immediately. "Are you using again, Caitlin? What did I say to you?"

"Me? Heck no. I haven't been using since before I went inside. I'm clean now. Been clean ever since I got out."

Their eyes simultaneously dropped to the crook of Caitlin's left arm, and Caitlin immediately pulled her sleeve down to hide the track marks.

She pulled her knees in tight, chin tucked down, as if trying to make herself smaller. "Okay, so sometimes I get a little low. It's nothing, Stace. Seriously, I can handle it."

Stacy pressed her lips firmly together and let her eyes lift briefly to the ceiling. "You know Amy died, right?"

"Yeah, yeah, I heard."

"You wanna be next?"

"It's only a taste—"

"It's not *only a taste*, Caitlin. It's never only a taste." Angry now, Stacy went to the window, hands jammed in her pockets.

"Aw, c'mon, Stace. Don't be mad at me. *Please?*" Caitlin said in a tiny voice.

She sounded truly repentant. But then, she always did. When Stacy looked back, she had her chin on her knees, head tilted looking up at her. "So is that the only reason you came here? Just to kick my ass?"

"No, it wasn't. Like I said, I just need a phone. I gotta call someone."

"You gonna tell me what it's about?"

"Best I don't."

Caitlin leaned over and pulled one of the cardboard boxes closer. She rummaged through it a moment, then pulled out an old flip phone. "Use this one. Keep it if you want. The guy's an asshole."

"Thank you."

"Stacy?"

"Yeah?"

Caitlin looked away, dragging her lower teeth along her upper lip before meeting Stacy's gaze again. "I ah…" She winced. "You got any money? I could really use it now."

Stacy had the twenty-five dollars gate money down her bra next to the photograph. If she thought Caitlin would buy a meal, she wouldn't have hesitated. "Not a dime," she lied, pocketing the phone as she went for the door.

"You're leaving already?"

At the doorway, she turned to regard Caitlin again. "I have to. I'll be back, though. And when I do, you better be clean."

"I will be."

"Make sure you are. 'Cause if I find out you're not, I might just kill you myself."

Then she left.

CHAPTER FOURTEEN
DAY ONE: 7:48 PM—ELIZABETH

By the time she had halfway recovered from the revelation Eileen Grant had dropped on her, Elizabeth realized she didn't have enough time to interview any more of the women today. She had immediately called for Warden Glassy, who had accompanied her down corridors divided by remotely opened security doors to the front entrance. Just as she stepped across the threshold, her phone beeped three times, indicating messages.

"Oh, I have coverage," Elizabeth said, surprised.

Glassy scanned the parking lot, hugging herself and rubbing her upper arms as if noticing the chill wind for the first time. "When the building was designed, they put in some kind of blocking equipment so that cell phones don't work within the prison. I should have warned you about that."

"It's fine. To be honest, it's nice to not have it ringing every two seconds." The message on the screen indicated she'd missed five calls and had three messages. "Only five calls. The media hounds must have given up."

"I find that doubtful," Jennifer said wryly.

Just as she was about to leave, Elizabeth paused and turned to face Jennifer. "Why didn't you tell me that Lois Hankerman, the woman who'd been convicted of smuggling the drugs into the prison, was your sister?"

Jennifer Glassy's mouth widened into a humorless smile. "And I suppose we can thank Eileen Grant for telling you that. I should have known she would."

Elizabeth didn't respond, just cocked her head, waiting for the response.

The other woman met her gaze, then briefly dropped her head. "It wasn't relevant, Mrs. McClaine. The case was resolved. Justice has been served."

"Do you believe she did it?"

She let her gaze reel out across the parking lot before answering. "It doesn't matter what I believe. An investigation was carried out and she was found guilty." She lifted her head an inch. "I was as surprised as anyone."

"I'm glad you place such faith in the legal system. I wish I could say the same."

Jennifer Glassy nodded once, declaring the meeting over. "Good luck, Mrs. McClaine. You're going to need it."

Jennifer Glassy had walked back in through the front doors without another word, leaving Elizabeth to walk to her car. Now, an hour later, after going over and over the information in her head, she was just pulling into her driveway when her phone rang. She cut the engine and answered it.

"Elizabeth, it's Penny. Where are you?" she said in a hushed voice.

"What's wrong?"

There was a moment of silence while Elizabeth imagined Penny moving to another location for privacy. Sure enough, when she spoke again, she sounded guarded. "When are you going to be home?"

"I'm in the driveway right now. Why?"

"I'm at your place. Delaney's here. He wants to see you."

Elizabeth glanced up in the rearview mirror, only now noting the late model black sedan parked across the street. "I'll be right in."

As soon as she opened the front door, Holly came shambling down the stairs to meet her, arms out for a hug, big smile on that beautiful round face. Despite those first few years when Elizabeth had struggled to come to terms with her child's disabilities, these days she never saw her daughter as a Down Syndrome sufferer. Even the scar from the second surgery to correct the cleft lip and palate was barely visible, although even with the best speech therapist, Holly's words were still thick, the *r* rounding out as *w*, and her *s* forming as *f*, causing the word "dress" to come out "dweff."

"Mommy, Mommy," Holly cried, as Elizabeth enfolded her in her arms and kissed the top of her head. She smelled of strawberries and cream, felt like a thousand summers in her arms.

"Hello, baby. Has Katy given you some dinner?"

The reply came with a mischievous grin. "I had hot dogs."

Despite the impediments, Elizabeth could hardly believe the leaps and bounds Holly's communication had made. There were days when she just wanted to sit and listen to her daughter, reveling in the words she never thought she'd hear from her.

"Oh, really? Hot dogs? What about vegetables?" Elizabeth asked, smiling.

The child made a face. "I don't like them."

Elizabeth narrowed her eyes and leaned to her daughter in mock reprimand. "Tomorrow, you eat vegetables, okay?" And she touched her briefly on the nose before putting down her briefcase.

Holly's smile broadened, but only momentarily. Drawing in a deep breath, she stepped back, her expression unusually serious. "Mommy, may I go to a dance?"

Elizabeth blinked at her, wondering where on earth this came from. "A dance?" She slipped off her coat and hung it over the stairway newel post, feeling a million horrors clanging around inside her. "What kind of a dance?"

Holly's hands flapped with excitement. "It's a school dance. I got a note in my backpack. From my teacher."

"I see. And who would you go to this dance with?"

The child clasped her hands at her chin, twisting left and right. "I will go with Cheryl. She's my best friend. Daddy say, if you say yes, he will take us."

Despite the threat of tears forming, Elizabeth found herself smiling. *Oh, my baby, how you've grown. Please don't grow any more.*

"Well, I cannot think of a better person to go to a dance with than your best friend. Of course you can go."

"Can I get a new dress?"

"I think it's the perfect opportunity to get a new dress."

"Fank you, Mommy." Holly threw her arms around Elizabeth, hugging her tightly while Elizabeth wrapped her daughter in her arms and planted another kiss on the top of her head.

Holly's head went back, looking up at Elizabeth. "Can we get my new dress from Boo Beeba? They have pretty dresses."

"You mean Rue Xeeba?"

"Yeff."

Without knowing why, Elizabeth felt herself stiffen. "We're not going to Rue Xeeba, my darling. We will find you the prettiest dress in all Ohio, but somewhere else."

"But Mommy—"

Elizabeth was about to respond when she glanced up to see Detective Delaney standing in the doorway, Penny just behind him, both watching.

She shuffled her daughter along, saying, "You go to your room and get ready for bed, young lady. We'll discuss this later." While Holly departed, climbing back up the stairs, Elizabeth turned for the living room and Delaney followed. "And to what do I owe the pleasure of this visit, Detective?"

He waited until she sat on the sofa and eased off a shoe before replying.

"I hope your interviews with the women in Carringway were worth your while," he said. From the look on his face, he wasn't expecting much.

"A few interesting comments, but nothing earth shattering. What's happening at your end?" She massaged her stockinged foot, then slipped the other shoe off, and relaxed back with her legs crossed.

"We found the bracelet. Stacy had cut it off and it was found it just this side of Euclid Avenue."

"So I heard. Not exactly a big surprise, was it?" Elizabeth said just as Katy, her housekeeper, entered, nodding in deference at her employer. "Coffee for me, thank you, Katy. Detective?"

"Not for me, thank you." When Katy had departed, he went on, saying, "We also found Gayleen Charms's car. It was parked out near Terrence Street."

Elizabeth slipped one foot up beneath her, her arm resting along the back of the sofa. "Why there?"

"She had been inside with a woman who lives there. I had an officer call on her but she says she hasn't seen Stacy since she was released several months ago."

"And you think she's lying?"

"Probably." He dug into his coat pocket to bring out what looked like a stack of envelopes bound together with a rubber band. "We found these in the car, though. On the passenger's seat."

He passed them to Elizabeth who flicked through the envelopes, turning them every couple so she could read the address. She frowned up at him. "They're all addressed to Wayne Lettes—Tyler's father."

"It seems he's moved. One of my officers dropped by there earlier and said that a Mr. Traynor who lives there now told him a young woman knocked at the door, asking where Wayne Lettes was. He gave her these."

"Oh, no. So where would she go from there?"

Delaney lifted his shoulders in a shrug. "That's the $64,000 question. But at least we found the tracking device. It was down a gulley nearby.

Looks like she threw it from the car. And Mr. Traynor confirmed he was the one that gave her the letters, so it fits."

"And you've looked through them all?"

"Most of them. It's obvious from what she writes that she never had any intention of sticking with the program. In the first letter four months ago, she says something about it all going wrong, and how she has to find Tyler. In the next few, she outlines a plan where she expects Wayne Lettes to help her. I'm betting that would have been a surprise to him because he's had virtually no contact with Tyler in the last three years."

"So why would she ask him?"

"I'm guessing she didn't know. She told him in the letters not to contact her because any communications could get intercepted. Which they probably would have."

Feeling that stab of a father's betrayal of a child from her own past, she handed the letters back. "Best-laid plans, I guess."

Delaney took them and tucked them back into the inside breast pocket of his coat. "I'm sorry it turned out like this, Elizabeth. If it's any consolation, you're probably not the first Stacy's put one over on."

He'd misread her—she didn't feel that Stacy had put one over her. She nodded once, but said nothing.

"There is one other interesting development, though. Nancy Pattrenko's office had a call from Wayne Lettes."

Elizabeth lifted her eyebrows. "The same Wayne Lettes, I suppose?"

"It's the very one. All of a sudden he's desperate to see his son."

Elizabeth's head jerked back. "After all this time, that's a conspicuously ominous change of heart, wouldn't you say?"

"I would."

"And you think Stacy's asked him to contact the foster parents so she can find Tyler."

"Seems likely."

"But of course you're not going ahead with this visitation, are you?"

Delaney bunched his mouth, clearly reluctant to reply. "I don't see why not. I've asked Nancy Pattrenko to contact Kay Heathers from Child Services and arrange a meet for nine o'clock tomorrow morning. As the parole officer, Nancy's been known to attend meetings between the children and their parents, so it makes sense."

Elizabeth's jaw dropped. She sat forward, both feet on the floor. "Let me get this right: you're planning to put a little boy in a potentially dangerous situation so you can, what? Ambush his mother?"

Delaney drew a patient breath and slowly raised his eyes to a point just above her head. Probably regretting telling her, Elizabeth thought.

"Elizabeth, this could be a legitimate request by the father, so we need to honor it. Tyler will be perfectly safe. We'll have a solid police presence in the area. Kay said she'll arrange to take him to a shopping mall, maybe McDonald's, get him a Happy Meal. He'll have a nice time."

"So your officers are going to, what? Jump out and arrest her in front of her child? He's a little boy. What's he supposed to think when the police drag his mother away?"

For some moments, Delaney just stared at her, his expression unreadable. Then he said, "You seem to have conveniently forgotten that Stacy May Charms attacked her social worker and put her in the hospital."

Elizabeth was flabbergasted. She got to her feet, pointing off towards the door, her voice raised and her face flushed with anger.

"She was *seventeen, goddammit.*" Elizabeth said, leaning in so he got the full force of her outrage. "She was barely more than a *child herself.* And maybe if her lawyer hadn't done a half-assed job, she wouldn't have wound up in prison at all."

Detective Delaney drew in a heavy breath and dropped his head a moment, his patience seemingly thinned to the edge of frustration. "I don't make the laws, Elizabeth. I just uphold them. If you want to continue with your inquiries, that's fine. But I have a job to do. If I find you're withholding information or getting in my way, I'll lock you right out and bring any attempts to continue with your own to a very abrupt halt. Understood?"

Elizabeth nodded and sat down.

"I'll see myself out," he said, and went to the door. Just before leaving, he paused, looking back at her. "And obviously I don't need to remind you that any information coming your way will be forwarded straight to my desk."

"You do not," she replied in a tight voice.

Just after he'd gone, Penny appeared in the doorway. "Youch. You need anything for those scorch marks?"

Elizabeth collected up her shoes and got up. "I'll live."

Penny slipped her sleeve back to indicate the time. "Well, I hate to be the bearer of more bad news, but you have thirty-one minutes before the Business Awards start."

"Talk to me upstairs while I dress."

Penny followed Elizabeth up to her bedroom, an elegant space decorated in soft greens and buttery yellows, the king-size bed adorned with plumped pillows and a hand-embroidered coverlet that matched the décor in both color and style. On the bed lay Elizabeth's navy business suit. Katy had laid it out, along with matching shoes and purse.

Elizabeth strode across to her walk-in closet and flipped on the light. Her encounter with Delaney had left a sour taste in her mouth. Perhaps he simply couldn't understand what a mother would do for her child, or the pain the rejection of that child's father caused.

"Your suit is over there," Penny said, pointing to where the garments were laid out in plain sight.

With nothing more than a passing glance at the suit, Elizabeth stepped into the closet, raking through the hangers. "Over my dead body."

"You're not wearing it?"

She ignored her secretary, instead moving garment after garment along the rail until she plucked off one hanger, then a second, and moved to the full-length mirror in the bedroom, holding a short-sleeved black dress trimmed with silk at the hem and sleeves against herself, then switching to a vibrant rose-colored strapless cocktail dress with a silk wrap. "Which do you think?"

"Are you going straight to the Business Awards or have you secretly signed for a new series of *The Bachelor*?"

"The rose one, I think," Elizabeth said, switching the dresses again, then nodding toward the rose-pink one.

"You can't be serious," Penny said as Elizabeth flung the dress on the bed and went in search of shoes to match.

Emerging with a pair of stiletto-heeled shoes under one arm, Elizabeth unclipped her earrings and moved to the dresser. She dropped the shoes on the floor and stepped into the dress, wriggling it up over her hips and slipping her arms into the sleeves. "I've never been more serious. So do you want to know how I got on in prison?"

"Oh, God, I hope I don't ever hear you say that again."

"Guess who I met?"

Penny sat on the bed with her legs crossed, watching her. "Not a clue. Shock me."

She turned, a secretive smile tweaking up one side of her mouth as she dragged the zipper halfway up the back of the dress. "Who was the biggest name in the financial columns a few years back?"

Shaking her head and frowning, Penny said, "You'll have to give me more."

Elizabeth stepped across, turning so her secretary could zip her into the dress. "Okay, then: Averil Cerventes took over from her."

The two lines between Penny's eyes deepened, then her eyes flew open. "You mean Eileen Grant? What the hell happened to her? It's like she just vanished without a word."

"Well, hello—prison."

"No! Why?"

"Can't say—sworn to secrecy. Suffice to say that when Warden Glassy said that Eileen, quote, 'didn't fit the criteria for the program,' she wasn't kidding." She turned to her trusted employee, brows raised, her voice serious. "And that information goes nowhere, understand?"

Penny made a show of zipping her lips, twisting an imaginary key, and tossing it aside. "Not a word."

Elizabeth drew her hair back in both hands, attempting to pull it into a knot at the back.

"Let me get that." Penny got up and crossed to stand behind Elizabeth, who immediately took a seat on a vanity chair in front of the mirror. Penny deftly swept her shoulder-length blonde hair up into a French roll at the back of her head, clasping it into place and sweeping the sides back.

"Thank you. I can never get it to do that. Anyway, it turns out that Eileen was in the same work detail as Stacy for the past four months. This is immediately following the big drug debacle I told you about that resulted in the death of Amy Dixon—Stacy's friend. It turns out one of the contracted physical therapists was bringing in drugs—Lois Hankerman." Elizabeth paused, looking up to gauge Penny's reaction in the mirror.

"I guess where there's opportunity," Penny said absently as she tucked a few stray strands in and sprayed them into place.

"Well, get this: Lois Hankerman happens to be Warden Glassy's sister."

Penny's eyes widened on Elizabeth's in the mirror, her expression one of horror. "No! How the hell did Glassy wind up with her sister working there?"

Elizabeth gave her a meaningful shrug. "Private prison? Different rules maybe?"

"Still sounds kinda hinky to me."

"And that's not all. The official story about why Stacy switched work detail *and* dorm, is that she had a big falling out with one of the other inmates. It sounded vicious, a fight. Nyla Guthrie, the other woman, broke a couple of Stacy's ribs. A couple of the women I spoke to seemed to think it was a big set-up, that they planned it together."

"Yeah, but two busted ribs is pretty serious. Anyone say why?"

"Nope, not a word. But if Nyla had anything to do with Amy's death, I could see it getting serious. Stacy had helped her get clean. But by all accounts, she didn't fight back—just stood there and took the beating because it would have counted against her for the release program."

"But if it got her moved out of the dorm, and the work program, maybe that was the whole point. Maybe this Nyla or whatever wanted her out of the way so she could keep selling drugs or whatever."

"I have no idea." Elizabeth let her gaze drift across the dresser, then absently picked up her lipstick while she tried to link all the information she'd learned. Something had snagged in the back of her mind, something one of them had said but she'd ignored. "Eileen wanted to tell me something, but she wouldn't in front of Kathy Reynolds. She ended up saying something weird about magic fairy dust or some such. Get me an appointment at the Women's Reformatory. I want a visit with Lois Hankerman. If she's in solitary, maybe she's more likely to talk."

"Will do," Penny said and made a note on her phone.

"Then get me a background check on the prison officers there, will you? I think that'd be as good a place as any to start with."

Her secretary made a pained face. "All of them?"

"Maybe just the ones in that block. Start with Kathy Reynolds with a 'K' and Patricia Tomes. Also another woman named Helen something-or-other and a Hispanic woman. I didn't meet either of them but their names were on the roster in Glassy's office. See if there's anything suspicious in their pasts. I'd start with the Forbes listings. See if there's anyone on their payroll we can cozy up to. Or better yet, get me Diana Du Plessis on the phone."

"Now?"

"Right now."

Penny picked up Elizabeth's phone and found the speed dial programmed into the seventh slot. Diana was the reporter who had befriended Elizabeth when Holly was taken. Ever since, they'd stayed in touch—not close, but close enough.

"Miss Du Plessis," Penny said into the phone. "I have Elizabeth McClaine here. She'd like a moment of your time."

Penny handed Elizabeth the phone.

"Diana. How are you?"

"Better than you by the sound of it."

Elizabeth could hear the smile in her voice.

"Then you can probably guess what I'm doing."

The humor warmed Diana's voice. "Getting into your most outrageous dress for the Business Awards dinner tonight?"

"You know me too well. I need a favor."

"Name it," said Diana.

"I need a background check on the prison officers at Carringway private prison." She waited a beat, then said, "Can you do it?"

"Do you know who you're talking to?"

Elizabeth smiled. "I do."

"You understand that I can't divulge any of my sources."

Giving Penny an encouraging nod, she said, "I'd prefer it that way."

"When do you need it by?"

"Soon as you can."

Elizabeth gave Diana the names of the officers in question then hung up and passed the phone to Penny before leaning into the mirror where she swiped on mascara, then twisted her lipstick up and applied it. Finally she got up and slipped her feet into her spike heels, gave herself a dab of her Chanel No 5, and struck a pose.

"So? Given we're still talking *The Bachelor*, how would I rate?"

Penny stood back, viewing her employer from top to toe. "Elizabeth, if I were that way inclined, I'd marry you myself."

CHAPTER FIFTEEN
DAY ONE: 8:39 PM—STACY

The sun had gone down and despite the time of year, the evening temperature had turned chilly, the air damp. Worse yet, while Gayleen's car was a heap of junk, Curta's car had just enough gas to get it to the next gas station. Stacy had put her head down and pumped in four dollars' worth, which was all she figured she could spare out of the twenty-five, causing the guy behind the counter to put his hand out for the cash, saying, "Gee, road trip across America, is it?" Stacy wanted to tell him that at least she wasn't stuck in some hellhole in the middle of nowhere, making smart-ass comments to the customers who paid their wages, but that would only make her conspicuous, which she definitely didn't want. So instead, she smiled and said, "It's my mom's car. I just gotta get home."

The guy rang it up and she left, muttering and wondering, in reality, how far four bucks' worth of gas would get her.

When she got back in the car and twisted the key in the ignition, the gas indicator had barely moved. Hopefully it was enough to find Alice Rasmussen.

Alice was a dyed-in-the-wool heroin addict who lived in an apartment block somewhere on East 46th. How she ever got out of prison was anyone's guess. After seven months in Carringway with her, Alice was the last person Stacy wanted to spend time with, but all her other ports of refuge had already been exhausted. So with a light foot on the gas, she'd tapped the turn signal, swerved out of the forecourt, and headed west along Carnegie.

The apartment building, while not palatial, was a far cry from Curta's. Even the area where it was located was better. Stacy locked the car and headed across the street and entered the lobby. The elevator light showed the car on the top floor, so she opened the door to the stairwell and stepped through. She took the stairs two at a time until she hit the fourth floor and exited into a narrow hallway with apartment doors leading off in both directions. Feeling as if the whole world was watching, she hunched her shoulders and lifted her collar, then rapped on the first door to her left.

The door opened and a black woman with her hair wrapped in a towel opened the door. "Yeah? What do you want?"

"I'm looking for Alice Rasmussen. I was told she lived in this building."

The woman's face registered disgust, but she tipped her head toward the end of the hallway. "Lives down there—apartment E. Let's hope she's not having another damn party," she said and shut the door.

Stacy walked to where the woman had indicated and paused in front of a battered door, the brown paint chipped and showing the previous olive green shade beneath, a crooked letter E nailed at eye level.

Did she really want to be around Alice? But, where else could she go? So she knocked and waited. Finally, the door cracked and Alice peeped out.

Alice was a ghost of the person she'd been in prison. The last time Stacy saw her she'd put on weight and begun to radiate, if not health, then something akin to it. Drugs had undone all that. Now she had dark rings under sunken eyes, and her complexion had paled to a sickly gray. Her hair had thinned to the point where her scalp was apparent through the strands, and her teeth were discolored, the edges corroded by the drugs she'd taken over the course of her life. She widened the door and leaned on the frame, hugging herself as if she was cold.

"Stacy? Hey, what are you doing here?"

Stacy glanced back down the hallway. "Can I come in?"

"Ah, yeah, sure." Alice stepped back, waited for Stacy to enter, then closed the door. "Don't mind the mess. I gotta get around to cleaning up. So what's new?"

Stacy moved into the tiny living room and looked around. The apartment might have been nice if it wasn't such a shit-heap. The kitchen was stacked with dirty dishes and the tiny dining table was cluttered with dirty ashtrays, a couple lengths of rubber tubing, a few disposable lighters, and four empty soda bottles. Stacy guessed the trash hadn't been taken out in a while because the whole place stunk of rotting food.

"I just needed a place to hang out for a while, if that's okay." She figured Alice didn't need to know more than that.

"Yeah, sure, sure." Leaving her visitor standing, Alice crossed to the two-seater sofa and sat with her legs curled up under her. "Take a seat," she said, indicating one of the dining chairs. Stacy pulled out a chair, wiped the crap off it and sat with her hands on her knees, wondering why she even came here.

"I saw you got out on that program," Alice said.

"Ah, yeah. I was pretty lucky."

"Lucky? Stacy, that was genius. Man, they must have been so pissed when you just walked off like that."

Stacy blinked at her. It wasn't until now that she realized just how many people this would have affected—Elizabeth McClaine, for a start. "Yeah, I guess," she said, nodding. She knew this was a bad idea. Now she needed an excuse to leave.

Alice picked up a plastic pack and papers and began rolling a cigarette while she spoke. "Want a smoke?"

Stacy waved it away. "Nah, I'm good."

Concentrating on tucking the shreds of weed into the papers, Alice made a face. "I been watching the news. Do you know how many politicians have got their asses kicked for backing that program? It was just on the TV: everyone runnin' for cover, and making out they voted against it, all those big-ass politicians saying they don't know who got the program rubber-stamped 'cause it sure as hell wasn't them, and all blamin' each other." She ran her tongue along the edge of the paper and went on, saying, "And then they showed that Elizabeth McClaine on her way to some fancy party, all dressed up like Christmas on a plate, and she's sayin' how you're the best one for the program, and how she believes in you and all that blah-de-blah. I'm like, 'Lady, are you for real?' But she's going on, sayin' like, how she has *faith* in you and she'll *get to the bottom of why you ran*—like she could. And here you are right here in my apartment, givin' it to her behind her back. That's so hilarious."

Stacy felt anger rise so fast it shocked her. "I'm not 'giving it to her behind her back.' She tried to help me. I appreciated it."

Alice flicked the lighter, held the flame to the end of the joint and took a drag on it, holding it down and blinking through the smoke as she spoke. "Yeah, some help, huh? Rich bitch like her wouldn't know her ass from a trip to the moon." Alice held out the joint, offering it to Stacy.

"Nah, thanks. Will you excuse me? I gotta make a phone call."

"Sure." Alice turned her attention to the joint, picking off bits of charred paper and cursing. Stacy moved through to the tiny kitchenette, took out the phone Caitlin had given her, dug in her pocket for Wayne's number, and dialed. The phone rang once, twice.

"Answer the thing, dammit," she growled softly.

On the sixth ring, Wayne picked up. "Yeah?"

"It's me. Did you make the call?"

"Hold on," he said. For a while all she could hear was his breathing, then she heard a door close. "You there?"

"I'm here."

"I made the call. They're gonna have Tyler at the McDonald's on East 55th. You know the one?"

"Yeah, I know it."

The place was a stand-alone, right out in the middle of nowhere. If it had been in a shopping mall, she could have blended with the customers. The location of this place wasn't going to make it so easy. "So what time?"

"Ah. Nine o'clock tomorrow morning."

"*Tomorrow?*" Stacy said and glanced back at Alice, who was too busy smoking her joint to notice. "Why did you make it tomorrow? I said today."

"They said they can't. It has to be tomorrow."

"Shit."

"Well, I did what you asked. I kept my side of the bargain, now you can put up your side. I don't wanna ever hear from you again," he said, and the phone went silent.

Stacy tucked the phone back into her pocket, felt the edge of something as she did, and pulled out Elizabeth McClaine's business card. She'd forgotten that Mrs. McClaine had given it to her on the way home, telling her if she needed anything—anything at all—she was to call. What she needed was her son, needed to know he was safe. And right at this minute she needed help, so she pulled the phone out again and dialed the number on the card.

CHAPTER SIXTEEN
DAY ONE: 8:59 PM—ELIZABETH

By the time the limousine had swerved to the curb at Elizabeth's house, it was almost an hour after the awards dinner was set to begin. Elizabeth had left instructions for Penny to call Kay Heathers and find out where the meeting was to be held between Wayne Lettes and his son, but not to make a big deal out of it. If Kay chose to tell her, that was fine. If she chose not to, then they'd have to find another information source, although they weren't exactly thick on the ground.

As she'd left the house, a swarm of waiting reporters rushed her, closing in to the point of almost crushing her, until the driver stepped in, asking them to move back. Just before getting into the car, she made a general statement to the media, saying that whatever had transpired causing Stacy May Charms to break her parole, Elizabeth had every faith in her, and that she was still convinced Miss Charms was the best candidate for the program. When the reporters pushed forward again, mics held high, a barrage of questions flying, Elizabeth had told them she had nothing more to say, then got into the car and left.

During the thirty-five minute ride, her phone had rung three times: the first two calls from Penny, telling Elizabeth she'd managed to wheedle the meeting venue out of Kay, then updating her with news reports—

most of which were interviews with various political figures from both sides of the House. Seemed everyone was now either denying all knowledge of the program, or insisting they didn't know how it had gotten through the first vote. The final call was from a number she didn't recognize, so she let it go to voice mail, before switching the phone off.

As the car swept into the covered entrance in front of the conference center, a waiting concierge stepped forward to open her door, then another escorted her to the ballroom, where she was announced at the door and her coat taken. She walked down three steps into a brightly lit ballroom echoing with the murmur of conversation and paused to get her bearings. When a passing waiter proffered a tray of champagne flutes, each filled to the brim and with lines of tiny bubbles trailing up the sides, Elizabeth gave the tray an aching look, and asked for soda and lime.

"Right away, ma'am," he said and vanished towards the bar.

Elizabeth skirted the room slowly, taking a moment to look over the crowd. In the far corner she could see the Wheelwrights, laughing and talking animatedly with another couple and a man with his back to her wearing a dark, well-cut suit. The Wheelwrights had once been close acquaintances of her and her then-husband, Richard, although technically, the Wheelwrights had been more Richard's business associates. As if feeling her gaze in their direction, Marianne Wheelwright turned to let her eyes skim the room before stopping on Elizabeth, who smiled and dipped her head. In response, Marianne gave her a slightly awkward nod, then turned back to the circle, leaning in to say something that caused the others to turn and glance Elizabeth's way before closing in, huddled almost shoulder to shoulder while they continued their conversation.

So this was how it was going to be. The waiter returned with a tray holding a single champagne flute. Elizabeth took the glass and sipped. "Thank you," she said and raised it in a small toast to him.

He bent slightly at the waist and stepped back, then vanished into the crowd once more.

Across the room, she spotted Charles McClaine, her father-in-law. He turned, scanning the room like a barracuda searching for minnows until his focus came to her. He gave her a quick, cool smile and also returned his attention to the couple he was in conversation with.

"Nice to see you, too," she muttered under her breath, and turned to pick up a shrimp canapé from the buffet, popping it into her mouth as she continued to survey the crowd.

These were people she knew and worked with, and yet right now she felt as though she had an invisible force field surrounding her, preventing anyone from approaching. Off to her left, she spotted Rebecca Dean, the wife of Cleveland's deputy mayor. Rebecca fluttered her fingers at Elizabeth in a brief wave, a welcoming smile on her face, which Elizabeth responded to in kind, until Rebecca's husband leaned over with a reproachful glance at Elizabeth and whispered something to Rebecca. Rebecca looked momentarily pained, then gave Elizabeth a sorrowful glance, before looking away again.

Elizabeth clutched her purse under her arm and moved on, casting a contemptuous eye over the business suits and the women's conservative gowns as she circumnavigated the room. Glancing down, she was beginning to wonder at her own wisdom in choosing this dress instead of the one Penny had advised her to wear, when a voice behind her said, "You look beautiful. I only wish I could have dressed you."

She spun around to find Clay Farrant behind her, looking suave and relaxed, tall champagne flute in hand. Only now she realized that he was the one the Wheelwrights had been in their little tête-à-tête with. She took a sip of her drink, then looked him over, saying, "I hope you didn't come all the way over here just to say *I told you so*."

His expression was one of mock horror. He touched his fingers to his chest. "Me? Why would I do that?"

"Weren't you the one in the media with your 'learned' views on the early release program, baying for the blood if it went ahead? Oh, and feel free to correct me if I got that wrong."

Dimples formed two perfect brackets that framed his mouth when he smiled. He wobbled his head side to side, trying to marry up her version of the events with his.

"If I remember rightly, that's not exactly what I said. It was never the program I was against." He glanced around, leaned to her conspiratorially, and dropped his voice. "Contrary to what you might think, I'm not stupid enough to spit on one of the governor's pet projects just when I've hit the Favorites list. It was your choice of candidate I was opposed to, not the program."

She looked away, took another sip. "At least you're honest. More than I can say for some around here."

"I've been called worse." He ran his eyes slowly down her dress, stopping on her legs. "And I mean it, I wish I could have dressed you. There's nothing like showing off your wares on a beautiful woman for good advertising."

"I don't wear your designs. They're a little too young for me," she said, then mentally kicked herself for making the type of age comment she regularly chastened others for making. Ever since she'd hit fifty, she'd found herself more confident inside her own skin, but ironically, less confident with what was happening on the outside—a line here, a wrinkle there. Somehow they all seemed to counterbalance the wisdom and confidence that gave her that inner self-assuredness. It was a double-edged sword and she hated it.

Clay tipped his head, eyebrows lifting to a peak. "I hear there's a certain school dance coming up. If I can't dress you, then I'd be honored if you'd allow me to showcase one of my designs on your daughter."

Elizabeth cut him a look, instantly both suspicious and protective of Holly. "How did you know about that? What do you know about my daughter?"

He clutched his champagne flute between finger and thumb so he could hold both hands up to her. "Whoa, hold it right here. It's my business, Elizabeth. I keep tabs on every opportunity." The smile broadened again. "And while I'm a little embarrassed by all this fuss, you don't win Most Progressive Enterprise and Businessman of the Year without keeping your ear to the ground."

"I thought it was your fabulous operational and logistical blueprint that was responsible for all the success. Or has the business community of Cleveland suddenly developed a sense of haute couture?"

He laughed. "You want to beat the Chinese in our own market and pay your workforce what they're worth, you have to have all your ducks in a row these days. I like to think my ducks are in pretty good shape."

She let an appraising gaze travel his full height. "I'm sure your ducks are exactly where you need them." Another sip. "So you still haven't told me why you've trodden over the red-hot coals to come talk to me."

He turned, looking over the other attendees, all of whom were now immersed in conversation and trying to look as if they hadn't noticed the two of them together.

His eyes rose to a point just above her head while he found the words. "I may just be able to help you."

"Me?" she said in surprise.

He leaned in, his line of sight directed over her shoulder. Elizabeth could feel his breath on her neck. "Don't take this as gospel, but a little bird tells me you're out in the … let's say … social wilderness at the moment."

He straightened and their eyes met.

"Well, how gallant. And you'll do what? Hunt down Stacy May and bring her back bound hand and foot, and flung over your shoulder like a sack of wheat?"

He laughed, dimples deepening, eyes sparkling, obviously enjoying the moment. "Well, the truth is, I have no more idea of where Stacy May Charms is than you do. If I did, you'd be the first to know. See, the thing is, I don't know if you keep abreast of the markets, but I'm told that when

Rue Xeeba floats on the stock market, I'll be sitting in a pretty good position." He gave her an appraising look. "I'd be happy to help pave the way back into the fold for you."

She drained the glass and put it down on the table behind her, shifted her weight while she regarded him. Penny was right, he really was good looking. "And why would you 'pave the way' for me?"

"Because this project you've been working on is the governor's baby. If anybody's going to help save it from going out with the bathwater, I'd like to be the one who's—well, if not holding the towel, at least keeping it warm."

"Oh, I see," she said, tipping her head back before meeting his eyes again. "You have *political* aspirations. Right. Now I get it."

He grinned again. Those dimples. "You make it sound like a death sentence." He took a second to regard those standing nearby and shifted to cut them off. "It's a smart move. Once the company floats, and there's a management team onboard and all the extras and doodads that go with it, my time will free up. I'm hoping I'll come out with enough cash and connections to be a contender. I think I could do some good."

"*Extras and doodads?* I can guarantee if you use that kind of language around my father-in-law he'll be running for the hills with all your potential shareholders right behind him. And if you want my advice, he's exactly the kind of ringleader you need to get the best share price."

He grinned, hands spread wide. "You see? That's what I love about you. You're straight up, honest." The smile faded. "I mean it, Elizabeth, if you need anything—anything at all, call me. I'd be more than happy to do whatever I can. And if I might be so bold, do it while I still have the numbers on my side."

Behind him, Elizabeth spotted Christine Wentworth cutting through the throngs and heading straight for them at a brisk clip. In her early thirties, Christine wore her blonde hair pulled harshly back from her face and heavy rimmed eyeglasses that might have looked vulgar on anyone else, but great on her. Her perfect skin was lightly made up, highlighting her sharp blue eyes. Standing no taller than five feet two without shoes, what she lacked in height Christine made up for in her reputation as a tough negotiator and iron-fisted business woman. Even tonight, her gray pencil skirt cut to the knee and double-breasted jacket over a plain navy blue blouse formed the perfect image of a woman who didn't take prisoners.

Following Elizabeth's line of sight, Clay turned, just as Christine approached with the corners of her lips creasing into a thin smile.

"And here she is," Clay said, with an outstretched arm, "my secret weapon. Elizabeth, have you met Chrissie?"

Elizabeth felt something inside her turn sour. "No. Lovely to meet you at last," she said, forcing the warmth into the words.

"Likewise," Christine said with a small tilt of the head. She immediately turned to Clay, slipping a beautifully manicured hand into the crook of his arm—the gesture of possession and familiarity not lost on Elizabeth.

"Clay, Harvey and Wynonna Benson are waiting to see you. Will you excuse us?" she said to Elizabeth, as if she were dismissing a servant.

Clay Farrant executed a brief bow. "We'll catch up soon." He gave her a regretful smile, then walked away with Christine guiding him by the arm, his hand already extended towards a waiting group of devotees.

After just over an hour Elizabeth had been roundly ignored by everyone in the room except the one man she least expected to speak to, and the one woman she found herself irritated by. Feeling conspicuous and somewhat regretting her choice of evening wear, she called for her coat and asked for the limo her father-in-law had arranged to pick her up out front and drive her home.

Just as her car pulled up in front of the conference center, she turned on her phone, noting that same unknown number had called her another four times—no message.

The driver got out and rounded the car to hold the door for her, and the second she got in and the door closed, she hit the speed dial, calling Penny. The line picked up after three rings, Penny saying, "That was quick. So how'd it go?"

"Did you catch it on the TV?"

"Ah, yep."

Nothing more. Just "yep," Elizabeth noticed.

The driver got in, started the car, and edged it toward the street.

"So how did I look? Did I come across okay?"

"You looked great. So tell me what happened. Who'd you speak to?"

Elizabeth sat back and turned her head to the passenger's window, watching the street lights sliding by as she spoke.

"Only one person spoke to me the whole night—Clay Farrant."

Penny's tone rang of something like horror. "Seriously? What did he have to say?"

Elizabeth rolled her eyes. "He said I looked beautiful."

"That bastard." There was a hesitation, then Penny said, "He *is* a bastard, right?"

"He's rallying support so he can make a run at the governor's seat."

"You think that's the only reason he spoke to you? What if it's not? What if he's interested in something else? You could do worse, you know—handsome poster boy for Ohio manufacturing, cozy little mansion for two, your social standing reaching the stratosphere in two minutes flat."

"I'm fifty-five. He must be, what? Thirty-eight, thirty-nine?"

"So you're saying a younger man can't be attracted to an older woman—especially a beautiful, intelligent one?"

Again, Elizabeth felt herself running down that same alley—the age issue.

"It doesn't matter, anyway. Christine Wentworth was there, *obviously* with him."

"Oh, Miss Sourpuss? Lucky him. But what difference does that make?"

"According to those in on the social grapevine, Christine Wentworth isn't just president of his manufacturing empire; word is there's a romantic connection between them."

"So?"

"Oh, get out of here. I'm not making overtures to someone who's already in a relationship. Anyway, I think it's just his way of soliciting for political support. It's the old back-scratching: you look after me and I'll look after you. The last thing I intend to do is spend the entire term of his governorship as one of his political cronies, bowing and scraping because he once cast a favorable eye on me, thank you all the same."

"Up to you, doll. But like I said, you could do a whole lot worse."

A couple of beeps in her ear indicated another call coming in. Elizabeth looked down at the phone. It was the same number. Sixth call tonight.

"Listen, I gotta go, Penny. I have another call. I'll call you first thing." And she hung up, switching from one call to the next.

"Elizabeth McClaine," she answered.

CHAPTER SEVENTEEN
DAY ONE: 10:02 PM—STACY

Stacy had been stalking around Alice's apartment between repeated attempts to call Mrs. McClaine, watching the stupid girl dope herself up to the eyeballs. She couldn't help shaking her head and wondering why Alice did it. It was only now as she made the sixth call that she realized that the battery indicator had dropped to the last two bars and she'd neglected to get the charger. She was just about to cut the call when the line picked up.

Stacy moved to the corner of the kitchenette with her hand to the side of her mouth, shielding it, and whispering so Alice wouldn't hear. "Mrs. McClaine, it's me—Stacy."

There was tense silence for a couple of seconds, then Mrs. McClaine said, "Stacy? Where are you? What's happening?" She sounded more concerned than angry.

"I can't tell you. I just … I just wanted to tell you I'm so, so sorry for what I did. Like, running out the way I did."

Out in the living room, Alice was curled up on the sofa, elbow jammed against the armrest, head leaning on her fist while she watched some reality show on the TV, talking to the cast and telling them what to do as if they were there in the room with her.

Stacy turned back towards the tiny window that overlooked the parking lot outside where she'd left Curta's car, and dropped her voice again. "I have to find Tyler. Do you know where he is?"

"No, Stacy, I don't. Child Services has him at a very good foster home, and I know that you requested to have him moved several times but—"

"It's not that," Stacy said, interrupting her. "Someone's after him. They threatened to kill him."

Another tight silence, then Mrs. McClaine said, "Who told you that?"

Stacy turned back, checking Alice, who was still watching TV and smoking. "I got a photograph. It was left in my cell, couple of days before I was released. I found it tucked down into my bedding. It's a picture of Tyler coming out of his school. Someone drew, like crosshairs on it, like they're gonna shoot him or something. Then they wrote *He's first, you're next* on the back of it."

"Why didn't you tell me?" The shock in her voice reverberated down the phone line.

"I couldn't." Realizing her own voice had risen, she lowered it again, saying, "I didn't get the chance to say anything because there was always someone around. I didn't know who I could trust."

"You think it was someone inside the prison?"

Stacy switched hands with the phone while she opened the window to let some fresh air into the apartment. "It has to be. But they must have a connection on the outside, too."

"Why would they want to hurt you or Tyler? Is this something to do with the drugs they found?"

Stacy huffed in frustration. There was so much to this thing and no time to go into it. "Listen, I can't tell you right now. Just make sure Tyler's safe, will you? Please?"

"He is safe, Stacy. I can promise you that. He's with a good family that loves him. Kay Heathers said he's very happy with them. She makes regular calls on them and they look after him very well."

"Yeah, but if someone can get close enough to take a photo of him—"

"Stacy, I have the assurance of the police that Tyler is fine. Your parole officer, Nancy Pattrenko, is assisting wherever she can. Listen, where are you? I'll come straight over and pick you up."

"You can't. You'd have to turn me straight in."

"I wouldn't do that."

"Oh, yeah?" Stacy said. "So we'll both end up in adjoining cells? Me with another two years for running, you for aiding and abetting? Thanks, Mrs. McClaine, but I don't think so." There was another silence, and Stacy said, "I'm sorry. It's not your fault. I should have thought this out better."

"It's okay, Stacy. I'm working on it at my end. We'll figure it all out."

A knock at Alice's door made Stacy turn, and her heart rate jumped. "Listen, I gotta go."

"Wait, Stacy, please."

"Just make sure Tyler's safe. Nothing else matters." And she hung up and turned the phone off.

In the living room, Alice had crossed to the TV and turned it down. They shared a tense look, and when the knock came again, Alice went to the door, opened it a crack, and peeked out.

Alice clapped her hand to her chest and threw the door wide, saying, "Jeez, you nearly gave me a heart attack. What are you doing here?"

A thin guy walked in, dirty jeans, sweatshirt over a plaid button-down shirt, his face blotchy with zits and stubble. His bleary, drug-reddened eyes went straight to Stacy.

"There's a party. Who's this?" he said, jerking his chin at her.

Alice shut the door and followed his line of sight. "This is Stacy. We were inside together. She just broke parole and needs a place to hang for a while."

"Well, gee thanks, Alice," Stacy said. "Nice cover."

"Aw, don't be like that," Alice said, like a kid who'd had her internet privileges taken away. "This is Bug. He's got a warrant out on him, so he's hardly gonna head straight downtown and throw your ass to the cops, is he?"

Bug looked from Alice to Stacy and made a bored face, saying, "Yeah, whatever. Are you coming or not?" he asked Alice.

"So you wanna come to a party?" Alice asked Stacy.

"No, I don't. You go, I'll … just hang here."

"Aw, c'mon. Why do you have to be such a Miss Pain-in-the-Ass Goody Good all the time? Come, it'll be fun."

Stacy pocketed the phone and went for the door. "Listen, I better go. Thanks for … y'know, everything."

Alice's shoulders dropped and she frowned in disappointment. "Sure, whatever. You want some … I dunno, maybe some crack or something? I could get you some."

Stacy put her hand up, saying, "No, seriously…"

Alice said, "Well, I got nothin' else. I'd give you something to eat but all I got's a can of tuna, but seriously, it's been open like, two weeks and even I wouldn't eat it."

Bug had already drifted back out into the hallway, eager to get away. He leaned back in through the door, a hand on each side of the frame, saying, "C'mon, Alice, let's go."

"Nah, you keep it," Stacy told her. "But thanks anyway." Then a thought occurred to her. "Oh, wait. You got any plastic bags, you know, trash bags or something?"

Alice looked at her like she'd gone nuts. "Ah, yeah. Over in the kitchen. Second drawer, I think. There's some shopping bags over in the corner there," she said, pointing.

Stacy found two trash bags in the kitchen drawer and three plastic bags filled with trash down behind the sofa. "Got any old clothes you don't want?"

Bug leaned in the door again. "Are you comin' or not?"

"I'm coming, you idiot. Just wait. Take anything you want," she told Stacy. "I gotta go."

"Yeah, sure. This is great. Thank you."

Alice hovered in the hallway, peering back in every now and then until Stacy had what she needed. Alice closed and locked the door behind them then went to the elevator where Bug pressed the button.

Stacy told them to have a good time, then took the stairs back to the lobby. There was no sign of them when she stepped out, so she pushed through the front door, trotted straight to Curta's car, and got in. The clock on the dash read 10:32 p.m.

She had less than twelve hours but it may as well be a week. She fired up the car and pulled out, heading across to East 55th, to the McDonald's Wayne had said they were taking Tyler to.

The four dollars' worth of gas had easily gotten her this far. Keeping an eye on the gauge, she drove slowly to East 55th, where the sign outside indicated the restaurant would close in twelve minutes.

Stacy drove a little farther down the street and parked a block away. She lifted the bags she'd taken from Alice's place, along with Gayleen's wig and dress, got out, locked the car, and hurried back. She entered the restaurant with seven minutes to spare. A guy in a greasy McDonald's uniform watched her head straight for the bathroom at the back. He was probably just looking forward to closing up and going home and not having to deal with some vagrant that was going to hold him up.

Closing the stall, Stacy picked out the dress and put it on, adorning it with several of Alice's scarves (still with price labels and security tags attached, she noticed) and wrapped them around her neck and across the lower part of her face. Then she tore a hole in the largest trash bag and pulled it on over the top. When she checked in the mirror, she looked exactly how she'd intended—homeless.

Outside, the sound of the wall-mounted TV set covering a football game went abruptly quiet. It was immediately followed by the voice of one of the waitresses announcing that the restaurant was closing, and, after thanking the empty booths for their patronage, she advised all customers to make their way to the exits.

Stacy stuffed the bags with the items she wasn't wearing, slipped on a pair of sunglasses, and shouldered her way out of the bathroom. She was just about to head for the door, when she turned to the girl slouched behind the counter and said, "What can I get for a couple of bucks?"

The girl tossed a glance at the cabinets. "Couple of dollar burgers?"

"I'll take 'em," said Stacy.

The girl stuck them in a bag, folding the top over and running her fingers along the crease. Stacy dug in her pocket and counted the money onto the counter. The girl scooped it up, and gave her the change, saying, "Thanks, but I'm sorry, you'll have to take it out. We're closing." Stacy thanked her, wished her a great evening, and went to the door just as a young guy crossed in front of her, opening it for her and ushering her out before locking up behind her.

Outside, the rain was pattering down—the kind of rain that gets into everything, saturates everything right down to the skin before you know what's happening. She pulled one of the small plastic bags from her pocket and dropped both shopping bags between her feet while she tied it over her head. Head down and blinking against the rain, she hurried across the parking lot, eating the burgers as she ducked into a grassy area between the restaurant and the neighboring car wash. It was the perfect vantage point. From here she could see the front doors and either way down the street. She found a bench under a couple of straggly trees that leaned overhead, providing a minimal shelter, and settled in.

Tyler would arrive at nine in the morning. The plan was to keep the place in sight. With nowhere to park nearby except the McDonald's parking lot or the Burger King across the street—which cops would likely patrol—that meant she'd have to sit outside. Last thing she could do was miss him again. The second she saw him arriving, she'd cut straight back to the car, then return and park where she could see them leave. Then she'd follow. It would be split-second timing. She'd have to be in exactly the right place at the right time.

She wasn't holding her breath.

If there was one thing she'd learned in the last twenty-four hours, it was that the best-laid plans never worked out the way they should. But right now, she was too tired to think straight, so this was what she had.

She tore the second trash bag down the seam and laid it out on the bench with one of the shopping bags as a pillow. Then she lay down with the upper half of the bag over her, arms around herself for warmth, and prayed to God that He'd keep Tyler safe.

CHAPTER EIGHTEEN
DAY TWO: 6:14 AM—ELIZABETH

Elizabeth jerked awake to the ringing of the phone on the nightstand next to her bed. She'd tossed and turned after a night of terrifying dreams, all of which ended with Stacy May Charms slowly falling backwards, arms spread wide, crying out in anguish as she disappeared over a cliff, or out over a building ledge, the blue sky clouding over behind her. In every one, Elizabeth dashed forward, crying out her name, but always just a fraction too late to save her.

When the phone stopped, and immediately began ringing again, she heaved out an irritated breath and reached across to pick it up, rubbing her eyes and blinking hard at the screen as she drew it across in front of her.

The instant she saw the number she sat up with her knees drawn up, wide awake. She cleared her throat, then hit the button, saying, "Detective Delaney. It's a little early, isn't it?"

Without preamble, he said, "What was our agreement, Elizabeth?"

She frowned. "What do you mean?"

"You told me you'd bring any information straight to me."

"I haven't had any information to bring," she replied.

"And what about the six phone calls you received from Stacy May

Charms? I'm assuming it was her that called you. Or are the phone records wrong?"

His words hit her like an ice pick to the chest.

The calls! But how …?

"You've been monitoring my phone?" she asked, horrified.

"We're the police, Elizabeth. Do you think we're stupid? We checked the incoming calls on your line and picked up the number last night. When we ran a check, it turned out to belong to a man who claims Caitlin O'Hare had stolen it from him. Caitlin O'Hare, for your information, was a cellmate of Stacy May's. Tell me it's a coincidence, and I'll come over there right now and arrest you for obstruction."

"I was going to call you."

"When?"

Elizabeth had never heard him so angry. She felt like a schoolgirl caught smoking behind the gym.

When she stuttered while her brain scrambled for an answer, he barked, "So what else haven't you told me?"

The fury in his voice made her wince. "I told you, I didn't get anything. I spoke to Nyla Guthrie who told me Stacy's friend—the one that died—and I quote, 'had it coming to her.' Then I spoke to an economist who told me all about herself before advising me that there's no such thing as fairy dust—which I'm rapidly beginning to believe. And then I spoke to Cissy Pettameyer, who turned completely psychotic when I wouldn't shortlist her for the next program selection. Satisfied?"

"And what did you and Stacy May have to chat about the six times she called?"

"We talked *once*. I was at the Ohio Business Awards last night. I had my phone off." A pause. No reply. "I'm telling you the truth," she insisted, hating the near-break in her voice.

"And?"

"Stacy thinks someone's after her son. I told her Tyler is safe, and that the home he's in is a loving and caring environment, and that she had nothing to worry about." There was a tense silence during which Elizabeth realized the severity of the situation. "And I didn't tell you because—"

"—because you took it upon yourself to withhold information—information I distinctly asked you to hand over to me. In other words, you've ignored me, and because of your own arrogance, you could have endangered a child's life, just so you could keep the whereabouts of a known fugitive from the police. Do I have that right?"

He had every right to be angry. The disappointment in his voice hurt the most. "Look, I'm sorry—"

"Let me tell you how this is going to run from now on." His voice was low, serious. Elizabeth dug her teeth into her upper lip and raised her eyes to the ceiling with her breath held, waiting.

"You will not make any further inquiries into the whereabouts of Stacy May Charms or the circumstances surrounding her flight. Do you hear me?"

"But—"

"I've called the wardens of both Carringway Prison, and the Ohio Women's Reformatory, requesting that they refuse any requests from you for admittance to question any prisoner in their facilities. Do you understand?"

Elizabeth let out the breath she'd been holding. "Yes, I do."

"And if I find out that you have acted against my instructions, I'll have you arrested for obstruction of the police in the course of their duty. Am I making myself perfectly clear?"

"Yes, you are."

"Then I'll bid you a good day, Mrs. McClaine."

He hung up, leaving Elizabeth shocked to the core and holding the dead phone to her ear. She reached across and put it back on the cradle, considering her situation for a moment before leaning forward with her forehead pressed to her knees.

What the hell had she done?

*****

Elizabeth took her time over breakfast, still smarting from the tongue-lashing Delaney had given her. She kept telling herself that she'd done nothing wrong, that what she'd done wasn't just in the interests of Stacy May Charms, or the Charles McClaine Foundation, but in the interests of the governor's program. Of course she was going to do what she could to correct the situation.

But every time Delaney's voice rang back through her mind, she cringed, knowing he'd been right. She should have told him about the threat to Tyler straight away. *What had she been thinking?*

The newspaper lay folded on the table next to her. She lifted it and shook it out. The whole saga had been run on the front page under the headline: "Early Release Comes Earlier for Stacy May." Beneath it was the Instagram photograph of Stacy making her getaway. The article began, "Police were left red-faced when Elizabeth McClaine's first successful candidate for the governor's early release program went on the run minutes after her release…"

Sickened by a welling sense of dread and humiliation, Elizabeth tossed the first few pages on the floor and flicked to the business page. Taking up a quarter page was an article about the business accomplishments of Clay Farrant. Above, the picture showed Clay holding up his award for Top Businessman, Governor Straussman on one side with his arm around Clay's shoulder in a father-like pose, Christine Wentworth on the other side with a triumphant smile.

"Jerk," she muttered, and closed the paper, setting it aside and wondering where that prick of jealousy had risen from.

When she looked up, Holly was watching her over the table, a piece of toast in her hand, jelly smeared across one cheek. "Are you sad, Mommy?"

"No, I'm not sad, sweetie. Mommy has a lot to think about today."

"When can we go buy a dress for the dance?" she asked, turning the toast to study it before deciding where to take the next bite.

"Not today. Let me check out some stores online, okay?"

"Okay." She didn't sound happy, but knew well enough this wasn't the time to argue.

When the front doorbell chimed through the house, Katy appeared from the kitchen, saying, "Finish your breakfast, Mrs. McClaine. I'll get the door."

She disappeared through to the front entrance where Elizabeth could hear voices. When Katy returned, she was carrying a large square box, cellophaned across the front, swathed in pink ribbon, and containing twelve dark red long-stemmed roses.

Katy gave her a meaningful smile and handed the box across. "These are for you."

"Who from?" she said, taking them and lifting the lid to find the accompanying card, although she had a sinking feeling she knew without even looking.

The card read: *Lovely seeing you last night. How about dinner? Clay.*

"Terrific," she said without emotion, and tore the card from the paper, crumpling it up in one hand while she put the flowers to one side. Last thing she needed in her life was another womanizer.

Katy hovered a moment, obviously confused by Elizabeth's reaction. "Shall I put them in water?"

"No. Take them home," she told her. "I don't want them."

Katy frowned in surprise. "I can't take them, Mrs. McClaine. They were sent for you."

"Can I have them?" Holly asked, reaching for them.

Elizabeth put her hand on her daughter's, saying, "Katy's taking them.

She works very hard and I think she deserves them more than us. I'll buy you your own flowers when we get the dress. Okay?"

Holly put her elbow on the table, head slumped against her hand, lip jutting. She'd lost interest in her breakfast.

Was there anyone who wasn't mad at her right now?

Holly put her toast down, then got up without a word and took her plate to the kitchen, leaving Elizabeth sitting at the table, hands clasped to her lips, and feeling like the worst mother in the world. When the phone rang, she called, "I've got it," and leaned across to pick it up.

"Elizabeth," he said.

Her shoulders dropped. "Clay," she said in a tone that still sounded chilly despite the warmth she'd tried to inject into it. "Nice of you to call."

"Did you get the flowers?"

"I did, and thank you. But you really shouldn't have."

"So how about that dinner I mentioned? Friend of mine just opened a new restaurant on the other side of town—best seafood you ever tasted."

"Well, I'd love to," she lied. "But I have so much going on at the moment."

"I'm sure you do," he said.

She gave it a beat, then got up and walked across the dining room to look out the window over the sprawling yard out back. The rain from last night had let up and blue sky was appearing between the cloud breaks. "I, ah … I'm lying. I don't have much going on."

"You found Stacy?" He sounded surprised.

"No," she said bluntly, her mind seesawing with indecision before pressing ahead, while a voice somewhere down in her gut warned her against it. "I had a call this morning from the detective heading the search."

"Oh. Good news, then?" he asked.

"Not really. He's told me not to pursue any inquiries into Stacy's flight, 'or the circumstances surrounding it.' His words."

"Ouch."

"Ouch is right."

Another brief silence.

"So what are you going to do?" he asked.

Outside, a flock of birds was descending onto the lawn where Katy had thrown the crusts from breakfast.

"I don't know. He threatened me with arrest."

"You're kidding. I can't imagine the governor being thrilled to hear that. I overheard him saying he's keen to get this program back on track. Is there anything I can do?"

"Well," she said, feeling the knot in her stomach tighten. "Now that you mention it…"

"Just say the word, Elizabeth."

She made a pained face, then said, "No. It doesn't matter."

"Now, c'mon, don't do that to me," he said, the grin coming through in his voice. "Tell me what you were gonna say."

"Like I said, it doesn't matter," she said, bending at the waist with her head in her hand and silently cursing herself for even thinking of it. She straightened, saying, "Seriously, it's nothing. I shouldn't have asked."

"You want me to put a word in the governor's ear to get your investigation running again? Is that it?"

She drew in a deep breath and rocked her head right back. "I'd do it myself, but you know…"

"It would be better coming from someone else. I get that. I don't know when I'm seeing him, but I'll see what I can do."

She clutched the phone close to her ear, feeling like a teenager waiting for a boy to ask her for a first date. "If you can't, it doesn't matter," she added hastily.

"I'll give it my best shot. But ah, you know, the primaries are coming up. There's talk of Straussman stepping down, letting some young blood in."

An unintentional snort escaped her lips. "Now that I'd like to see."

"Why? You think he won't?"

"I think he's there for at least another term, Clay," she said. "I'd just about stake my life on it. If it was worth anything right now," she added flatly.

"Well, either way I need to position myself to back the right horse. I'd have to choose my moments, if you know what I mean. You understand."

"Oh, look, I completely understand. Forget I spoke, Clay. Truly, I'll work something out."

After making excuses to avoid dinner with him tonight, she ended the call and hung her head, humiliation washing back and forth like a spring tide. When the doorbell sounded again, she groaned, saying, "What now?" and calling to Katy, "I'll go."

Penny stood on the doorstep, briefcase in hand. "You weren't at the office."

Elizabeth widened the door and Penny entered, giving her boss a worried look. "Are you okay?"

"I'm great." She closed the door and went back to the dining room with Penny following.

"I had a call from Delaney. He's threatened to arrest me for obstruction of a police investigation. Then he called both the prisons I was to visit and told them not to admit me."

"Whoa!" Penny deposited her briefcase on the floor and rested one hand on the back of a chair, other hand on her hip. "So what brought that on?"

Elizabeth folded her arms, defensive. "Stacy called me. Last night. Apparently, Delaney was monitoring the calls. He called me at just after six this morning to kick my butt for not telling him."

"Great wakeup call."

Elizabeth frowned at a point just in front of her. "You know, I was just thinking." She let the idea take shape, then said, "What's the time?"

Penny checked her watch. "Seven forty-two. You've got that look on your face. What are you cooking up?"

"Did you bring your car?"

A flinch, indicating the obvious. "How else would I have gotten here?"

"Did you bring your phone?" Elizabeth asked.

"You ever seen me without it?"

"Good. Come with me." Elizabeth headed for the stairs.

"Where are we going?"

"I think it's time I took you to breakfast," she told Penny over her shoulder.

Penny followed her upstairs, responding in a suspicious tone, "That's nice. What's the catch?"

"No catch. Just don't expect eggs Benedict." Elizabeth pushed her bedroom door open and went in. "We're going to McDonald's."

CHAPTER NINETEEN
DAY TWO: 7:43 AM—STACY

Almost the second Stacy's head had hit the bag she was using as a pillow, the heavens had opened and the rain started falling, streaming down like someone had turned on a tap. Despite pulling the trash bags over her head and tucking her feet up, the rain seeped through, leaving wet patches on her jeans, her sweater, and saturating her hair. When an icy raindrop trickled down her collar and around her neck, she knew even the dumbest homeless person wouldn't sleep out in weather like this. So she'd pulled the trash bag over her head, gathered up her two plastic shopping bags, and gone in search of shelter. Head down against the deluge and squinting into a sea of shattered streetlights, she turned the corner to her left and found a bus shelter. It was dry, and from here she could still see the entrance to McDonald's, so she'd flicked the water from her hands and ruffled it out of her hair. After shedding the wet garments and tucking them away, she'd spread out her trash bag on the bench, and again, using one of the bags as a pillow, she lay down.

No sooner had she wrapped her arms around herself for warmth and found a semi-comfortable position with the restaurant in her line of sight, when a couple entered the shelter. Apparently also homeless, the two talked in low voices, warily glancing back at her every now and then as they set up their own sleeping arrangements on the opposite bench before settling in.

Stacy had lain awake, shivering with the cold and listening to the rain pelt against the Plexiglas and the hiss of tires speeding by. For the briefest moment, she guessed she'd drifted into something approaching sleep, because when she shuddered awake at just after twelve, feeling like she had a knife in her back, the homeless couple had disappeared along with one of her bags.

"Oh, you're kidding me." She sat up, rolling her shoulders, and tilting her head left and right to stretch the kinks out, then lifted the remaining bag onto her knee, searching through the contents.

"Bastards." She pressed the remaining items back down into the bag again.

Gathering up the few things she had left, she slung the shopping bag over her shoulder and returned to the car. She may as well sleep in some comfort, head back here by eight. Even if they were early, there was a chance she'd find a good position from which she could catch Tyler and whoever was with him as they went in.

But she had to get some dry clothes on.

At the bottom of the bag was a pair of jeans and a sweater Alice had discarded, probably too large for Alice's emaciated frame. Switching to the rear seat, she slid across to the middle and arched her back against the seat back while she maneuvered her jeans down to her feet and kicked them off, then took off her sweater. It was a struggle even getting Alice's jeans up over her hips, but after wiggling side to side and holding her breath, she finally got them up. She couldn't zip them, but that didn't matter; the sweatshirt came down far enough to hide the zipper. She flicked the hood up over her head and took a look in the rearview mirror.

Perfect.

Well, almost perfect. After pulling Tyler's toy car out of the pocket of her wet jeans, she dug out her keys, got into the driver's seat, and hit the road.

The first all-night launderette she came across turned out to be just around the corner. She parked in a spot across the road, got out and ran to the front door, where she pushed her way inside, toting her one remaining bag and wondering whether Tyler would remember her.

It wasn't the first time she'd wondered; wasn't the first time that sliver of fear had carved an enormous hole in her chest. What could be worse? A child you love enough to do anything for who doesn't even remember you.

Would he still have memories of those first two years he'd lived with her? Or would these last three with so few visits have erased them, replacing them with a bond with his foster mom that no one could break? Stacy couldn't think of a worse fate for a mother. All she could do was hope that with time, he'd come to love her the way she did him, and if he didn't, that somehow he'd come to know that everything she'd done, she'd done for him.

The inside of the launderette was warm and smelled of fabric softener and soap. She selected a dryer at the rear of the place and tossed in her rain-dampened clothing, removing her socks as an afterthought and throwing them in as well. Just as she had slipped the first few quarters into the slot, two women pushed through the front door, talking and laughing about some party they went to last night. They glanced her way and moved to the machines opposite.

Keeping her back to them, Stacy picked up one of the tattered magazines left for the customers and pulled her hood down in front, head bent low, pretending to read. Behind her, the chatter had dropped to a few whispers. She could feel them watching her.

She sat for as long as she could, but when the silence behind her echoed over the machines, she got up, opened the dryer before it had completed the cycle, and took the clothes out. She stuffed them into the plastic shopping bag, exited the launderette, and hurried back to the car.

When the clock on Curta's dash told her it was 8:34, it was time to go. She knew what she had to do, where she had to go. But she needed Mrs. McClaine to know. If anything went wrong, she had to know that she'd make sure Tyler was taken care of. So she pulled out the phone, switched it on, and waited for it to connect to the network.

The instant the bars appeared in the top right corner, the phone beeped, telling her she'd missed eleven calls.

Eleven? Who would be calling eleven times?

First, she checked messages—nothing. Next she checked the numbers that had called. Four were from a number she didn't recognize, the rest had been blocked. Was it the guy Caitlin had gotten it from? What if it was Wayne, telling her they'd changed the arrangements?

For a second she was lost in indecision. Then she dug out Mrs. McClaine's card, comparing the number that had called with all three numbers printed after her address. It was none of those. She found Elizabeth McClaine's cell phone number and was just punching it in, when the phone rang in her hand. She stared at it, noting the number was blocked, so she hit the button, and held it to her ear, but said nothing.

"Hello, Stacy." It was a man's voice—not one she knew.

Frozen in place, heart pounding, she kept the phone pressed to her ear, listening.

"Stacy, this is Detective Delaney," he said. She hung up at once, switching the phone off and casting it into the passenger's seat as though it was something deadly.

How did the cops get the number? Had Mrs. McClaine turned her in? Surely she wouldn't. What if they'd spoken to Caitlin? Or Wayne? What if he called the cops straight after she'd spoken to him? Or his girlfriend?

Whatever. When it all came down to it, it didn't matter how they knew. They just did. But from now on, Stacy would only be able to switch the phone on for short periods of time. Verna Harris two cells down in C-Block had wound up with a seven-year stretch after the police had tracked Verna down by locating the areas her cell phone was in use. Verna had been oblivious to the fact that her whereabouts were practically common knowledge across the entire Cleveland Police Department, and the way she told it, she was coming out of Chuck E. Cheese in the Great Northern Plaza when forty-two cops descended on her and threw her ass in jail. Then again, everyone knew that Verna wasn't exactly a criminal mastermind, so even if the cops hadn't picked her up using the cell phone, it wouldn't have been long before they got her some other way.

Checking the street in front and back, Stacy fired up the car, put her foot to the accelerator, and pulled out, heading back to McDonald's.

If her luck would just hold long enough, she might catch up with her beautiful boy. It was one date she didn't want to miss.

CHAPTER TWENTY
DAY TWO: 8:54 AM—ELIZABETH

Elizabeth sat in the front passenger's seat of Penny's car, directing her to drive this way and that, until Penny finally said, "Elizabeth, I have GPS. We'll find the damn place," and Elizabeth sat back, one elbow resting on the window frame, and the knuckle of her forefinger pressed to her mouth while she focused on the passing landscape.

As they rounded the last corner, Elizabeth sat up, saying, "Here it is. Park over there."

"No, I'll park over here," Penny replied as she spun the wheel and guided the car into the Burger King parking lot directly opposite, where she pulled into a spot facing the street.

"Oh, this is even better," Elizabeth said, twisting around in her seat, eyes searching the area. "I can't see her."

Penny pointed out the windshield. "There's Nancy Pattrenko."

Across the street, they could see the woman walking into view. At around five-three and thickset, Nancy must have been in her late forties, hair dyed plum red and drawn harshly back from her face, heavy features without makeup, scowl lines obvious even from this distance.

Elizabeth huffed. "Couldn't she have put something over her hair?

Look at her. She looks like a traffic accident. Stacy gets one look at her and she'll run."

"Does Stacy know what she looks like?"

"Of course she does. They met several times in prison to discuss the terms of her parole. It was one of the conditions of her release."

Penny sat forward, her gaze riveted to the shrub garden at the corner of the restaurant. "What's that guy doing over there?"

Elizabeth shifted in her seat to follow Penny's line of sight. Sure enough, a guy in a windbreaker and sunglasses was crouched, ostensibly to tie his shoe, but the moment he placed his finger to his ear it was obvious he was wearing a mic.

Elizabeth groaned. "Oh, my God. He'll be one of the police stakeout team." She leaned right across, head pressed to the passenger window so she could see down the other side of the restaurant. "There's one on the other side. They may as well have worn their uniforms and brought signs, the idiots. What time is it?"

Penny slipped her sleeve back. "Two minutes to show time."

Right at that moment, Elizabeth's phone rang.

"Dammit," she said, and scrambled through her purse to find it. Lifting it, she turned it to check the screen. "It's Diana."

"Answer it. I'll keep watch," said Penny, ducking her head to get a look down the alleyway next to the restaurant.

Elizabeth hesitated. She was just about to hit the button, when Penny said, "Wait up. There's Kay Heathers with Tyler. Over there." Again, she pointed.

Sure enough, a gray-haired woman in her late fifties, early sixties maybe, walked toward the restaurant, a small boy next to her, his hand in hers.

At six years old, Tyler Charms was a slim child with fine dark hair cut squarely around his face. He wore a padded blue parka a couple sizes too big for him, track pants, and sneakers. Together they turned towards the front doors of the restaurant, Kay clearly nervous, darting looks up and down the street as she pushed open the doors and they moved inside.

Either side of the building, both police officers had vanished.

"What now?" asked Penny.

"We wait."

Penny leaned one arm over the steering wheel, angling herself around so she could see further down the street. "Is that her?"

Elizabeth sat forward in time to see a young woman approaching the restaurant, head down, sweater hood pulled up and furtively glancing around, but the wig clearly visible beneath; Gayleen's flowered dress hanging below the sweater, jeans below over dirt-covered sneakers, plastic shopping bag in hand.

"That's her. That's the wig and the dress she was wearing in the photo. I'm sure of it. What do I do?"

"There's nothing you can do. We just have to—" Penny began, but almost at once, three suited officers approached the girl, two from in front, one materializing from behind.

The girl stopped short on seeing them, visibly stiffened, then turned, apparently opting to turn back, but the officer right behind her closed in. All at once, she threw the shopping bag two-handed at the nearest officer, who fended it off with a swipe of his hand. He made a grab for her but she ducked under his hand and took off at a run. She tore down the side of the McDonald's with the three right behind her. Out of nowhere two police cars appeared, lights flashing, sirens whooping.

"Get going, follow them," Elizabeth ordered, but Penny had already switched the ignition and slammed the car in reverse. She swung out of the lot so fast Elizabeth grabbed the door, then they hung a right onto the main road, almost hitting a car that came out of nowhere. Elizabeth pointed down the alleyway adjacent McDonald's. "Down there. I just saw her. Keep going straight along and we'll follow."

Penny pressed her foot to the floor and they shot forward, then slowed at the next intersection. The driver behind leaned on his horn and Penny yelled, "Ah, shut up!"

"There she is." Sure enough, the hood had blown back and the wig was half off. She fled across the intersection one street down, running parallel with Penny and Elizabeth, the three cops and two cars following close behind her.

"Man, she's fast," Penny remarked.

"Next intersection—go, go, go," Elizabeth yelled, waving her forward like General Patton signaling his troops to advance.

Once again, Penny hit the gas and they lurched forward until they were at right angles to the next street. At the dead end of the alleyway, they could see the girl clinging to a chain-link fence, kicking out at the cop beneath her as she tried to scramble over.

"Down there, go," Elizabeth yelled, pointing again.

"I'm going, I'm going! Oh, shit!" Penny said as the two police cars swerved in behind them and flew down the alleyway to screech to a halt in a V formation.

Penny backed up, then threw the car into drive and they hurtled down the street, coming to a whiplash-inducing halt behind the police cars.

Elizabeth threw her door open, jumped out, and ran to where the cops had tugged the girl down from the fence and pounced on her, rolled her onto her stomach and cuffed her hands behind her back.

"If you've hurt her, the governor will be told and your asses won't be worth squat," Elizabeth told Delaney, who was just getting out of the second car. Together they walked quickly over to where two of the pursuit policemen were breathing heavily, one bent with his hands on his knees trying to get his breath, while the third took the girl by the shoulder and jerked her over onto her back.

She had a hole in one knee of her jeans, a bloody graze showing through. The wig had come off and her nose was bloodied, probably from the fall. She looked up, eyes reflecting the same horror on the faces of everyone surrounding her. She had the same coloring, same hairstyle, but it was not Stacy May Charms.

CHAPTER TWENTY-ONE
DAY TWO: 9:06 AM—ELIZABETH

"So who's this?" Elizabeth demanded, gesturing towards the girl as the two officers lifted her to her feet and took her to a waiting car.

Delaney had his phone to his ear. He turned away briefly, speaking in a low voice, watching as the one of the officers placed a hand on the girl's head, assisting her into the back of the patrol car, while the other went around to the driver's side and got in. The detective hung up, pocketing the phone as he turned to Elizabeth, his face expressionless. "Officer Turner found at least two ounces of marijuana on her. She'll be taken down to the station for questioning." He looked away, trying to avoid her furious gaze.

"Oh, thank God. We can sleep easy in our beds again." Realizing the level of sarcasm was one step over the line, she said, "I'm sorry, Detective, that was uncalled for."

Finally he turned to face her, hands in his pockets. "Elizabeth, I'm every bit as keen to find Stacy May Charms as you are—"

Elizabeth gestured toward the departing car. "So how did that girl get those clothes? Those were the ones Stacy was last seen wearing. Did she rob her? Did she beat her up and leave her to die somewhere?"

Delaney tipped his head back, searching for patience. "She said she found them. In a bus shelter."

"Seriously? And you believe that? And it's just some crazy coincidence she happened to be walking to the very same McDonald's in the very same clothes?"

"I don't know, Elizabeth. But whatever happened, I have it on good authority that Stacy May Charms can look after herself. I very much doubt that she's lying dead somewhere."

He started back to the car, so she followed, speaking at his back. "So are you any closer to finding out why she ran?"

"No, but I'll be sure to ask her when I find her."

"This is all about drugs coming into Carringway Prison. Everything I've found out points to it."

With something close to forced patience, Delaney paused to let his eyes sweep the alleyway behind her. "I've spoken with Warden Glassy. She assured me they're on top of the drug issue and there's nothing more to investigate. They found the culprit and took the appropriate action. What else do you want me to do?"

"And what about Tyler?"

Delaney pressed a finger and thumb to his eyes, then dropped his hands, clasping them in front of him. "I know this is tough for you. I know it must bring back some terrible memories. But he's safe, Elizabeth. He's with Officer Pattrenko and Kay Heathers. Now, if you don't mind—"

"And what about the photograph? Doesn't that mean anything?"

He swung around, eyes narrowed on her, his patience instantly morphing into thinly disguised outrage. "What photograph?"

Elizabeth felt a cold jolt of realization hit her. She hadn't told him. "The photograph Stacy said she got. I haven't actually seen it myself."

He said nothing, just stared, eyes blazing, nostrils slightly flared.

She took a faltering breath and folded her arms tightly across herself, feeling foolish. "When I spoke to her last night, Stacy told me she got a photograph of Tyler. It was left in her cell a few days before she was released. It showed Tyler outside his school, and the image of him was circled to indicate crosshairs, like someone might be going to shoot him or something. Whoever left it had written something like 'He's first and you're next' on the back." She drew her shoulders in, hugging herself a little tighter while she dropped her gaze to the ground between them, waiting for the onslaught.

"And when were you planning on telling me this?"

She looked around briefly before meeting his fiery gaze, lifting her chin like a kid caught smoking in her room. "I did tell you that Stacy thought someone was after her son. I would have told you the rest of it but you were too busy kicking my ass to listen," she said, and mentally kicked herself because now she was acting like that same kid.

He sucked in an infuriated breath and let his eyes drift.

"Listen, this is pointless," she said. "We're both looking for Stacy, and yes, I admit I was out of line. I should have told you about the photograph. It wasn't intentional; I simply got carried away defending her. I'm sorry."

He said nothing, dipped his head in a brief nod.

"Detective … Lance, I need to find her. She ran because she genuinely thought Tyler was in danger."

He was about to say something else when his phone rang in his pocket. He dredged it out, checked the screen, frowned and answered, saying, "Kay."

The frown deepened and his head dropped as he listened.

"When?" he asked. He listened for a moment, then said, "So where were you? Whoa, whoa, slow down," he said, patting the air as though she could see him.

Elizabeth could hear the garbled voice on the other end. Kay Heathers sounded distraught.

"What's happened?" Elizabeth asked.

Still on the phone, Delaney put up his hand to her and turned away. "Stay where you are, Kay. I'll be right there."

"What's happened?" Elizabeth asked again as Delaney put the phone away and gestured for his car to be brought around.

"Kay Heathers says that she went to the bathroom and when she came out, Tyler and Nancy Pattrenko were gone."

Elizabeth followed as he walked quickly to the car and got in. "Gone? Gone where?"

"That's what I aim to find out." He slammed the door just as the car swerved around, eased past Penny's car and took off.

"Follow them," she ordered Penny like the hero in a movie pursuit.

By the time Elizabeth and Penny got back to the restaurant, Delaney was interviewing Kay Heathers, who had both hands to her face, tears rolling down her cheeks while two officers with radios and notebooks interviewed patrons and staff, taking notes and calling the information in.

Kay's face was flushed, her eyes red, her brow deeply furrowed, the distress aging her ten years. "I came out and they were gone," she kept saying, looking from Delaney to the doorway as if they might reappear at any minute. "I looked in the bathroom, out back, everywhere. They'd just vanished."

"How long ago was this?" Delaney asked.

The woman bit her lip as she played the events back in her mind. "Maybe five minutes? Just before I called you. I searched everywhere," she said again.

"Did Ms. Pattrenko say she was taking Tyler anywhere at any time?"

Kay took out a handkerchief and wiped away the tears. "She didn't say anything. I'd just gotten Tyler an Egg McMuffin…. I know it's not the best breakfast, but you know what kids are like."

As she spoke, Delaney nodded and rolled his hand, urging her to continue. "Did you see which way they went?" he said, interrupting her.

She gave him a sharp look, visibly shocked by the suggestion. "Of course not. I was in the bathroom. I just told you that."

One of the officers who'd run the girl to the ground in the alley crossed from the counter, angling himself around, eyes on the parking lot outside while he spoke to Delaney. "Guy behind the counter said he saw a woman with red hair and a kid walk out onto the street and get into a car. The guy said the kid was crying. He didn't get a make on the car."

"Did he see which way they went?" Elizabeth asked before Delaney could.

"Didn't see," the officer replied, addressing his remarks to Delaney. "Thinks they might have gone south."

"Did he get a description of the car?" Delaney asked.

The officer shook his head. "Said it could have been gray or silver four-door sedan. Probably late model."

Delaney lifted his phone, hit the redial. "Get an APB out on a late-model, silver or gray four-door sedan headed south on East 55th. And get a chopper in the air."

He hung up and stepped away, relaying the details into the phone once again and barking out orders. Almost at once, Elizabeth's phone rang. She glanced at the screen and answered immediately, saying, "Stacy! Where are you?"

Delaney spun around, stared for a second, then ended his phone call.

"Mrs. McClaine?" Stacy began. She spoke again, saying something else but the call was breaking up and Elizabeth couldn't hear.

Delaney moved across in front of her, his hand out for the phone. "Give it to me."

Elizabeth tugged away and turned, placing one finger to her other ear, nodding and telling the girl, "Slow down, slow down, I can't understand what you're saying. Tell me that again."

Delaney still had his hand out, irritation carving deep lines into his features.

"She'll just hang up if she hears you," Penny told him in a matter-of-fact tone.

Between the occasional break on the line, Stacy's voice was strained, desperate. "What's happening? I just saw Tyler come out of the restaurant with Officer Pattrenko and get in a car. Where are they going?"

Elizabeth lifted her eyes to meet Delaney's. "Where'd they go? Which way?" she asked.

"South. I'm right behind them."

"Stay with them, Stacy."

"Ask her for the license plate," Delaney told her.

Elizabeth waved him away, saying, "Listen to me, Stacy—are you close enough to make out the license plate?"

"I can't. I'm two or three cars back. We're headed south on East 55th and we just stopped at the lights on … shit, I can't see the … hold it, we're stopped at the corner of something and East 55th."

"Where? What's the street?" Elizabeth demanded.

"Too late, we're moving. I can't lose them."

Elizabeth quickly relayed the information to Delaney who picked up his phone, hit the speed dial and stepped away.

"Can you give me your location—anything?" she asked Stacy.

"I'm trying, but…"

"But what? Are you okay?"

"I'm okay."

"Don't speed. Just drive carefully, and don't let that car out of your sight."

"What's happening? Where's Nancy Pattrenko taking him?" Stacy asked.

"I don't know. I wasn't aware she was going to take him anywhere. Stay right behind them, but not too close. I don't want to panic them."

"Wait, I…"

Elizabeth's throat tightened. "What is it? What's happened?" In the background she could hear the rise and fall of the car engine as Stacy slowed and sped up, probably weaving through traffic.

"I'm gonna catch up to them."

Elizabeth's entire body tensed. "No, don't. Just stay with them. Don't do anything rash. She might panic and crash."

"Ask her what car she's driving," Delaney told her in a gruff voice.

"Just be careful, Stacy," Elizabeth said. "Just be careful and tell me what—"

The phone had gone dead.

CHAPTER TWENTY-TWO
DAY TWO: 9:39 AM—STACY

Stacy switched the phone off, flung it into the passenger seat, and gripped the wheel with both hands. She could just see the car up ahead, the turn signal indicating right while the car moved to the far right-hand lane. At the first chance, she swerved in behind it, cutting off a guy behind her who leaned on his horn and shook his fist.

"Go to hell," she told him in the rearview mirror, then looked back just as the car in front took the corner. With her stomach rolling and her heart pounding, she followed, easing the car around the corner after the sedan. They were in the middle of nowhere—wide-open spaces between sprawling industrial buildings. They were the only two cars on the street. She pulled into a driveway and waited until the sedan was almost out of sight, then followed. Not too close. She didn't want to cause them to crash.

At the next corner, she saw the car in the distance pull down a driveway and stop. She slowed, wondering what to do next.

She inched forward then also stopped. As soon as she was out of the car, she ducked out of sight and ran down the side of the street until she spotted them.

Nancy Pattrenko stood in an open area, looking around expectantly,

Tyler next to her, his hand in hers. As soon as Nancy saw Stacy, the grip tightened and she pulled the child back towards her, saying, "Stay back."

The instant Tyler's gaze hit Stacy, his eyes lit up. "Mommy! Mommy!"

"Tyler?" she called.

He reached for her, his fingers spread, surprise and desperation widening his eyes.

"Tyler!"

But Nancy Pattrenko tugged him back by the hand, saying, "Stay back, Stacy. Just stop there, and back away."

In the distance, she could hear the *whop whop* of a helicopter approaching. The police, no doubt. But now that she'd gotten this close, Stacy couldn't just walk away.

"Mommy, Mommy!"

Pressing her mouth into a tight line, nostrils flared, Stacy put her head down and ran at the woman, yelling, "Leave him! Leave my son alone!"

Nancy pivoted on the spot, swinging Tyler around, hugging him in front of her. Tyler wailed and cried out, his hand reaching. Stacy scrabbled, trying to get to him, but Nancy elbowed back, fending her off. Furious, Stacy gripped her by the shoulder, wrenching her back around with one hand, tugging Tyler from her grasp with the other. She shouldered Nancy aside, sent her staggering, then dropped to one knee, taking Tyler in her arms and hugging him like she'd never let him go. Eyes closed, she lifted him and straightened, her face buried in his hair, smelling his sweetness, feeling the warmth and the frailty of his small body against hers, feeling his arms encircling her neck, and the ache in her heart.

But now she could hear the distant wail of sirens.

"Turn yourself in, Stacy," Nancy told her. "You take this child, it's kidnapping. You've got enough problems."

"Where were you taking him?"

Acknowledging the warning in her voice, Nancy raised both hands.

"Wasn't what it looked like. He was crying, wanted to go home. That's where I was taking him." She extended her hand. "Let go of him, Stacy. Let me take him home."

Nancy was right. Stacy couldn't just take Tyler and run now. She squeezed her eyes shut and let a single tear break and roll down her cheek. "Just let me hold him a little longer." She blinked hard and pulled back, gazing into her son's eyes.

"Mommy stay?"

"Oh, baby, I love you so much, but I can't. But I'll come back for you. I promise. *I promise,*" she said and hugged him in close for the last time. "Don't you ever forget me, cause I won't forget you."

Nancy still had her hand out. "Let me take him. I'll take good care of him. I promise."

She felt him pulled away, watched as Nancy drew him back with her.

"Give yourself up. This won't go the way you want."

Never lifting her eyes from Tyler, Stacy put her fingers to her lips, kissed them and blew while her chest tightened and her heart shattered into a million pieces. "I love you, baby. Just remember, I'll always love you." She looked up at Nancy, eyes fiery, nostrils flared. "If I find you didn't keep your promise and anything happens to my son, I'll come after you. That's a promise."

"Mommy," Tyler cried, reaching for her as she backed away.

She got in Curta's car, torn by the sight of Tyler's face, red and crumpled with anguish. He knuckled away the tears and watched her, his bewilderment plain even from here.

"I'll be back for you, baby," she said and started the engine. "I promise you."

And she put her foot to the gas and took off.

CHAPTER TWENTY-THREE
DAY TWO: 9:52 AM—ELIZABETH

Penny swerved the car at the last intersection and put her foot down. Up ahead they could see two police cars and a silver sedan, all with their doors open, and a circle of cops around Nancy Pattrenko. Everyone turned at the sound of the car racing up behind them and sliding to a halt in a cloud of dust and gravel. Delaney must have recognized it as Penny Rickman's because his face registered annoyance and he looked away.

Elizabeth threw open the door and got out, followed by Kay Heathers, who'd ridden with them. Striding angrily across to Delaney, she said, "So where's Stacy?"

His eyes rose to a point a short distance in front of him, his patience clearly thinning.

He tucked his tablet into the front pocket of his jacket, looking set to leave. "Ms. Pattrenko says she left a couple of minutes ago. At least now we have a description of the car. We've put out an APB and have a police helicopter looking for her. Believe me, we'll find her."

She followed him across to the first police car. "What about Tyler? Is he okay? Where is he?"

He nodded toward Kay, who had already gone straight to the second police car where Tyler had been buckled in. She was bent to the open door, speaking softly and stroking back his hair.

Delaney rammed his hands into his coat pockets. "He's fine. Kay Heathers will accompany him back to his foster home."

Elizabeth watched in silence as Kay got in beside Tyler, passing her a sorrowful glance before closing the door, then turning her attention to Tyler.

The moment the car pulled out and passed them, Elizabeth rounded on Delaney, pointing back along the street. "What the hell happened back there? Why did Nancy Pattrenko bring him all the way out here?"

Delaney drew an irritated breath as he watched after the departing car behind her. He looked like he didn't want to speak to her, but said, "That's what I intend to find out, Mrs. McClaine."

"I should hope so," she said, following him as he walked back to his car. "And don't think you've heard the end of this. I'm going to demand an inquiry into why this whole thing went so horribly wrong. You promised me this little boy would be in no danger. You told me—"

"Mrs. McClaine," he said, cutting her off as he turned back to her, one hand on the open car door, the other on the roof. "You can do whatever you like." Just as he started to get in, he added, "Oh, and by the way, it seems the governor and the police commissioner both agree that it would be in everybody's interests if you were allowed to continue your investigations."

"I see," she said. "And when did this turn of events come about?"

He leaned one elbow on the roof of the car. "Well, it seems *someone* in your circle of friends had a word in Governor Straussman's ear sometime last night. I guess it pays to know all the right people in the right places. He called me first thing this morning."

Her nostrils flared and her eyes narrowed on him. "And when were you planning on telling me this, Detective?"

"I just did," he said, and signaled the officer waiting by the other car. "Take Ms. Pattrenko on in. I'll join you shortly."

As the officer got into the second car, fired up the engine, and drove back the way they'd just come, Elizabeth stepped in, cutting Delaney off again. "Excuse me, Detective, but if the governor and the police commissioner have sanctioned my investigation, then I'd like to be present at the questioning of Nancy Pattrenko, if you don't mind."

He got into the front passenger's seat and lifted a bemused look on her. "As a matter of fact, I do mind, Mrs. McClaine. This is a police investigation and I don't care what the governor or the police commissioner say you can do, this is my case and you won't be present at any time during the questioning of a law enforcement officer. And that's an end to it."

Just as he closed the door, he muttered something she didn't catch.

Penny walked across to stand next to her. Together they watched the car perform a U-turn and take off the way they'd come.

"So what happens now?" Penny asked.

"You heard the man, we find out what the hell is going on, and we find Stacy May Charms."

CHAPTER TWENTY-FOUR
DAY TWO: 10:31 AM—ELIZABETH

Elizabeth had spent the entire trip back to her office with her elbow on the car window frame, head resting on her hand, staring out at the passing city without even seeing it. By the time they arrived back at the office, a headache was throbbing at the back of her skull.

"Are you okay?" Penny asked as she pulled to a stop at a traffic light.

Elizabeth leaned her head back, staring at the spot right above her head. "So where do I go now?"

Only a tense silence followed. She glanced across at Penny, who met her gaze briefly and said nothing.

"What? You think I should just leave it at that? Just walk away?"

Penny bunched her mouth, checked the rearview mirror. When the light changed, she pressed her foot to the accelerator and they moved forward.

Elizabeth kept her gaze fixed on her secretary. "You do, don't you? You think I'm chasing shadows."

"I just think, y'know, you're a smart woman, Elizabeth. Stacy broke the law, threw away all her chances. Why don't you just leave it to the police? I don't know what you're trying to prove."

"I'm not trying to prove anything. I'm trying to figure out why Stacy broke parole and ran in the first place."

At the next intersection, Penny hit the turn signal, eyes on the road as she took the corner. "You don't think that maybe she just ran because she could? Because the opportunity presented itself and she grabbed it?"

"Oh, not you, too." Elizabeth sighed and turned back to the window. "Stacy told me she was afraid for Tyler. That was real. She said she had a photograph of him that threatened someone was going to kill him. That's not chasing shadows."

"And what if it was just another inmate that was pissed off with her? What if she'd annoyed one too many people by getting an early release and one of her buddies inside decided it wasn't going to be all Happy Families? You said yourself that Cissy whatever-her-name-is turned out to be a complete nut job, that she was happy to step up for an early release no matter what she had to do."

"Stacy didn't believe it was another inmate, and neither do I. It had to be someone with access to the outside. Who else would be able to get the photograph? Who would know where Tyler was?"

"Well, there's Kay Heathers."

"And Nancy Pattrenko," Elizabeth added in a sour tone. "But why? What could anyone have to gain? There's no way Nancy would bring drugs into the prison … would she? And where was she taking Tyler?"

"I overheard her telling one of the cops she was taking him out of the danger zone because she was afraid for his life." Penny hit the brake, stopping at yet another traffic light.

"Afraid for his life? She abducts a child and tells the police she was afraid for his life? Who's she trying to kid?"

"She's a parole officer. Maybe she saw something that made her think she had to get the child out of the way."

"But why take him there?"

"Stacy was in a car right behind her. Maybe she spotted her following behind and just kept driving, believing they were still in danger. Who knows?"

"That's a lot of maybes, if you ask me."

Penny checked for oncoming traffic, then pulled the car into the parking garage, and into their allocated spot. As she took the keys from the ignition, Elizabeth felt the atmosphere in the car grow heavy.

"What?" she asked.

Penny drew her teeth along her lower lip, as though she was trying to pick her words, then turned to face her. "I know you have every faith in Stacy May Charms. I know you interviewed her and you had this ... this thing where you connected, right?"

Elizabeth said nothing, just sucked in her cheeks and waited for it.

"Think about it, Elizabeth," Penny said softly, counting points on her fingers, "One, there's no crime; two, there's no evidence of any crime; nothing to prove anything happened. Stacy ran. Okay, she says she's in danger, that Tyler's in danger, that someone's threatened them—but who? She says she doesn't know. So what else is she going to say? She was hardly going to admit that she didn't want to continue with the program, was she? That she was sick of being pushed around and told what to do and what not to do, and that she wanted her kid back so she could do whatever she wanted? I mean, an explanation like that isn't exactly going to fly, is it?"

"Are you done?"

Penny lifted both hands, dropped them in her lap. "I'm trying to play devil's advocate here, Elizabeth. I'm not saying you're wrong, I'm just saying that... " She turned to stare off across the parking garage.

"Something is definitely off. There's some kind of cover-up going on. I'm sure of it," Elizabeth said, although her voice lacked her earlier conviction.

"Jennifer Glassy said they got to the bottom of the drug trafficking. She said they found the evidence, and they convicted Lois Hankerman—"

"Yes, her own sister," Elizabeth interrupted pointedly.

"Even sisters screw up." Penny heaved a sigh. "Listen, Elizabeth, I know you want to believe that Stacy had good reason for bailing on her parole. God knows, I want to believe it. I know how hard you've worked on this program—sheesh, I was in your shoes, I'd be disappointed. But maybe," she said softly, focusing on a point low on the steering wheel before turning her attention back to her employer. "Maybe Stacy May Charms wasn't the right candidate for the program. Pure and simple."

"You're saying I made a mistake? That I just can't admit it?"

Penny bunched her mouth a moment. "There are probably other candidates who would be just as good. Obviously, the Charles McClaine Foundation wouldn't be involved because the child—or children—probably wouldn't have disabilities and therefore wouldn't be eligible for support, but the governor specifically asked you for your input on this program. He believes in you." She spread her hands, gave her an encouraging look.

Elizabeth got out of the car without another word and went to the elevator. Something deep down inside her had curled up into a ball, refusing to be pried open. But it wasn't dead.

When the elevator opened, the two women stepped inside, then turned silently to face the doors, each staring straight ahead until the doors reopened on the sixth floor, where Elizabeth's office was located. Stepping out first, Elizabeth went straight to the door and directed her gaze off down the hallway while Penny unlocked the office. As soon as the alarm was deactivated Elizabeth walked straight through to her inner chambers without a word.

Now, sitting at her desk with the sun streaming in behind her, she couldn't help wondering what on earth had been going on in Stacy May Charms's head. Had she really duped Elizabeth? Was she really that good? And was it fair to take it out on Penny, when all she'd done was point out what was rapidly looking like the truth—a truth that perhaps Elizabeth would prefer to close her eyes to?

"Penny!"

She appeared almost immediately in the doorway to Elizabeth's office. "Yes?"

"I'm sorry. I spoke out of turn. I didn't mean to take all this out on you."

Her secretary stuck one hand on her hip. "Coffee? I think we need one."

"I'd prefer a good stiff vodka martini."

Penny's eyebrows shot up.

"Well, I would."

"You start drinking again after all this time, I'll make you sorry twice over. I'll get the coffee."

While Penny disappeared to put the coffee on, Elizabeth drew together all the files strewn across her desk, all devoted to Stacy May Charms's application. It was hard to believe how much work had gone into the process. She stood the file folders on end, stacking them into a neat pile. Next to her, the phone rang—her personal number. Frowning, she picked up.

A woman's voice. "Elizabeth, it's Diana."

Diana Du Plessis. Elizabeth squeezed her eyes shut, silently cursing herself. She hadn't gotten in touch with her again. Here the woman was going out of her way for her, delving into the backgrounds of all the prison officers in Carringway, and all for nothing. Elizabeth pressed her fingers to her eyes, saying, "Diana, it's great to hear from you. What did you find out?"

"Not a lot, I'm afraid. I think the recruiters who brought all the officers in did their due diligence. We got files on all personnel except the kitchen staff."

"And?"

"Nothing that stands out. A few traffic offenses, one investigation into an incident, but the officer was cleared of any wrongdoing. Otherwise, no major convictions to speak of."

Elizabeth dropped her head, cradling it in one hand. That headache was coming back.

"I can't tell you how much I appreciate all you've done, Diana. Really."

"It's nothing. There was one small thing, though. Like I said, it's not major but you may like to be aware that one of the prison officers is in a relationship with another law enforcement officer."

"Is that unusual?"

"Not at all. Let's face it, if cops didn't marry cops, the world's police forces would be a pretty lonely place. This is slightly unusual because it's a lesbian relationship."

Frowning, Elizabeth said, "Again, I can't see anything wrong with that."

"There's nothing at all wrong with it. I just thought I'd bring it to your attention while I had you on the phone."

She picked up a pen, said, "Okay, so who have we got?"

"Well, apparently an officer by the name of Patricia Tomes, one of the senior prison officers in Carringway, is in a live-in relationship with a parole officer in the Cleveland central area."

Elizabeth's heart did a flip. Her eyes lifted to a point straight ahead of her. "And what's the name of this parole officer, Diana? Can you tell me?"

"It's Nancy Pattrenko."

Diana said something else, but Elizabeth wasn't listening. She was already out of her chair and calling Penny from the other office.

"Switch the machine off. The coffee's going to have to wait."

CHAPTER TWENTY-FIVE
DAY TWO: 11:45 AM—STACY

Stacy had turned the car and headed east, in the direction she'd come from, then looped around on a side street and come back a mile or so west of where she'd left Tyler with Nancy Pattrenko. Then she'd headed for East 40th Street. When the sound of the helicopter hammered through the air to her left, she'd pulled into a parking lot outside a factory, ducked down, and waited. Sure enough, it banked and flew on over. With any luck, they'd have assumed she'd put her foot down and headed south. Maybe if she'd had enough gas, she might have done exactly that. As it was, she guessed she had only enough to get to the next station, so she'd given it another ten minutes, then hit the ignition and driven on through to Woodland Avenue and merged with the traffic.

If her original plan had gone right, she'd have had Tyler and been out of the state by now. It didn't. No point dwelling on it, she could only work with what she had. Whoever had threatened Tyler, had murdered Amy. She'd have bet her last dime on that. Chances were, she'd never get Tyler back. Maybe she'd never see him again. But while she had the chance, she could at least find the bastard who thought they could threaten her child and kill her friend.

To do that, she needed information. The blouse Amy had found had been sent back to Carringway by the same company that had received it—Millcreek Fashions. None of the inmates had given a fat rat's ass about who Millcreek was. But if Eileen was right, that's where she had to start looking. Maybe from there she could pick up enough clues to figure out who had the most to gain by shutting Amy up and keeping Stacy under wraps. And the only place she knew to get information was probably the last place the cops would look for her.

It took just a little over twenty minutes to drive across town. Cleveland Public Library Downtown would have been a better bet, but with only nineteen dollars in her pocket and a gas gauge tipping the red zone, she'd have had to park ten miles away. This way, she'd get the same information without spending a cent.

First pass, she cruised straight by University Heights Public Library, checking out the lay of the land. Nothing out of place, nothing unusual, and no cops. So she parked down a side street under the trees and walked back.

A woman with short brown hair and a name badge introducing her as Caron looked up from behind a large reception desk just inside the front doors, and smiled as Stacy approached.

"Good morning. How can I help you?"

Stacy drew a breath and gave the area a quick scan. "Ah yeah, I was wondering if I could use a computer."

"What time did you book for?"

Book? Shit, this could get awkward.

"Ah well, I was going to but then I … y'know, I forgot."

Caron gave her an uncomfortably long look, then snapped to, saying, "Okay. What about your library card? Do you have it with you?"

Sliding her hands in her back pockets, Stacy twisted back to give the door behind a quick check. "No, I don't. I left it at home." She pinched the bridge of her nose briefly then stuck her hand back in her pocket. "Listen, I'll go back home and get it," she said as she backed up a couple of steps.

"Well, hold on a sec. Let me see what I can do. After all, you're already here." Caron leaned in, squinting at her computer screen, clicking her mouse and swiping it across the mouse pad.

Had she recognized her? Her body language was difficult to read. Or was Stacy just being paranoid? She could leave right now, but she needed the information.

She flicked her eyebrows. "Yeah, sure. Thank you."

Caron's lips relaxed into the shape of an O while she searched. Then she smiled. "Oh, look, you're in luck. We've got two computers free at the moment. Can I just take your name?"

Their eyes met.

"Kay Heathers," Stacy replied without blinking.

"Then if you'd like to come this way, Kay, I'll show you where to find the computers."

She got up and walked off through a set of double doors. Stacy hesitated, and shot a look back at the front doors again. Her gut said, *Run.* Her head said, *Go get the information.*

Caron paused at the door, waiting for her. "This way, Kay."

Feeling like she was wading through quicksand, Stacy followed. They walked past racks of books, down corridors, through silent rooms of people sitting at tables and reading. No security. They kept walking until they turned a corner and entered an area lined with desks on which the computers sat, all sectioned off from each other.

"Second from the end," Caron said, pointing. "And here's the password."

Stacy took the card from her. If Caron had recognized her and was about to call the police, her acting skills were pretty good. If that was the case, she didn't have much time. She walked briskly down to the computer two back from the window, entered the password, and typed "Millcreek Fashions" into the search engine.

When the results came up, she went straight to the fifteenth page, which is where she'd found it when she'd done the same search in her computer studies while she was inside. Sure enough, there it was. It was just a few lines in among a whole bunch of blah: the mention of the company name picked out on some company registration form or other, and a couple of names she didn't recognize. She drew across a pencil and paper seemingly provided for such occasions, and noted the names down: Maryanne Louise Crane-Thorpe and Christine Amanda Redfern Wentworth. When she entered Maryanne Louise Crane-Thorpe into the search bar and hit *Images*, a series of pictures came up. She clicked on one to find a middle-aged woman with sharp features, short curled gray hair, and the brand of stiff smile you get only with money.

Christine Wentworth was much younger—maybe late twenties, early thirties. The images showed her in business suits, with clutches of business guys, and at some big-ass function where she was arm in arm with some old guy, champagne glasses raised in a toast.

Sneering at the stupid things the rich think are important, she tucked the note with the names on it into her pocket, but over the top of the computer she picked up a security guy in the distance. Dressed in black with security emblems on the upper arms of his shirt, pot belly hanging over his pants, he was making his way across the front of the building outside, headed for the front door at a brisk pace.

"Shit." She closed down the search and got up. Moving quickly back the way she came, she exited through the double doors and turned down a hallway to her left where she ducked between two shelves of books and walked to the end. Finding no other way out, she paused at the far end of the bookshelf where a woman was reading the back of a book.

"Have you read this?" the woman whispered to her, showing her the cover.

Stacy glanced at the cover, then back down to the main aisle. "No. I'm actually more into crime," she replied, and squeezed past her. "Will you excuse me?"

Ducking from the end of one stack of shelves to the next, Stacy was halfway back to the exit when she heard voices.

"In here?" a guy asked.

"In the computer room." Caron's voice, the sneaky snitch. Stacy had pegged her as a tattletale. Why didn't she listen to her gut?

When the two walked quickly past the end of the shelving, Stacy caught a glimpse of the same security guy, Caron right behind him, pointing. They exited toward the computer room so Stacy hurried to the door they'd just entered through and started toward the front door.

"Hey, you!" The security guy.

Stacy didn't even turn around. She took to her heels, switching and stepping around people in the way, and heading for the front door. She shoved the door open, skipped down the steps, and turned left. A glance over her shoulder told her the security guy was right behind her. She picked up the pace, but she could hear his steps gaining on her. Surprised at his speed, she tucked her head down, turned left and sprinted down the street beside the library to find a plastic garbage bin on wheels positioned in the middle of the sidewalk. She slowed long enough to grab the handle and swing it around behind her. She heard the empty rumble as it hit the ground and rolled. She looked back to see the guard attempt a leap over it but his foot caught. He went down, hands first, but in seconds he was up again. She took off, zigzagging around a couple who were headed to their car, then crossed the street just as a car swung around the corner and slid to a stop with a blast of its horn. She spun around the front of the car and kept going, sprinting past parked cars and driveways, under trees, over a kid's bicycle, and hurdling another fallen bin. When she looked back this time, the security guy was still there, cheeks flushed but still gaining.

What the hell?

She made a sharp right into a driveway, sprinted to the end and vaulted over a small fence into the back yard.

A shoulder-height hedge all around—the only break, a small wooden gate leading into the rear section.

On the porch behind her, a black dachshund startled into life with a howl. It tore down the steps and came after her, yipping. And now she could hear the guy's footsteps pounding down the driveway.

What to do?

Then she spotted a ball. She ran toward the rear gate, scooping up the ball on the fly and throwing it over into the rear yard, then dived under the hedge, head down and rolled with her knees tucked up. The dog followed the trajectory of the ball with its eyes, little head going up with the rise, then falling with the ball. It raced to the back gate, barking. The second the security guy came barreling around the corner, the dog spun around and went for him, yipping and dancing. Ignoring the dog, he went straight to the back gate, both hands on it as he looked over, searching. Thinking he'd lost her, he bent with his hands on his knees, breathing heavily. When he turned, his face was scarlet and squeezed in agony, sweat glistening on his forehead and forming dark patches under his arms and down his back.

He trudged wearily back toward the driveway with his hands on his hips and his head tipped back, sucking in air. Soon as he'd disappeared around the corner of the house, Stacy rolled through the hedge into the neighboring yard and crept along the length of the hedge until she hit the sidewalk. Down the street, she could see him ambling back towards the library shaking his head.

Thank God six months of sitting on her ass studying hadn't diminished her fitness. She checked the time and crouched, waiting until the guy turned the corner.

For now, she'd gotten what she came for. The trip to the library had probably pinpointed her position to the cops, but it got her some names. It wasn't much. But it was a start.

So she trotted back down the road, looked both ways, then headed back to the car.

CHAPTER TWENTY-SIX
DAY TWO: 12:05 PM—ELIZABETH

From the moment Elizabeth had put the phone down, she was in motion. She'd ended the call then immediately dialed Delaney, who answered on the second ring. She'd asked him what, exactly, had transpired during the interview with Nancy Pattrenko. After stalling a moment, obviously preferring not share any more information than he had to, he had informed her that Ms. Pattrenko had been "suspended from duty pending an investigation into her actions."

Elizabeth asked him if the woman was under arrest, to which he'd said, "Mrs. McClaine, Nancy Pattrenko is an officer of the law, and if there's any hint of wrongdoing in her actions, believe me, she'll feel the full force of the law."

"*She took a child.* Without permission; without authorization. How can you not see that as 'wrongdoing'?"

"Ms. Pattrenko has made a formal statement in which she claims that she took the child from a situation where she felt his welfare was compromised and removed him to a place of safety."

He sounded like a police procedural manual. A typical butt-covering stance the police take when defending their own, Elizabeth thought. But she wasn't done.

"Okay, so then she drove this 'compromised' child out to the middle of a backwater industrial area—why exactly?" Her voice had risen and her heart was racing. She didn't care. She wanted answers.

"She was being followed, Mrs. McClaine. As you well know—by Stacy May Charms. And at the time, the child's safety was her primary concern. She acted in his best interests and has been released on her own recognizance."

"And what about the fact that Nancy Pattrenko is in a live-in relationship with Patricia Tomes, who happens to be a prison guard at the very prison Stacy was incarcerated in? Doesn't that mean anything?"

The few seconds of silence on the line suggested the news had come as a surprise. If it had, he wasn't rising to it, because he replied with, "Mrs. McClaine, I've questioned Ms. Pattrenko to my full satisfaction, and I've taken the appropriate action. Now if you don't mind, I have a stack of paperwork to complete, and other cases to attend to. Good day."

And he'd hung up.

Elizabeth slammed her phone down and grabbed her purse and coat, repeating to Penny that Nancy Pattrenko had been "suspended, pending an investigation into her actions."

Penny's eyebrows shot up. "Are you serious? She basically abducted a child. Where's the doubt?"

Elizabeth shrugged into her coat and closed down her computer. "Tell me about it."

"So where are we going?"

"*I'm* going to visit Nancy Pattrenko. Get me her address. The police might be happy with her explanation, but I'm not."

She followed Penny through to her desk, watching as she tapped out a query into the search engine, then said, "Here it is." And wrote it down.

"Thank you. I don't know how long I'll be. If anyone calls, tell them I'll call them back tomorrow. What are you doing?" she asked as Penny shut down her computer and grabbed her own purse.

"You don't think I'm missing out on this, do you? Besides, who's gonna navigate?"

"My GPS," Elizabeth had replied, but Penny was already standing at the door, waiting to lock up, saying, "We'll take my car. And remind me to increase my personal injury insurance when we get back. I think I'm gonna need it."

Now, almost a half hour after entering the address into the GPS in Penny's car, and following the indicated route, they turned into a narrow back street lined on either side with two-story single family homes, and slowed as they approached the address listed in the White Pages under Pattrenko, N. B.

Elizabeth pointed to a pale green house across the street, a flower garden neatly tended along the front, love seat out on the porch. "There it is."

Penny pulled the car to the side of the road. "What are you going to say?"

"Whatever comes up."

Elizabeth got out of the car, closed the door and crossed, following the small path that led up to the front door. A small placard next to a brass bell read: *Beware: Cats on duty.*

Ignoring the bell, she rapped on the upper panel of the door and waited. Finally, a shadow appeared on the other side of the glass, and the lace curtain twitched momentarily aside. There was a moment's hesitation, and the door opened.

Nancy Pattrenko's cheeks were flushed, her hair bedraggled, her eyes puffy. She stood in the doorway, staring her visitors down, until Elizabeth said, "May we come in?"

The woman looked them both over. "What do you want?"

"I need to talk to you."

"I got nothing to say to you," she said and went to close the door.

"And what about Patricia Tomes?" Elizabeth said, just as the door narrowed to the point of closing.

A hollow silence followed, and the door opened again.

Nancy cast a suspicious look over both women. "What about her?"

"I believe you're in a relationship with her."

For a second, Elizabeth thought she was about to slam the door in their faces. Instead, she widened the door, saying, "Wipe your feet. I just cleaned the place." And stood back for them to enter.

Penny followed Elizabeth inside to a neat living room, decorated in muted greens and pinks, floral sofa and two matching chairs, each with embroidered throw cushions positioned neatly on the seats. On a rough-sawn oak coffee table sat a glass vase of white tulips, the green of the stems blending perfectly with the surroundings.

Nancy closed the door and returned to an armchair where she'd apparently been sitting reading a paperback novel, but remained standing, arms crossed in front of her, gripping her elbows.

"What's this about?"

No offer for them to sit. It was obvious she didn't want them there any longer than necessary.

"Then it's true that you and Patricia Tomes are in a relationship?"

"What's that got to do with you?" she asked, shooting a look at Penny as though the question was her fault.

"It was you that took the picture of Tyler Charms, wasn't it?" Elizabeth said—a statement rather than a question. It was a brave call—a guess at best, but even if she was wrong, she wanted to see the woman's reaction to the idea.

"What picture?"

"The one outside his school. With a woman."

The sides of Nancy's mouth pulled down and she shook her head, as though wondering where this was going. "So?"

"Why did you take that picture? Who asked you to?"

Again, her eyes went to Penny and back before she replied. "I took lots of photos of him. Trish asked me to. She said she wanted one for Stacy

May Charms. She said it was like, a gift for her or something. I knew where he went to school. I've attended a couple of meetings between the social worker and the paternal grandmother. I didn't see a problem."

"Don't you think you should have reported it?"

"Why? Trish is my life partner. I live with her. She asks me to do her a favor so she can do someone else a favor, you think I'm gonna make a federal case out of it?"

The reasoning might have seemed sound under normal circumstances, but these circumstances were anything but normal. Elizabeth looked her straight in the eye and asked, "Did you know there was a threat on Stacy's son's life?"

The woman's face clouded over. Once again, her eyes shifted to Penny and back. "Who from?"

"That's what we're trying to find out," Penny said. "So when you go driving off with the very child in question, *without permission*, it makes us kind of nervous."

Visibly shocked by the news, Nancy's jaw dropped and she spread her hands. "I didn't know there was a threat on his life. Who told you that? Why didn't Delaney tell me there was a threat? I thought we were just waiting for Stacy May."

"Then why did you drive off with him?" This from Penny.

She blinked a couple of times. "I, I just…"

"Oh, c'mon," Penny said, jabbing a finger at the woman. "You did it because that threat came from *you*."

Clearly horrified by the allegation, Nancy Pattrenko took a step back, both hands up. "I swear, I didn't know anything about it. One minute everything was fine, next thing I look up and the officers are gone, Delaney's gone, no sign of Kay. Tyler started rocking back and forth, smacking his head against the back of the chair over and over and saying, 'Home, home.' I'm thinking, 'Holy crap, the kid's gonna knock himself out.' I tell him to stop, and next thing he's howling. Everyone's turning around looking at me like I'm trying to kill him. I called Detective Delaney. He didn't answer. I didn't know what was going on, so I said, 'Okay, let's go,' and I took him."

Penny jabbed a finger at her, teeth clenched, lips peeled back like an angry dog, saying, "Listen, lady," but Elizabeth cut her off, placing a restraining hand on her arm, holding it for a second.

"Thank you, Penny. I'll take it from here." She waited for Penny to take a step back with a nod of surrender, then turned back to Nancy. "Who told you to take him all the way down East 55th?"

Nancy stuck her hands on her hips. "No one. I got in the car, headed back to Tyler's foster home, next thing there's a police helicopter headed our way. I turned into Crayton Avenue. Soon as I got to an open space, I got out to wait for the police. That's when I saw Stacy May running at us. I thought she was gonna attack me."

"And Trish Tomes didn't tell you to take him anywhere?"

The shocked expression on Nancy's face said it all. "Hell, no. Why would she?"

"But you did tell her about the setup? The sting to catch Stacy May using Tyler as bait."

Nancy hesitated a moment, considering the charge. "Well, I wouldn't say he was used as *bait*."

"You told her, or you didn't."

Breaking eye contact, Nancy chewed her upper lip before answering. "Maybe ... I guess. You know, you talk. She's my partner."

"And you didn't think it might be a breach of that child's privacy?"

Nancy Pattrenko's expression sharpened. "Trish is my wife. I talk to her. I can't see what any of this has to do with her, anyway." She folded her arms, defensive now, eyes darting from Elizabeth to Penny and back.

Elizabeth didn't see any point in pushing it. "Where's Patricia Tomes now?"

Her arms tightened across her chest and her head dropped briefly. "I don't know."

Penny leaned in, one hand on her hip. "Oh, come on. Let's cut the bullshit here." When she got a sharp look from Elizabeth, she said, "Seriously? You think she has no idea?"

"I'm telling you I don't know, okay? She didn't come home last night. She texted me from work, said she was doing another shift. That was at two this morning. Nine o'clock, I tried calling her because the graveyard shift finishes at eight and she still wasn't home." She dashed a knuckle across the end of her nose and dropped her gaze momentarily to the floor.

"Wait a second, are you saying she sent you a text from the prison before her shift ended?"

"So?"

Elizabeth frowned. "She couldn't have texted from the prison. They have a system built in that blocks all cell phone usage. You can't call; you can't send or receive texts—you should know that. But you got a text from her while you were at McDonald's, didn't you?"

Elizabeth could see by the look on the woman's face she was right.

"That's why you didn't notice Kay leave to go to the bathroom. You were too busy texting back to see when she'd be home."

Nancy raised both palms to the ceiling. "I wanted to know where she was. She should have been home hours ago. I've texted her, tried calling her, but nothing. I even called into Central to see if there've been any traffic accidents. Nothing, zilch, nada. Her last text just said not to worry, that she'd be late again. But I am worried. She usually calls."

"Has she done this before—worked late and not come home?"

"Some." She shrugged, as though it wasn't of any importance.

"And you didn't tell Delaney any of this?"

"Why would I? Trish hasn't been missing twenty-four hours. He'd tell me she'd got a flat tire or something. He'd say if she's still not home tomorrow, report it then. It's standard procedure. And besides…"

"And besides what?" Penny said.

Nancy regarded them both, then shuffled from one foot to the other. "She's been … I dunno, different lately. Kind of distant. Coming home late; all tears one minute, then angry and yelling the next. She said it's all about work, but I thought…" A shrug.

"You thought she was seeing someone else."

A long silence followed. Nancy dropped her gaze as her face puckered. She pressed a palm to one eye, swiped it away, then looked up at the ceiling, swallowing hard before nodding. "I thought that's what was going on. All of a sudden she's buying new clothes, running up her credit cards on gadgets. She got a new car. She didn't even need a new car."

"And you didn't tell Delaney any of this?" Elizabeth asked.

"Like I said, why would I?"

"Does he know you and Trish are a couple?" Penny asked.

Nancy dropped her head and looked away, no reply. None needed.

Penny let out a deep sigh and looked to Elizabeth. "So where was Trish Tomes when she sent that last text if she wasn't at work?"

"Do you have any idea?" Elizabeth asked Nancy.

"I don't know where Trish is," she said. An expectant silence hung in the air, then she said, "But I might know where her car is."

CHAPTER TWENTY-SEVEN
DAY TWO: 12:45 PM—STACY

The needle on the gas gauge was pointing to the red zone just past empty. Curta's car was old—no indicator to tell her how many miles she had left. Stacy guessed whatever gas she had wasn't going to get her far. Leaning across into the passenger's footwell, she located the phone and turned it on—one bar on the battery indicator. She had to be quick.

She opened the internet browser and the phone scanned, searching for connectivity. When the home page showed on the screen, she tapped in the URL for the White Pages and did a search on Maryanne Louise Crane-Thorpe. The page opened, but the phone bleeped twice and the screen went black.

"Terrific."

She tossed the phone back onto the seat, started the car and gently put her foot to the gas. Wayne once told her that cars have way more gas in the tank than the indicator shows. She had nineteen bucks left. That wasn't going to last long. Which is why she hadn't put more gas in the car in the first place. But if her memory served her right, there was a gas station a few blocks down.

With her lower lip clamped between her teeth, she turned left at the lights and pulled into traffic. Right up ahead she spotted the Sunoco sign and her shoulders dropped in relief. She hadn't realized how tense she'd been until now. She blew a long slow breath out between pursed lips pressed her foot to the gas and hit the signal light to cut into the next lane when the car coughed and the engine died.

"No, no, no," she said over and over, like the words would make it not true. She twisted the key in the ignition and the car roared into life again.

Then died.

Horns began tooting almost immediately, cars veering around her as irate drivers let her know what they thought.

"Yeah sure, I'm doing this for fun," she yelled after a guy who gave her an offensive hand sign as he shot past her.

"Oh, please, please," she begged and twisted the key again. The engine turned over and over with a *whirr, whirr* sound, but didn't catch.

In her rearview mirror, she could see the traffic piling up, cars waiting then pulling out so they could go around her. Only now, the traffic next to her had slowed. Her face crumpled and she leaned forward with her head against the steering wheel. When she looked up, a cop on a bike was weaving through traffic on the other side of the street.

"Oh, please, this can't be happening."

She slumped in the seat, arms over the steering wheel. How could it have come to this? Caught after everything she'd been through, just because she'd been stupid enough to run out of gas.

"It's okay, I got it," called a man's voice from somewhere just behind her. The cop on the bike signaled in return, then pulled the bike around into the street opposite and roared off.

Stacy checked the rearview mirror. Behind her all she could see was the front grille of a tow truck, amber lights flashing.

When a knuckle rapped on the window, a tiny spark of hope ignited in her chest. She turned the key in the ignition so she could lower the window, and looked up.

"What's the problem?" he said.

He was big and burly, same build as Bear Traynor, same Indians cap, same manner, but without the mellow bearing and carrying a little extra weight around the middle. He had one hand on the roof of the car while he bent to talk to her.

"Ah, I just ran out of gas, is all."

"Well, you can't stay here. You're holding up traffic. I got a call in asking me to get you out of the way."

He glanced behind him to where the cars were now backed up right down the street, but were now sedately maneuvering around them.

"How much is this going to cost?" she asked as she got out and followed him back to the truck, flattening herself against the car every now and then to let another vehicle pass.

The guy waved a couple of cars by. "Sixty bucks for the tow, ten for every day it's in the yard."

"Don't you have any gas with you?"

"Nope," he said with a one-sided grin. "Just sold the last of it, and you're stopped in a no parking zone." He pointed. "Sorry, I gotta tow it. Go sit in the cab of the truck while I get your car loaded up. We'll talk about payment in a bit."

Instead of getting into the truck, she cut between the truck and Curta's car and went to stand on the sidewalk among a collection of onlookers. Yes, she could make a run for it, but a) she'd be on foot, and b) there was no way she'd leave Curta's car here. So it wasn't a choice.

"Door's unlocked. Go ahead and get in," he said as he walked back to the driver's door of the truck.

She gave the people to one side of her a self-conscious glance, wondering if any of them would recognize her, then walked quickly to the tow truck, pulled open the door and hoisted herself in.

The guy came back and slid into the driver's seat then waved out the window, fingers splayed, indicating for the traffic behind to make way. When the traffic stopped, he pulled out and steered the truck into the space in front of Curta's car, and backed up. He got out, and the truck whined and jolted as the front of Curta's car lifted.

Stacy slumped back in the seat. There was no way she could pay for this. That meant she'd lost Curta's car. What was she going to tell her? Stacy felt sick.

The guy opened the driver's door and slid back into the cab with a sideways look at her. "You're lucky I happened along. I don't come out this way much." And he turned the ignition.

"I can't believe I ran out of gas," she said flatly, while she stared out the windshield.

He put his hand out the window to stop traffic again, then pulled out. The truck engine droned up the scale as they picked up speed.

"You got a specific place you need to get to?"

"Just the gas station. I got nowhere else to go." She turned her head to the window, furious with herself. Then she turned back to him, "Do you know a guy named Bear Traynor?"

The grin said it all. "The Bear? Course I do. Everybody knows him. Why? You a friend of his?"

"Yeah, I am."

"Sure," he said and grinned, as though that's what everyone told him.

"No, seriously, I am."

He gave her a sideways glance, still not convinced. "So where do you know him from?"

"Ah, we met at his house."

He pulled to a stop at a red light and checked the rearview mirror. "You want me to call him?"

What did she have to lose?

"Yeah, sure. Why not?" she said, wondering why the hell she'd even suggested it.

The guy picked up his radio and called in. Almost immediately, the line crackled to life and she recognized the voice coming back.

"Hey, Craig buddy. What can I do you for?"

Craig slipped a look across at Stacy. "I got a lady here says she's a friend of yours. Name's …" He lifted his eyebrows to her.

Goodbye frying pan; hello, fire, she thought. "Ah … tell him it's Shelly."

He relayed the information and there was a brief silence on the line. "I'm just over at the depot. Are you nearby?"

"Right around the corner. We'll be over in a couple of minutes," Craig replied happily, seemingly not noticing Stacy place her finger and thumb to her eyes in utter despair.

Craig pulled to the far right lane and turned into a narrow street. Up ahead she could see a wrecker's yard surrounded by a tall chain-link fence, two steel gates standing open and behind them, cars and trucks all piled up on either side of a dusty driveway. They bounced down a rutted track and came to a halt behind the truck she recognized as Bear's.

Craig pulled on the parking brake and waved as Bear ambled over. Stacy unbuckled her seat belt, opened the door and slid from the cab, wondering what Craig planned to do next. She hugged herself and wandered around, pretending she hadn't noticed the two guys go into a huddle, flicking glances her way every now and then. Finally, Craig motioned back to her, saying, "Well, she's all yours now. Up to you, buddy. Good luck."

He got in his truck, lowered Curta's car to the ground, then took off.

Bear watched the departing truck clatter back down the driveway, waving to it before turning to Stacy. "Well, hello again."

She watched Craig come to a halt at the street, turn left, and take off. She was beginning to wonder if she'd have been better off running. But that wouldn't have worked for long. She tucked her tee shirt in at the back and dropped her head. "Listen, I wasn't entirely honest with you yesterday."

"What? About the name? Or about the reason you were in my house?"

She gave the landscape behind her a quick look. "Just the name."

He twisted his mouth to one side while he thought, then said, "I kinda guessed that, Stacy. It is Stacy, isn't it?"

"Ah, yeah." She shifted uncomfortably, folding her arms, then sticking her hands in her pockets, then folding her arms again.

He ran his tongue over his lower lip and passed a thoughtful look at the front gates before speaking.

"So what happened? How'd you wind up here?"

She sighed heavily and shook her head. "I ran out of gas."

The corners of his mouth drew back to create creases on either side. "You're kidding."

"Nope. Middle of the great escape, I run out of gas. Worst. Fugitive. Ever."

"Well, lucky for you, I got ten gallons of gas in back there." He walked back to his truck and she followed along like a little dog hoping for a snack.

"I don't have enough money."

"You can pay me back," he said over his shoulder.

"What? You're still gonna put gas in my car?"

He swung a look on her as he strode back to his truck, but said nothing.

"What are you doing? I thought you were going to turn me in."

He opened the door of his truck and paused, his brow crumpling while he contemplated his reply. "I should. I know that. There's an APB out on this car. Cops all over are looking for it." She waited, wondering what the hell was coming next.

He narrowed his eyes on a point just across the street, then dropped his head briefly. "I felt kind of bad throwing you out of the house the way I did. I coulda done something else."

"Yeah, like what? Gotten arrested for aiding and abetting a wanted fugitive? That'd be real smart."

Brow still furrowed, he reached across, thumbed something off the truck's windshield. "Fact is, I should have tried to do something. I should have helped you instead of throwing you out like that."

A short, sharp laugh burst from her lips. "Hell, if I was you, I'd have kicked my ass out the front door way sooner than you did."

He gave it a beat, considering his reply. "You know, ever since you busted into—" He held up one hand, then amended his words to, "I mean, ever since you *visited* me, I started reading up in the papers about your case. About you getting out on that early release program. It kind of got me thinking."

She hugged herself, wondering where this was going. "Okay."

"You were looking for your son, right?"

"Yeah."

"Did you find him?"

The memory of Tyler's tiny body pressed to hers, the smell of his hair, the warmth of his skin, all flooded back, along with the knowledge she might never see him again. It welled up in her chest, tightening her throat and threatening to drop her straight into that deep, black pit of depression again.

"Yeah."

"Is he okay?"

She felt her lower lip tremble. "He's okay."

"Good. 'Cause I don't know why you got put away in the first place, but that program, all those requirements you had to meet and all the stuff you had to go through; you must'a wanted to see him real bad."

"I did."

"Papers said you had to go back to school while you were in prison. And you graduated even though you were working in some program after your school lessons, then you were doing parenting classes at night. Is that right? You did all that?"

Thinking back now, she wondered how she'd ever gotten through it all. A quick nod. "Yeah, I did."

"Y'know, some people with all the money and luxuries in the world don't do that."

"I guess."

"That takes a lot of guts. A lot of determination."

"Don't make me sound like the good guy, Bear. I'm not. I screwed up. I've done some dumb things, made some stupid decisions."

His eyebrows lifted while he tilted his head. "We don't always take the right path the first time."

The kindness in his voice brought a lump to her throat. She dropped her head so he couldn't see her palm away a welling tear. Then she looked up again, straight into his eyes. "I don't even know why you're wasting your time on me, Bear. I got chances I didn't deserve; let down people who were only trying to help me. This turned out to be the worst plan of my whole life. Everything I touch just goes from bad to worse."

He folded his arms across his chest. "So what happens now?"

Speaking straight, no self pity, no hiding from the truth, she said, "I'll get caught. It's only a matter of time. I guess they'll make an example of me, running like that. A whole bunch of politicians ended up looking real stupid. I doubt they'll let me out again anytime soon." He was watching her. "My son's safe—for the moment. But I've made some promises. If I can't do anything else, I need to keep them before they put me back inside and throw away the key."

"You gonna tell me?"

"Nope."

"You need help?"

"I can't ask you to do anything else. As it is you could get arrested for doing this much."

He let his gaze reel out across the yard, then nodded as though he'd come to some kind of decision. "When I met you, I didn't see a bad person. Or a stupid person. I saw someone with a problem—a big problem. I turned my back on you and I shouldn't have. Now, you've got a little boy out there wondering why his mom doesn't come get him like she was supposed to; maybe wondering if she doesn't want him anymore."

Another pang of guilt and sorrow lanced through her. "I'll get him back one day. I don't know when, but when I do, I want to be able to look him in the eye and know I did everything I could for him." That welling sense of loss threatened again. She fought it back, pressed her lips together, found control again.

"And that's why I want to help you. So let's get your car gassed up, and you get out of here. 'Cause the way I see it, if you don't finish what you started, you might as well have left your boy where he is and just kept running, disappeared into the wild blue yonder and never come back. He'd have been better off that way."

That one blunt truth punched the air out of her. She didn't know what she must have done to deserve such a break. But she wasn't about to question it.

"You can't know how much I appreciate this. I'll pay you back, I swear." She tucked her hands into her back pockets, following him back to his truck where he leaned over and grabbed a red plastic gas can and went to Curta's car. While he waited for the gas to funnel into the tank, he looked up.

"Did you need something else? 'Cause now's your chance."

She shuffled from foot to foot, fighting past the bravado, past the pride, and said, "Yeah. I know I just said you can't do anything else for me, but can I ask you for one more favor?"

"Shoot."

"Can I look up an address on your phone?"

Without replying, he removed the funnel and replaced the cap on Curta's tank. Then he dredged his phone from his shirt pocket. She stepped in next to him, lifting her head to watch as he opened the browser.

Somewhere in her chest, a tiny flame burst into life—a flickering ray of hope rekindled and fanned into life. She could do this. She could finish what she started.

"You got a name?" he asked.

"Maryanne Louise Crane-Thorpe."

He tapped it in. "That's some fancy name," he said while they waited for the results. "Here it is. That's some address an' all. You gonna tell me who she is?"

"Less you know the better, don't you think?"

She followed him to the cab of the truck where he tapped it into the GPS and pointed. "That's the most direct route to the address she's listed under."

"Got it."

He gave her a long steady look. "I'm not gonna regret this, am I?"

"I just want to talk to her, that's all. I promise."

He held her gaze, then said, "Okay."

"Thank you. I really mean it."

"Just find what you need to make everything right. If I can do anything to help, gimme a call." He wrote down his cell phone number on the back of a card and handed it to her.

"Can I ask you something?"

He looked up, waiting.

"Why are you doing this? I mean, what do you get out of this?"

He broke eye contact and hesitated a long while. "My mom died when I was six. I spent a long time in and out of foster homes. Nobody who hasn't lost their mom would understand."

"I'm sorry."

"Don't be. That was my journey. This is yours. Now, go find what you need to get yourself out of this hole you've dug, then get that boy of yours back. Take him home where he should be, with his mom. That's the promise you made the day you signed onto that program. And I'm not gonna stand by and let you break it."

CHAPTER TWENTY-EIGHT
DAY TWO: 2:08 PM—ELIZABETH

As it turned out, one of the gadgets Trish Tomes had purchased, along with her new car, was an online auto tracking system.

"So you've been tracking her movements?" Penny asked her.

"Not all of them," Nancy replied defensively, as though she found the very idea offensive. Then she tipped her head in concession. "Okay, maybe some. But not always. Just the last few days."

"And where's she been going?" Elizabeth asked.

"Work and back. Then someplace down south, out in the middle of nowhere. She's been there a couple of times. Stays an hour or so, then comes home."

"Do you know why?"

Nancy shrugged. "No idea. And she didn't say."

Penny chipped in, saying, "Did you ask her?"

The horror at the very suggestion registered on Nancy's face. "Why would I? I trust her." Noting the skeptical looks, she added, "Well, I did before this."

"So do you know the address she's been going to?" Elizabeth asked.

Nancy nodded. "Sure. It comes up on the system. It uses GPS to locate the car."

"But how do you track the car?"

"I told you—online."

"Surely you'd have to have a password to get into it, though, wouldn't you?" Penny had addressed the question to Elizabeth, but Nancy replied.

"You do. Trish gave it to me. I didn't have to ask or anything. Just said, 'Here you go.'"

Somewhat surprised, Elizabeth asked, "Then why would she give you the password to the tracking system if she was having an affair? You could just track her down, find out where she's been?"

"I guess she trusts me." It was clear the very idea brought with it a certain amount of self-recrimination. Nancy drew back one side of her mouth and looked away. "Or at least, she used to."

"Do you know where the car is right now?" Elizabeth asked.

"Yeah. It's in the same place it was last night when I looked. Same address: out in the middle of nowhere."

"Then let's go," said Elizabeth.

*****

Penny clutched the steering wheel with both hands, knuckles white and foot hard on the accelerator for almost the entire thirty-four-minute journey south on I-77. Beside her in the passenger seat, Elizabeth sat with one hand on the dashboard, the other gripping the seatbelt, staring wide-eyed and, at times, open-mouthed at the oncoming vista flying at them on the road ahead; every now and then, saying, "Do we have to go so fast, Penny? Maybe we should slow down a little."

In the rear seat, Nancy Pattrenko didn't seem to notice the speed. She stared out the window, muttering, "Yeah, right. And how am I going to explain this? 'Oh, hey yeah, we were taking a quiet drive in the middle of nowhere, and I just happened to recognize your car?' I don't think so."

"We'll cross that bridge when we come to it," Elizabeth told her without taking her eyes off the road ahead.

Penny hit the turn signal and slowed to veer off the freeway and along the first of a crisscross of back streets the GPS was now indicating.

"You know what I don't get?" she asked. "How did Tyler know Stacy? I mean, how long is it since he saw her last? Kid must have a memory like an elephant."

Nancy sat forward, hands gripping the backs of the seats, eyes on the road ahead while she spoke. "Well, don't forget he lived with Stacy for three years before she went away. And then Kay Heathers said that as soon as his foster family found out Stacy was being released, they started telling Tyler he'd be going home with his mom, and that he'd be living with her. They got photos of her and everything. She said he was so excited about it. He might have learning difficulties, but he sure knows who his mom is. Makes you think, doesn't it?"

The image of Tyler, of how small and innocent he looked, sent a stab of pain arrowing into Elizabeth's heart. "That little boy will be crushed if she doesn't come home. What's he going to think? That she doesn't want him?"

"I doubt she'll be home anytime soon," Nancy said grimly. "Delaney seems to think they'll have Stacy back in custody by the end of the day. They're expecting her to be up for sentencing first thing Monday morning."

Penny passed Elizabeth a horrified look. "Monday morning. They have to know something we don't. How long does that give us?"

Elizabeth checked her watch. "It's almost three now. Somebody wants this brushed under the carpet as soon as possible. We've still got tomorrow, though." All at once aware of how little time they had, she lifted her purse, dredged out her phone, and scrolled through her contact list until she came to the listing for Grant Alders. In his early sixties now, Grant had been the family lawyer for as long as her father-in-law, Charles, had been wealthy—a sure testament to his success. She hit the send key, put the phone to her ear, and waited.

Grant picked up on the sixth ring, just as Penny swung the car in through a gateway and followed a dusty back road, seemingly heading towards a building some half mile or so farther up ahead.

"Grant, it's Elizabeth McClaine," she said, trying to inject a note of good humor into her voice that she didn't feel. "How are you?"

"I'm fine, Elizabeth. What can I do for you?" Straight to the point. No time for small talk.

"I need you to represent a client of mine in court. She hasn't been arrested at this point, but from what I've heard, she soon will be."

There was an unhealthy pause at the other end of the line. "I see. You mean Stacy May Charms?"

"That's correct. The police have indicated that they'll be making an arrest by the end of the day so I need to get some representation for her right now. I'm afraid that if she goes back to prison, they'll make an example of her."

Another pause, and a deep sigh. "Elizabeth, this really isn't my field."

A flash of anger shot down her spine. How much money had her family shoveled his way over the years? When she spoke this time, her tone was firm, but polite. "Then I'd like you to find someone whose field this is."

"And what do you expect them to do?"

A second flash of anger made her cheeks flash hot. "Keep her out of prison until I can find out what the hell is going on. What do you think I expect them to do?" The fury in her tone surprised even her.

Penny cut her a flabbergasted glance but said nothing, just swiveled her eyes straight back to the road and kept driving. Avoiding her gaze, Elizabeth turned her attention to the passing landscape, somehow even more determined now.

"Well, can you do it, or do I have to find someone else?"

"Let me see what I can arrange," he said. "I might be able to get one of our guys to look it over, see what they think—"

She cut him off mid-sentence. "Seeing what they think isn't good enough. She's already had one lousy lawyer; she needs someone on her side." She glanced across at Penny, who made a doubtful face. "I want him up to speed and with a solid game plan before Monday. That means she'll need someone on the case tomorrow at the latest. And if you say you can't do it, I'll be forced to take this up with Charles. That's not a course of action either of us wants. Am I making myself clear here, Grant?"

"Tomorrow is Sunday, Elizabeth—"

"I don't care if tomorrow is Christmas Day. I want him on the job first thing in the morning. Now can you do it or not?"

She pressed her fingers to her forehead, frustrated that no one ever seemed to take her seriously anymore. All she could hear down the line was the sound of Grant Alder's breath, then a clearing of his throat as he went to speak.

"Well, I guess we can get Jay Templeton on it. He's young but he's had some criminal defense experience," he replied. "He's a bright guy, came into the firm last fall. Plus, he can do it pro bono."

A sly reminder that Elizabeth might have the position, but she didn't have the money. Determined not to be goaded, she said, "Then I suppose he'll have to do."

By the time she ended the call and put her phone away, her cheeks were burning and her heart pounding. She couldn't remember the last time she felt so infuriated. Why was everyone so focused on Stacy May's actions instead of looking for the reasons behind them? Was it so much easier just to lock her up and forget about her? Just because a few politicians had been left red-faced?

Penny's eyes flicked across to her, then back to the road.

Feeling like she owed her secretary an explanation, she said, "He's putting one of their junior lawyers on the case—a young guy he says has had some criminal defense experience."

"How much experience is 'some experience'?" Penny asked.

"It'll have to be enough."

She'd tried to sound upbeat, but the bleak look Penny slipped across at her said it all.

"I know, I know. Just drive, will you?" Elizabeth said.

CHAPTER TWENTY-NINE
DAY TWO: 3:08 PM—STACY

Bear had told Stacy to stick to the back streets. According to the police frequency the tow-truck drivers listened in on, the police had received a report of Stacy's car parked in an empty lot on Union Avenue. By all accounts, every cop in the vicinity had responded, and when they got there, it was some poor schmuck with the same make of car, in a compromising position in the back seat with his girlfriend. But at least that had kept the cops busy for a while. And given Stacy a momentary advantage.

The gas Bear had put in took the indicator to just under half a tank. Stacy kept her foot light on the pedal. No point in wasting what she had. And there was no way of knowing how much she'd need. Now, twenty minutes after pulling out of the wrecker's yard, here she was on Chagrin River Road—might as well have been another world based on the difference in landscape.

Sun shafted through the leafy canopy overhead, dappling the roadway and strobing across the windshield as she drove along stretches of narrow, tree-lined street. Five minutes further on, the landscape opened up and she found what she'd been looking for—Velmont Boulevard.

Despite the fancy name, Velmont was a narrow lane that led off to the right and out into open fields, freshly mown grass on either side, trees forming a ridge across the top of the first incline. At first, Stacy thought Bear must have got the street wrong. She checked the address and turned up the lane, driving slowly until she saw the first house and almost ran off the road. A massive gray structure, it looked like something out of one of those shiny-paged books all about home decorating—all manicured lawns and hedges and fountains, behind which stood a house that six families from Stacy's neighborhood could probably occupy without ever running into each other.

"Holy shit."

Passing one enormous home after the other, she drove steadily along until she came to the address she was looking for, a wrought-iron gate across the driveway and high brick walls on either side, behind which she could see a forest of tall trees. The name welded into the ironwork over the gate read:

MENDELLSON ESTATE
Private Property of M & PJ Crane-Thorpe

"This is it. This is definitely it." Her heart fluttered. This was her only lead. She could not mess it up.

Fifty yards or so past the gate the street widened into a bay cut into the trees to allow cars to pass. She pulled the car in, wiggled into her dry clothes, and looked herself over. Not exactly fashion runway material, but at least she didn't look homeless.

The gate was locked, walls too high to climb, no gap she could squeeze through.

But there was another way in. She walked quickly back to Curta's car, got in, and started it up. Inching back and forth, she maneuvered the car closer and closer to the brick wall until a clunk from the front fender told her she couldn't get any closer. When she got out, the car was wedged in perfectly, so she climbed up onto the hood, then onto the roof. From here she could just make out the driveway through the trees, winding up a slight incline. With both hands on the top of the wall, she jumped, hoisted herself over, and dropped on the other side.

How much money would you have to have to live in a place like this? The front yard looked like a state park. She headed for the driveway, following it up toward the house, wondering what she was going to say when she got there. Best plan, she figured, was what she'd thought of on the way here—to say she wanted a job with Millcreek, telling them she heard they had vacancies. Maybe Maryanne Thorpe-whatever would tell her who to contact. That'd give her an in. It was a long shot, but what else did she have?

The driveway was longer than she'd counted on. It wound around a couple of turns, cutting through a sparse forest of oaks and firs with squirrels scuttling across the leaf litter and up branches, until the house came into view. An enormous cream-colored place, it looked like a replica of some Spanish castle with balconies with wrought-iron railings, and roses and some kind of vines trailing up them.

Hanging back behind one of the trees, she scanned the gardens right across to the far tree line on either side of her: not a soul in sight. If anyone got antsy, they could call the cops and she wouldn't see the light of day for the next ten years. With her heart in her mouth, she walked on up the garden path, across the huge circular driveway out front, and up the broad, stone front steps to a pair of expansive wooden doors. A bell hung at one side. She rang it and clasped her hands in front of her, circling her thumbs around one another while she waited. After a few seconds, the door opened and a woman looked out—dark hair caught up in a bun at the back, dark eyes, a slash of red lipstick. Stacy would have guessed she was around forty, maybe fifty.

"Hi. I'm looking for Mrs. Thorpe."

The woman looked over Stacy's shoulder, scanning the tree-line. "How did you get in here?"

Stacy thumbed back over her shoulder. "The gate was open," she lied. "I just walked in."

Stacy followed the woman's gaze, then leaned into her line of sight. "So is Mrs. Thorpe here?"

"I'm sorry, Mrs. *Crane*-Thorpe isn't available at the moment," the woman said in a snotty tone. "Now if you don't mind, you can show yourself out again."

She went to close the door, but Stacy interrupted her, saying, "When will she be available? I need to talk to her."

The door opened slightly. "May I ask what it's about?"

"Who is it, Celia?" A woman's voice from somewhere in the house. The echo indicated a large open area and that the woman had spoken from up on a second-floor stairway.

"A young lady asking to speak to you, ma'am," Celia called up over her shoulder.

Footsteps clicked down stairs, then across the marbled floor. The door widened and a woman peered out—short gray hair caught up in stiff curls, eyebrows arched severely over hooded lids, a pale blue ring circling each iris of her hazel eyes, which meant the woman was elderly. Certainly older than the image Stacy had seen on the internet, which must have been taken some years back. But it was definitely the same woman.

"Mrs. Crane-Thorpe, I'm sorry to bother you, but I was wondering if you had any vacancies at Millcreek."

The woman frowned as deeply as a face full of Botox would allow and shared a questioning look with Celia.

"I'm sorry, I don't know what you're talking about."

"I looked you up—on the internet. It said you were on the executive board of Millcreek Fashions and I was told you might have some jobs." She looked from Mrs. Crane-Thorpe to Celia and back. Both of them frowned out at her.

"I'm sorry, young lady, but I think you must have the wrong person."

"No, I don't. Millcreek Fashions. Maybe if you just tell me who's in charge, I can go talk to them."

"Go and have my car brought around," the woman told Celia.

"Look," said Stacy, a little irritated now, "All I want is—"

"I don't have time for this right now. I suggest you go and check your facts. There's no one here on any board of executives for a Millcreek or anything else. Good day."

And the door closed in her face.

Stacy swore under her breath, then realized she wasn't going to be able to get out of the front gates until the woman left. She hammered on the door with the side of her fist. "Hey, I can't get out. You'll have to open the gate for me!"

When no one responded, she muttered a few choice words, then started back down the driveway. When she got to the street, sure enough, the gates were still locked.

Now she'd have to wait until the woman brought her car down.

A minute later, the automatic mechanism hummed into life and the gates slowly parted. Stacy stepped back as a white Mercedes swept down the driveway behind her and paused until the gates were fully open. Maryanne Crane-Thorpe sat in the back seat, eyes glued to something in her hand—probably her phone. The car swung out of the driveway onto the road and turned right.

Stacy walked out behind them and watched the car depart down the lane.

The woman had lied and Stacy intended to find out why. She hurried back to Curta's car and pulled back out onto the road, following until the Mercedes was just in sight. She eased the car to the side of the street and waited until it had crested the first hill, then pulled out after it.

There was more than one way to skin this cat.

CHAPTER THIRTY
DAY TWO: 4:32 PM—ELIZABETH

Nancy was right—the address indicated on the GPS tracking system was out in the middle of nowhere. After driving down a long dusty road lined with the occasional abandoned house, they came to a dry riverbed where the bridge had collapsed and never been repaired. Nancy got out of the car and strode over to the flimsy white wooden barrier that had been placed across the entrance to the bridge and leaned over. After scanning the surrounding stony ground populated only by the odd naked sapling, she bent to pick up a sign that lay on the ground next it.

"Sinkhole," she called, pointing to the sign. Shaking her head, she tossed the sign back down and trudged back to the car. "River runs right into it and disappears. No wonder everybody moved out."

Penny backed up, swung the car around, and retraced their original route back to the main highway. The new route took them down a pot-holed back street lined on both sides with bare saplings. A mile or so later, Penny guided the car past a roadside Dumpster and a stack of cardboard cartons next to it, tied in neat bundles and waiting for collection, and down a long, narrow lane. After another couple of hundred yards, the lane opened into the front entranceway of what looked like an old freight storage building surrounded by a sagging chain-link fence. Penny pulled the car to a stop and cut the engine. All three women sat in silence, listening to the *tick, tick* of cooling metal under the hood while looking the place over.

Covered mostly in plywood siding, the place stood two stories high, a rusted tin roof dipping into visibility at the front, a garage door standing open to the left with a white truck reversed into the loading bay. The front reception area consisted of a set of double wooden doors, both closed, the glass windows boarded up, a lopsided sign next to them with an arrow pointing to the rear of the building alongside a few words handwritten in Spanish.

Penny joined her, a hand on one hip, the other across her brow, shielding her eyes from the sun while she read the sign over on the building frontage, lettered in black italics.

"*Millcreek Fashions*. Who in their right mind would run a business way out here?"

Nancy peeled off, striding towards the front double doors. She grabbed both handles and shook them, then turned to Elizabeth and Penny with a quick head shake, indicating they were locked.

"This way." Elizabeth set off for the loading bay with Penny following along behind. When a man appeared on the dock, Elizabeth called, "Excuse me, I need to speak to one of your managers?"

The guy looked back at the main building where he'd come from, and replied in Spanish with a shrug.

Penny huffed in disgust. "He says there's no one here. Thinks we came down in the last rain."

"A manager," Elizabeth called to him. "*Quiero ver al gerente*—your manager," she added.

The guy raised both palms and shook his head, meaning, "I don't understand."

"Yeah, like hell you don't," mumbled Penny.

At that moment, Nancy joined them, walking quickly from the other side of the building, thumbing back over her shoulder. "Trish's car's here, all right. Around the other side."

"Where?"

They retraced their steps, following Nancy past the front entrance and down the opposite side of the building where several cars were lined up in a makeshift parking lot.

Nancy pointed down the line. "The one on the end. Dark gray Lexus."

Elizabeth and Penny followed as she marched off down the line of cars to a dust-covered dark gray Lexus at the end, the front grille almost touching the side of the building, windows rolled right up.

After running an appraising eye over the car, Penny let out a soft whistle. "Whoa! Very nice. How'd she afford to buy a car like this?"

"Told me she saved up for it," Nancy replied. Her dubious flinch told Elizabeth even she didn't believe it.

Elizabeth tried the door first. "It's locked." Then she bent to the passenger's window, cupping her hand to the glass as she peered in. "You sure it's hers?"

Nancy pointed at the plates. "Registration's hers."

"So where is she?"

"'Scuse me. What are you doing here?" It was a woman's voice, calling out to them from behind.

All three turned in unison to see a dark-haired woman in hip-hugging jeans and a slim-fitting blouse walking towards them. She looked in her mid- to late thirties, black hair tied back, suspicion forming two lines etched into her forehead between her dark eyes. She paused a few yards from them. "This is private property. Didn't you see the sign?" she asked, jerking her head back toward the driveway.

"I drove right in here. We didn't see any sign," Penny said.

Gesturing towards the Lexus, Elizabeth said, "Can tell me where the owner of this car is?"

The woman's line of sight crossed to the car. She made a dismissive face before meeting their gaze again. "I don't know. It's been there since yesterday but I don't know who owns it. No one here, I can tell you that much."

Moving back a few paces, Elizabeth looked up and across the building. "What do you do here? Are you a garment manufacturer?"

Somewhat defensive now, the woman folded her arms, glancing up the signage above. "This is a private business. You're not supposed to be here."

"We're looking for the owner of this car—Patricia Tomes. Do you know where she is?"

"I don't know anybody by that name."

"Do you mind if I come in and ask your employees if anyone knows where she is?"

The woman shifted her weight from one foot to the other, head tilting. "They don't know anything. Like I said, the car's been here since yesterday."

"Can't we just ask?"

The corners of her mouth dropped into an irritated scowl. "I think you better leave now."

Penny tugged Elizabeth's sleeve. "I think we should do as the lady says."

The three of them walked to Penny's car, each passing the occasional glance back to where the woman stood her ground, glaring after them until they reached the car.

Elizabeth pulled out her phone. "That's it. I'm calling Delaney." She dialed, waited, but the phone went straight to voice mail. "Lance, call me when you get this message. It's Elizabeth."

"We're leaving?" Nancy said. "Just like that? What about Trish? I need to know she's okay."

"We'll find her. Look, she could have simply broken down and pulled in here. She could have called for a cab and gone home while the car gets picked up. She could be back at your place right now, waiting for you," Elizabeth said, although she didn't believe it herself.

"You think?"

While Elizabeth and Penny got back into the car, Nancy cast an aggrieved look back at the building. "Gimme a sec, will ya? I'm gonna try her." Nancy pressed buttons on her phone and waited. After a few moments, she shook her head and hung up. "Nothin'. She's not there," she said and got into the back seat.

"Well, if the people at Millcreek Fashions don't want to tell us who they are, and what they do, I know someone who might."

Penny slipped the key into the ignition. "Who are you calling?"

Elizabeth punched in the number and put up her hand, gesturing for Penny to wait while she put the phone to her ear. The phone rang twice before it was picked up.

"Well, hello," he said. "Tell me you've changed your mind about dinner."

Slipping into the front passenger seat of Penny's car, Elizabeth cast a quick look back to find the woman standing with her arms folded, still watching them. She forced a smile into her voice, and said, "I wish I were. But alas, I'm going to ask you another favor."

"Another one? This is becoming a habit."

As if she wasn't already aware of that. "Listen, I need some information about a company in the fashion industry. I'm guessing you'd know most of them."

The smile in his voice lightened his tone. "Michael Corleone once famously said, 'Keep your friends close, and your enemies closer.' I've survived many a dip in the road living by those words. Hold on a sec, will you, Elizabeth? Yeah, what is it?" In the background she heard a voice, and she heard him answer, "Thanks, Chrissy. Tell Governor Straussman I'm on the phone and I'll call him right back."

For Elizabeth's benefit, she would have bet, letting her know he was still in tight with Walt Straussman. She gave Penny a pained look, then he was back on the line.

"Sorry about that. Now, who are we talking about and what's the interest?"

"A little fashion company out in the back of the boonies—place called Millcreek Fashions. It's running out of an old delivery depot, by the look of it, located thirty minutes south of the city, out in the middle of nowhere."

"Millcreek?" he said. "Nope, never heard of it. Wait a second, I'll ask Chrissy." She waited while a muffled conversation took place. Then he was back. "She says she's never heard of them. What's this about?"

"I was just trying to find out if they were a player in the industry. You know: who runs it, who owns them, that kind of thing."

"Well, neither of us has heard of them and believe me, anyone worth knowing would be on Chrissy's radar. She's like a bat." More serious now, he asked, "Is there anything I can help with, Elizabeth?"

Now she felt in his debt again and wished she hadn't called him. "No, truly. That's all I needed."

"No explanation? Come on, Elizabeth, you can't just call a guy up, pick his brains, and dump him."

Feeling somewhat cornered, as though having called him she now owed him a few words of explanation, she said, "It's nothing. Just something someone said. I thought it had to do with Stacy May Charms. Obviously, I was wrong."

"You think someone at this Millcreek might be helping her? Maybe harboring her or something?"

"I doubt it. If they are, they're certainly not saying."

"You mean you're there now?" The concern in his tone rang clear. "Elizabeth, if these people are doing anything illegal, and you've been asking around about their business, it could make them very nervous. You have no idea the lengths some of these lowlifes will go to keep their operations off the radar. If you think Stacy's out there, call the police, let them deal with it."

She looked back to where the woman was striding purposefully back to the front entrance of Millcreek Fashions with her phone to her ear. She shot Elizabeth a look, then went inside and the door slammed shut behind her.

"Do you think?"

"Absolutely. Tell me where you are, I'll have someone come get you."

"There's no need. I'm here with my secretary. We're leaving now."

She thanked him and hung up, then closed the door and put her seatbelt on.

"Clay's never heard of them," she told Penny. "He said to leave, let the police deal with it. He thinks if they're doing anything illegal, they could start getting antsy, and I agree."

Nancy sat forward, worried. "So that's it? What about Trish?"

Elizabeth turned in her seat. "What do you want us to do? Storm the place? They're not letting us in." Seeing the concern in Nancy's face, she said, "Listen, I know you're worried, but as soon as I get hold of Delaney, I'll tell him everything—about the car, the tracking system, everything. But right now, Clay thinks it's probably not a good idea for us to stick around out here. We should go."

"Don't have to tell me twice." Penny hit the ignition and put the car into reverse.

In the back seat, Nancy folded her arms and scowled out the passenger window, saying, "I'm not happy about this."

"Duly noted," Elizabeth told her and dialed Delaney's number again. Again, it went straight to voice mail.

"Where the hell is he? Remind me to call his office when we get home," she told Penny.

"Will do." After swinging the car around in a wide semicircle, Penny put it into drive, heading back the way they came.

Sitting forward between the seats again, Nancy said, "You were talking to Clay Farrant, right?"

Penny addressed her in the rearview mirror. "She sure was. Handsome, rich, single; thinks Elizabeth is a beautiful and talented woman. He wants to take her out to dinner and treat her like a princess. Of course, in Elizabeth's eyes that makes him a skunk," she added.

"I didn't say he was a skunk." Somewhat irritated by the comment, Elizabeth turned to the passenger window and found herself pouting. "He's already spoken for. I told you that. And besides," she added in a defensive tone, "he's not my type. I'm discerning."

"Hon, you married Richard McClaine. How discerning would you have to be?"

Elizabeth flicked her secretary a razor-edged stare.

Penny looked suitably shamed and said, "Sorry. "I'm just saying."

Nancy snorted. "Trish went to school with Clay Farrant. She said he always had some scheme or other going on. They called him the Magician. Anything he put his hand to miraculously turned into cash. Now they're calling him the Magician of Manufacturing. Rich or not, I gotta say, he wouldn't be my type, either." Picking up on the loaded silence that followed, she added, "I mean, if my preferences went that way."

Penny twisted the wheel, checked for traffic, and guided the car slowly down the potholed lane, heading for the exit. "Well, he hit all the right notes when he launched his Rue Xeeba brand, that's for sure. He's got stores opening up all over the country. Once that baby floats on the stock exchange, both he and Christine Wentworth will be raking it in." She did a face shrug. "If he asked me out, I, for one, would not spit in his eye."

"Let's drop it, shall we?" said Elizabeth. The whole subject had somehow struck a nerve. After putting her phone away, she leaned her elbow on the window frame, wondering why she seemed to be the only one who gave a damn about the reason Stacy May had run. And what about a little boy whose only wish was to be with his mother? Didn't he matter?

But hidden among all these questions, something else had emerged deep down in her gut. It was a gnawing doubt she just couldn't seem to shake. And no matter how hard she tried, it just kept getting stronger: was she really doing this for justice? To prove to the world they'd underestimated her choice of candidate? Or was she terrified that she'd been wrong about Stacy May Charms all along?

Penny hit the signal light and brought the car to a halt while she checked each way for traffic. To the left of them sat the Dumpster and the stack of papers and cardboard cartons.

"Wait. Stop here a second." Elizabeth snapped off her seatbelt and checked the lane behind them for cars before opening the door.

Penny frowned across at her. "What are you doing?"

"Just give me a minute."

Elizabeth got out of the car and stepped through the long, dusty grass at the side of the lane to the trodden area in front of the Dumpster. When she lifted the top, the stink that hit her made her face crumple and she automatically dropped the lid. She turned her face away—old food, rotten fish, by the smell of it, all covered in plastic bags and cardboard tubes that had once held rolls of fabric, all mixed together in a toxic cloud. Elizabeth clapped a hand over her nose and mouth, and waited for her stomach to stop roiling.

"What is it?" Penny called from the car.

"Oh, dear lord, I have no idea, but it stinks."

Penny had gotten out of the car to join her. "What do you expect? You go opening Dumpsters sitting on the side of the road in the sun, they're gonna stink. What are you looking for?"

Still holding her hand to her nose and mouth, Elizabeth stood grimacing while she waited for the nausea to pass, when her attention snagged on the flattened-out cardboard cartons neatly stacked in bunches tied together with twine.

"I need a knife. Or some scissors or something. What have you got?"

By now, Nancy had also gotten out of the car to join them, a puzzled expression tweaking up one side of her lip. "I don't carry scissors, but I've got this." She yanked a set of keys from her pocket, selected a tiny blue pocket knife with a two-letter logo on the handle and flicked out a tiny blade. "It's not too sharp. I use it for doing my nails. Trish got the pink one. What do you want it for?" She passed it across.

"That'll do." Elizabeth took the knife and squeezed one finger beneath the twine on the first stack of boxes, and sawed the tiny blade back and forth until the ties gave way and the boxes cascaded apart like a deck of cards. She lifted the top carton and turned it—nothing on the reverse side. The second one was the same—all packaging documentation had been removed, leaving an empty square of rough white paper where it had been torn off.

Penny moved a little closer, taking and stacking the discarded cartons as Elizabeth sorted through them. "What are you looking for?"

On the underside of the second-to-last box in the pile was a torn label with a partial address scrawled across it that read: *Carringwa—*

"This is it." Angling the flattened cardboard towards Penny, Elizabeth tapped the label with her fingertip. "Carringway Prison. I'd bet my life on it. This is how the drugs are being smuggled into the prison. I *knew* it. I *knew* Stacy May Charms had a damn good reason for breaking parole and running. She figured out how the drugs were getting in and now someone wants to shut her up."

"I don't understand," said Penny. "How could anyone ship drugs into the prison from this place? And in cartons? That's a lot of hooch."

"It's somehow incorporated in the fabric. Or the buttons, maybe. I'm sure of it."

"So why didn't Stacy just tell you about it when she had the chance?"

"Because every time I spoke to her, we had a prison guard in the room—either Trish Tomes or Kathy Reynolds. Who knows, maybe she even thought I was involved."

Penny finished the thought. "So if she didn't know who she could trust, she figured she was safer not trusting anyone."

"Exactly. Stacy and Amy were both on the same work detail when, somehow, they both discovered how the drugs were coming in. Now Amy's dead. Stacy said she was murdered but no one believes her. They think she was just another drug addict who'd gotten hold of a syringe that Lois Hankerman brought in. But I don't think that's what happened. Stacy said Amy would never use again, that someone killed her. And that's why Stacy ran. And whoever is behind this *Millcreek*," she said, waving dismissively toward the building they'd just left, "is the same person who's running the drug operation. That's the person who murdered Amy and threatened Stacy *and* her son. And knowing what happened to Amy, Stacy's got no doubt that they'll act on that threat. Her son was in real danger."

"Why didn't she just tell Warden Glassy? Why break parole and run? I mean, she could have told me, couldn't she?" This was from Nancy, who had followed them back to the car and gotten in while listening to Elizabeth.

Elizabeth twisted in her seat to face her. "Okay, think about it: Stacy and Amy discover drugs being smuggled in, right? It's a well-run operation. It would have to be. In a prison like Carringway, there's a gauntlet of security checks and metal detectors to run. They'd pick up anything coming into the place. I know, I've seen how many checks visitors are subjected to."

"Everyone is. It's Corrections policy," Nancy told her.

"So the only way you'd get something in through the back door is if someone in a position of authority knows what's going on and approves those shipments. So who can Stacy trust that she can tell? You? The prison officers? I doubt it. She can't even talk in front of them. Then Amy dies, and Stacy gets the threat: 'You tell anyone what you know—you die. Or worse still, here's a picture of your son.

Connect the dots, you don't have to be Einstein to figure out what would happen to him.'"

"Hey, wait a second there. You're talking about the picture I took? You're saying Trish has something to do with this?"

Nancy's protest went unanswered while Elizabeth went on, each of the pieces of the puzzle seemingly slotting neatly into place with every point. "So now she can't trust the prison officers, she can't trust me, she has nowhere to go. Who can she tell? Jennifer Glassy? Hardly. Glassy was the one running the investigation that had her own sister convicted of drug smuggling and tossed into the Women's Reformatory. And maybe it wasn't Lois at all. Maybe it was someone trying to shut her up as well." She lifted her eyebrows at the other two women and waited for the idea to percolate.

"So what choice does Stacy have? Stay in prison? Hope something doesn't slip out that puts her son's life in jeopardy? No, she comes up with a plan. She has to save her son. So she takes the first opportunity she gets, and she runs."

She looked from Penny to Nancy, waiting for objections.

Nancy came up with the first one. She'd been frowning deeply while she listened, eyes narrowed on a point just in front of her while she followed along in her mind.

Eventually, she bunched her mouth and tipped her head to the negative. "Nope, sorry. I just don't buy it. There's no way you'd get anything into that place. You don't know what it's like. You give 'em half a chance, you got no idea what people try to smuggle in. And if you're talking suppliers, everything, and I mean *everything* that goes into that prison is logged and checked then rechecked. Trish told me that Glassy's totally anal about security—even more so since Lois Hankerman was arrested."

"Exactly. So what's the conclusion Stacy is going to come to? That it has to be someone on the inside. Now all she can do is find her son and hope the two of them can disappear forever. Come on, let's get back. We've got a lot of work to do."

Penny hit the ignition, put the car in gear, and eased out of the lane into the main street, heading north. "Where are we going next?"

"You're on research duty. I want the names of anyone even remotely associated with Millcreek and I want you to dig out any connections you find with Trish Tomes—regardless of how loose."

Nancy sat forward again, clearly offended. "Well, hold on a second. I don't like this idea that you think Trish has been dealing in drugs. That's nuts. She just wouldn't do that."

"You said yourself Trish has been acting strange lately—angry one minute, crying the next. What if her job is being threatened? Or worse, what if she's being blackmailed? What if whoever's threatening Stacy is also threatening to kill you if Trish doesn't do what she's told? That's a more likely explanation for why her car's out here in the middle of nowhere. And why she's been coming here these past few nights. Somebody's got her under their thumb and they're applying the pressure."

Penny slowed the car, indicated, then swung back to the main highway again, checking the rearview mirror before hitting the accelerator and swerving across two lanes, cutting off a driver who leaned long and hard on his horn in response. She ignored him, saying, "So you think it's Jennifer Glassy who's bringing in the drugs? Why would she? Money? You think she'll risk her job, *and* throw her sister into the can, just to make a few bucks on the side? You gotta admit, it's a stretch."

Elizabeth didn't even blink when they swerved into the fast lane and Penny slammed her foot to the floor, rocketing them over the speed limit. As far as she was concerned, the faster they got back, the better. Everything in her mind reinforced her theory and if Nancy was right and the police were expecting an imminent arrest, they didn't have a minute to lose.

After mulling over the details a minute more, she turned in her seat, addressing both Penny and Nancy. "Okay, so this is what I'm thinking:

what if Lois found out what was going on first? What if she discovered heroin being smuggled into the prison and who was responsible, and went to her sister to tell her what she knew? Maybe it's one of the other contractors. Or a supplier. Maybe it's someone Glassy can't afford to fall out of favor with. Lois threatens to go to the authorities. And when Glassy can't convince her to keep her mouth shut, she does the only thing she can—has her framed, then arrested and thrown into solitary confinement."

"That's a lot of what-ifs and maybes," said Penny. "Especially just to keep a few extra bucks rolling into the place."

"Too many ifs and maybes for my liking," Nancy added sourly. "You're saying that Warden Glassy would turn a blind eye to drugs coming into her own prison, then frame her sister and have her arrested? I don't see it."

Elizabeth picked up her phone and hit the redial. "Well, there's only one way to find out what's really going on in that place." After several rings, the call was picked up, and she said, "I'd like to speak with Jennifer Glassy, please."

"Just a moment," the woman at the other end said, but in less than a minute she was back. "I'm sorry, Warden Glassy isn't available at the moment. Can someone else help you?"

Elizabeth checked her watch—after five already.

"No, I need to talk to the warden. Has she left for the day?"

"She's been called away to an incident. She's down in the infirmary. Can I take a message?"

"Yes. Tell her that Elizabeth McClaine called and that I'll be there in forty-five minutes for a meeting with her. And tell her it would be advisable to make sure she's available, because this is a matter of absolute urgency."

CHAPTER THIRTY-ONE
DAY TWO: 6:08 PM—STACY

Stacy had followed the Mercedes back into the central city, ducking down back streets to avoid the cops, then emerging further along, convinced she'd lost the car, only to pick it up in the distance.

But sooner or later, someone was bound to spot her license plates and call it in. After an intense internal debate that came down on the side of abandoning the pursuit, she was about to cut down the next street to her right and take off, when the left indicator light on the Mercedes flickered and the car slowed.

Three cars back, Stacy also slowed. When a gap in the traffic opened up, the Mercedes swung across into the parking garage of a tall corporate-looking building that was all glass and steel cut in angles, and disappeared down the ramp. Stacy drove on a ways, and found a parking place just around the corner. No time to feed the meter. She locked the car and walked quickly back. Keeping her head down, she hurried down the main street and entered a brightly lit lobby, marbled floor, vaulted ceilings, light shafting in from the floor-to-ceiling windows. The place looked like a museum.

In the center of the lobby, a concierge sitting behind a broad desk looked up as she approached.

"Excuse me," she said. "Can you tell me where the stairs are? My sister left her phone with me. She's parked in the basement and I have to get it back to her."

"The elevators are just back here," he said, thumbing over his shoulder. "Take one of the first four. They'll take you straight to the parking garage."

"Be faster to take the stairs," she told him. "And better exercise."

He gave her a quizzical look, then leaned forward and pointed past her, this time across to her left. "Just over there."

The second she was through the door, she hit the stairs, flying down them until she came to the lower landing with a sign next to the door that read: LI PARKING GARAGE.

Out in the gloom, rows of concrete pillars stood with maybe twenty, thirty parked cars scattered between. Around the corner, same story. Saturday, the place was almost deserted. On a weekday the place would be packed. At the sound of an engine echoing dully across the space, she ducked down behind an SUV in the front row. A dark gray Toyota sedan went by. She waited until it rounded the first bend then straightened.

No sign of the Mercedes. She threaded her way across a couple of near-empty rows in case the car was sitting behind one of the pillars.

No sign of it.

Across in the next row, a guy got out of the gray Toyota that had just passed her and headed for the elevator. After pressing the call button, he turned to watch her.

Keeping her head down, she swerved away and walked to a nearby car. "Yup, that'd make my day—lose the target, then some random guy turns me in," she muttered under her breath while she pretended to unlock it.

Conscious that the owner would have unlocked the car by now, she waited until he glanced up to check the elevator light panel, then ducked down until she heard the bell ding and the doors slide open. When she bobbed up, the doors were open and she caught a glimpse of Mrs.

Crane-Thorpe in the back of the elevator, and the guy sliding a card down a slot, and pressing a button just before the doors met. A couple of seconds later, the letter G lit up on the panel above. She trotted across and watched the numbers climb, noting only now that there was another parking level below the one she was on. The elevator stopped on the first floor, then moved on.

How many people were in the elevator? It didn't look full, but she was sure the woman wasn't on her own. The elevator door next to her opened and three people stepped out. She didn't even look, just kept her eyes glued to the light. The numbers climbed without stopping: 26, 27, 28, then slowed. Number 29 remained illuminated. The car stopped again on 32, then began descending again. The woman had obviously gotten off either on 29 or 32. She hit the call button and when the elevator next to her opened, she got in. Right next to the number panel was a sign stating that key card access was required for the upper floors. Which meant that the guy with the swipe card probably got off at 32.

She hit the button marked G and burst into the lobby the second the doors parted. The concierge was pointing a couple back to the elevators. She walked double-time past him and over to the lobby where, as she'd expected, a metal background iodized into a gold color, black tiles lettered in white and set into slots to spell out the names. No sign of Millcreek on 29. Or on 32. Or on any others.

A dead end.

The concierge lifted his eyes as she approached.

"Yeah, me again. Can you tell me if there's a company in this building named Millcreek Fashions?"

"Not that I'm aware of."

"Are you sure? Like, maybe it's a part of another company or something."

He said nothing, didn't even blink.

"I see. Okay, thanks."

So the company wasn't here. She'd hit a brick wall. It was a long shot, but disappointing all the same. But why would the woman deny her involvement with Millcreek? She didn't even flinch when Stacy mentioned the name, so it wasn't like the company name had changed or she'd resigned from the board. She'd have at least shown recognition.

No matter. She had one more cat in the bag, one other name to follow up. If only she'd gotten the address from Bear while she had the chance. Too late now. Across the lobby, the concierge scanned the area from glass windows to elevators, from the potted plants in the corner across to where Stacy was, and stopped on her with his eyebrows up.

"Just one more thing," she said as she headed towards him.

He recognized the name right away. When he gave her the pitying look someone might save for the terminally stupid, she wanted to say, "Hey, not all of us sit around reading the financial columns in the can," but as Curta always said, you catch more flies with honey than with vinegar, so she kept her remarks to herself.

The concierge leaned his elbows on the desk, hands laced under his chin, speaking to her in a slow, deliberate tone. "I'm afraid even if I knew Miss Wentworth's home address, I'm sure you're aware I couldn't give it out."

"So you know who she is?"

His eyebrows went up again, as if to say, "Are you kidding?"

"Okay, so can you tell me where I can find a phone book?"

He shifted, as if his patience was coming to an end. "If you're looking for Miss Wentworth, may I suggest you visit her in her office on the 29th floor."

Stacy blinked at him, then looked across at the elevator bank. "She's up there?"

"Could be. She usually works Saturdays until six or so. Although," he said and made a show of checking his watch, "you may have just missed her."

"Okay, thanks." She hustled across to hit the elevator button and waited with her arms folded and her head down.

Behind her, one of the elevators dinged and the doors slid open. In back of the car she got a glimpse of Maryanne Crane-Thorpe talking to a man next to her. Terrified the woman would recognize her, Stacy kept her head down and fell into step with four executive-looking women who got out of the car she was waiting for, and walked with them until the elevator door closed again.

Then she raced for the stairwell.

"Excuse me," the concierge called after her. "Would you mind—"

But she was already through the door, thundering down the stairs two at a time, swinging around the railing at the midway turn, sneakers squeaking on the pivots until she got to the lower parking garage. She cracked the door and peeked out just in time to see Mrs. Crane-Thorpe, scarf billowing out behind her as she walked back to her car, arm in arm with a younger man. Following a short distance behind, but obviously with them, was the woman Stacy recognized from the same Google search as Christine Wentworth. The photo she'd seen on the internet must have been a recent one because she looked exactly the same. Stacy slid in behind one of the concrete pillars, straightened, and peeked out. The car reversed up, did a 180-degree turn, and sped in her direction. She ducked around the back of the pillar until it swished by, then watched as it cornered at the far end of the row and disappeared up the exit ramp.

If her gut was right, and if luck was still on her side, she knew where she had to go next.

CHAPTER THIRTY-TWO
DAY TWO: 6:49 PM—ELIZABETH

After dropping Nancy back home with instructions to keep an eye on the tracking system for any further movements of Trish's car, Elizabeth told her emphatically that whatever happened, she was not to follow. She was to call immediately and they'd decide what to do from there. She also advised her to call Trish's phone at regular intervals, and if she picked up, ditto: call without delay.

Nancy told them if Trish were in any danger, she'd know it in a heartbeat, that Trish would have told Nancy if she was in trouble, and they'd have dealt with it together because that's the kind of relationship they had.

Elizabeth didn't bother reminding her that over the past few months, the poor woman had displayed God only knew how many signs of distress, sure indications that something was terribly wrong, but in each case, every cry for help had gone unnoticed. Then again, she was hardly one to talk. Look at what had happened in her own relationship. She and Richard had fallen so far apart in what everyone thought was the perfect marriage, and yet when the final curtain fell it was almost as if she'd been living with a total stranger. *It's what happens, sometimes,* she thought. *You don't always know the person you love as well as you think.*

Quite apart from that, what would be the point in laying guilt on Nancy and making her feel even worse than she already did?

For now, Elizabeth's only hope in getting to the bottom of this whole fiasco, she thought, was to track down the weak spot in the prison supply line that had allowed Millcreek Fashions to smuggle drugs onto the premises, leaving a woman dead and an innocent woman to take the blame, and Stacy May Charms with no hope of seeing her son grow.

Having picked up her own car, she'd headed straight out for Carringway—a trip she knew so well now, she could have made it blindfolded.

Dusk had drawn a black curtain over the landscape, creating large blocks of oily black shadow across the front of the prison as she drove down Carringway Drive and in through the front entrance. In contrast to the bleak façade, the interior lighting at each of the barred windows lent the place a deceptively warm atmosphere within.

Elizabeth pulled the car to a halt at the gate where the barrier arm lifted and the guard on duty waved her straight through. She turned right at the end of the approach and into the public parking lot where she pulled into the first available spot.

After taking a moment to rehearse the points she needed to take up with the warden, she got out and locked her car, tucking her purse under her arm as she walked to the entrance. At the visitors' reception area, she was met by a waiting prison officer.

"Mrs. McClaine?" the woman asked sharply.

"Yes. I have an appointment with Warden Glassy."

"She's expecting you." She gestured for Elizabeth to follow, then walked off.

Elizabeth trailed her down a hallway past two interview rooms and halted at the gated entrance where the duty officer carried out all the usual formalities of identification and signing in. Feeling the eyes of the remaining administration personnel following her as she passed, she kept her head high and continued on down the familiar route until they reached Warden Glassy's office. At the door, the officer gave two short raps on the upper wood panel and waited.

"Come in." Glassy's voice, from within her inner sanctum.

The officer pushed the door open and stood back holding it, waiting for Elizabeth to enter.

"Thank you," she said, moving past her.

The prison officer withdrew with a nod of her head, then closed the door, leaving her alone with the warden.

Warden Glassy was sitting at her desk, her legs crossed, both arms along the armrests of her deep-seated black leather swivel chair. She dipped her head briefly in greeting. "Come in, Elizabeth. Take a seat," she said, indicating one of the chairs facing her. She looked exhausted.

Elizabeth took the closest chair and sat down. "Thank you for agreeing to see me at such short notice."

An icy smile curled the corners of the warden's mouth. "You say that as if I had the choice. What's on your mind, Elizabeth?"

"Stacy May Charms. What else?"

Jennifer Glassy leaned forward to position a pen at the edge of her blotter before sitting back again. "And what exactly did you want to discuss?"

The tone was cool, all business. None of the pleasantries they'd exchanged throughout the months they'd spent assessing and selecting candidates for the governor's early release program.

Letting the moment stretch, Elizabeth placed her purse on the floor next to her and also crossed her legs. "I think she knew exactly how those drugs were brought into the prison. Maybe she even knew who brought them."

Jennifer Glassy tilted her head. "Yes, and so do I. And I told you that when you last came here asking the same questions, Elizabeth. I carried out the investigation myself. We found a syringe in Amy Dixon's cot, track marks on her left arm, and enough narcotics in her system to fell an ox. Then we found several containers of high-quality heroin in the physical therapy clinic, in Lois Hankerman's locker. But you already know all this. I don't know why we're going over old ground here."

Shifting uncomfortably in her chair, Elizabeth continued, undaunted. "I don't think this is old ground. I think those drugs are still coming into the prison. And if they're not, someone's planning to bring them in."

"To what end, Elizabeth? Money?"

Shocked at the response, Elizabeth said, "Well, of course money. What else?"

"Because for whoever might be planning such an ill-advised operation, the payoff simply wouldn't be worth it. Even those on the work schemes don't have the kind of cash you'd need. Do you know how much these women earn? Twenty-five cents an hour. Tell me how that's going to make anyone rich." She sat forward, leaning her elbows on her desk again, irritation radiating from her steely blue eyes. "Do you have any idea what security procedures we have in place to prevent contraband coming into this facility? Procedures I put in place?"

"I'm not talking about someone walking in the front door with a few ounces of marijuana in their pockets. I'm talking about heavy-duty drugs being brought in by your own suppliers. Drugs that have already taken the life of one of your prisoners."

A look of utter incredulity slowly squeezed Jennifer Glassy's features until her face had twisted into a contemptuous scowl. "*What* suppliers?" She spread her hands wide. "How would any of our suppliers get any illicit items in here? If you can tell me that, I'd be most interested."

The criticism of Warden Glassy's job—of her security systems—had hit a nerve. Elizabeth should have expected it. But somewhere deep down in her gut, she felt the first real twinge of uncertainty. "I'm not talking about all of your suppliers—just your fabric suppliers."

"You mean Millcreek Fashions?" Not a question. A statement of incredulity.

Bingo! thought Elizabeth. "Oh, so you admit that Millcreek is one of your suppliers?"

Jennifer raised one hand, dropped it on her desk in utter disbelief. "I'm sorry, Elizabeth, I don't see where this is going."

"Trish Tomes is where this is going. Can you tell me where she is right now?"

"How would I know? I'm not her immediate supervisor. I don't keep track of every officer in the place. And if she's not on the premises, we certainly don't keep tabs on all our employees once they leave the building. Who does?"

Elizabeth tamped down her welling frustration and moderated her tone. "I'm asking has she been in to work today?" When Jennifer just stared at her, Elizabeth dropped her shoulders. "Humor me, Jennifer. You're not the only one answerable for your actions here. I have reports to submit to my board as well. All I'm asking is that you check your records and confirm when Trish Tomes was last seen here. Please."

From the look on her face, Jennifer Glassy was wavering between arguing and simply telling Elizabeth to get out and never come back. Finally she picked up her phone, pressed a couple of buttons, and sat back, stony-faced and with her eyes set accusingly on Elizabeth. "Get me Susan in HR. I need to follow up on one of our officers."

There was a long pause, then Glassy smiled, her voice softening as she leaned her head back, blinking at a point just off to her left.

"Hi, Susan, I'm sorry to bother you so late in the day, but I need some information on one of our C-Block officers—Patricia Tomes. Can you tell me when her last shift was completed?"

A couple of nods. "Uh-huh. So she wasn't on the roster for last night?" Another pause, a couple more nods, then she frowned up at Elizabeth. "Thank you, that's all I needed to know." She hung up and clasped her hands across her lap, her expression one of self-righteous indignation. "She left yesterday after her normal shift. She hasn't been seen since."

"And what time was that?" Elizabeth asked.

Glassy gave her an intense glare before replying. "Her normal shift ended at two. She wasn't scheduled to work the late shift."

"Her partner said she got a text from her, saying Trish Tomes was signed on to work the graveyard shift. She didn't turn up this morning. Her partner hasn't heard from her since."

Glassy took a moment before answering. "I really don't see the significance. Maybe she got waylaid somewhere. Maybe she got stuck in traffic. Or had some important business to attend to in the city. How would I know?"

"Trish Tomes's car was located at Millcreek Fashions, not an hour's drive from here. According to the tracking unit she'd had fitted, it had been there some hours."

"Why are you telling me this?"

"You don't find it odd that one of your own officers was at the premises of one of the suppliers of your prison?"

She spread her hands in astonishment. "Why should I? Trish Tomes was the one who brought in the deal with Millcreek. She's been there several times over the past few months, discussing the terms of the deal. I appreciated her help."

Elizabeth jerked in her seat as though she'd been physically struck. "Trish Tomes is the one who brought in the sewing contract for the prisoners to complete? And you allowed this?"

"Why not? It was perfect timing. Trish came to me saying that a friend of hers ran the place and they were looking for a manufacturing company that could turn out low-cost garments to supply a number of contracts they'd recently won. The deal was … fortuitous. Everything came together at exactly the right moment. And the terms of the contract turned out to be quite lucrative for the prison. The board has been more than happy with the results, which makes the shareholders happy, and that makes me happy." She straightened in her chair. "I probably don't have to remind you that we're a private organization, Mrs. McClaine. Our shareholders have every right to demand a return on their investment. We need contracts like these to maintain profitability." Still frowning, she titled her head, saying, "I don't know what you think Millcreek is doing, but let me tell you, you're wrong. We did a thorough investigation into the company background of Millcreek Fashions, and by all accounts, they're a very reputable company. Any supply organizations we deal with are required to submit to a full examination of their business processes and procedures and account for their financial stability. We're not stupid. Despite what some people may think."

Refusing to rise to the derisive tone, Elizabeth pressed on. There were too many unanswered questions for her liking. "Then are you saying that Millcreek supplies the fabric for the garments you make?"

Glassy pushed her chair back. "I'll remind you that I'm under no obligation to answer these questions," she said.

"I'd hate to go running to Governor Straussman on this, Jennifer."

Warden Glassy's expression ran the gamut from frustration to a flicker of anger while she considered this, then settled into resignation. "Of course they supply the fabric. It's part of the deal. They also send us the designs for each garment run. Where else would we get them from?"

"Can you show me your shipping area? Maybe run me through the security procedures you've put in place? Like I said, humor me. Walt Straussman's going to ask the same questions. And you're not the only one answerable to an executive board."

Looking as though she was nearing the limit of her patience, Warden Glassy got up from her desk and moved straight to the door. "I'd be more than happy to. This way, Mrs. McClaine."

CHAPTER THIRTY-THREE
DAY TWO: 7:04 PM—STACY

Caitlin's building looked even more depressing in the early evening light. No street lighting out here. Just an entire block of derelict buildings waiting for some developer to come along and knock down to make way for a new shopping mall, or a parking lot.

Stacy slowed past the building, looking it over. This time of night, the local inhabitants had surfaced. Small groups of figures stood huddled together in doorways, while several nondescript bodies sat with their backs to the wall beside battered shopping carts, cardboard sheets, and coats arranged over them to keep out the rain. A few looked her way as she turned down the side of the building, but she lost them as she rounded the last corner and pulled the car into the parking lot she'd seen from Caitlin's window. After locking the car she walked quickly around to the front of the building and squeezed through the gap between the front doors once more.

Inside was in total darkness except for a faint rim of light outlining a door down the corridor she'd gone down last time. Not Caitlin's door.

She stood totally still, listening and waiting while her eyes adjusted, then made her way in the direction of Caitlin's room.

"Cait?"

Movement. Up ahead to her right. Then nothing.

Stacy sidled along to the doorway and slipped inside the room.

"I can see you," a guy's voice sang. Not the paranoid one. "Come outta there or I'm coming in after you."

She stayed where she was. "Where's Caitlin?"

"She ain't here."

"How long's she gonna be?"

A snigger. "A long, long time. Who're you? What do you want with her?"

Did that mean she'd moved on? Surely she'd have said. And who was this guy?

"How long's a long time?" she asked.

The beam of a flashlight stabbed her in the eyes. She angled her head to one side, hand shielding her from the glare.

"You tell me who wants to know."

"I'm a friend of hers. She was going to loan me a cell phone."

In the ambient glow of the flashlight, she could just make out the guy—tall, a halo of frizzy hair, something metal pinned to his shirt. Her heart skipped a beat.

"Listen, I've obviously missed her. I'll catch up with her later."

"Don't move."

"Who you got, Mitch?" Another guy. Shorter than the first. The beam swept briefly across him, and back.

"Some bitch. Says she's a friend of Caitlin's or something."

Not cops. Just two dickwads. One, she could have taken. Maybe. If he wasn't armed.

Two? It was doubtful. Especially in the dark.

"Listen, I'm just going to turn around and leave. I don't need any trouble. Okay?"

The click of a hammer going back. Dammit. Now she could see it— small, shiny black barrel, his enormous fist making it look like a kid's toy.

"Let's see what you got. Empty your pockets."

"I don't have anything."

"Search her," the guy with the gun said.

Stacy took a step back, both hands up. "Don't do this."

"Don't do this," mimicked the second guy in a wheedling voice.

The first one laughed, but from somewhere out front someone yelled, "Cops."

"Shit! Let's go," said Mitch.

"What about her?"

"She gets this." He raised the gun, arm level with his shoulder, finger around the trigger.

Stacy gasped. "Please, no."

He squeezed the trigger and nothing happened.

"Dammit!" he said.

"You got the safety on, you moron. I told you not to put the safety on." This from the second guy.

Then a third guy came crashing through the double doors. "Cops. Get out."

The three of them turned and fled on down the corridor, crashing into each other in their panic to escape. Out front, a brilliant beam of light sliced into the central area through the gap between the front doors. Outside she could hear voices calling for the chains to be cut, orders snapped out, dispatching officers left and right, followed by the sound of footsteps and the first thud of the ram on the front doors. With each successive thud, the wedge of light widened.

Stacy made a dash for Caitlin's room, hunting among the rags and boxes and crap in the ambient light. No sign of Caitlin. In the second box she found a Nokia phone, and grabbed it just as the front doors crashed open with the pounding of boots and cops yelling orders. All around squatters were yelling, running down stairways, only to be met by cops and running back up again with a pack of cops right behind them. Stacy hoisted Caitlin's only chair, swung it, and smashed the window. Using her elbow, she knocked out a few remaining shards, then climbed onto the ledge and rolled out, dropping just below it as a guy came running through the parking lot from the rear of the building, with a gun and yelling, "It's a raid! Get out!"

Two shots rang out from the window right above her head. She looked up to see a cop leaning out, following the guy in his sights. The instant he withdrew, she did a duck and run around the side of the car, opened the door and slid in behind the wheel. She fired it up and drove down the side in the direction the guy had come from. Two cops coming up the driveway stopped short.

She flattened her foot to the floor and the cops jumped aside, firing after her. She swung the car around, almost losing it on the turn. She straightened and crashed through a chain link fence at the side of the property, then swerved onto a second driveway. Three cops were running down the side of the building as she passed, but by the time they got to the entrance, she'd spun the wheel and was already heading south.

In the rearview mirror she could still see lights.

Was it just a raid on a drug den? Or did someone report her being there? Who knew? But for now, she had a phone, and she had an idea.

And that was all she needed.

CHAPTER THIRTY-FOUR
DAY TWO: 7:32 PM—ELIZABETH

Elizabeth followed Jennifer Glassy through another series of security checks and waypoints to the rear of the building where she stopped at a locked door with a sign affixed that read: RESTRICTED AREA: AUTHORIZED PERSONNEL ONLY BEYOND THIS POINT.

Glassy stopped in front of the door, and turned to Elizabeth with her hands clasped behind her back. "This is as far as you go. I can't allow you to go any further."

"What's in there?"

"Our loading docks. All of our shipments, food and laundry supplies—everything we need to run the prison comes in through here."

"Would you mind showing me the security measures you have in place?" Elizabeth asked.

"Yes, I would mind. Strictly speaking, you shouldn't even be in here. It's against Corrections policy to give out any information on security. I'm sure you understand that."

Elizabeth shifted her weight. "So bringing me all the way down here was a big charade—your way of telling me to mind my own business?"

For the longest time, a palpable tension hung between them. Then the warden said, "I can tell you this much, Mrs. McClaine: every, single shipment that comes through those gates—every truck, every pallet—*everything*, is searched, numbered, logged, checked, and rechecked. Each and every driver who comes through those gates has security clearance before he can even set foot on these premises, and every one of them carries identification in full view until they leave. For every second they're here, they're accompanied and overseen by prison personnel. We use metal detectors, screening, and full body searches if we have to. We follow Corrections procedures to the letter in this facility, because failing to do so is more than my job's worth."

It was all rhetoric. Elizabeth had spent enough time on the periphery of the political arena to know hedging when she saw it. Even so, deep down was a clanging feeling of disappointment. Even from the glimpse of the security she'd already seen, she couldn't see how anyone could bring contraband onto the premises.

"You mentioned drug dogs."

Warden Glassy tipped her head in resignation. "Drug dogs are expensive and we don't always have access to them. But my officers are well trained, and you wouldn't even believe some of the stories they could tell. You'd have to get up pretty early to get anything past them."

"Do you always use the same officers?"

"We have a total of seven on various shifts. They've all been screened and each officer submits to a personal search on both arrival and departure each day. I hope that satisfies your doubts, Elizabeth, because that's the end of the tour." And they exited back into the hallway again.

As they headed back to her office, Warden Glassy made a point of running through the basic procedures in case of riot, disaster, or blackout. By the time they got there, Elizabeth felt as though she knew the place inside out, and yet still couldn't see how a mouse could get in through the security systems she'd seen without detection.

"I'm not saying we're perfect," the warden told her as she opened her door, crossed her office, and took her seat again. "We do everything we can with the personnel we have."

"What if some enterprising supplier simply tosses a package over the fence and someone on this side picks it up? You're saying that never happens?"

The warden's cheeks flushed and her expression stiffened. "Anyone who approaches the outer perimeter is intercepted and questioned. But frankly, I can't see a major operation the size you're talking about tossing their product over the fence. And if there are any flaws in supplier security, I'd welcome someone to come in and tell me where they are."

"So you're telling me Lois Hankerman simply walked in through the front door with a bagful of heroin and a syringe in her pocket?"

"As I told you, security has been tightened considerably since then."

"But surely she'd have to have help on the inside."

The subject was evidently raw in the warden's mind. She shifted in her seat and when her response came out, it was stilted, sounding practiced. "The drug found in her possession was heroin. In fact, we believe Lois did bring in it with her. Who knows how she got the syringes in through the security checks, but evidently she found a way. She was trusted, knew every angle in the security processes, knew the admissions personnel. Someone on my watch got lax. Doesn't matter whether it was my sister or the Queen of England. The situation resulted in someone walking in with drugs on their person. It shouldn't have happened. And believe me, it won't happen again." In the following silence, she turned her attention to closing a couple of files on her desk and stacking them neatly to one side, before meeting Elizabeth's gaze again.

"You don't believe your own sister would do that. You must know her better than that to have even had her working here."

Jennifer Glassy's expression hardened. She folded her hands in her lap and cocked her head.

"I have a job to do here, Mrs. McClaine. People seem to think that because we're contracted by the state, this is just another bureaucratic money pit." She leaned forward, jabbing her index finger on the desk as she spoke. "Well, guess what: this is no different than any other job—I have budgets to meet, company performance objectives to achieve, KPIs coming out of my ass, and after two savage staffing cuts, I'm supposed to keep an under-resourced workforce safe and content doing a goddamn tough job on a pay scale that's frankly insulting." She sat back, spitting out the words now.

"Our investors don't care what happens inside these walls. They don't care about the Stacy May Charmses or the Nyla Guthries of this world. They couldn't give a damn about the welfare of my staff or the inmates. That's my brief. That's my job. All they care about is the return on their investment—the bottom line."

Seemingly surprised by her own sudden outburst, the warden turned to the files again, shifting them as though their presence offended her. Having regained her icy calm once more, she lifted her head high, her lips a tight line.

"Is there anything else you need to know, Mrs. McClaine?" She made a point of checking her watch, then said, "I have a tight schedule and I'm supposed to be meeting my husband for dinner. He's practically forgotten what I look like and I'd like to be there on time in case he winds up wining and dining a total stranger."

Elizabeth rose from the chair. "Then I guess that's all for now. But you haven't heard the end of this."

CHAPTER THIRTY-FIVE
DAY TWO: 8:07 PM—STACY

The sun was long gone. Between the overhead rooftops, the moon had risen, threading long fingers of shadow between buildings, turning alleyways into black tunnels, its blue-white reflection mirrored over and over on glass like a kaleidoscope. The building she'd visited earlier looked different at night—somehow colder, harsher, the edges sharper. An array of floodlights on either side of the front doors shone out across the wide entranceway, like a warning, like a lighthouse saying, "Don't come any closer."

Keeping one eye on the street, Stacy walked briskly up to the front door and peered in. In the center of the lobby, she could see the desk where the concierge had sat, empty benches left and right between the potted plants, all quietly washed in the subdued nightlight. She crossed to the far left of the windows and cupped her hands to the glass, squinting in at the board with all the company names tiled over it. *Floor 29: Farrant Beta Holdings.* Maybe she'd heard of it. Maybe she was imagining it and mixing it up with something else.

She went back to the wide double doors, tried them. Locked. To the right was a single door that exited out to the east side of the building, probably for employees to leave after hours. She went over and tried it—also locked.

What now?

She walked as far as she could down the side of the building, then back. No way in down there. Inside, a strip of light widened across the rear of the lobby as an elevator opened. The doors stood open for a few seconds, then closed behind a dark figure in a suit and carrying a briefcase. He strode across the lobby, momentarily pausing to search his pockets, presumably for his phone, because his eyes were fixed on it all the way to the single exit door.

Stacy swung around with her back to the wall and waited. The door sucked open, swinging right around in a full arc, almost smacking her in the face, then began hissing closed while the guy walked off down the street. She let it swing halfway back, then grabbed the handle, pivoted inside and dropped into a crouch as it clunked shut again.

Silence all around.

No canned music. No background hum of air conditioning. The place radiated icy emptiness. A quick peek confirmed the guy had gone, so she straightened and tiptoed quickly across the lobby to the elevators and pressed the up button. Almost immediately, the car behind her opened with a waft of aftershave. She stepped inside, hit the button marked 29, and turned to face the doors.

The car rose, speeding up until it reached 28, then slowed to a stop on 29. The doors opened onto a dimly lit marbled lobby with a sign on the wall that read: FARRANT BETA HOLDINGS.

Behind a set of double glass doors, she could see a shiny chrome and black reception desk, three hallways leading off in different directions behind. She got out and tried the doors. The left one opened. She slipped inside, wondering what she was going to do next— her plan hadn't involved getting this far.

A door at the very end of the left hallway swung open and a wedge of light expanded into the hallway as a man exited with a bunch of papers in his hand, heading for the front desk. He looked up, straight at her, and froze.

She backed up a couple of paces. "Sorry, I think I got the wrong place."

"Stacy? Stacy May Charms?" He inched closer, head angled and peering at her as if in disbelief.

Her mouth dropped open.

"What are you doing here?" he asked softly. "Elizabeth's been looking everywhere for you."

Adrenaline flashed through her veins. Flight or fight. Which was it going to be?

He inched closer, one hand up. "It's okay. You can trust me. My name is Clay Farrant. I'm a friend of Elizabeth McClaine's. She told me everything that's happened. She's worried sick about you."

The tension in her shoulders eased. She glanced back at the front door. "Where is she?"

"I don't know. Last time I talked to her, she was asking about some little manufacturing company way out in the boonies."

"Millcreek," she supplied.

His brow crinkled. "That's the one. You know it?" As if suddenly remembering his manners, he said, "Listen, you must be starved. I don't have much here, but can I get you a drink? A snack maybe?"

In her experience, people who said "Trust me" were the last ones to trust. Her gut said, *Run.* Her stomach said, *Stay long enough to get fed.*

She nodded once. "Okay, thanks."

"Come, this way." He gestured toward the door he'd exited from. "We'll talk in my office. Security checks in here every half hour. Plus they've got cameras." He pointed.

Behind her were two small cameras mounted on the ceiling, swiveling from the elevator to the entrance, the red in the lens showing like an eye. Another two the same, just inside reception.

He showed her the flat of his hand—a stop sign. "Don't worry. It's okay. They'll call up, but—"

A buzz from the telephone console on the reception desk cut him off.

With an *I-told-you-so* shrug, he leaned across and hit a button on the console as he lifted the receiver. "No, it's fine. I forgot to call down to say I was expecting someone. Sure, thanks." And he hung up.

"See? Nothing to worry about," he told her. "Come in and I'll get you a drink. Maybe something to eat."

He walked back to the doorway and waved her over, smiling. "C'mon, I don't bite."

Behind her, the elevator door had closed, the light on the panel illuminating the number 7. She followed him slowly, keeping a distance between them.

"What do you do here?"

"We import and distribute fabric." He gestured to a row of graphics in frames along the hallway as he passed them, then disappeared into his office, calling back, "We have a number of subsidiary companies that we supply, like Tammy Frank and Rue Xeeba."

The name snapped into her memory. The fashion label.

"Come on in. Don't be shy."

He was across to a bar when she entered. It was fully stocked with bottles and liqueurs and glasses, a refrigerator at the center. About the size of the last house Stacy lived in, Clay Farrant's office was situated on a southwest corner of the building, two walls consisting of floor-to-ceiling glass that looked out over the city. She'd never seen anything like it. Out there she could see lights blinking forever, cars zipping along the streets like toys. An expansive black desk stretched across one corner of the room, plaques and awards displayed on shelves behind it. On one corner of the desk was a newspaper open to the business section. A picture midway down. Clay Farrant with the governor. The caption read: *Clay Farrant Ohio Businessman of the Year.*

Clay turned from the refrigerator with a bottle of juice and a pack of cookies. He placed them on the desk, rounded the end of it, and sat.

"Take a seat. Tell me what's going on."

She lowered herself into the seat opposite him, took a tentative sip of the drink.

"Go on, eat."

She opened the pack of cookies, took a bite. She hadn't realized just how hungry she was. "Millcreek is what's going on."

He leaned forward on his elbows, sharp eyes watching her. "Elizabeth said she went there. She thinks someone's smuggling drugs from there."

She spoke through a mouthful of cookie crumbs. "Yeah? What else did she tell you?"

He frowned while he collected his thoughts. "Ah, that someone murdered a girl named Amy? Is that right?"

She paused with the cookie halfway back to her mouth. "Yeah." She took a bite, watching him.

"And that someone threatened your son. That's unbelievable. Listen, I'm going to call Elizabeth, tell her you're with me. Okay?"

She hesitated while she considered it. Couldn't see a reason not to. "Sure," she said, and lifted the drink to her lips.

He punched in a number, hit a button and the *burr, burr* of the phone ringing burst from the speaker. It rang several times then went to Elizabeth's voice mail, her voice inviting them to leave a message.

His shoulders sank as he hung up. "Damn. Not answering. I know, let me try her other line." Again, he punched in a number, this time lifting the phone to his ear. He waited a moment, then lifted his eyes on Stacy. "Hey, Elizabeth, thank God I caught you. I have Stacy May right here with me. Yeah, I know, it's incredible. She walked right into my office. Listen, remember what we talked about?" He gave Stacy a flick of the eyebrows—a sign of reassurance, that everything was in control. "I suggest we meet up, figure out what to do next. At Millcreek? Sure. We'll be there in…" He checked his watch. "A half hour or so." And he hung up.

"You're right. Whatever is going on has something to do with Millcreek." He got up, drew his jacket from the back of the chair and shrugged into it, saying, "She wants us to meet her there."

Stacy sat frozen in the chair and looked up at him. "So you know where it is?"

"Sure—," he began, then cut himself off. "She just told me."

She eyed him for a few seconds, then got to her feet and stuffed the remaining cookies into her pocket.

"I better go. I have somewhere I gotta be."

He rounded the desk and paused in the doorway. "But I just told Elizabeth we were on our way. She's expecting us."

Their eyes met, and her gut tightened. "Then she'll have to be disappointed. Excuse me."

When he didn't move, she squeezed past him, both of them in the doorway. Feeling the heat of his body against her, she pushed past him and went for the front door. It was locked. She shook the handles.

Behind her, he said, "You know, I can't just let you go. You wouldn't get far anyway. I doubt you'd make the lobby."

This time, she froze; then turned slowly, only now noticing the swirl in her brain and blurring of her vision.

"I'm afraid you're going to take a short nap," he said.

"This is bullshit," she slurred, as the room spun out from under her.

CHAPTER THIRTY-SIX
DAY TWO: 8:42 PM—ELIZABETH

Nighttime had dropped the temperature to a chilly forty-two degrees by the time Elizabeth exited the front doors of Carringway. Buttoning the front of her jacket for warmth, she walked quickly back to the parking lot, where her car sat in a hazy pool of yellow light cast by the overhead security lights. Two beeps from her phone indicated she had a message. Opting to get out of the cold first, she opened the driver's door and slipped in behind the wheel where she hit the ignition and switched the heating on, rubbing her hands together to get warm before digging her phone from her purse.

Two calls from Penny, one call from a number she didn't recognize. Only one message. She was just about to hit the message button, when the phone rang in her hand. Recognizing the number as the second call she'd missed, she hit send and cautiously answered with a flat "Elizabeth McClaine."

Nancy didn't even bother with the formalities. She jumped straight into a garbled stream of words that Elizabeth couldn't make sense of. "It's gone! The car's gone. It went off the radar and I've got no idea where it went."

"Hold on just a second," Elizabeth told her, gesturing her to stop, despite the fact that she couldn't see her. "Slow down and tell me what happened."

"Nothing happened. I went online to check on it and it's gone—vanished off the screen. I clicked all kinds of buttons and tabs and shit, but nothing happened. It's still gone."

"Let me get this right—are you saying the car's gone? Or just the signal?"

Frustration raised her voice to a shout. "How would I know? All I know is it's gone."

"Calm down, Nancy. Where was the signal last time you checked?"

"Same place—Millcreek. Then it just disappeared. I don't know if the car's gone, or if someone turned it off, or if Trish is driving the car, or what."

"And the system doesn't tell you?"

"Who knows? I tried every goddamn button on that website but I can't find a thing. I'm going out there."

"No, wait—"

"What for? This is my wife we're talking about. She's been gone twenty-four hours, not a damn word, and now her car's disappeared. I should have done something sooner. I should have listened to my gut. Now she could be in real trouble. I'm not waiting another minute."

"Nancy, slow down. Call the police. Tell them what's happened and report her missing."

"Do you know how long that'll take? The hell with that. I'm going out there now."

Floundering for a better plan and failing to come up with one, Elizabeth said, "Okay, then I'll meet you out there. And stay in your car until I get there, okay?"

When all that echoed back down the line was an electrically charged silence, Elizabeth said, "Nancy. Do not get out of that car until you see me. You hear?"

"Yeah. I hear you," she said and hung up.

The GPS still held the location of Millcreek. She tapped the screen, setting the location, and changing the route so she didn't wind up at the same collapsed bridge. Then she put the car in gear and headed for the exit, phone in hand while she dialed Delaney's number. The line opened, rang several times, then went to voice mail.

"Lance, where the hell are you? Call me. Now!" she said, then hung up and tossed it onto the passenger's seat.

Millcreek was a half hour away. For the first ten minutes she spent the time running various scenarios through her head, backtracking, and starting all over. By the time she got back to the interstate, her brain felt like it was swimming around in ever-decreasing circles in an ever-deepening pool, so she tapped the next CD lined up in the player and wound up the volume, letting Taylor Swift lighten the mood with *Shake It Off* until the GPS guided her back down the narrow lane, past the Dumpsters, and into the parking lot of Millcreek Fashions.

Elizabeth pulled to a stop at the front gates, cut the music, and looked the place over.

Total silence all around.

The building stood at the end of the lane like an abandoned fortress, the angles of the roof and the concrete apron around the loading dock picked out in the watery moonlight against a backdrop of black on gray countryside.

No sign of Nancy. Or anyone else. The place exuded emptiness, the windows creating black voids like eyes in the walls.

Feeling the first twinge of uncertainty tighten in the pit of her stomach, she hit the gas and drove past the front of the entrance, wondering what on earth she'd been thinking driving all the way out here before speaking to Delaney. It wasn't until she swung the car around and pulled into the lot to park beside the only other car there that she let out a long breath, more relieved to see Nancy's car than she'd have guessed.

Despite her warnings, Nancy wasn't in her car. Elizabeth cut the engine and sat for some moments, listening—nothing out there but the breeze in the dried grass and the occasional whoop of a distant bird. The entire place was in darkness.

She was just reaching for her phone when a knuckle rapped on the window next to her. Elizabeth let out a yelp and clutched her hand to her chest.

Nancy appeared at the window with a flashlight under her chin like something out of a horror movie. "It's me, Nancy," she called through the glass. "I'm sorry, I didn't mean to scare you."

Elizabeth undid her seatbelt and opened her door with her heart hammering against her chest. "I told you to stay in your car. Why aren't you in your car?"

Oblivious to her annoyance, Nancy turned and drew the beam in a wide arc across the front of the building and into the surrounding bushes. "She's not here. Car's gone. I looked all around, but nothing. Not even a tire track. What did you find out?"

The night air was even colder out here. With the chill biting right through to her skin, Elizabeth tugged her collar up and crossed her jacket lapels in front of her. Now she was wishing she'd worn something warmer than a skirt and jacket.

"I found out that to get anything illegal into Carringway, you'd need Criss Angel and a prison riot." When Nancy gave her a look, she added, "Apart from tossing a package over the fence and hoping it hit the spot marked X, I can't see how you'd get a mouse in there. There's security on their security." She huffed out a breath that clouded in front of her. "That's if you believe everything Jennifer Glassy says."

"Told you."

Elizabeth gave her a scathing look, then said, "So where did you look?"

Nancy turned to regard the building again, directing the beam of the flashlight like a pointer as she spoke. "All around the back there, down the west side, tried the front door. Place is shut up tighter than a fish's ass. There's a door out back by the loading dock. With a bit of luck, I think we could get in through there." She strode off.

Horrified, Elizabeth shouted, "Wait! You can't just walk in there. It's private property." When Nancy ignored her, she slammed her car door and went after her, talking to her back like an angry child following her mother through a shopping mall. "I thought you said the place was locked up. Did they leave one door unlocked?"

"Nope."

Striding briskly to keep up with her, and glancing back over her shoulder in case of unexpected company, Elizabeth followed Nancy around to the rear of the building, where the thin circle of light from Nancy's Maglite picked out a short stairway leading to a single wooden door, a glass panel in the upper half.

Both women stood at the foot of the stairs, looking up.

Elizabeth spoke first. "So how are you going to get in? Bust the door down?"

Nancy fished in her pocket and produced what looked like a collection of dental tools attached to a ring, which she held up and jingled. "No need for any damage. I got these. Here, hold this."

She handed Elizabeth the flashlight, then mounted the stairs and ran her finger over the lock, studying the keyhole before selecting the right pick. Then she got to work.

Elizabeth followed her up the stairs, angling the light down over Nancy's shoulder while she worked. When something out in the surrounding darkness let out a howl, she whipped around, sweeping the light left and right, eyes wide and her heart thumping. All she could see were the gnarled and naked outlines of the boxelder and oak trees creating a twisted tangle of shadows in the distance.

"Will you shine that thing over here?" Nancy snapped. "This is tough enough without doing it in the dark."

Elizabeth stepped in a little closer, hugging herself while she angled the beam down to where Nancy had her face two inches from the lock, her ear angled to the keyhole like she was breaking into a bank vault, while her fingers gently twisted the pick this way and that in the lock.

It was taking longer than Elizabeth would have expected. "Where did you learn to do this stuff? Crime school?"

It netted her a sharp look. "What? Not going fast enough for you? Do you want to try?"

A deluge of caustic responses flooded Elizabeth's mind, but she stuck with, "I'm curious, that's all."

Nancy paused long enough to pass her a doubtful look, then continued on. "Hon, you been around criminals long as I have, you learn stuff."

Elizabeth gave the darkened landscape another scan. "But isn't this breaking and entering? What if somebody comes? What if they have security guards stopping by at regular intervals?"

The lock clicked and Nancy straightened to pocket the lock picks. "Then we can ask them where Trish is." She snatched the flashlight back, twisted the handle, and shouldered the door open to peer in.

"You don't have a gun?" Elizabeth hissed at her back. "Why don't you have a gun?"

Nancy cut her an accusing look. "Nice spotting, Mrs. McClaine. And correct, right now, I don't have a gun. I was required to surrender it, thanks to you and Detective Pain-in-the-Ass Delaney. Now, are you coming or not?" she said, and disappeared inside.

Elizabeth hesitated. The choices weren't what she'd have wished for: unlawfully entering the premises Nancy had just broken into or staying outside in the cold and dark with whatever was howling out there in the woods. When a second howl wailed from the darkness, she flinched, then hurried inside after Nancy.

"This is definitely breaking and entering," she told Nancy in a harsh whisper. "We could go to prison for this. We could end up spending the next couple of years alongside whoever it was that taught you how to break into places. *And* Stacy May," she added, and felt sick.

Ignoring her, Nancy directed the light up to the ceiling, then all across to a wire-embedded window that looked out across the darkened loading dock. A desk sat against the west wall of the room, topped with an old computer, a stack of battered-looking files, and an old phone. It looked like the shipping office of a company straight out of the eighties.

Nancy picked up the phone, listened, then put it down again. "These here are what you call *exigent circumstances*. I have probable cause to believe that Trish is somewhere on these premises, and in serious danger. You get in my way, she won't be the only one," she added, and pushed past her to exit into the next room.

In here, Nancy ran her hand up and down the wall, then flipped on a switch. The single bulb hanging in the center of an empty break room illuminated the area with a pale, white light. The place smelled of garbage and refried beans.

Nancy wrinkled her nose and sniffed. "Smells like a Mexican restaurant in here."

Elizabeth's upper lip twitched at the dirt-encrusted surfaces. "I'm surprised they have electricity. Do they ever clean the place?"

"They've probably got a generator housed somewhere close by." Clipping the flashlight to her belt, Nancy headed for the only other door leading from the room. "This way," she said as she pushed the door open and strode off into the darkness.

Elizabeth followed, figuring she had few other choices. "We shouldn't be doing this," she hissed at Nancy's back. Even at a whisper her voice echoed off the grimy walls in the gloom. They walked past deserted offices devoid of furniture or fittings, graffiti across every surface in thick black lines spelling out illegible words that had been struck through in red, only to be overwritten with some other illegible message.

"How can this be a legitimate business? Look at the place. How could they have gotten clearance to supply the prison?"

Nancy said nothing, just kept walking, opening doors, flipping on switches, searching into empty rooms before moving on to the next.

Elizabeth followed close behind, almost running into her every time she stopped, then starting after her again. "You'd think someone would know something. I thought at least one of the women I spoke to at Carringway might have some clue. But nothing."

Nancy angled her head back to speak. "Who'd you talk to?"

"Cissy Pettameyer."

A snort and a shake of Nancy's head told Elizabeth she didn't have to say more.

"Then I spoke to Eileen Caston. She used to go by the name of Eileen Grant. A respected financial columnist—stuck in prison for…" Elizabeth cut herself off, realizing that she'd been on the verge of breaching someone else's privacy. "…well, crimes."

"Whoa! Imprisoned for crimes, huh? Who'd'a thought?"

Elizabeth could have done without the comments. "And as for Nyla Guthrie—she gave me the creeps."

Nancy stopped to regard Elizabeth. "Trish told me that woman was way smarter than anyone gave her credit for. What'd she have to say?"

"*Pfft*. Nothing I'd consider smart." A wave of anger swelled at the cruelty of Nyla's words. But the feeling that something had snagged in the back of her mind surfaced again. Nancy had walked on. "No, wait a second," she said, speaking to herself rather than to Nancy. *"Amy got what she had coming.'* No, that wasn't it."

Nancy had walked on. When she realized Elizabeth was no longer following, she stopped. "What are you doing?"

"That's not what she said."

"Who?"

"Nyla. I thought she'd gotten the wording wrong—but what if she didn't? What if she was trying to tell me something?"

"Why? What did she say?"

Squeezing her eyes closed for a second, Elizabeth ran the scene through her mind once more. Again, she could see Nyla Guthrie sitting across from her, her face creased into that ugly smirk.

"I kept thinking she said, 'Amy got what she had coming to her.' And I remember thinking she didn't get that right. But what she actually said was, '*Amy's got* what she had coming.'" She lifted her eyes to meet Nancy's. "What if it's a message?"

A shrug. "Saying what? That could mean anything. Could just mean Amy got what she had coming. Trish said Amy was a total train wreck. She'd have sold her own grandmother for one whiff of coke. Maybe she was saying her death wasn't exactly a big shock to anyone." And she walked on down the hallway

"Maybe." Elizabeth wasn't convinced. She walked on behind Nancy. "According to Warden Glassy, Stacy was furious about Amy's death. She insisted Amy had gotten clean. And Stacy wasn't stupid. Surely she would have known if she was stoned or not. And besides, if Nyla Guthrie was half as smart as Trish says, how could she get a simple expression like that wrong?"

"So?"

"So what if she meant that Amy was supposed to get something, and now she's got it."

"Same difference, isn't it? She's dead." Nancy continued on down the hallway, opening doors, flicking on lights and peering in. "Trish!" she yelled at the top of her voice. The sound reverberated down the corridors.

"Shhhh!"

"What? You worried about the neighbors hearing?" Nancy snorted and pressed on.

Irritated by Nancy's flippancy, Elizabeth rolled her eyes and followed after her, still talking at her back. "No. What I mean is: what if she was due to get something, what if it was something that was put into her personal effects?"

Nancy was leaning in through a doorway, hands rested either side of the frame. She cut a smirk back over her shoulder at Elizabeth. "Like what? Drugs? You think the releasing officers are gonna come across a bunch of drugs and go, 'Oh, hey, this must have been Amy's personal stash. Let's send it to her folks?' I don't think so." And she walked on.

Elizabeth cast a sour look after her, but Nancy was right. The prison staff would check anything they sent home to the grieving family.

It seemed like every time she got hold of a thread of information, it came to an abrupt end. "Okay, so what about money? What if Amy had money and that was what Nyla was talking about? What if she had a stack of cash due to her—or … I don't know." She raised both hands and dropped them in frustration.

Another snort from Nancy. "Yeah, all that money would be really worth waiting for. Those women earn a whole twenty-five cents an hour. A king's ransom," she said, and chuckled. "Her folks are probably out looking at Trump Towers investment opportunities on the strength of it."

"Seriously? You're giving me sarcasm?"

"Listen, even if Amy was rolling in dough—which I seriously doubt—she wouldn't have gotten paid out straight away. Takes weeks to work through all the bureaucratic bullshit that's involved, if you'll excuse my French." She cast her eyes to a point above Elizabeth's head and made a face, one side of her mouth hooked up in thought. "Only things they send back to the next of kin are their personal effects that they had in prison, and anything they came in with. That's it. Anything weird would have been taken out." And she moved on again. "You're barking up the wrong tree."

"Okay, so maybe I'm reaching, investigating all the angles and coming up a little short. But something was going on in that prison. There's no doubt in my mind."

"Sounds like some of those angles you're checking out are a little obtuse, if you ask me." Nancy stopped in her tracks and spun around, eyes searching the hallway behind Elizabeth.

Elizabeth also spun around and looked back. "What? What is it?"

Pushing past her with her hand up like a stop sign, Nancy angled her head, listening. "Shh. I thought I heard a car."

"What? Oh, *shit*! I knew we were going to get caught. I *knew* it!" She could just see the look on her father-in-law's face, on Walt Straussman's face. On *Penny's* face. "Oh, God, please don't let it be a car," she groaned in a tiny voice. "Please don't let it be Penny."

Nancy strode off in the direction they'd just come from. "This way."

"What? Where are you going?"

"To see who it is."

"No, wait!" Elizabeth hurried after her. Just as Nancy went to turn the last corner heading back to the shipping office again, Elizabeth reached out and grabbed the back of her shirt, halting her in her tracks.

Nancy turned with a look that made Elizabeth snap her hand back and fold her arms protectively across her chest. "Listen, let's think this through. If someone's out there, why are we running out to meet them?"

"Because it could be Trish," she said.

She leaned around Nancy to peer down the darkened hallway in one direction, then the other. "And what if it's a security guard? Or … or what if it's that woman coming back to check on the place?"

Nancy jabbed a finger towards the office door. "And what if it is Trish? I left a message for her on the counter at home, and on the message on the phone saying I was coming out here. What if she's driven all the way out here looking for me?" Without waiting for a reply, she marched off again.

"Dammit!" Elizabeth spat out, then hurried after her, following along like a scolded puppy. "I'll call Delaney. I'll ask him to come out here, take a look around. I mean, that's his job, right? We'll go back to our cars, call him up—"

"And say what?" Nancy stopped, hands on her hips. "'Ah, listen, Detective, we just broke into this here building, and there's no one here. But I think I heard a car, so would you mind driving way out into the boonies and checking it out for us?'"

Elizabeth stiffened. "You *said* we weren't breaking and entering. You *said* this would be considered exigent circumstances."

Nancy shrugged and walked on. "I say a lot of shit. Doesn't mean you had to go along with it. But I also said I need to find Trish. I want to know what the hell is going on just as much as you do. I want to know where her car is, I want to know where she got all that money, and why she hasn't come home. Now are you helping me or not?"

Elizabeth felt the words hit her like a slap in the face. She hurried after her. "All *what* money? You told me she'd saved up for that car."

Nancy turned down the next hallway, striding out and speaking over her shoulder. "All the money she's been spending lately. She thinks I'm stupid. Thinks I don't know. But I see her credit card bills. I see the payments going out."

Elizabeth grabbed her by the shoulder and jerked her around. "Why didn't you tell me this?"

Nancy's eyes narrowed on her. "Because you would have thought she was guilty of something, of smuggling drugs or whatever. You'd have had her wrapping up stashes of heroin and smuggling it into that prison for a bunch of poor-as-shit prisoners who'd roll on her quick as look at her. And she's not stupid. She wouldn't do any of that." Then she walked on, shaking her head angrily and muttering.

For a moment, Elizabeth stood there blinking at the woman in sheer astonishment. Then she hurried after her again. "So why didn't you ask her where the money came from? What the hell is wrong with you?"

Before she could answer, two cracks like distant gunshot cut the air. Elizabeth gasped, both hands clapped to her chest. Then felt foolish when Nancy dredged her phone out of her pocket, saying, "Dammit, I thought

I set that on vibrate. Cool message alert, though, huh?" She checked the screen and her eyes flashed wide. "*Shit!* It's Trish."

"Trish?" Elizabeth leaned over Nancy's shoulder so she could see the wording on the screen. "What did she say?"

Nancy rocked her head back, pressed the phone to her bosom, and heaved out an enormous breath. "Oh, thank God. She says, 'I'm home, I'm hungry and I'm … well, she's home."

Elizabeth didn't need the rest. The shake of Nancy's head was enough. She watched as she began tapping out a reply.

"Goddamn, that's a relief."

"How do you know it's her?"

"It's her usual message. It's what she always texts." She hit the send key, pausing while the message went out. When the phone bleeped, indicating the message was sent, she stuck the phone in her pants pocket again and rubbed her hands together. "Right, we're outta here."

"What about the car you heard? You're just going to walk out there?"

"It was probably just the wind."

Elizabeth stood aghast, staring after her. "And that's it? You don't care that there's something illegal going on in this place? That Trish could be involved?"

Still walking back to the door, Nancy said, "Frankly, Mrs. McClaine, I couldn't give a fat rat's ass about this place. Not my job. All I know is that Trish is home, and that's all I wanted. I'll see you around."

And she left Elizabeth standing there, glaring tight-lipped after her.

CHAPTER THIRTY-SEVEN
DAY TWO: 9:31 PM—ELIZABETH

At Elizabeth's insistence, Nancy had conducted a quick search across the docking bay, then the parking lot. After reporting back that there was no sign of a car, and insisting it had probably been the wind she'd heard, she'd gotten in her car, swung it in a wide arc across the concrete apron out front of Millcreek, then headed for the exit.

Elizabeth stood hugging herself and watching the taillights recede down the lane and disappear. Then realized Nancy had just driven off with the only flashlight.

"Dammit." She turned to survey the building once more. Whereas it had looked like the Black Hole of Calcutta when they'd first arrived, now it was lit up like Times Square, the lights they'd turned on blazing at almost every window.

"Oh … *crap!*" Fists balled at her sides, and muttering curses against the woman for leaving her to lock the place up, she headed back around to the rear of the building and up the stairs.

Without Nancy there, the atmosphere inside the building had taken on an eerie calm. Far above, the tin roofing creaked, and the walls seemed even icier than they were ten minutes ago. For a second, Elizabeth thought she heard a scratching sound, like something small scrabbling through the walls.

Pulling the sides of her jacket close in across her chest and folding her arms against the chill, she trod quietly down the hallway, intending to switch each light off as she made her way back. But just as she reached to flip off the last one down the hallway, she noticed a closed door a pristine sign affixed to the upper half.

WORKROOM: AUTHORIZED PERSONNEL ONLY

Elizabeth checked behind her, then the door. Her stomach clenched and the hairs on the back of her neck stood up. In the deathly quiet, she tiptoed down to the doorway and leaned her ear to the upper panel.

Nothing. Not a squeak.

She put her fingers on the handle. It turned.

Her heart leaped into her throat and a shot of adrenaline hit her system.

With her lip caught between her teeth, she put her fingertips to the door and gently pushed. It creaked open.

The space inside was bathed in that same oily darkness. Running her fingers down beside the door frame, she located two switches. When she flipped them on, six neon tubes set in three pairs across the ceiling flickered with a plinking sound, then flooded the room with an icy white light.

Elizabeth stood in the doorway with her hand pressed to her heart, scanning the room.

"Hello?"

A chilled emptiness echoed back.

She stepped across the threshold and gave the place a long look. Four large square worktables stood pushed up against each other to form one large square in the center of the room. Each side of the work surface held two sewing machines threaded with an industrial size spool of black thread and along each side of the tables, a steel measure had been attached. At the far end of the room, rolls of fabric were stacked on end.

She moved quietly inside and ran her fingers along the nearest tabletop. Clean. Not a speck of dust. Behind her the wall was stacked two deep, and almost to the ceiling with bulging cardboard boxes, each with the address crossed out and numbered in thick black crayon. Elizabeth walked to the end of the table and scanned the area from this side. Just under the table next to her, she spotted a plastic trash can. She pulled it out and ran her hand through the layers of tiny black labels inside, each embroidered with a Millcreek Fashions logo.

She plucked one out and studied it. A couple of short cotton threads were attached at each end of the label, as though it had been cut from the garment. She dropped it back and spotted a carton pushed under the table; same black crayon marks across the side. She dragged it out to find the upper flaps hadn't been sealed, just tucked down. Inside was a jumble of garments made from a soft beige silk. She drew the top one out and shook it out: a blouse, scooped neckline, darts at the waist, label on the neckline that read *Millcreek Fashions*.

The fabric felt soft, sensuous. If it wasn't real silk, it was as good as anything she'd seen.

Across the room, twenty or so rolls of the same fabric stood on end, lined up against the wall. She crossed to lift the unfurled end of an outer roll between her fingers. Same softness, same quality. She put it to her nose and took a cautious sniff, then realized that if the fabric had had drugs of any kind embedded in it, she had no idea what it would smell like.

When the ring of her phone cut the silence, she jumped and let out a squeak.

"Shit!"

She dredged it from her jacket pocket and checked the screen.

"Oh, great timing," she said, and answered. "Clay. What a surprise."

"Elizabeth. I'm sorry, I know it's late."

"No, it's fine." In the background she could hear the thrum of an engine. "Are you driving?"

"Just left my office. Tough meeting. I got to wondering what you're doing."

She glanced around the room. "Ah, nothing much."

"How about I pick you up and take you to that restaurant I was telling you about? You can tell me how a beautiful woman ends up spending Saturday night doing 'nothing much.'"

She picked up the tag and ran her thumb across the embroidered lettering—gold stitching on black, the threads dangling from each end. "Answer me something first."

"Shoot."

"Why would someone order garments, then cut the labels off?"

He considered it for a second. "Maybe they put the wrong label on. Or if they were selling those garments under a different brand, perhaps. I don't know, why?"

"Did you find out anything about Millcreek Fashions?"

A pause, then he said, "I didn't know I was supposed to be looking. What's going on, Elizabeth?"

She crossed to the unfurled roll of fabric again and picked up the end. "Okay, so do you have any idea how you'd embed fabric with drugs? Like heroin, maybe? And how you'd get it out again?"

"How would I know something like that?" Suddenly his tone was serious. "You're not out at Millcreek again, are you?"

She wanted to lie. Experience had taught her she was a hopeless liar. "I just dropped by to see if anyone knew where Trish was."

His tone became stern. "Elizabeth, get out of there right now. If those guys come back and find you there, you could be in real danger."

She felt like a kid being scolded by her father. "I'm leaving now."

"Wait a second."

She waited. For the longest moment, all she could hear was the sound of his breath.

"Okay, I've got it on the GPS. I'm coming over there."

Fine, but how was she to explain how she got in here? She touched her fingers to her forehead, eyes squeezed closed, annoyed now. "You don't have to do that, Clay. There's no one here and I'm leaving right now."

"Go back to your car and wait there. If anyone comes before I get there, just hit the gas and drive. Do you hear me? But unless that happens, don't leave until I get there."

Almost exactly what she'd told Nancy to do.

"No, seriously, I'll leave right now."

"I'm ten minutes away on the state highway," he said. "I'll see you soon."

And he hung up.

Elizabeth rolled her head right back and stared up at the night sky.

"Dammit!"

CHAPTER THIRTY-EIGHT
DAY TWO: 10:03 PM—ELIZABETH

For what turned out to be closer to fifteen minutes, Elizabeth sat in her car wishing she'd insisted on meeting Clay back in the city. Why she couldn't just drive off was anybody's guess. She had just made up her mind to leave and then call him back once she was on her way, when headlights appeared at the end of the lane. They swept across the darkened building and stopped on her car.

She waited until she heard the car door slam, then got out, holding her hand up to shield her eyes from the brilliance of the light.

"Clay?"

"It's me." He left his car door open and rushed to her. "Are you okay?"

The temperature had plummeted. Only now did she realize how cold she was.

She rubbed her upper arms. "Just a little cold."

"You look freezing. Here, take this." He shrugged out of his jacket and drew it around her shoulders.

"Thank you." Feeling the intensity of his eyes on her, she stepped back and looked away.

He raised both hands. "I'm sorry. I didn't mean to—"

"No, it's fine, I'm just..." Now she felt foolish.

Recognizing the awkwardness of the moment, he smiled and dropped his hands to his hips, then looked back at the darkened building. "So what are you doing out here?"

She pulled his jacket in around her, glad of the warmth. "It's a long story."

He tipped his head toward to the late model black BMW he'd driven up in. "Let's go back to my car. It'll be warmer."

She walked to the car, feeling his hand on the small of her back, guiding her. She waited while he opened the passenger door, then she slipped inside hunching her shoulders against the cold while he closed it. The seats were warm, pale gray to match the exterior; an extravagant-looking console between the seats; custom-made steering wheel. The scent of warm leather and aftershave wrapped around her. He circled the front of the car, cutting through the glare of the headlights, then got in and closed the door. The leather creaked as he twisted in his seat, elbow resting on the seat back, the knuckle of his forefinger at his lips while he regarded her.

"So what do you think is going on? You think Stacy's been out here?"

She lifted her hands, dropped them. "No. It's a long story, but we tracked a car out here, a prison officer's—Patricia Tomes. Now, the car's gone. I have no idea where. Maybe Trish took the car and went home. Maybe we're worried for nothing."

"But you don't think so." He hit a button and the heating kicked in, warm and comforting on her stockinged legs.

She looked back at the building. "I know this might sound stupid, but I think whoever runs this place is smuggling drugs into Carringway Prison in the garment labels."

His eyebrows shot up. "Seriously? Why? What makes you think that?"

"There's a whole stack of boxes full of garments in there with the labels cut out. Why would they do that? I mean, how much heroin could you get in the label?"

He shrugged. "Not much. Do you know who's behind it?"

"Someone inside Carringway—someone with enough money, and in the right position to get the drugs in there. It has to be. It's all I can think of."

He reached out a hand and touched her gently on the arm. "But why is this your problem? Why don't you leave it to the prison warden? Or the police? Did you tell them?"

Good question. She'd found herself asking the very same thing so many times now it had practically become a mantra. But didn't Eileen Grant tell her to trust her gut? Wasn't that what she was doing?

"If I don't find out what's going on, Stacy May Charms will finish up spending a big chunk of her life behind bars, and a little boy will be without his mother when he needs her most. And it's all just because of someone else's greed. One girl has already lost her life over this. I can't let it go."

Another silence. He stroked the sides of his mouth while he mulled it over.

"And this other girl—the one that died—you think she knew something?" he asked.

"I'd bet money on it. I'm also beginning to think something was sent to her parents after her death, something incriminating. When they got it, they didn't realize the significance of it."

He twisted a little further around in his seat, frowning, head resting on his knuckles. "What do you think it could have been?"

Elizabeth felt drained. Exhaustion and dehydration were bringing on a headache. She touched her fingertips to her forehead, then dropped her hands back into her lap. "I have no idea."

"Have you spoken to the parents?"

"I don't even know where they live."

A half grin creased one side of his face. He got out his phone. "I'll bet you fifty bucks I can find it."

She watched him tap the screen and wait.

"What was her name? The girl that died?"

"Amy Dixon. Why?"

He tilted the phone in her direction. "Obits. How long ago?"

"Oh, great idea." She leaned a little so she could see the screen. "About four months ago. She was from Cleveland."

He moved around, leaning a little closer to her and angling the phone so she could see it.

"Bingo! Here it is. It says: 'Amy Marie Dixon. Nineteen years, gone too soon. Beautiful only daughter of Ron and Sara. You're always in our hearts.' Does that sound like it?"

The words brought Elizabeth a stab of sadness. She nodded, felt the lump in her throat. Clay was already tapping again. She angled her head again. "What are you doing?"

"Looking for their phone number."

She checked the time. "Now? They'll be asleep, won't they?"

The number was up on the screen, his finger poised over it. "Your call."

She hesitated. If it were her, would she mind being woken by someone who may have found her daughter's killer? "Go ahead."

He hit the button and handed her the phone. It was already ringing. She turned away from him, hugging herself and gazing out into the night while she waited. On the sixth ring, the answering machine picked up, inviting her to leave a message, or to try them on a cell phone number, which was rattled off at the end. She relaxed, let her shoulders drop while she relayed the message to Clay, then hung up.

He tipped his head. "So let's try the cell phone."

"You think?"

He lifted his eyebrows again.

So she tapped the number in and waited. The phone rang five times. She was about to give up when the line opened and a weary voice answered. "Hello?"

"Mrs. Dixon? Sara Dixon?"

A brief hesitation, then a cautious, "Who is this?"

Feeling dreadful now, and wishing she'd left it until morning after all, Elizabeth said, "Mrs. Dixon, this is Elizabeth McClaine. I run a funding trust that's involved with one of the young women in Carringway Prison. I'm so sorry to call this time of night, but it's a matter of some urgency."

She glanced across at Clay, who nodded encouragement.

Sara Dixon's breath rasped down the line. It sounded as though she was repositioning herself in bed. After a moment, she said, "What's this about?"

How to put this gently?

Another look at Clay.

Another reassuring nod.

"It's about Amy, Mrs. Dixon. I'm so sorry for your loss, and I hate doing this to you, but I have reason to believe that she didn't die by her own hand."

The reply was a tight whisper, as if her throat had tightened. "I know she didn't." A brittle silence stretched into a ragged breath. "What have you found?"

"It's only a hunch. I can't promise you anything, but I need to see what the prison sent home after Amy's death. I think there's something among her personal effects that could prove she was…" Elizabeth closed her eyes tightly, as though that might soften the words. "…well, that her death wasn't accidental."

Another hesitation. When Sara Dixon spoke this time, her voice was strained but firm. "The prison sent a package of her things home. I'm sorry, I know this sounds terrible, but I … I haven't even looked in it. I couldn't." The final word hooked in her throat, reducing it to a whisper. Elizabeth felt her own eyes welling.

"I'm so sorry." Elizabeth swallowed hard, then steeled herself for the next question. "Would you mind if I came over tomorrow and took a look at it? I promise you, I would use all care and respect."

"We're not at home. We're staying with my mother in Boston." In the background a man's voice mumbled something. "Can you hold on a second?"

It sounded as though her hand had gone over the phone while a muffled conversation took place in the background. Elizabeth figured it was Ron Dixon. Clay tipped his head into her line of vision, eyebrows up, as if to say, "Well?"

She nodded once and Sara Dixon was back.

"Are you there, Mrs. McClaine?"

She turned away from Clay to gaze out the window and pressed the phone hard to her ear. "I'm here."

"There's a key under a geranium pot on our front porch. If there's something among Amy's things that'll prove she didn't take those drugs, you have my full permission to go into the house and find it."

Elizabeth motioned to Clay and he took a pen and notebook from his jacket pocket. She took down the address, thanked Sara Dixon, and hung up with a promise that anything they found that could be evidence would be taken straight to the police.

"So what now?" asked Clay.

"I'll go there tomorrow."

He waggled his eyebrows, gave her one of his poster-boy grins. "Why wait?" he said and started his car.

CHAPTER THIRTY-NINE
DAY TWO: 10:52 PM—ELIZABETH

Clay had offered to follow Elizabeth back to her house, then take her in his car to the Dixons' house on the waterfront. Elizabeth had declined the offer, telling him that she didn't want to put him to any more trouble than she already had. In fact, she was tired and after that awkward moment back at Millcreek, she didn't want to have to rely on him if she needed to leave. So she'd driven the forty minutes to Amy's house with him following. Now, here she was parked in front, looking up at the darkened windows and wondering why the hell she let him talk her into coming here tonight instead of tomorrow morning.

The house was in total darkness. A two-story frame construction, built in the style of a Cape Cod, it somehow exuded an atmosphere of abandonment—as though Amy's death had drawn out all the life and happiness, leaving nothing but an empty shell.

The lights of the BMW behind her died, and the car door opened and closed. Clay walked to the window of Elizabeth's car and dropped into a crouch so he was eye level with her. They both looked up at the house.

"You sure this is the place?"

"This is the address Sara Dixon gave me. Only one way to find out for sure." She yanked the key from the ignition, got out and closed the door, locking it with the remote as they crossed the street and approached the front door. Sure enough, the key was where Sara had told her. She slid it into the lock and paused.

Clay's eyes met hers. "What are you waiting for? They're not home."

"It just feels weird going into someone else's house."

"They said you could."

He was right. Sara Dixon wanted to know that Amy's death wasn't by her own hand. Elizabeth had offered them a fine thread of hope that she could prove it. But what if she was wrong? What if she'd raised their hopes for nothing? She turned the key in the lock and pushed the door open.

The interior smelled stale, as though the place had been locked up for months. When Clay flipped on the light, they found themselves in an open entranceway, a staircase to the second level right in front of them, a formal living area to the left. Clay moved into the living room and switched on a table lamp. The place was furnished in soft peach colors, dark brown leather sofa, a fireplace with a gray and black stone mantle set into the far wall. Deep peach-colored floor-to-ceiling drapes covered most of the remaining wall. Clay drew the corner back to reveal a set of French doors leading out into a barbecue area, a covered pool just beyond.

Clay opened the door, peered out, then closed the door again. "Nice place. How long are they gone for?"

"I have no idea." Suddenly saddened at the thought of what these parents must have gone through, Elizabeth turned for the stairs. "Sara said the package was in Amy's room. It'll be up here."

At the top of the stairs a wide hallway led toward the rear of the house. The first room had been turned into a library with mahogany wood shelving standing on each of the three walls facing her; a second fireplace stood facing three deep-seated leather armchairs set around a glass coffee table.

"Not in here." She flipped off the light and moved on.

The next room on the right was clearly Sara and Ron's, the third a bathroom, and finally Amy's room, evident by the plaque on the door with her name embellished in red and surrounded by butterflies.

Just as Elizabeth placed her hand on the door, that welling sense of sorrow seemed to suck the breath from her. This had been the Dixons' only child. They'd lost her—their precious daughter stolen from them. Elizabeth had come so close to losing her own child. She dropped her head, closed her eyes a moment while she wrestled for control.

"Are you okay?"

How could he even ask? Was it because he'd never known what it was to have a child? Someone so beloved that the loss of them was almost unbearable?

Without answering, she pushed the door open and flicked on the light, almost afraid to enter.

Amy's bedroom was decorated in pastel blues and pinks, the bed set with a dozen or so teddy bears. On the wall above was a framed copy of the Serenity Prayer: "…the serenity to accept the things I cannot change, courage to change the things I can, the wisdom to know the difference."

Amy had had the courage. Elizabeth wondered if perhaps it was the wisdom that had failed her.

Clay stood close in behind her, peering over her shoulder. "What's wrong?" he asked again.

Without replying, Elizabeth stepped into the room, feeling like an intruder sullying the memory of the Dixons' beloved daughter.

"Don't touch anything," she told Clay. "We're just looking for the box."

He lifted his hands briefly and dropped them as if to say, "Understood."

There were no boxes or parcels evident. Whatever Sara Dixon had received from the prison, she'd tucked it away out of sight. Perhaps preferring to remember her as the child they'd had, not the child they'd lost.

A mirrored door stood ajar to Elizabeth's left. The closet. She moved over to it and placed her fingers to the handle. She gently pushed it open to find two rails of clothing running from the doorway to the rear wall. She moved down the rows, searching the floor beneath the dresses and shirts, then the shelves above. At the end was a brown cardboard box a little larger than a shoebox, wide clear tape running top to bottom and side to side forming a glossy T on the front. Amy's name and address were visible beneath the tape, handwritten in wide black marker pen.

Elizabeth reached up and took the parcel down just as Clay moved into the closet behind her.

"Is that it?"

She turned the box to find the prison's stamp on the underside. "Looks like."

Wishing now that she'd come here alone, she waited until he'd exited the closet, then carried the parcel out to the dresser and set it down.

They both stood there looking at it.

"Well? We've come all this way. You gonna open it?"

She shook her head.

"I'll open it later. We should leave."

"Why not now? What difference does it make?"

Something in his words pricked at the back of her brain. She turned to regard him. "I don't have anything to open it with." It came out a little more harshly than she'd meant it to. She gave him a brittle smile, trying to lighten the moment. "And I'm not breaking my nails on it."

"Here, use this." Clay reached into his pocket and took out a pocket knife, black, with a two-letter logo.

At the sight of it, a montage of images flashed through her mind: the flattened cartons, the awards dinner, Eileen Grant's parting words—*what were they?* Almost at once, she felt the color drain from her face, the sickly sensation of acid rising in her stomach. Seemingly without noticing the shift in her demeanor, he leaned past her and slit the tape before tucking the knife back into his pocket. With a quick tilt of his head, he moved back. As if he'd opened a car door for her. As if he'd done something gentlemanly.

But that feeling in her gut had swelled and the flesh on the back of her neck began to prickle.

She turned and gave him a forced smile. "Thank you."

"Open it." His tone lacked the previous warmth now.

Feeling the intensity of his gaze on her, she turned, pressed her thumbs between the flaps on the top of the box, and eased them apart. Then closed them, both hands holding it down.

"I know. Why don't I take this home and do it later? I don't want to waste any more of your time than I already have."

This time when she turned, the smile was gone. The chilly glint in his eye mirrored the shift in his demeanor. "I think you should do it now. Don't you?"

She didn't want to, but she had to ask. "How did you know where Millcreek was?"

"You told me," he said.

"I don't believe I did." She dropped the forced smile. "What's in there?"

A zero-degree grin, both palms raised. "How would I know? There's only one way to find out. Open it and see." Another tilt of the head, hands on his hips, suggesting she had no other option available. "You want me to do it?" The words were more like a threat than a suggestion.

Her chest tightened and a flush of adrenaline hit her system. When she spoke this time, the words hooked in her throat, causing her to swallow involuntarily mid-sentence. "No. I'll do it."

Turning to the box once more, she pressed both thumbs in under the outer flaps, then eased the opposing ones apart. Inside was a stack of garments neatly folded in a clear plastic bag. Alongside it, and tucked down the side was a second bag containing a toothbrush, deodorant, a cup, and a number of assorted toiletries.

Keeping her eyes on the parcel, but keenly aware of his proximity, she made a feeble search, then went to close the box again. "I don't think there's anything here."

"You didn't look very hard." His voice came over her shoulder, standing so close now that she could feel his breath on her neck.

Almost paralyzed by his overwhelming presence, she slowly lifted the toiletries out of the box and placed them on the dresser. Then she lifted the plastic bag of garments, set it alongside the first. Now that she'd removed everything from the box, she could see a familiar line of fabric lying along the center of the folded garments, like something hidden between the underwear and tee shirts and towels. Parting the layers of the plastic surrounding them, she pressed her fingers into the stack, and drew out a fine cream blouse made from the very same fabric she'd seen in the workroom at Millcreek Fashions. Fascinated, she slipped it from the pile and shook it out, then held it up by the shoulders, studying it—the seams, the back, the darts, the label …

The sight of the wording sent another blast of adrenaline through her. Her breath caught and her eyes widened.

"Rue Xeeba?" Her words were a hollow whisper.

Scrunching the blouse to her chest, she turned to him, frowning. "I don't understand."

A cool grin deepened those dimples into creases. "And here was me thinking you were the smart one."

She lifted the bunched blouse. "This?"

He reached up, took it from her.

"Took you long enough. For a while there I was worried you were going to give up." He shook the garment out, studying it from top to bottom. "Lucky for me, you hung in there. I have been searching *everywhere* for this." He lifted the blouse briefly, like a toast. "Thank you."

"This is about … Oh, for crying—!" She dropped her hands to her sides as those words rang out in her head. "*There is no magic wand.* That's what Eileen Grant told me. I didn't understand what she was trying to say. But she was referring to this," she said, dismissively flicking a hand at the blouse. "*You* were what she was talking about. *The Magician of Manufacturing*."

Another tip of the head, that smile deepening the dimples again, as if acknowledging a compliment. "That's what they call me. And they're not wrong, you know. I am pretty damn spectacular."

When she spoke this time, her voice was low, resonating with the hatred and rage that roiled in her gut. "Spectacular at what? You don't have any 'groundbreaking business model.' That's all bullshit."

He flinched theatrically on the word, sucking in air like he'd been burnt.

"*Elizabeth*. Such dirty talk. Keep it up, I love it."

She took one step back. "All your amazing workforce initiatives are a crock of shit—an industrial empire built on prison labor. Twenty-five cents an hour," she spat out. "No downtime, no sickness or absenteeism to have to pay for. No vacations messing up your precious production line. Just top-quality products at slave labor prices. *Oh*, and just a little murder or two to keep things running smoothly."

He threw up a hand, seemingly amused. "Whoa there. I can categorically say that I did not murder anyone."

"And what about Christine Wentworth? What did she have to do to keep your dirty little secrets covered?"

One side of his mouth tugged back in a regretful smile. "Oh, boy, she's a tough cookie," he said, as though he'd had to pull out all the stops but finally succeeded. "She's a terrific gal, but I doubt she'd have approved of our logistical arrangements. She kept threatening to go out to Millcreek. Seriously, I was running out of excuses to keep her away."

"And you expect me to believe that? I doubt you'd have stopped her. Another little pawn in your game. Another mug to do all your dirty work. After all, you wouldn't want to do anything that might wreck your precious business plan, not until you got the best share price on the stock market." She glared at him, more disappointed than she could have known. "*Why?* Why do all this? Was it about the money? Or was this all about sitting in Walt Straussman's chair while someone else picks up the pieces? Playing your fiddle while Rome burns."

One side of his cheek twitched and the self-assured smile evaporated. He screwed up the blouse in one hand and shook it at her. "It's just business, Elizabeth. You think we can compete in this market? Huh? You think I'm stealing jobs from hard-working Americans? The hell I am. If prison labor wasn't making these, who do you think would be? We'd be slugging it out with Bangladesh, Mexico, China. Not Americans. Our cost of labor wouldn't be in the same ballpark."

"You think this is about the ethics of using prison labor?"

He ignored her, shouting now. "People like you with your bleeding-heart ideals and your sanctimonious attitude have no idea how the world works, Elizabeth. I worked my ass off to get to where I am. Me," he said, beating his fist into his chest. "No handouts, no rich daddy to help me along. Just me."

"Oh, what a guy."

His expression soured and his voice dropped. "Do you know how many do-gooder assholes tried to stand in my way? Let me tell you, there were a lot. And I beat every single one of them at their own shitty little games. Me—*The Magician*. And I did it all with this." He stabbed his finger to his temple. "I outsmarted every asshole that tried to knock me down, and I walked away the winner."

The hatred in her gut twisted. "Oh, like you outsmarted Amy Dixon? You murdered an innocent child. And for what? Because she found *a blouse*? Because Eileen Grant put all the pieces of the puzzle together and figured out your little scam?" She spat out a breath of disgust. "And what about Stacy?"

"Stacy May was doing fine until *you* decided to let her out of prison. So technically, this is your fault."

Elizabeth's eyes flew open. "My fault? Oh, of course. And that's why you were so eager to help me find her. Well, weren't you just the good Samaritan?"

His demeanor cooled. "When you're in business, you have to make tough decisions."

"I can't believe what I'm hearing."

He jabbed a finger at her. "Stacy was warned not to apply for that program. I had to shut her down."

"Because you were terrified that once she was out, so was your secret. So that's why you came kissing up to me? All the flirting, asking me on dates?"

He shook his head, seemingly amused again. "Don't take it personally, Elizabeth, but older women aren't really my thing. Not when I can have my pick of any girl I want."

"Screw you," she said.

"Oh, Elizabeth," he said, and reached to brush away a stray wisp of hair on her forehead. "You keep this dirty talk up, I could get to like you after all."

She slapped his hand away. "I wouldn't let you touch me if my life depended on it. Where's Trish Tomes? What have you done with her? Or did you use a magical wave of your hand to make her disappear?"

His expression morphed into one of mock sorrow. "Unfortunately, our Trish became somewhat ... bothersome. Then Kathy Reynolds came to me with a much better deal. I offered Trish an exit package. She refused. I had to let her go." He lifted his shoulders briefly. "Strictly business. Nothing personal."

She didn't want to ask. But she had to. "So where is she now? What did you do with her?"

"I didn't do anything with her." The grin spread slowly once again as he spoke. "Now, if you'd been half as smart as you think you are, you'd have realized you've been driving past her for the last two days."

Elizabeth clapped both hands to her mouth, one over the other. "Oh, God. She was in that Dumpster."

"Like I said, my friend has the best seafood restaurant in the city. I dropped by, picked up a little insurance against anyone digging too deep. You know, you cannot rely on anyone these days. Those trash collectors were supposed to pick up on Saturday morning. So what was I supposed to do?"

"You bastard. You covered her in garbage. You threw her away like a piece of trash."

He said nothing, just stood there blankly regarding her.

Behind him was the open door. To her left, a heavy photo frame—a picture of Amy as a child.

Elizabeth snapped her hand out for the frame but he beat her to it, hooking her around the waist with one arm and jerking her back, knocking the frame from her hand. She stumbled backwards, cracking her elbow on the dresser, but managed to stay on her feet. As soon as she'd collected herself, she went for the door but he grabbed her again, swinging her around and throwing her backwards.

She had to get to the door, had to get out. She ducked and made another dash, but this time he grabbed her, running her backwards and slamming her into the mirrored glass on the closet door. She felt the glass behind her shatter. Before she could gather herself, he was on her again. This time he grabbed her by the front of her jacket, drew her straight up, and slammed her against the door again and again, smashing her against the broken glass until her vision blurred and her legs went out from under her. When he let go, she slid down the door with a thousand tiny slivers of glass slicing into her scalp, hooking into her jacket, and knifing into her back until she hit the floor.

Despite the vibrations echoing through her head, she tipped her head up far enough to see him standing a few feet in front of her. He ran the back of his hand across his mouth, watching her. She twisted around, one hand flat on the floor to ease herself up, but her movements were slow, her actions jerky and mistimed. She went to get up, but her knees buckled, so she dropped to her hands and knees and lifted herself, ready to go, like a runner off the blocks, but he grabbed her, flipped her onto her back, and swung one leg over to sit astride her, his knees pinning her elbows. She twisted and kicked under him, desperate to free her arms as he reached into his jacket and pulled out a tiny vial.

He popped the top with his thumb, saying, "Open wide. A pharmacist friend of mine formulated this. It's a little like Rohypnol, no memories, no residue in the system, only this is much faster acting." He clamped one hand on her forehead and pried her jaw down with the hand holding the vial. "C'mon, Elizabeth. Just relax. You won't feel a thing."

His grip was like a vice. She felt her lips pried apart, felt two drops of bitter liquid hit her tongue. She jerked her arms loose and fought against him, head rocking from side to side, fists pounding on his chest, at his arms, and his face until tiny dots of blackness popped across her field of vision and spread into black splotches. Again she clawed at him, but her head was swimming, her strength draining. A floating sensation flooded her brain, pressing in, tightening.

When she opened her eyes, Clay Farrant, Amy's room, and everything around her blurred, and swirled.

Her arms relaxed, her body gave out, and she felt herself swept away into a sea of nothing.

CHAPTER FORTY
DAY THREE 5:22 AM—STACY

Stacy figured it must have been close to dawn when she woke. She could see the line of pale light around the door. She had no idea of the time—just a vague memory of walking out of the elevator in the parking garage on Jell-O legs, her arm clamped under Clay Farrant's; him telling a security guy she'd had too much to drink; her looking back in desperation, but the guy just chuckling and walking on. Then flashes of a car trunk, the smell of leather and new carpet; Kathy Reynolds peering into the car at her, then seeing Mrs. McClaine, but she couldn't remember the context, or the correct sequence of events.

She sat up and swiveled her back to the wall, waiting for her head to stop spinning. Then she checked herself over.

No damage. Apart from a screaming headache. Could have been worse.

But she was locked in a closet. So it could have been better as well.

She rolled onto her knees, gave it a second, then used a shelf to pull herself to her feet, swaying for a moment while she got her balance.

What the hell did he put in her drink? Her tongue felt like it had been scrubbed with Drano. This shitty closet wasn't helping. Dust hung thick in the air along with the smell of something dead. A rat, maybe.

First thing, she checked her pockets—pulled out the toy car. Tyler! He was in more danger than ever. She had to find him, keep him safe. But first, she had to get out. Running her fingertips down each side of the doorframe, she finally came to a switch. She flicked it and light flooded the space around her and drove a lance of pain through her temples. She turned away with her eyes closed, stomach rolling until she felt herself stabilize. Not Clay's office. He wouldn't leave her there. This would be somewhere out of the way, somewhere no one would find her.

That bastard. Now the pieces were all falling together. Now she could see the whole picture. And she knew why. The memory of him speaking to Mrs. McClaine shimmered back, asking her to meet him. What if she'd agreed? It didn't bear thinking about.

Of course the door was locked. No matter how many times she jerked the handle. Pounding her shoulder into it didn't do any good, either. So she pulled out the phone she'd gotten from Caitlin and switched it on.

Full battery. "Thank you, thank you," she muttered over and over as she dug the card from her pocket. She tapped in Elizabeth McClaine's cell phone number and held it to her ear. Instead of the blips and bloops of the phone dialing, an automated message said, "You have zero dollars credit." And hung up.

"Oh, you are shitting me. Thanks a bunch, Caitlin."

No way to get help. That meant she had to find a way out. So she stuck the phone back in her pocket and searched the closet. The space was around eight feet by three. No air-conditioning vents, no windows.

Behind her the shelves ran floor to ceiling, all the way along, stacked with old stationery. If she'd learned to pick a lock, maybe she could have used a paper clip. Might have been useful. Hell, she'd been inside with twenty women who could have done it in their sleep. Stacy never even bothered to ask.

Shaking her head at the irony, she went from shelf to shelf, searching—staplers and stacks of yellowed paper and files and dusty office shit everywhere. Nothing useful … until her eyes dropped to a paper knife in a small satin-lined box. Beneath it was a collection of them, all with damaged boxes, all with the Beta Farrant corporate logo on the front of the boxes and engraved into the handles. Client gifts, maybe. Probably the rejects.

She shook one from the molded case and returned to the door. The doorknob was one of those old ones. Like they'd had back home. Dropping to one knee, she inserted the tip into slot on the handle shaft and pulled, just like Wayne showed her the time she got locked in the bathroom. Sure enough, the handle popped off. So far, so good. Next, she pressed the tip of the knife into the tiny gap in the side of the plate.

The plate also popped off.

She slotted the tip of the knife into the upper screw holding the door handle mechanism on. The screw was in tight and the blade snapped. So she grabbed another knife. Same thing happened, so she got a third and a fourth. By the fifth, the screw turned a fraction and this time the blade didn't break. With the tip pressed firmly into the slot, and her shoulder to the door, she twisted the knife until the screw came loose. She spun it several times until it wobbled out and fell at her feet. She rattled the handle but still it held fast.

The lower screw was easier. It twisted almost at once. She spun it out, then levered the inside plate off.

Now she had a hole in the door with the spindle of the handle sticking out. But the door wouldn't budge.

"Goddammit!" she yelled, and thumped the door with the side of her fist.

There had to be something on the shelves she could use. Moving from one to the next, tossing stationery and crap aside, she searched every inch until frustration tightened the muscles in her jaw and left her wanting to punch something. Or kick something.

She grabbed a hardback day planner for the previous year and whacked the end of the spindle.

Still nothing.

Infuriated, she whacked it over and over until the spindle went through the cover of the diary and the diary hung impaled on the shaft. She stood back and kicked it with the flat of her foot once, then twice, and the door flew open with the guts of the handle dangling from the other side.

Now she had to get to Mrs. McClaine. On a desk in the corner sat an ancient computer, a big boxy monitor, dirty keyboard. When she moved the mouse, the screen burst into life requesting a password.

She entered *1111*.

Nothing. She tried *0000*.

Still no dice.

Then she entered *1234*, and the image changed to a Microsoft screensaver. Pulling out the single wooden chair she slipped behind the keyboard.

"Find my phone," she muttered, as she tapped the words into the Google search bar. It was a trick she'd learned in Carringway to find a missing cell phone.

The computer was slow as a wet week. The cursor went around and around, but finally the page popped up requesting a password. What the hell would it be? Mrs. McClaine wouldn't be stupid enough to use something simple on her Google account. It'd be something personal.

But what?

She typed in *Elizabeth*.

Incorrect password. Two more attempts.

Elizabeth McClaine.

Wrong again.

"Oh, God, what do people use?"

One more attempt. Then it would lock her out.

Stacy tipped her head right back with her eyes shut tight. What would she use? What would Stacy use if it were her? Her eyes flashed open and she typed in:

Holly.

The screen snapped to a map. Stacy leaned in, studying it.

"Holy shit. What's she doing way out there?"

She kicked back the chair and went for the door. At least she knew where Mrs. McClaine was. With no car, no phone, no time, she'd never make it. That didn't mean she wouldn't try.

CHAPTER FORTY-ONE
DAY THREE: 5:55 AM —ELIZABETH

The distant ringing of a phone and the clatter of stones just below Elizabeth's head woke her. She was curled up on her side, hands and feet bound, a strip of duct tape stretched across her mouth to her cheeks on either side. Beneath her was a layer of thick plastic. It crackled and slipped against the carpeting under her. Darkness all around. The smell of leather upholstery and car fumes laced the air with a hint of Chanel. She was in the trunk of a car—her car. Her center of gravity moved with the motion, sliding back and forth on the plastic with each turn, the hum of the engine reverberating.

From up ahead in the cabin of the car, a phone rang—her phone; she knew because it was the ringtone she'd designated for Delaney. It rang several times, then stopped. Almost at once, the car turned hard left and the rattling of stones intensified, as though the road had gotten worse. The throb in her head and the fumes in the confined space turned her stomach. If she vomited, she'd choke. So she swallowed back, forced herself to relax.

After a few moments, the engine slowed, along with the clattering. They were drawing to a halt.

Fear surged in her gut. She twisted her wrists, writhing against the bindings, desperate to free her hands, but the plastic ties bit into her flesh without giving. She had to get out, had to get away. Farrant had everything to lose. He'd murdered to keep the charade going; he'd murder again. Now she was at his mercy and there was no way he'd let her go. She had to do something.

But what? She was bound hand and foot. No way to open the trunk. No way to escape. By the time they'd reached whatever destination they were bound for, she'd be back in his control again. She'd never felt so helpless.

She wanted to cry. Tears welled in her eyes. A sob rose in her chest and burst from her mouth, followed by a second.

Then the image of Holly flashed into her mind. She could not leave her. She could not die—not here, not at the hands of a madman. Holly needed her mother, needed her at home. Almost at once, a second image flooded in—of Stacy May Charms, a mother whose son needed her.

Stacy was a fighter. She'd fought tooth and nail to get out of that prison, to save her child. She'd turned her back on the inmate hierarchy system, put herself in the firing line, allowed herself to be bullied and beaten. But she didn't give up. She'd stood tall and believed in herself; she'd backed herself and followed through. Gut determination.

Now it was Elizabeth's turn.

By the time the car came to a stop, her heart was pumping, her resolve fierce.

The engine died and she heard the car door open, then the thud as it closed. Gravel crunched as footsteps moved down the side of the car and the trunk opened. Blinding white light knifed into the tiny space. Elizabeth closed her eyes against it, then turned her head, cracked her eyes to look up.

Clay Farrant stood over her, shirtsleeves rolled up.

"Guess what, honey, we're home."

Right there, right then, she couldn't have hated him more.

I will not give in to you, you bastard.

He tucked the keys in his pocket, ducking his head as he bent into the car trunk, and slipped his arms under her shoulders and knees. Then he drew her up into his embrace. Like a lover, a newlywed. The initial strength of his grasp shocked her, but her resolve and hatred doubled.

He carried her, regarding her every now and then as he spoke. "Do you know what I found?" he asked in an amiable tone, as if they were friends in a conversation over drinks. "A sinkhole. Do you know what that is?"

He staggered a little, then bent, partially dropping her unceremoniously onto the stony ground. She could see him standing over her, arching his back, as though he might have strained it, while he scanned the area.

"All the times I've been out to Millcreek, I had no idea. Funny the things you find out. Kathy Reynolds told me about it. She asked me what I did with Trish. I said, 'Trash, what else?' You know what she said? She said, 'Why didn't you just throw her down the sinkhole?' I'm like, 'What? You're kidding me, right?'" He shook his head in amusement.

"Only wish I could have seen Trish's car go down there. Kathy told me it slid down the side there, then got stuck. She's thinking, 'Holy shit, it's not gonna go.' But then all of a sudden, the nose tipped and down it went. *Whooo*," he said, planing his hand like a kid mimicking the downward path of an airplane. "Shame I missed it. But that's okay. I'll get to see yours go over."

Elizabeth glared up at him. Anger flared, heating her cheeks. Again, she struggled against the restraints.

"Oh, Elizabeth, you're never going to break those. They're cable ties. They're made like that for a reason."

He took a few steps away. Fifty yards or so beyond him, she could see the bridge—the one the GPS had led them to on the first trip out here. Silhouetted against the red of the sun just spilling over the horizon, Clay stood against the dismal landscape with his back to her, fists on his hips, looking out over the immediate area as though he was there to value the place.

"You know, the first time I came out here, this is where my GPS brought me. Apparently, this road used to be the main thoroughfare to the quarry out here. Then one day, the ground opened up and swallowed half the bridge." He turned a bemused look on her. "Imagine the surprise on the face of the guy driving over it. Wish I'd seen it."

The distant sound of a car engine made him turn around, casting a suspicious eye back down the road they'd just driven in on. Elizabeth tried to turn but the restraints would only let her get halfway. Not enough to see.

"Well, there's a surprise. I see we have company." The joviality in his voice was gone. He hiked his pants up, then stood square on, feet slightly spread, waiting.

Behind her, the car was approaching. She could hear the stones rattling on the underside. It rumbled to a point a few yards from where Elizabeth lay, then skidded to a stop.

The door immediately opened, then slammed, followed by the sound of footsteps in the gravel.

"What the hell do you think you're doing, Farrant?" Nancy's voice.

A tiny fist of hope bloomed in Elizabeth's chest. She let out a relieved breath and let herself relax. She wanted to cry out Nancy's name. She wanted to hug her.

Clay gave out a brief snort of laughter and dropped his head. "Parole Officer Pattrenko. Wow. You got me cold. How on earth did you find me?"

Nancy came to a halt no more than a few yards behind Elizabeth.

Elizabeth twisted around, desperate to see her.

Nancy made a derisive noise. "You're an idiot, that's how. When you started Trish's car up again, the tracking system reset itself. Pointed all the way out here."

"Oh, that pesky tracking system."

A hollow silence hung between them. In that silence, Clay's grin widened, and Nancy's bravado seemed to falter. Somehow, that fine balance of power that had emerged with her arrival had now swung back into Clay's court.

When Nancy spoke this time, the bluster was gone. Her voice lacked its initial authority. "Untie her."

Clay looked all around. "Why should I untie her? How about you untie her?"

Another tense silence. Elizabeth twisted around again. Nancy stood just within her peripheral vision.

She jerked her chin in her direction. "You okay, Mrs. McClaine?"

Elizabeth grunted beneath the tape and nodded.

Nancy shuffled a second, then slowly moved forward, eyes locked on Clay while she dug in her pocket and produced her little knife. Clay moved back, both hands up.

"She's all yours."

Nancy said nothing. Placing the tiny knife between Elizabeth's wrists, she began sawing rapidly at the cable tie. All the while, Elizabeth murmured against the tape over her mouth, begging her to hurry.

"I hear you. Just hold on till I got your hands free," Nancy told her.

Just behind her, Clay was moving closer. Elizabeth squealed, eyes wide on Clay.

Clay grabbed Nancy by the collar and yanked her back. Nancy rolled once, then leapt to her feet. "What are you gonna do? Scare me to death?"

Clay's lip twitched. With lightning speed, he lunged at her, his hands going straight for her throat, but Nancy twisted away and swung the knife at him, gouging into his arm and knocking him off balance.

He staggered a second, chuckling and checking his arm where she'd hit him. "Oh, so that's the way you want it." He grinned and tucked his shirt in. "Trish told me you wouldn't go without a fight. But then, she was easy. She just lay there—"

Nancy's face flashed scarlet with rage. She flew at him, fist clenched, knife going for his throat, and screamed, "You asshole!"

This time Clay was ready. He grabbed her wrist, took the hit in the stomach while he pried the knife from her hand and shoved her back. She ran at him again, caught him off guard, but he grabbed her by the shirtfronts, and the knife dropped from his hand. Ignoring it, and gripping her tightly, he drew her straight up and slammed her down on the rocky ground. Without missing a beat, she rolled to her side, shifting her weight to get up, but his foot came up, kicking her hard in the chest, knocking her backwards with the wind punched out of her.

"Nancy! Oh, no, please don't," Elizabeth begged into the tape.

Just a few yards from her, Nancy lay gulping for air. She lifted herself on one elbow, but this time Clay dropped onto her, straddling her, face turned from her as she hammered at him, but his reach was longer, and his hands were already around her throat, her face swelling. She clawed at him, frantic now, pounding on his chest, at his arms, trying to loosen his grip, but he kept his head turned and his hands tight on her throat for what felt like a lifetime. Finally Nancy's movements slowed, and died to nothing.

"No, no, no," Elizabeth mewed over and over.

Breathing hard now, Clay got up, his attention back on Elizabeth.

"You bastard," she yelled against the tape while she fought against the bonds.

He raked a hand through his hair and tucked his shirt in again, before bending down and scooping Elizabeth up in his arms, hoisting her briefly to reposition her. When she writhed against him, his grip tightened, his fingers pressing painfully into her flesh. He carried her around to the driver's door of her car, lowering her weight onto his knee while he opened the door, then angled himself around and slid her into the driver's seat, lifting her feet into the footwell.

She frowned up at him.

In response, he leaned one elbow on the roof of the car and bent down to her. "You're taking a little trip. Unfortunately, unlike the Terminator, you won't be back." He took a cable tie from his pants pocket, threaded it through the one around her wrists, then looped it around the steering wheel, securing it with a tug. "This way I get rid of you, and the car. A two-for-one deal. It doesn't get better than that," he told her with a wink.

She jerked at the wheel, yanking left and right but the cable tie held fast.

Through the open door she watched him scan the area, then select a rock the size of a melon. He lifted it and returned to the car, grunting with the effort as he dropped it next to her feet. Elizabeth moved in her seat, twisting around so she wouldn't have to touch him while he positioned the rock over the accelerator. That's when she realized the car was angled straight at the bridge. Her heart skipped a beat and she struggled again, terror flaring in her chest and burning her cheeks, but the bindings held fast and bit into her skin.

For a moment he disappeared from sight. She watched in the rearview mirror as he opened the trunk, then closed it. Returning, he gave her a brief look, one that might have said *I'm sorry*, but knelt to wind duct tape around the rock, fastening it to the accelerator. After three complete circles of tape, he severed it from the roll with the knife.

One knee on the stony ground next to the car, he caught Elizabeth's eye, held it. "I guess this is goodbye. Shame I didn't get to know you better. You could have been useful to my election campaign." He twisted the key in the ignition and the car burst into life with a roar, the engine screaming under the acceleration.

"Excuse me, will you?"

He leaned across, and the car jerked as he slipped the gearstick into drive. Over the roar of the engine and the wheels spinning, a voice behind him yelled, "Hey, asshole."

His head whipped around and Elizabeth looked up just in time to see

Stacy smash a rock down square on the crown of his head. He fell back, hand going to his scalp. Scrambling to his feet, he checked the blood on his fingers and stepped wide of her.

"You little bitch." He met her defiant gaze. "How did you get here?"

"I ran. Took a shortcut. Millcreek's just over that hill," she said and thumbed over her shoulder. "Now get away from her."

Clay straightened, then lunged at Stacy with frightening speed. They wrestled for a moment, then both disappeared from Elizabeth's sight.

No time to follow them. Elizabeth had both feet stamped on the brake pedal, but the car strained against the braking system and slewed left, the front now facing a gap between the skeleton of a dead tree, the stony dip into the sinkhole just to her right. The engine roared as the wheels spun in the gravel, digging deep, carving out two ruts, until little by little, Elizabeth felt movement, felt the tires bite into the stony ground. When it inched forward, she squealed.

To her left, she spotted Nancy on the ground. Blood soaked her shirt, the ashen cast of her face emphasizing the red of her hair. Just beyond, Stacy was backing away from Clay, taunting him, searching for a better position, but he moved up and leaped at her, swinging wide, and again, Elizabeth lost sight of them.

The car inched forward and slid right as the wheels bit in, then sped up as the wheels found traction. It bumped over a ledge of rock and hit the stony ground below, creeping closer and closer to the edge of the sinkhole. She shrieked against the tape, leaned back hard just as the front of the car dipped and stopped with the underside caught on the ledge, and the engine died.

A gasp of relief. A few breaths. Elizabeth tried to turn, desperate to see where Stacy was.

That relief came too soon.

Beneath her, the body of the car teetered on the rock ledge, gently seesawing for a moment before the nose dipped, and the front wheels touched down. All she could see was a funnel of gravel in front of her—the vortex. Without thinking, she stamped on the brake again, but the grind of stone on metal told her the car was edging forward, slipping into oblivion. She howled into the tape and writhed in her seat, yanking at the bindings holding her to the steering wheel. Tears welled, but just as the first broke and trickled down her cheek, the car door opened and Stacy leaned in, the blade of a paper knife going straight to the cable tie.

"Hold still, Mrs. McClaine. I'll get you out of here." The stones beneath Stacy's feet began sliding under her, sucking her down like a child on a sandy bank. She pedaled against them as she sawed back and forth with the knife. The tie around the steering wheel sprang apart but the car was sliding now, carried along by the cascading wall of shale, and Stacy along with it.

Once again, Clay rose up behind her, grabbing Stacy by the back of the collar and jerking her out of Elizabeth's view. Again Elizabeth stamped on the brake. It made no difference. Down next to the brake, she spotted Stacy's knife, Beta Farrant logo on the handle. Elizabeth folded over, shoulder pressed against the steering wheel, hands bound but reaching, stretching, until her fingertips connected with the knife. With one last lunge, she gathered it between her fingers, held it fast as she sawed back and forth until the ties around her ankles sprang apart, and she sat up. The car skewed around in the gravel, sliding sideways now and threatening to tip. She leaned her weight against the door, twisted the knife in her fingers, and placed it between her teeth.

With not another second to spare, Elizabeth grabbed the door handle, shouldered it open and fell out, leaving the car to slide. In looser gravel now, it twisted around, gliding faster towards the center. Ignoring it, she scrambled against the loose stones beneath her, found them slipping and sliding under her, and her along with them. Scrambling against them, her hand reached out, found a tree root. She grabbed it, held fast, offered up a little prayer. With the knife still caught between her teeth, she hauled herself up until she felt the knife against the tie around her wrist and slid it jerkily back and forth, but the edge was blunt and the cable tie held.

Walking one hand over the other, Elizabeth inched farther up the tree root, pulling herself up. No sound from above. It wasn't a good sign. She kept hauling until she found the rock ledge the car had caught on. Still clinging to the tree root, she drew one knee up and clambered onto the ledge. An overwhelming sense of exhaustion washed over her, but she could not give up. Just above her, the tree that had sent the root out stood stark and solemn against the background. She'd never get to it.

To her left, a shadow loomed.

"Mrs. M! Grab my hand."

Stacy gripped the tiny tree with one hand, crouching as she reached with the other. Elizabeth felt Stacy's fingers brush hers.

"Just a little more," Stacy urged.

Elizabeth stretched, felt Stacy's fingers curl around her wrist and lock, felt herself being drawn upwards, shoulders aching, muscles taut until she crested the top and fell to her knees.

Stacy stood over her, hands on her knees, panting. Elizabeth tore the tape from her mouth, but when she looked up, Clay Farrant was to her right, maybe fifty feet away, face bloodied and set with fury, striding toward them.

"Stacy, look out!"

Clay ran at her, grabbed her by the back of the jacket and swung her around. Stacy crashed to the stony ground and rolled. She went to get up, but not quick enough. Clay was on her again, straddling her with his hands around her throat.

"No, no, no." Elizabeth dragged herself to her feet, limbs aching. She scooped up a rock and half ran, half shambled toward him. His head swung around, but too late. She brought the rock down on him again and again, her movements automatic and so frantic that the sound of two cars and the wail of sirens hardly penetrated her consciousness.

All she could think of was stopping Clay. All she could think of was saving Stacy.

Clay folded beneath her and fell to one side just as two hands grabbed her and pulled her off. She spun around, the rock ready, her jaws clamped in anger. Delaney gripped her by the shoulders, holding her at arm's length while another officer dropped beside Stacy. Over Delaney's shoulder she could see two officers with Nancy, one with a shoulder radio, calling for an ambulance, the other checking her vitals.

The rock dropped from Elizabeth's hand. "Nancy! Stacy!"

Delaney drew her gaze, saying, "They're both okay, Elizabeth. It's all okay. You're safe now."

She faltered a moment, then relaxed against him, felt his arms hesitate, then encircle her. A sob welled up so fast she couldn't stop it. It burst from her lips and she howled like a child while he tightened his hold on her.

"It's all okay. It's all going to be fine," he whispered into her hair.

CHAPTER FORTY-TWO
MONDAY MORNING: 10:30 AM—STACY

The courtroom was smaller than Stacy had expected. More like the judge's office. Or his chambers, or whatever. Judge Henley was an older man, gray frizzy hair clipped neatly around the sides, gray moustache, a pair of black-rimmed eyeglasses sitting low on the bridge of his nose. He sat at a wide, pale wood table, papers spread before him. Didn't look up as they entered. He obviously knew who they were.

Stacy entered between Jay Templeton, the lawyer Mrs. McClaine had called in, and the bailiff. A thin man in uniform, the bailiff escorted her to the front row of seats, then left them to take up his position to the right of the judge's table, staring at the rear wall, hands behind his back. Behind them, on a single row of seats, Warden Glassy perched anxiously next to Penny Rickman.

No sign of Mrs. McClaine. A jolt of panic tightened Stacy's chest.

Where was she? Was she okay?

When the door opened, everyone looked up in expectation. Curta Brixton entered wearing a wide, blue flowered dress and matching hat. Clearly discomfited by her surroundings, she tugged at the scarf around her neck, then crossed to sit with the maximum number of seats between her and the only two other women there.

Stacy gave her a smile and Curta returned the smile with a little finger wave and a nod of encouragement.

Judge Henley lifted his head, peering over the glasses as he ran his eyes across the sparse gathering. "If we're all here, we may as well get underway."

Next to her, Jay Templeton let out a slow breath. He sounded nervous. She leaned towards him, whispering, "Where's Mrs. McClaine?"

He whispered back. "She's getting discharged from the hospital today."

"Oh."

The judge looked up, met Stacy's gaze. "Are you well enough to continue?"

"Yes, sir … Your Honor. I'm fine."

"You've taken quite a beating. If you feel you need to take a break at any time, you tell me."

"Thank you, Your Honor."

He smacked his lips and lifted a file in front of him. "Then we'll begin. Stacy May Charms, I've been going over the files here. My recommendation for anyone who violates their parole is an immediate additional two years to be added to their sentence, running consecutively." He held her eye, waiting. "You know what that means?"

She dropped her head, then looked up. "Yes, sir, I do."

He swiped off his glasses and leaned back in the black leather chair, one arm along the armrest, the other holding the stem of his eyeglasses to the corner of his mouth while he studied her.

Jay Templeton made a small movement forward. "Sir, if I may—"

"No, you may not, Mr. Templeton. I have your notes here. I can read them any time I like. I want to hear what Stacy has to say."

Feeling herself in an unwelcome spotlight, she said, "Sir, I've done some stupid things in my time."

His eyebrows shot up. "I don't think anyone's going to argue with that."

"Three years ago, I hit out at someone who was just trying to help me. That was stupid. I see that now. But for a long time when I was inside, I was angry. I thought it was everybody else's fault. Then when I started on the sewing program…" She paused while her mind went back to that day, that brief moment that made everything she'd done so far worthwhile, and made her heart glow. "I can't tell you how I felt, you know? It was like, 'Man, I can make stuff. I can really do something. Something good.'"

His eyes narrowed on her, but he nodded. "I get that. That's why Warden Glassy over there is so supportive of these programs." He crossed his arms over his chest, resting one elbow on his wrist, stem of the glasses to his mouth again, but still listening.

"And believe me, sir, I appreciate that. The prison programs gave me an education—gave me chances I might never have got." She blinked at a point just in front of her as she tried to arrange her thoughts, then looked up. "But I missed my son something terrible. Every day I wondered where he was, what he was doing.

"So when this program came up, I jumped at it. All I could think about was being a good mother, the mom I always wanted to be. Tyler—my son—he has learning difficulties. He's about two years behind the other kids now, but that's only going to get worse unless he has constant support. He'll get further and further behind the older he gets. That's not gonna get better if he's in and out of foster homes. But I could take care of him, help him. 'Cause I love him. And that's what you do for someone you love, right? I know it's gonna be tough sometimes, but I'm the one should be taking care of him. Me. No one else."

The judge nodded. "And what would you do for money? You can't live on fresh air."

"I could work while Tyler's at school. While I was inside, I started doing a little of the design work. Some of my designs ended up getting used in the Rue Xeeba range. They said they were good. So y'know," she shrugged. "I kinda thought I could do some night school classes, maybe get a job doing design work. Or whatever."

"And that sounds very commendable. But you ran out on that one opportunity that could have gotten you all of that."

She dropped her head. "Yes, sir." She tightened her grip on the note in her hand, the one she'd received from Bear that simply said, "Good Luck." Right now she needed all the luck she could get.

Judge Henley leaned forward on his elbows, waiting. "So are you going to tell me why we're all sitting here now?"

Stacy chewed her lower lip, then began. "It started when Amy came to me. She said she found something. It was a blouse that got sent back from Millcreek Fashions. That's the company we supplied finished garments to. We could tell right away the blouse that came back was one of ours, because it was one of the ones Amy had sewn. She could just about sew a straight line, but buttonholes? No way. Even though the machine does it all, she screwed them up every time. That's why she got put on sending and receiving, packing up boxes of garments, signing for the fabric and stuff that came in."

"This was…" He pushed a paper aside on his desk and put on his glasses while he checked the details. "…Amy Dixon?"

The pain knifed her in the chest. Just as it did the day Amy died. When she spoke this time, her voice was strained. "Amy was a good friend. She'd worked so hard to get clean. You know, she just needed someone to watch out for her sometimes. She always trusted the wrong people."

"So you looked after Amy?"

"Kind of. I did what I could. But I know she wouldn't have killed herself. Someone murdered her. Someone inside the prison."

"And at the time, you had no idea who."

A quick shake of the head. "They said she died of a drug overdose, but she wouldn't have. I know it. Then Lois Hankerman got arrested and charged with bringing drugs into the prison. Everybody knew she didn't do it. She wouldn't have. She was straight up. But no one had any idea who did, and once Lois was gone and everyone blamed her for Amy's death, it was like nobody cared anymore."

Again, he nodded. "So when you signed up for this program, you decided what? That you'd just run?"

"No. I wanted everything to be just right. It was a great opportunity. So I studied hard, I worked hard. But a couple of months after I applied for it, Amy found the blouse, and next thing, she was dead. Then, just after I found out I'd been selected for the program, someone left a photograph of Tyler in my cot. It shows him crossing the street outside his school with some lady, and it had, like, crosshairs over it. Like someone was threatening to shoot him. On the back, it said, *He's first, you're next.*"

"Is this the one?" Judge Henley slipped the photograph out of a file and pushed it across the table.

"That's it."

"What did you think this photograph was telling you?" he asked.

"I didn't think it. I knew it meant that if I got out of prison, they'd kill Tyler, then me. I'd seen what they did to Amy. And Lois. I had no doubt in my mind that they'd do what they said."

"So why didn't you tell the warden about this?"

She turned around to find Warden Glassy watching her.

"Because she would have started an investigation, like she did when Lois got arrested. But it wouldn't have done any good. Whoever got Lois Hankerman put away also murdered Amy, and got away with it. I'd promised Amy I'd look after her. And I didn't. And by the time any investigation got started, it would have been too late. They already knew where Tyler was. They'd have murdered him. And my whole life, everything I've worked for, it would have all been worth nothing. I might as well spend the rest of my life in prison 'cause it wouldn't be worth a thing without my son in it."

Judge Henley waited a beat, then gathered the papers on his desk.

"Okay, I think I've heard enough."

Jay Templeton shuffled nervously. "Ah, Your Honor, may I have a moment? I'd like a chance to offer—"

"No, I have everything I need, Mr. Templeton. You may sit over there while I think about this."

Jay turned, scanned the room, hesitated a second as if he wasn't sure what to do, then scooted across next to Penny. She leaned while he whispered something, then he shook his head, obviously dismayed.

The judge twisted his mouth to one side in deliberation and leaned back in his chair. "You know, I've been doing this a long time, Stacy."

"Yes, sir."

"It might surprise you to find out that Warden Glassy over there is a close friend of mine. And I know for a fact that she's as keen to keep young people from wasting their lives in prison as I am." He laced his hands over his belly as he spoke. "And believe me, I see them come, and I see them go. Time after time. It's such a waste of young lives, not to mention taxpayers' money."

Stacy had no idea where this would go. It could fall to her, or against.

"And yet," he continued on, "I see the same young people doing the same stupid things over and over. And I wonder why in God's sweet name they don't learn. Do you understand what I'm trying to say here?"

"Yes, sir, I do."

"I would love to let you out again, give you that chance that you've been working so hard for. But…"

She knew it. That *But*. It hit her in the chest like a sledgehammer and her heart hit the floor.

"The way I hear it," he said, "your mother is not willing to have you reside with her. And I don't blame her. Do you?"

Stacy felt the air sucked right out of the room. "No, sir."

"So even if I wanted to re-release you, you have one immediate problem of having nowhere to go, and a second immediate problem of the leg bracelet you have to pay for. And that's around fifteen hundred dollars, according to the Department of Corrections."

Her eyes widened. "Oh. I didn't know they cost that much, sir."

"Sir? Your Honor?" A voice behind her—Curta. "Sir, if Stacy's okay with it, I can sell my car that she borrowed and loan her the money for the bracelet. I never use the car. Got the thing back this morning and I don't need it. We could come to some arrangement, and then she can pay me back over time. I wouldn't charge her interest or nothin'. I owe this girl my life. I could tell you what she done for me, but it would take the whole rest of the day, Your Honor." All at once, she realized everyone was staring at her. Her cheeks blazed apple red while her eyes darted around the room. "I mean, that's if she's released, of course," she added, and sat again, clinging to the seat in front for support under the weight of the sudden attention.

Henley frowned. "Well, that's very kind of you, ma'am, but Stacy needs to find a way of paying you back for that loan. That means finding a job."

"The offer still stands, sir," Curta said, half standing, then collapsing back, drawing her enormous purse onto her lap, both hands gripping the top of it.

Stacy turned, smiling and mouthing out the words "thank you," before turning back to the judge.

"You certainly have a lot of people going to bat for you."

"I do, sir. And I'm truly grateful."

He leaned his elbows on the table, chin resting on his knuckles, frowning. "So what am I to do with you, Miss Charms?"

"Your Honor, if I may?"

Judge Henley let out a long, weary sigh. "Yes, Mr. Templeton," he said with forced patience.

"I have a petition to present to the court on behalf of Parole Officer Nancy Pattrenko. She's requested permission to have you consider Stacy

May residing with her for the duration of her parole period, if it pleases the court."

Henley drew the corners of his mouth down. "Well, that's a very nice gesture, but isn't Miss Pattrenko in the hospital?"

"She's expecting to be discharged in a couple of weeks. She said she has a room Miss Charms can stay in, and she says she thinks the company will be good for her after the loss of her partner. Although," he added in a low voice, "that's probably neither here nor there."

Judge Henley turned a questioning look on Stacy, who felt her mouth drop open.

"Seriously? Nancy Pattrenko wants me to stay with her?"

"That's a generous offer," Henley told her. "What do you think of that?"

A broad smile cracked Stacy's face. The first grin she'd mustered in days. She placed her hand over her mouth in disbelief, then dropped it again. "I'd think that's an incredibly generous offer, sir."

"So do I."

"And I'd work day and night to pay for the bracelet. And I promise you won't see me back here again."

"I'd better not," he said. "But that leaves us the next couple of weeks that you'll need to stay somewhere."

Jay leaped to his feet again. "Your Honor, I believe we have a solution for that problem, too."

*****

Curta had been the first to throw her arms around Stacy, hugging her and sobbing into her shoulder, until the bailiff told them they had another case and asked them to please move on.

Stacy had told Curta she'd pay her back whatever she owed her for the car—somehow—but Curta had waved it away and told her just to keep in touch, that that was all she wanted. Then Stacy had been swept out into the morning air by her supporters and a clutch of journalists.

Now, outside the courthouse in the brilliance of the sunshine, Stacy tipped her head right back, feeling the warmth, soaking in real freedom for the first time in three long years. How a person could take this for granted, only someone who'd never been inside would know. This was the first day of a long line of good ones. She'd make sure of that.

The clearing of a throat a few feet in front of her snapped her out of the moment and back to the courthouse steps. Standing a few feet in front of her was Bear, a bunch of tulips and daisies in his hand.

"I'm really happy for you," he said, and handed her the flowers. "Congratulations."

She took them, put them to her nose. "Thank you."

The small crowd of supporters had thinned to but a few. Only one journalist remained. Obviously, good news doesn't rate so well. She scanned the steps and along the street each way.

Bear followed her gaze, seemingly picking up on her disappointment but misreading it. "You need a ride?"

"Can't." They both looked down at the bracelet on her ankle. "But thank you."

"Oh, right. Well, this one better stay there."

They both smiled, a little awkward, until she felt a hand on her elbow. Jay Templeton. "We should go."

"Sure."

They walked to the curb to the waiting car. The door opened and she hesitated, still searching. She was about to get in, when a second car raced up and drew to a halt behind them. The door flew open and Kay Heathers jumped out, saying, "Oh, thank heavens we caught you." She hurriedly opened the rear door and Tyler scrambled out. For a second, he looked around, a little bewildered. But the instant he spotted Stacy, he shambled over, reaching for her and calling, "Mommy, Mommy."

Stacy dropped to her knee, arms outstretched while he stumbled into her embrace. "Oh, baby, baby," she said, and planted a firm kiss in his hair. "Mommy thought you'd forgotten."

"Mommy come home," he said.

Kay Heathers bent next to him. "You remember what I said, Tyler? That you'll be home with Mommy soon, but Mommy has to find a house especially for you and her to live in."

Tyler's little face dropped and his eyebrows went up in the middle. "Mommy home?"

"Soon. I promise."

His little face puckered and Stacy's heart broke into a million pieces. How could something she'd wanted so badly carry so much pain?

"Oh, Tyler," she said, and pulled him in, feeling him fold into her, his shoulders heaving with the first sob as his arms tightened around her.

"Oh, sweetheart, please don't cry." She tightened her embrace for a second, then pulled back, ducking her head to catch his eye. Thumbing the tears away, she said, "Hey, guess what I still have." She waited until his eyes lifted on her, then she pulled the toy car from her pocket.

Tyler reached up a tentative finger and touched the car, his eyes widening as though mesmerized by it. "Mommy car."

"I know, but you know what? I'm giving it to you to look after. This is my promise that you're coming home one day soon. And you'll never go away again."

She drew him back into the embrace, felt his arms circle her and tighten like he'd never let go.

"Mommy an' Tyler house?" he said into her hair.

"Mommy and Tyler's house," she said.

CHAPTER FORTY-THREE
MONDAY: 3:04 PM—ELIZABETH

Elizabeth shook out the skirt she'd been wearing the day before and checked it over—ruined. A tear down the side, dirt ground into the seat that she'd never get out. She balled it up and tossed it into the hospital trash can and continued hurriedly packing the pajamas, the robe and the toiletries Katy had brought in for her the previous night.

She couldn't wait to get away. Hospitals gave her the creeps. Ever since she'd lost her mother, the smell of antiseptic and floor wax nauseated her, made her feel small and insignificant. It was almost as though on some deep level she still blamed the hospital for her mother's death.

The flowers could stay. A huge bouquet from Richard, another from Charles, her father-in-law. She suspected they were token gestures of apology. Not that her ex or his overbearing parents had made the effort to bring them in person. They'd simply picked up the phone and had them delivered, or gotten one of their underlings to do it. It would be weeks before they could look her in the eye again. Only once the hoopla had died down and Charles could talk about investment opportunities without the name of Clay Farrant coming back to bite him. But eventually, he'd be back. Nothing would again cut his ties with Holly, his only granddaughter.

Behind her, a tap on the door to her private hospital room made her turn.

"Come in."

The door opened and Detective Delaney peeped around, looking a little out of place.

"Detective," she said in greeting, and continued packing.

He moved into the room and crossed to the foot of the bed, watching her zip up the bag and place her purse next to it.

"They tell me you have Stacy May Charms as a house guest until Officer Pattrenko is discharged from hospital," he said. This seemed to amuse him.

Elizabeth lifted her head high, chin up. "Why not? She might be an ex-convict, but she's a kid who found herself in a no-win situation. Even the judge saw that."

"So you've discharged yourself. Against hospital advice?"

She paused, both hands rested on the top of her overnight case while she regarded him. "I'm fine. A few cuts and bruises, but otherwise, I'll live."

There was no way she would admit to the pain she was still suffering, or the nightmares that had woken her during the night. The bruising on her face and the welts around her wrists would fade, and she'd go back to her life as it was. "Besides, Penny's organized some home help. She'd kill me if I told her to cancel it now." When he gave her a doubtful look, she said, "Anyway, I have a ton of work waiting for me at home and it's not doing itself. "

Feeling ill at ease under his scrutiny, she dropped her eyes to the bag, drew the zipper up. "I guess I should thank you for coming along when you did. How did you know where we were?"

He hesitated, apparently considering his response. "Ms. Pattrenko had the forethought to call in and leave me a message with the location Patricia Tomes' car was last recorded. Something I wish you'd done."

"I didn't know where the car was." She looked away. "Anyway, I tried to call you. I left you a message. You didn't get back to me."

She didn't intend the accusation in her tone. She knew he didn't deserve it.

When he spoke, his voice was soft, reassuring. "Elizabeth, when I got that message I was already investigating the disappearance of Patricia Tomes. That's why we arrived when we did."

Elizabeth's mouth dropped open. "Why didn't you tell me?"

"I was trying to distance you from all this. Stupid, I know. I should have known what a stubborn, obstinate, hard-headed woman you are, and that you'd carry on regardless of what I said."

Her grip on the overnight bag tightened. "Clay Farrant murdered Amy Dixon and Patricia Tomes. I hope he goes to hell for it."

He shuffled, looking slightly less at ease. "Believe me, we're doing everything to see that he does." He let his gaze drift around the room before coming back to her. "Elizabeth, you could have been killed. If we'd been two minutes later…" He shook his head and let the implication hang.

Feeling a little sheepish now, she fumbled with her purse, drew out her car key. "So what happens now?"

Delaney nodded, lips pursed in thought. "He's under arrest for kidnapping, assault with a deadly weapon and in connection with the murders of Amy Dixon and Patricia Tomes. New evidence pointing to Kathy Reynolds for the murder of Amy Dixon means Warden Glassy will be lodging an appeal for the retrial of Lois Hankerman. And once we're done, the FBI will be looking into allegations of conspiring to misrepresent information leading up to the float of his company on the stock market. All going well, he'll be away for a long time."

"And what about Christine Wentworth? You can't tell me she knew nothing about this."

"That's what she maintains."

She gave him a dubious look. "Seriously? That's what she's saying?"

He flicked his eyebrows, the gesture one of cynicism. "Apparently, Clay started up Millcreek under his mother's name without her knowledge. Of course, now her precious son is up for so many charges, she's suddenly decided to retract her earlier statements and gotten her own lawyer."

"Oh, what a great mom."

He tipped his head and smiled. "We'll get her to recant. It's only a matter of time. Turns out he had deals with four other prisons—two in Indiana, a couple in other states, all apparently signed off by her."

She turned to face him and smiled, more relieved than she could know. "So they'll get him on forgery as well. Good. "

Delaney gave her a long, hard look. "It is good. As long as we secure a conviction."

Her smile faded. "What do you mean, as long as you get a conviction? All you have to do is go to Millcreek. You'll find all the evidence you need. Nancy and I saw their operation—saw everything."

He cut her off, saying, "Are you saying you were invited onto the premises?" His eyebrows rose, waiting for her response.

"Well, no. But everything's right there. All you have to do is get a search warrant and you'll see."

"We went out there with a search warrant just this morning."

"And?"

He raised both hands, and dropped them again. "And nothing. The place is empty. Clean as a whistle."

She blinked at him. "But it wasn't. We saw—"

He glanced down at his hands. "You can bet your bottom dollar that if we bring evidence forward under those circumstances, Clay Farrant's attorney will find some way to throw it out as having been solicited by the police and therefore inadmissible. Then they'll fire a breaking and entering charge right back at you and Nancy. The press could have a field day with that and any testimony you offered would be deemed questionable."

That bastard. He must have called in the entire cleaning crew to gut the Millcreek operation the second he hung up from speaking to her. No wonder he was in such a rush to get out. His undoubtedly illegal workforce was probably already paid off and on their way out of state.

"But he'll still be charged with murder in the first degree, won't he? I mean, he was the one behind Amy's death. And Trish Tomes's."

Delaney spread his hands. "Clay Farrant has already hired the best criminal defense in Ohio. According to Farrant, he has no idea of Kathy Reynolds' whereabouts, or who put Patricia Tomes' body in that Dumpster. And, as he's pointed out numerous times, setting up supply programs with prisons is perfectly legal. Lots of companies do it. Now, he's laid the entire scheme at the door of Christine Wentworth."

"Who, naturally denies all knowledge."

"Naturally."

"But surely you don't believe her?"

He shrugged.

"Well, I'm happy to testify. And I'm positive Nancy Pattrenko would. And what about the women in Carringway? Can't you question them?"

"I could. They're unlikely to talk. They know what happened to Amy Dixon, and to Stacy May. They don't want to be next."

A sickening silence hung in the air while she processed the information.

"You're saying he could get out?"

"It's unlikely. He attacked three women and he was found with Trish Tomes's cell phone in his possession. Apparently, he'd been texting messages to Nancy Pattrenko after Trish was dead, trying to throw her off the track. We found Trish's body in the Dumpster and traces of blood in his car. Next time," he said and jabbed his finger at her like a father warning his daughter about curfew, "you do exactly what I say, when I say it."

She dropped her head a moment, then met his gaze, held it. "Thank you. I mean it."

He said nothing, just nodded and walked out, leaving the door to hiss closed in his wake.

Elizabeth's hands were trembling, her heart pounding. Suddenly alone, it was only now that she realized how badly the whole series of events had shaken her. She lifted her purse, unclasped it, and found her phone. She scrolled through until she came to the entry three slots down, and hit send.

"Hello, Penny? I'm ready when you are," she said.

"I'm leaving right now. Traffic being what it is, I'll be there in around twenty minutes," she said and hung up.

Elizabeth put her phone back into her purse and moved across to the window.

Out beyond the glass lay Cleveland, a beautiful, vibrant city—the city she'd grown up in, the place she'd always come back to. It was where she'd found love, and lost it, only to find the real love of her life: Holly, the child she came within a hair's breadth from also losing. It was the place she'd finally made peace with herself, found herself, found her place in.

For the first time, doubt lay sour in the pit of her stomach.

What if Clay Farrant had disposed of Trish's phone? What if Delaney hadn't arrived when he did?

She hung her head and the first sob burst from her lips.

She couldn't wait to get home.

CHAPTER FORTY-FOUR
MONDAY EVENING: 5:32 PM—ELIZABETH AND STACY

Elizabeth leaned her head to the crack in the door, hand raised to knock. Inside she could hear the sound of voices, soft and gentle.

Maybe she should just leave them.

Absolutely. This was their time. She dropped her hand, about to tiptoe away, when the room fell silent, and Stacy called, "Mrs. McClaine?"

Elizabeth hesitated, then pushed the door open. Stacy sat cross-legged on the floor with Tyler, on his knees, running a red toy car back and forth on the carpeting. Already, a picture of the two of them had been set on the nightstand next to Stacy's bed: Stacy and Tyler with their heads pressed together, both smiling into the lens, the joy obvious in both.

"Oh, hey," Stacy said, and went to get up.

Elizabeth put up a hand. "Don't get up. Stay there."

Settling back into her cross-legged position with her eyes on her son, Stacy said, "I can't tell you how much I appreciate everything you've done for me."

"You don't have to."

The brief but sad smile that came back almost broke Elizabeth's heart.

A ragged breath from Stacy. "Yes, I do. If it wasn't for you, I wouldn't have got Tyler back. I wouldn't have—"

"Hey," she said, interrupting her. "This," she said, gesturing at the two of them. "This is all I wanted. And besides, if it wasn't for you, I might not be here, either."

Stacy smiled. Then drew a preparatory breath. Elizabeth froze, wondering what was coming next.

"Is there something else you need?"

"Ah, yeah." There was a moment's hesitation while Stacy collected her thoughts. "Listen, you've been really terrific, and I appreciate everything you've done, but I was wondering if I could ask one more thing."

Elizabeth felt her chest tighten. *Did she want to leave? Was there somewhere else she preferred to be?*

Stacy got to her feet, hands slipping into the back pockets of her jeans, avoiding eye contact. "I was wondering if … y'know, I know how much you've done for me, but …" She shuffled on the spot. "I'd really love it if Tyler could stay—maybe just one night. If that's okay."

The relief washed through Elizabeth like a tidal wave. She smiled, suppressing the urge to laugh at herself for being so afraid to lose this little family from her life already. "His bed is all made up, and his foster mom said it'd be fine. I'll call you both when dinner's ready."

Tears welled in Stacy's eyes. She dashed them away on her sleeve and shook her head, "I can't tell you…" she said and held her breath, pushing back a wall of emotion.

"Then don't even try," Elizabeth said softly, and closed the door.

The End

ACKNOWLEDGMENTS

To all those who supported me in the writing of this book:

Laura Hunter: first reader, head cheerleader, supporter, and enthusiast. She kept me on an even keel even through the stormiest seas.

Sara J. Henry (author of *Learning to Swim* and *A Cold and Lonely Place*): Editor and friend, Sara's structural editing is a sight to behold. Not to mention the hilarious editing comments she leaves.

Linda M. Au: Friend, author, formatter, proofreader extraordinaire. She went above and beyond, and came through for me when I needed her. She'll probably edit and reformat this acknowledgment.

Rob Williams: Friend, sounding board, and knowledge base. He's put me right on so many occasions I don't know what I'd have done without him.

My Girl: my inspiration, my gift, my treasure. I miss you more than you could know.

OTHER BOOKS BY CATHERINE LEA

The Candidate's Daughter
The Contestant

Made in the USA
Lexington, KY
20 February 2016